Michelle Smart's love affair with books started when she was a baby and would cuddle them in her cot. A voracious reader of all genres, she found her love of romance established when she stumbled across her first Mills & Boon book at the age of twelve. She's been reading them—and writing them—ever since. Michelle lives in Northamptonshire, England, with her husband and two young Smarties.

Melanie Milburne read her first Mills & Boon novel at the age of seventeen, in between studying for her final exams. After completing a master's degree in education she decided to write a novel, and thus her career as a romance author was born. Melanie is an ambassador for the Australian Childhood Foundation and a keen dog-lover and trainer. She enjoys long walks in the Tasmanian bush. In 2015 Melanie won the HOLT Medallion, a prestigious award honouring outstanding literary talent.

GW00319959

Discover more at millsandboon.co.uk.

A PASSIONATE REUNION IN FIJI

MICHELLE SMART

CINDERELLA'S SCANDALOUS SECRET

MELANIE MILBURNE

MILLS & BOON

First Published in Great Britain 2019
by Mills & Boon, an imprint of HarperCollins*Publishers*
1 London Bridge Street, London, SE1 9GF

A Passionate Reunion in Fiji © 2019 by Michelle Smart

Cinderella's Scandalous Secret © 2019 by Melanie Milburne

ISBN: 978-0-263-27361-8

MIX
Paper from
responsible sources
FSC® C007454

This book is produced from independently certified FSC™ paper
to ensure responsible forest management.
For more information visit www.harpercollins.co.uk/green.

Printed and bound in Spain
by CPI, Barcelona

A PASSIONATE REUNION IN FIJI

MICHELLE SMART

This is for Keanu Reeves,
my teenage object of lust
who, like a fine wine, grows only better with age.

CHAPTER ONE

LIVIA BRIATORE CLIMBED the metal steps to the sleek jet's cabin, her heart hammering so hard she felt the vibrations in the tips of her hair. The sun was setting, the growing darkness perfectly matching the darkness that had enveloped her these recent months.

The flight crew, the same crew from when she'd first boarded this plane over two years ago, greeted her warmly but with questions ringing from their eyes.

Livia responded with a smile but the effort was such the muscles of her mouth protested. She didn't think she'd smiled once these past four months.

Sick dread swirled in her stomach. Clamping her teeth together, she straightened her spine and raised her chin, then stepped into the luxurious cabin where she was destined to spend the next twenty-six hours flying to Fiji.

Immediately her senses were assailed by the familiar smell of expensive upholstery mingled with the musky yet citrusy scent of the man on the plush leather seat, a laptop open before him.

She almost doubled over with the strength of the pain that punched through her stomach.

The first time Livia had stepped on this plane her

heart had pounded with excitement and anticipation. Her body had run amok with brand-new feelings.

That first time in this plane, taking off from this very same airport in Rome, she had been filled with more happiness than she had known existed. The man whose attention was currently fixed on his laptop had hardly been able to wait for take-off before dragging her into the bedroom to make love to her.

All that was left of the flame of the passion that had seen them married within a month of meeting was ashes.

She blinked the painful memories away and forced her leaden legs forward.

She'd made a promise and she would keep it, however much it hurt.

The plane had four luxury window seats facing each other with the aisle between them. Massimo had raised his partition and when she took the seat diagonal to his, all she could see of him were his shoes. They were as buffed and polished as they always had been, a quirk she had thought adorable. Her husband was the least vain man she had ever met but he always took pride in his footwear.

She fastened her seat belt then laced her fingers tightly together to stop herself giving in to the need to bite her nails. She'd had an expensive gel treatment done on them the day before, masking that they were all bitten to the quick. She didn't want Massimo to see them like that. She couldn't bear for him to look at her and see the signs of her broken heart.

Livia had patched her heart back up. She'd licked her wounds and stitched herself back together. That was the only good thing about her childhood. It had taught her how to survive.

She would survive the next four days too. Four days and then she need never see him again.

The captain's voice came over the tannoy system, informing them they were cleared to take off. His words brought Massimo to life. The partition acting as a barrier came down as he closed his laptop and stored it away, then fastened his seat belt. Not once did he look at her but Livia was aware of every movement he made. Her heart bloomed to see the muscles of his tall, lean body flex beneath the expensive navy shirt with the sleeves carelessly rolled up, the buttons around his strong neck undone. No doubt he'd ripped the tie he would have worn to the conference from his neck the moment he'd left the venue. A maverick even by usual standards, Massimo conformed to rules only when *he* judged it necessary. She supposed the engineering conference in London he'd been guest of honour at had been an occasion he'd decided was worthy of bothering with an actual suit.

Livia only knew he'd been in London because his PA had casually mentioned it in her email when they'd been making the arrangements for today.

It wasn't until the plane taxied down the runway that the soulful caramel eyes she had once stared into with wonder finally met her gaze. It was the briefest of glances before he turned his attention to the window beside his head but it was enough for Livia's stomach to flip over and her throat to tighten.

Massimo's face was one she'd been familiar with long before they'd met. Employed as his grandfather's private nurse, she'd stared at the large Briatore family portrait that had hung in his grandfather's living room too many times to count. Her gaze had always been drawn to the only member whose smile appeared forced. It was a beautiful face. Slightly long with high cheekbones, a strong Roman nose and a wide firm mouth, it was a chameleon of a face, fitting for a construction worker, a banker or a poet. That it belonged to one of the richest self-made billionaires in the world was irrelevant. She would have been drawn to that face no matter who he was.

Seeing him in the flesh for the first time, in the church his sister was getting married in, had been like having all the oxygen sucked out of her.

The first time she'd seen him smile for real her insides had melted as if she'd been injected with liquid sunshine. *She* had brought that smile out in him. She couldn't even remember what she'd said, only that after hours of sidelong glances at each other throughout the wedding ceremony and the official photographs, she'd gone to the bar of the hotel the reception was being held in and suddenly the air around her had become electrified. She'd known before even turning her head that he'd come to stand beside her. Her tongue, usually so razor sharp, had tied itself in knots. Whatever she'd said in those first awkward moments had evoked that smile and in that instant all the awkwardness disappeared and it was as if they had known each other for ever.

And now he couldn't even bring himself to look at her.

She had no idea how they were going to get through a weekend with his family, celebrating his grandfather's ninetieth birthday, pretending to still be together.

Massimo watched an illuminated Rome disappear beneath the clouds and tried to clear the hot cloud that was the mess in his head.

When he'd agreed to speak at the engineering conference in London, it had made sense to fly to Rome afterwards and collect Livia en route. It had been logical.

He'd assumed that after four months apart, being with her again would be no big deal. He hadn't missed her in the slightest. Not that there had been time to miss her with all the hours he'd been putting in. Without the burden of a hot-tempered wife demanding his attention, he'd been able to devote himself to his multiple businesses just as he had before she'd collided into his life and torn it inside out. The day she'd left, he'd bought himself the bed for his office which the mere suggestion of had so angered her. He'd slept in it most nights since. It was far more comfortable than the blanket on the sofa he'd used the nights he'd worked late and decided it wasn't worth driving home.

He hadn't anticipated that his blood would become hot and sticky and his hands clammy just to land in his home city and be under the same sky as her again.

And now that she was here, in the cabin of his plane, every cell in his body, dormant all this time apart, had awoken.

He could curse his logical mind. Why hadn't he insisted she fly to Los Angeles, where he was scheduled to refuel, and board his plane there? He couldn't have her fly all the way to Fiji separately from him—that would defeat the whole purpose of her being there—but he could have engineered things so they only had to spend a minimal amount of time on his plane together, not the full twenty-six hours it would take to travel to the other side of the world.

For the return journey he would fly with her to Australia and charter a plane to fly her back to Italy.

He'd listed all the excuses he could have made to avoid bringing her with him but it had all boiled down to one thing. This was for his grandfather, Jimmy Seibua. His terminally ill grandfather, who'd taken a cruise from Rome to Fiji with his family and an army of medical personnel in attendance and had arrived on the island three days ago. This weekend was all that had been keeping his grandfather alive, this one last visit to the homeland he'd left as a twenty-two-year-old the spark giving him the fight needed to beat the odds. Jimmy would celebrate his ninetieth birthday on the Fijian island of his birth, now owned by Massimo, with the family he loved. His grandfather thought of Livia as part of his family. He loved her as a granddaughter. His only regret at Massimo marrying her was that it meant he lost the private nurse who had tended to him with such care during his first battle with cancer.

And, whatever his own feelings towards his estranged wife, Massimo knew Livia loved Jimmy too.

'Are you going to spend the entire flight ignoring me?'

Massimo clenched his jaw as Livia's direct husky tones penetrated his senses, speaking their native Italian.

That was the thing with his wife. She was always direct. If she wasn't happy about something she made damned sure you knew about it. For a long time the object of her unhappiness had been Massimo. Her declaration that she was leaving him had come as no surprise, only relief. Marriage to Livia had gone from being passionate and invigorating to being like a war zone. And she wondered why he'd spent so much time at work? The nights they had spent together those last few months had been with her cold back firmly turned to him. She'd even started wearing nightshirts.

He swallowed back the lump that had suddenly appeared in his throat and finally allowed his gaze to fall on her properly.

The lump he'd tried to shift grew but he opened his mouth and dragged the words through it. 'You've had your hair cut.'

Her beautiful thick, dark chestnut hair, which had fallen like a sheet down to her lower back, now fell in layers to rest on her shoulders in loose curls. It was lighter too, streaks of honey blonde carefully blending with her natural colour. Livia was not the most beautiful woman in the world but to his eyes she was stunning. It was the whole package. A sexy firecracker with a dirty laugh. He'd heard that laugh echo through the walls of the church while they'd waited for his sister, the bride, to arrive and when he'd spotted the woman behind it he'd felt the fabric of his existence shift. He'd grabbed the first available opportunity to speak to her and had been blown away to discover she had a thirsty, inquisitive mind. He'd been smitten. In Livia he'd found the woman he'd never known he'd been searching for. Or so he'd thought.

Her dark brown eyes, always so expressive, widened before a choked laugh flew from her mouth. 'That's all you can think to say?'

She didn't wait for a response; unbuckling her seat belt and springing to her feet.

She'd lost weight, he noted hazily.

Her kissable plump lips were tight as she stalked past him, the bathroom door closing sharply a moment later.

Massimo rubbed his jaw and struggled to get air into his closed lungs.

He hadn't expected this to be easy but it was a thousand times harder than he'd envisaged.

Livia sat on the closed toilet seat and hugged her arms across her chest, willing the threatening tears back. She hadn't expected this tumult of emotions to engulf her or for the ache in her chest to hurt so much.

She had shed enough tears for this man, so many she'd thought herself all cried out.

Massimo had never loved her. That was the truth she needed to keep reminding herself of.

But she had loved him. Truly, madly, deeply.

And in return he'd broken her.

The worst of it was he had no idea. For all his high intelligence, her husband had the emotional depth of an earthworm. She'd just been too blind to see it.

She closed her eyes and took three long inhalations.

There was no point in driving herself crazy with her thoughts. She had loved him once and while echoes of that love still beat in her heart they weren't real. She didn't love him any more. She was only there to honour the promise she'd made to him the day he'd let her go without a solitary word of fight to make her stay.

He'd wanted her gone. He'd been relieved. She'd seen it in his eyes.

Three more deep breaths and she got back to her feet and flushed the unused toilet.

She was Livia Briatore, formerly Livia Esposito, daughter of Pietro Esposito, Don Fortunato's most trusted clan member and henchman until her father's gangland murder when she'd been only eight. She'd been raised in the Secondigliano surrounded by drugs and brutal violence and she'd learned from an early age to show no fear. To show nothing.

Escaping Naples to study nursing in Rome had been like learning to breathe. Dropping her guard had not been easy—constantly checking over her shoulder when she walked a street was a habit it had taken many years to break—but she had forged a new life for herself and the joy it had given her had been worth the anxiety that had gnawed at her to be separated from her siblings. Life had gone from being a constant knot in her belly to being an adventure. She'd learned to laugh. With Massimo she had learned to love.

But her old protective barrier had never fully gone. It had sat patiently inside her waiting to be slipped back on.

To get through the next four days she needed that barrier. She needed to keep her guard up, not as protection against Massimo but as protection against her own foolish heart.

She took her seat and was not surprised to find Massimo working again on his laptop.

This time he raised his eyes from the screen to look at her. 'I've ordered us coffee. Did you want anything to eat?'

'I've eaten,' she answered with strained politeness, not adding that all she'd eaten that day had been half a slice of toast. Her stomach had been too tight and cramped to manage anything else. The countdown to seeing Massimo again had wrecked the little equilibrium she'd regained for herself.

It was hardly surprising that there was an awkwardness between them but they had a long flight ahead and she didn't want to spend it in uncomfortable silence. 'How have you been?'

He pulled a face and turned his attention back to his laptop. 'Busy.'

She dug her fake nails into her thighs. How she hated that word. It was the word he'd always used to justify never being there. 'Are you too busy to stop working for five minutes and talk?'

'I have data to interpret and an analysis to send.'

Two years ago he would have explained both the data and analysis to her, assuming rightly that she would find it interesting. The truth was she had found everything about Massimo interesting. Enthralling. The workings of his brain had never failed to astonish her. How could they not? This was the man who'd used his downtime from his computer engineering degree to create a web-based platform game that had taken the world by storm and which he'd sold upon his graduation for two hundred million US dollars. That money had been the linchpin for his move to America, where he'd formed his company, Briatore Technologies, whilst simultaneously studying for a PhD in energy physics, followed by a second PhD in applied physics and material sciences. His company, of which he was still the sole owner, now employed thousands worldwide, creating environmentally friendly solutions for many of the world's greatest carbon-related threats. He was on a one-man mission to save the planet one invention at a time. That he'd earned himself a fortune in the process was almost incidental. Only a month ago he'd been named in the top thirty of the world's most powerful people and in the top fifty of the world's richest.

It would have been so easy for him to make her feel stupid but he never had. Anything she didn't understand—which when it came to his work was most things—he would explain patiently but never patronisingly, his face lighting up when she grasped the finer details of something, like how a lithium ion battery worked and what carbon capture meant on a practical level.

She had been so thrilled that this man, clever, rich, successful and with a face and body to make the gods envious, had been as seemingly enthralled with her as she had been with him that she'd been blind to his emotional failings. Once the first flush of lust had worn off he'd retreated into the all-consuming world he'd created for himself, hiding himself away from the woman he'd married.

She wished she knew what she'd done to make him back away from her but every time she'd tried to get him to open up, the further into his shell he'd retreated.

The silence, filled intermittently by the sounds of Massimo tapping on the laptop's keyboard, grew more oppressive.

She watched him work. The familiar furrow of concentration was etched on his brow. How could he tune her out so effectively?

But as she watched him she noticed subtle changes. Flecks of white around the temples of his thick black hair that had never been there before. The full beard, as if he'd given up the bother of shaving altogether. Dark rings around his eyes as if he'd given up sleep along with shaving. Not that he had ever slept much. His brain was too busy for sleep.

Livia swallowed back the pang that had crept through her. Massimo was thirty-six years old; old enough to not look after himself if that was what he wanted.

He reached absently for the strong black coffee on the desk beside his laptop and took a large sip. His attention did not stray from the screen before him. He tapped something else onto the keyboard. The sound was akin to nails being dragged down a chalkboard.

Suddenly she could bear it no more. Jumping back to her feet, she took the three steps to him and slammed his laptop lid down.

CHAPTER TWO

MASSIMO CLENCHED HIS teeth together and placed a protective hand on his laptop to prevent Livia from snatching hold of it and throwing it onto the floor. 'What was that for?'

Diminutive though she was in height, in presence she was larger than life and right then, standing over him, she seemed magnified, the anger rippling from her in waves. 'We've been in the air for an hour and you've spared me only ten words.'

'Twenty-six,' he corrected through gritted teeth. 'I have spoken twenty-six words.'

'And now you're being pedantic as well as rude.' She pulled her hair together in a fist then released it. 'How are we supposed to convince your grandfather and the rest of your family that we're still together if you won't look at me or talk to me?'

'I'm not being rude. This is a very important time for me. On Monday we are running the prototypes on...'

'I don't *care*,' she interrupted with a cry. 'Whatever you're working on, I do not care. I'm here as a favour to you for your grandfather's benefit. The least you can do is treat me with some respect.'

'If I'm being disrespectful then I apologise,' he answered stiffly, biting back the retort of *what did you expect?* Livia had been the one to walk out on their marriage, not him. She had been the one to laugh in his face when he suggested they have a child. How did she expect him to be around her?

Damned if *he* knew how to act around her. Focusing his attention on the screen before him was the only tool he had to drive out the tumultuous emotions ripping through him. That these emotions were still there defied belief but Livia had always been able to induce feelings in him that had no place in his world, feelings that went far deeper than mere lust and friendship. She took up too much head space. She distracted him. That would have been easy to deal with if she'd only distracted his head when he'd been at home.

'I don't want your apologies. You don't mean it. You never do. Your apologies are meaningless.'

It was an accusation she had thrown at him many times and usually preceded an escalation of her temper, which only got wilder when he refused to engage. Massimo disliked meaningless confrontation, considered it a waste of energy, and would walk away when she refused to listen to reason.

Unfortunately, right now there was nowhere for him to walk away to. To escape to.

Keeping his own temper in check—keeping a cool head when all those around him lost theirs was something he took pride in—Massimo inhaled slowly through his nose and gazed at the angry face before him. 'What I'm working on is important. I'll be finished before we land in Los Angeles. We can spend the time between Los Angeles and Fiji talking if that's what you want.'

She laughed without any humour then flopped onto

the seat opposite his and glared at him. 'Great. You're going to do me the huge favour of talking to me if *I* want. Thank you. You're too kind.'

She'd folded her arms across her chest, slightly raising her breasts. He knew she hadn't done it deliberately—intimacy between them had died long before she'd called time on their marriage itself—but it distracted him enough for a sliver of awareness to pierce his armoury.

Livia had a body that could make a man weep. Even dressed as she was now, fully covered in tight faded jeans and a roll-neck black jumper, her feminine curves were undeniable. The first time he'd made love to her he'd thought he'd died and gone to heaven. Her virginity had surprised and delighted him. Surprised him because he would never have believed a twenty-four-year-old woman with such a dirty laugh and who carried herself with such confidence could be a virgin. Delighted him because it had marked her as his in a primal way he'd never experienced before.

Sex had never been a great need for him. When he'd shot up from a scrawny teenager into the frame he now inhabited, he'd suddenly found women throwing themselves at him, something that had only increased when he'd sold his web-based game after graduation and become worth a fortune. If he'd been in the mood he'd been happy to oblige, finding sex a satiating yet fleeting diversion from his work. Livia was the first woman he'd been truly intimate with. When they had first got together they'd been unable to keep their hands off each other. For the first time in his life Massimo had found himself consumed by lust.

The loss of that intimacy had not been his choice. Their marriage had disintegrated to such an extent that the nights he had made it home, they'd slept back to back. A man could take only so much rejection from his own wife before he stopped bothering.

Had she taken a lover? It was a thought that sent a stabbing motion plunging into his chest and for a moment he closed his eyes and breathed the pain away.

It was none of his business if she'd taken a lover and it would be unreasonable to expect her to have remained celibate during their separation. If not for his grandfather they would already be divorced.

'When did you last see your grandfather?' she asked suddenly, cutting through his attempts to concentrate on the screen in front of him rather than the bombshell opposite.

Livia felt only fleeting satisfaction to see the caramel eyes raise to meet hers.

'Why do you ask?'

'Because when I saw him the day before he set sail for Fiji he complained that you hadn't been in touch. I emailed Lindy about it.'

Lindy was Massimo's PA, a dragon of a woman who ran his business life. She was the only person in the world who knew their marriage was over in all but name. As far as their respective families were concerned, they were still together.

When they'd married, Livia had hoped Massimo's new status would encourage him to see more of his family but it hadn't worked that way. In their two years of shared life they had spent one Christmas with his family and that had been it. Livia had made numerous visits from their house in Los Angeles to Italy alone, visiting her youngest brother and dropping in on Massimo's family, all of whom she adored.

Since they'd gone their separate ways, her frequent visits had continued. They were used to her visiting alone so Massimo's absence had gone unremarked. Only Madeline, Massimo's sister, had the perception to see that anything was wrong but as she had a newborn child to take care of, her perception skills were less honed than usual. The ache that formed in Livia's heart as she held Madeline's baby only added to the ache already there but she would have been helpless to resist cradling the tiny bundle in her arms even if she didn't have a show to perform.

None of the Briatores or Espositos had any idea she was back on Italian soil permanently. Whenever she was asked about Massimo—who rarely bothered to message his family and had never met his niece—she would say he was busy with work, satisfied that she wasn't telling a lie. Massimo was *always* busy with work. Always. She'd lived with his grandfather as his private nurse for nine months and in that time Massimo hadn't made one trip home. She'd accepted the family line that Massimo was too busy to fly home from California regularly but had come to her own private conclusion during their marriage that it was nothing to do with his schedule preventing him from spending more time with his family. He simply didn't want to.

She would be glad when these evasions of the truth could be done with and they could tell his family they had separated. She hated lying, even if only by omission.

'Lindy mentioned it,' he admitted stiffly.

'Did you do anything about it?'

'I called him on the ship. He sounded fine.' His gaze dropped back to his laptop.

'He isn't fine.' Livia's heart had broken to see how

frail Jimmy had become. The elderly yet vital man who'd waged such a strong battle against his first diagnosis of cancer was fading, too weak to fly both legs of the mammoth journey to Fiji. It had been decided that a cruise was the safest way to get him to the other side of the world. Jimmy wanted to spend his ninetieth birthday with all his family around him, see corners of the world he'd never visited before and tread the soil he'd been raised on one last time.

Everything for him was now one last time.

'I know that.'

'Will you spend some proper time with him this weekend?' she asked. It was pointless adding that spending real time with Massimo was Jimmy's greatest wish. It was his parents' greatest wish too.

Massimo thought the gift of his money was enough. When he'd made his fortune, he'd bought his entire family new homes of their own and a car each. As his wealth had increased so had his generous gifts to them. It had been Massimo who'd paid for the private treatment during Jimmy's first diagnosis and all the associated costs including the agency fees for Livia's wages as his live-in nurse. It was Massimo who had bought the island his grandfather came from and spent a fortune building a complex for the entire family to stay on. It was Massimo footing the bill for the cruise the rest of the family were taking with Jimmy to reach the island. He'd chartered an ocean liner for their sole use.

Yet for all his generosity, he was spectacularly blind to the fact his family would much rather have his presence than his presents. He also seemed blind to the fact that time was running out for his grandfather.

'Yes.'

'You'll leave your laptop and phone switched off?'

'You know I can't do that.'

'I know you *won't* do that.'

His jaw clenched. 'We can talk about this later.'

She laughed mockingly. 'Later. Of course. Everything is always *later* with you, isn't it?'

Without any warning, Massimo slammed his fist against the panel beside his seat. 'And everything still has to be *now* with you. I said we could talk once I have completed my work but, as always, you don't listen. This is important and needs my attention. If you can't wait patiently for me to finish then I suggest you take yourself to the bedroom and give your mouth a rest.'

Massimo refused to feel guilt for his outburst, even when Livia's face paled before him.

True to form, she refused to let him get the last word, getting to her feet slowly and glowering at him. 'If anyone has a problem with listening it's you. If it doesn't involve your precious work then it's insignificant to you. It's been four months since you last saw me and you haven't even cared to ask how I've been. If I'd had any doubts that leaving you was the best thing I could do, an hour in your company has proven me right. You never cared for me. You've never cared for anyone.'

She walked away, not to the bedroom but to her original seat. There was dignity in the way she moved that, despite the acrimony that thickened the air between them, touched him. Livia was a strange mix of toughness and vulnerability, traits that had first moved him then infuriated him. Her toughness meant she did not know how to back down from an argument but the underlying vulnerability found her easily wounded. He'd never known the words to say to repair the wounds he'd unwittingly inflicted on her. Eventually he'd stopped trying.

Her partition rose and she disappeared from sight.

Massimo sighed his relief and rubbed his eyes. He hadn't slept in over twenty-four hours and was exhausted.

Ringing the bell, he ordered a fresh coffee when the stewardess appeared. Caffeine and sugar would keep him awake long enough to get his analysis done. Maybe then he'd be able to catch some sleep.

He tuned out Livia's husky voice when the stewardess turned her attention to his wife.

But he couldn't tune out her presence.

The data on the screen before him blurred. His head felt so heavy. All of him felt heavy, a weight compressing him from the top down and, even with the importance of the work that needed to be done, he found his thoughts drifting to the early days of their marriage, days when he'd believed nothing could come between them.

Nothing *had* come between them. Only themselves.

Livia tried to concentrate on the movie she'd selected from the thousands stored on the in-flight entertainment system—a system Massimo had had installed for her benefit—but the storyline passed her by in a haze. The first movie, a comedy, had passed her by too. This second one was a critically acclaimed thriller guaranteed to keep her tear ducts intact but, even with the sound on her headphones turned up high to drown out the incessant tapping of Massimo's fingers on his keyboard, he was all she could think about.

How had it come to this? How could a marriage

formed with such passion and joy disintegrate into such bitterness?

Movement caught her attention and she removed her headphones and straightened as the head stewardess approached to see if she would like anything.

'A blanket would be nice, thanks,' she replied. The air-conditioning on Massimo's jet was always set to freezing.

The blanket delivered, Livia was suddenly struck by the cabin's silence.

Lowering her partition, she looked across at Massimo.

He'd fallen asleep.

His laptop was still open but the man himself was fast asleep, upright in his seat, his mouth slightly open as he breathed in and out heavily.

A tightness formed in her chest as she watched until, without thinking, she got to her feet and padded over to him.

For a long time, hardly daring to breathe, she drank in the features of the man she had once loved so much. His Fijian ancestry was stronger in him than in his sister. His skin was a deep olive, his thick hair the most beautiful shade of ebony. She'd liked it when he forgot to cut it, and had spent many happy hours snuggled on the sofa with him, Massimo talking, his head on her lap, Livia content to simply listen to his wonderful rich, deep voice and run her fingers through his hair. It was the closest to peace she had ever felt in her life.

She'd tried so hard to hold onto what they had but he had slipped away from her with the same ease her fingers had run through his hair.

Her throat closed, Livia carefully draped the blanket she'd been about to use for herself on his lap. She wanted to press the button that would tilt the chair back and turn it into a bed but was afraid the motion would wake him. Struck again by the dark circles around his eyes, she wondered when he'd last had a decent night's sleep. Or the last time he'd had a decent meal.

The compulsion to reach out her hand and stroke her fingers over his high cheekbones, to feel the texture of his skin on hers, to run her fingers through his hair… it all hit her so fast that her hand was inches from his face before she realised what she was about to do and stopped herself.

Her heart thumped wildly and for a moment she couldn't breathe.

Putting her hand to her chest, she backed away, afraid to be this close to him.

Afraid of what it did to her.

Massimo's eyes opened with a start.

He blinked rapidly, disorientated.

His laptop was still open but had put itself into sleep mode.

Had *he* fallen asleep?

Getting to his feet to stretch his legs, he felt a sudden chill on his thighs and gazed down in astonishment at the blanket that had fallen to the floor.

Where had that come from?

He stared over at Livia. Her partition was still up but, standing, he could see her clearly. She'd reclined her chair and was watching something on the television with her headphones in. A blanket covered her whole body up to her chin.

'Did you put a blanket on me?' He didn't mean to sound so accusatory but the thought of her doing that…

Her face turned towards him and she pulled the head-phones off. 'Did you say something?'

Before he could answer one of the cabin crew entered. 'We will be landing in twenty minutes.'

The moment they were alone again, Massimo turned back to Livia. 'How long was I asleep?'

She shrugged.

He swore under his breath. He hadn't finished his analysis. Damn it, he'd promised the project manager that he would have it in his inbox before he reached the office that morning.

He bit back the demand he wanted to throw at her as to why she hadn't woken him and sat back down.

Livia had put the blanket on him. He knew that with a deep certainty and he didn't know if it was that simple gesture or that he was now behind on where he needed to be workwise that made his guts feel as if acid had been poured in them.

He felt close to snapping. Virulent emotions were coursing through him and his wife, the cause of all his angst, was reclined in her seat as nonchalant as could be.

But knowing her as well as he did, he knew her non-chalance was a sham. Livia did not do nonchalance.

Why had she put a blanket on him?

His eyes were better able to focus after his short sleep but, with their landing imminent, he put his laptop away and folded his desk up and secured it, all the while hat-ing that he was fully aware of Livia sorting her own seating area out, avoiding looking at him as much as he avoided looking at her.

Los Angeles couldn't come soon enough.

Not another word was exchanged until the plane had landed safely.

Needing to escape the strange febrile atmosphere that seemed to have infected his flight crew as much as them, Massimo grabbed his laptop and got to his feet but the moment he left his seat, Livia was there facing him in the aisle, holding her bag tightly, clearly ready to make her own escape.

He stepped to one side to let her pass but she stepped to the same side too.

Their eyes met. Their gaze held, only momentarily, but long enough for him to see the pain she had become a master at hiding from him.

A sharp compression lanced his chest, as if his heart had become a rose in full bloom, its thorns spearing into him.

And then she blinked, cast her gaze to the floor, murmured, 'Excuse me,' and brushed past him.

Massimo swallowed away the lump in his throat and left his plane by the other exit.

CHAPTER THREE

TWO HOURS AFTER landing in Los Angeles, they were cleared to take off for the second leg of their mammoth journey to Fiji.

Livia had returned to the plane before Massimo. She guessed he'd gone to the private executive lounge in the airport to work. She'd taken herself for a walk, keeping her phone in her hand for the alert that the plane had refuelled and she could get back on, and tried to get hold of Gianluca, her youngest sibling. He hadn't answered and hadn't called her back either. She'd had no wish to go sightseeing or do any of the things most visitors with a short layover at LAX would do. Just breathing the air brought back the awful feelings that had lived in her the last dying months of their marriage.

She hated Los Angeles. She hated California. She'd loathed living there. For a place known as the Golden State, her life there had been devoid of sunshine.

At first, she'd enjoyed the novelty of it all. Compared to Naples and Rome it was huge. Everything was so much bigger. Even the sky and the sun that shone in it appeared greater and brighter. But then loneliness had seeped its way in. She had no friends there and no means to make them. Unlike Massimo, who spoke fluent English, her own English was barely passable. The glass home they'd shared was forty kilometres from downtown LA. An intensely private man, Massimo had deliberately chosen a home far from prying eyes. There were no neighbours. The household staff spoke only English and Spanish.

She'd become sick with longing for home.

Massimo hadn't understood. He hadn't even tried.

But there hadn't been any sunshine since she'd left him and returned to her home in Italy either.

It was strange to experience taking off in her second sunset of the day. She should have slept during the first leg of the journey but sleep had been the last thing on her mind, the last thing she'd been capable of. The sun putting itself to sleep now in LA would soon be awakening in Rome.

She yawned and cast her eyes in Massimo's direction. His partition was raised again but she could still hear the tapping of his fingers on the keypad. So much for talking. Silence for them truly had become golden.

A member of the cabin crew brought her pillows and a duvet and turned her seat into a bed while Livia used the bathroom to change into pyjamas, remove her makeup and brush her teeth.

She thought of the plane's bedroom and its comfortable king-sized bed. An ache formed in the pit of her stomach to remember the glorious hours they had spent sharing it. Massimo would never begrudge her sleeping in it now but she couldn't do it. She couldn't sleep in a bed they had shared knowing that when she woke the pillow beside her would be unused. That had been hard enough to deal with when they'd been together.

Massimo was on his feet stretching his aching back

when Livia returned to the cabin clutching her washbag. It was the same washbag she'd used when they'd been married and his heart tugged to see it.

She looked younger with her face free from make-up and plain cream pyjamas on. More vulnerable too.

The threads tugging at his heart tightened.

'I'm going to have a nightcap. Do you want one?'

Surprise lit her dark brown eyes before they fixed on his own freshly made-up bed. 'You're finished?'

He nodded. 'My apologies for it taking so long. I didn't factor in falling asleep.'

Her plump lips curved into the tiniest of smiles. 'I would have woken you but you looked exhausted.'

She looked exhausted. Her seat had been made up into a bed for her too but, however comfortable it was, it was not the same as sleeping in a proper bed. 'Why don't you sleep in our bed?'

Now the tiniest of winces flashed over her face. 'I'll be fine here, thank you. You should use it—you only napped for a couple of hours.'

The only time he'd been in the jet's bedroom since she'd left him was to use the en-suite shower. Sleeping in the bed he'd shared with her…the thought alone had been enough to make his guts twist tightly.

To see the same reluctance reflected in her eyes twisted them even harder.

He removed a bottle of his favourite bourbon and two glasses from the bar as the stewardess came into the cabin with a bucket of ice. Massimo took it from her and arched an eyebrow in question at Livia.

She hesitated for a moment before nodding.

As the stewardess dimmed the lights and left the

cabin, he poured them both a measure and handed a glass to Livia.

She took it with a murmured thanks, avoiding direct eye contact, carefully avoiding his touch. He could smell the mintiness of her toothpaste and caught a whiff of the delicately scented cream she used to remove her make-up and the moisturiser she finished her night-time routine with. The two combined into a scent that had always delighted his senses far more than her perfume, which in itself was beautiful. The perfume she sprayed herself with by day could be enjoyed by anyone who got close enough. Her night-time scent had always been for him alone.

Had any other man been lucky enough to smell it since they'd parted?

She sat on her bed and took a small sip of her bourbon. As she moved he couldn't help but notice the light sway of her naked breasts beneath the silk pyjama top.

Her nightwear was functional and obviously selected to cover every inch but the curves that had driven him to such madness were clearly delineated beneath the fabric and it took all his willpower to keep his gaze fixed on her face.

But her face had driven him to madness as much as the body had. With Livia it had always been the whole package. Everything about her. Madness.

After a few moments of stilted silence she said, 'Are you going to get some sleep too?'

Massimo knew what Livia was thinking: that having his own seat made into a bed was no indication that he actually intended to get any rest.

He shrugged and took a large sip of his bourbon, willing the smooth burn it made in his throat to flow through his veins and burn away the awareness searing his loins.

'If I can.' He raised his glass. 'This should help.' Enough of it would allow him a few precious hours of oblivion to the firecracker who would be sleeping at such close quarters to him.

'How long do we have until we reach Fiji?'

He checked his watch. 'Nine hours until we land at Nadi.'

'We get another flight from there?' Livia already knew the answer to this but the dimming of the lights seemed to have shrunk the generously proportioned cabin and given it an air of dangerous intimacy.

What was it about darkness that could change an atmosphere so acutely? Livia had grown up scared of the dark. The Secondigliano was a dangerous place in daylight. At night, all the monsters came out.

The dangers now were as different as night and day compared to her childhood and adolescence but she felt them as keenly. With Massimo's face in shadows his handsome features took on a devilish quality that set her stomach loose with butterflies and her skin vibrating with awareness.

'I've chartered a Cessna to fly us to Seibua Island.'

'You managed to get the name changed?' She couldn't remember the original name of the island Massimo's grandfather had been born and raised on.

'The paperwork's still being sorted but I've been reliably informed it's been accepted.' He finished his drink and poured himself another, raising the bottle at her in an unspoken question.

She shook her head. Marriage to Massimo had given her a real appreciation of bourbon but too much alcohol had a tendency to loosen her tongue, which she was the first to admit didn't need loosening. It also loosened her inhibitions. She'd never had any inhibitions around Massimo before but to get through the weekend in one piece she needed them as greatly as she needed to keep her guard up around him. All of this would be easier to cope with if her heart didn't ache so much just to share the same air as him again.

'Are you going to buy a Cessna of your own to keep there?'

He grimaced and finally perched himself on his bed. The overhead light shone down on him. 'The yacht's already moored there and can be used as transport. Whether I buy a plane too depends on how often the family use the island.' The resort created on the island would be available for the entire extended family to use as and when they wished, free of charge. The only stipulation would be that they treated it with respect.

'Knowing your sister it will be often.' It was doubtful Massimo would ever use it. His idea of a holiday was to take a Sunday off work.

She caught the whisper of a smile on his firm mouth but it disappeared behind his glass as he took another drink.

'When did your family get there?'

'They arrived three days ago.'

'Have you been to the island yet?'

'I haven't had the time.'

She chewed her bottom lip rather than give voice to her thoughts that this was typical Massimo, never having the time for anything that didn't revolve around work. He'd jumped through hoops and paid an astronomical sum for the island but those hoops had been jumped through by his lawyers and accountants. He'd spent a further fortune having the complex for the family built but, again, he'd had little involvement past hiring the architects and transferring the cash. Livia had signed off on the initial blueprint for the complex in the weeks before she'd left him. She had no idea if he'd even bothered to do more than cast an eye over it.

There was no point in her saying anything. It would only be a rehash of a conversation they'd had many times before, a conversation that would only lead to an argument. Or, as usually happened, it would lead to her getting increasingly het up at his refusal to engage in the conversation and losing her temper, and Massimo walking away in contempt leaving her shouting at the walls.

In any case, Massimo's sidelining of anything that wasn't work-related was none of her business. Not any more. If he wanted to blow his own money on projects and assets he had no intention of enjoying then that was up to him. If he wanted to keep his family on the fringes of his life for eternity then that was up to him too. He wasn't an adolescent like her youngest brother, Gianluca, who'd been born seven months after their father's death.

There was hope for Gianluca. Unlike their other siblings, who had succumbed to life in the Secondigliano, Gianluca's humanity was still there. The question was whether he had the courage to take Livia's hand and join her far from the violence and drugs that were such an intrinsic part of the Espositos' lives before it was too late and he was sucked into a life of crime from which his only escape would be in a coffin.

It was too late for Pasquale, who like their dead father had risen high in Don Fortunato's ranks, and too late for Denise who had married one of Pasquale's equally ambitious friends and was currently pregnant with their second child. Livia's siblings and her mother all knew Livia's door was always open for them. Gianluca was the only one she allowed herself to hope for. He could still leave without repercussions just as she had but time was running out. He'd recently turned eighteen. Should Don Fortunato decide Gianluca was worthy of joining his guard he would strike soon.

The man Livia had married, a man who abhorred violence and anything to do with illegal drugs, had made his choice when he was only a few years older than Gianluca. He'd chosen to leave Italy and leave his family, just as his own grandfather had done seventy years before him. The difference was his grandfather had left Fiji for the love of his life, an Englishwoman, and set up home with her in England. When their daughter Sera had married an Italian, Jimmy and Elizabeth had moved again, this time to Italy so they could stay close to their daughter. For them, family came first above all else. They were as close as close could be. All except for Massimo himself.

He didn't want to change. He saw nothing wrong with how he lived his life, nothing wrong with keeping a physical and emotional distance from the people who loved him. That was the choice he'd made and Livia had to respect that. She couldn't change it. She'd tried. When the realisation hit that his emotional distance from his family extended to her too, along with the recognition that this too would never change, she'd had no choice but to leave him.

She hadn't clawed her way out of the Secondigliano to spend her life as a trophy in a glass cabinet masquerading as a home.

While she had spent the past four months trying desperately to fix herself back together, for Massimo there had been nothing to fix. He'd got on with his life as if she'd never been a part of it.

Finishing her drink, she put the empty glass in the holder beside her bed and got under the covers. 'I'm going to get some sleep. Goodnight.' Then she turned her back on him and closed her eyes.

Massimo lay under his bed sheets, eyes wide open. He'd drunk enough bourbon to tranquillise an elephant but his mind was too busy. Except now it wasn't the project he'd spent over a year working on that stopped his mind switching off.

Turning his head, eyes adjusted to the dark, he watched the rhythmic rise and fall of Livia's duvet. He guessed she'd been asleep for around an hour now. He always knew when she was properly asleep and not just faking it. When she faked it, she lay rigid in absolute silence.

They'd slept together the first night they'd met—once they'd got talking at the hotel bar he hadn't let her out of his sight—and both of them had known it was no one-night stand. He'd been dozing in the aftermath, Livia wrapped in his arms, his body thrumming with the delights they'd just shared, when she'd mumbled something. That was his first experience of her sleep-talking. He'd quickly discovered that she talked a lot in her sleep. Sometimes the words were distinct. He remembered the feeling that had erupted through him the first time she'd mumbled his name. It had been ten times the magnitude of what he'd felt to be offered two hundred million dollars for the stupid game he'd developed during his boring university evenings.

But her dreams hadn't always been good. At least once a week he'd had to wake her from a bad one. The darkness of the life she'd lived until she'd left Naples at eighteen still haunted her.

Had another man woken her from the nightmares since she'd left him?

He pinched the bridge of his nose and willed the pain spearing him away.

Livia's sex life was no longer his business.

The thought of her with a lover was something that hadn't even occurred to him until she'd stepped onto his plane and now it was all he could think of.

In the four months since she'd left him, his own libido had gone into hibernation. From the feelings erupting through him now, he realised he'd shut down far more than his libido.

He'd shut down long before she'd left him.

Their marriage had begun with such high hopes and such certainty. They'd both been too foolish to realise that it was nothing but lust, a flaming passion that could only burn itself out.

He'd been intoxicated by her. He'd never met anyone like her: tough on the outside but marshmallow-soft inside. Straight talking. Capable of lancing with her tongue. But tender and compassionate. Someone who would drop everything if she were needed. Someone who would give everything they had if it were needed. Massimo had never been one for showing his emotions but being tactile with Livia had come naturally. She'd brought that side of him out right from the start.

And then the tide had turned. His assumptions that he

would be able to continue his life and work in the same way he always had but with his beautiful, vivacious wife to come home to had been quickly dispelled.

He should never have married her, that was the truth of it, but he'd been so swept up in the need to tie her to him and make her his in every way possible that he'd blinded himself to what marriage to a woman like Livia would actually entail. It entailed far more than he could give.

It was still dark when Livia woke. Groping for her phone, she looked at the time and was relieved to see they only had a couple of hours left until they landed.

Creeping out of her bed so as not to wake Massimo, she took her overnight bag from the compartment and made her way to the bedroom. She needed a shower. It was pure misfortune that the main bathroom was reached through the bedroom.

The moment she opened the bedroom door and stepped inside, she realised her mistake. The bathroom light was already switched on and the scent of Massimo's shower gel seeped through the gap in the door. Before she could beat a hasty retreat, the door opened and he stepped over the threshold as naked as the day he was born.

Startled caramel eyes met hers. All the air flew from her lungs.

Seconds passed that stretched like hours as they did nothing but stare at each other.

A compression formed in her chest and tightened her throat.

For a man who rarely worked out, Massimo had a physique to die for. Lean but muscular, his deep olive skin had only the lightest brush of fine dark hair over his defined pecs and the plane of his washboard stomach. The hair thickened considerably below his abdomen to the huge…

Her own abdomen contracted, heat rushing through her pelvis as she noticed—couldn't *help* but notice—his growing erection.

The heat in her pelvis spread. It suffused her cheeks with colour and she tightened her hold on her bag, crushing it against her chest.

Slowly, his features became taut, his nostrils flaring. His caramel eyes swirled with something she recognised, something that should have her spinning round immediately and leaving. But she couldn't. Her feet were rooted to the floor.

He'd had more work done on his tattoo, she noticed dimly, trying desperately hard not to let her gaze fall back below his waist, trying even harder to contain the rush of sultry warmth flooding her veins. His tattoo covered the entire bicep around his left shoulder, all in bold black lines. The large sun, the centrepiece that he had once told her symbolised his rebirth and represented the way he strove for perfection in all he did, was encircled by sharks' teeth, which represented power, leadership and protection, and they were now encircled by spearheads. She didn't know what the spearheads represented but knew they must mean something to him.

Instinct told her they represented something to do with her.

The sensation in her fingers that had almost had her touching his sleeping face earlier tingled again. An ache to touch his tattoo. To touch him. A yearning to feel the heat of his powerful body flush against hers, to be swept in his arms and to lose herself in the wonder she had always found in his lovemaking. It all hit her so quickly that if he had reached out for her she would have fallen into his arms in an instant.

More seconds stretched without a word exchanged but with that thick, sick chemistry shrouding them.

And then Massimo closed his eyes.

When he next looked at her, the swirling desire had gone.

He'd shut down again.

He turned and walked back into the bathroom, locking the door behind him.

CHAPTER FOUR

LIVIA GAZED OUT of the window of the Cessna they'd transferred to after landing at Fiji's Nadi airport and soaked in the oval-shaped patch of land that rose like a majestic tropical oasis from the South Pacific below. Ringed with golden sand and light turquoise shores that deepened to ultramarine, Seibua Island was far more beautiful and exotic than even its namesake had described.

Livia had only ever travelled from her Italian homeland to the US; the scents that exploded through her airways when she stepped onto the small airfield were ones she'd never had the pleasure of smelling before.

She stared up at the rising sun before closing her eyes and savouring the sensation of the most incredible warmth on her skin.

Then she cast a glance at Massimo to witness his reaction at his first steps on his grandfather's homeland.

Far from savouring anything, he'd immediately headed to the waiting golf buggy and was introducing himself to its elderly driver.

Like Livia, who'd changed into a knee-length red sundress, Massimo had donned summer clothing too, opting for a pair of black canvas shorts and a fitted navy T-shirt with the cover of a hellraising rock band's album on it. Ever the chameleon, he looked as divine in these casual items as he did in a full dinner jacket but it only made her think that he never looked better than when he wore nothing at all, and she had to push hard to rid her mind of the vivid image of him standing before her naked. It was a battle she'd been losing for the past four hours.

She forced a smile at the two young men who were removing their luggage from the small plane and loading it onto a second buggy, and walked over to Massimo, who introduced her to the man he employed to run the island for him, first in English then in Italian for her benefit.

She shook the extended hand from the friendly looking man and carefully said, 'It is nice to see you.'

She caught the dart of surprise that flashed in Massimo's eyes but he said nothing about her attempt at English, indicating only that she should get into the buggy.

She slid into the back and was relieved when Massimo climbed in the front beside the driver.

'How long until we get to the complex?' she asked. The island was bigger than she'd envisaged. Naively, she'd imagined something around the size of a small field with a solitary palm tree as a marker.

'Not long. Five or ten minutes.'

Soon the thick, scented flora they drove through separated and the golden sand she'd seen from the air lay before them, glimmering under the glorious sunshine.

Stunned, she craned her neck to take in the thatched chalets nestled—but not too closely together—along the length of a high rock formation that ended on the shore of the beach. A long wooden bridge led the eye to a further thatched chalet that appeared to rise out of the ocean itself. On the other side of the thatched cottages and lower down, separated from the beach by a wall, lay the chalet designated for Massimo's grandfather. Beside it lay a handful of smaller though no less beautiful chalets. To the right of all these dwellings was the centrepiece, the huge, multi-purpose lodge behind which, virtually camouflaged by the coconut palms and other tropical trees and foliage that thrived on the island, were the structures that housed the great kitchens and the island staff's living quarters. Further to the right, where the beach curved out of sight, were the mangrove saplings, recently planted in their thousands to protect the island from erosion and rising sea levels.

Everything Massimo had envisaged for the island of his grandfather's birth had come to life in spectacular fashion.

The driver stopped in front of the main lodge and said something to Massimo before jumping out.

Livia's heart almost dropped to her feet when Massimo followed suit and held his hand out to her.

Confused at this unexpected gesture, especially since they'd spent the past four hours after she'd inadvertently walked in on him naked ignoring each other's existence, she stared into the caramel eyes that were fixed on her with an intensity that belied the easy smile playing on his lips.

A child's cry rang out and in an instant she understood. Massimo's family were already there. He was holding his hand out because they must be watching.

She reached out and wrapped her fingers loosely round the waiting hand.

At the first touch of her skin to his, her heart flew from her feet to her throat and her fingers reflexively tightened.

For that one singular moment in time, the world paused on its axis as she stared into his soulful eyes and a rush of helpless longing swept through her, long-buried emotions rising up and clutching her throat.

And then the ground beneath her feet began to spin.

These were emotions she'd buried for a reason—because they had never been returned with the same depth with which she'd held them.

Turning her head and blinking the brief spell away from her vision, she was thankful to see Madeline on the steps that led to the main entrance of the lodge holding her infant daughter, Elizabeth. Dropping Massimo's hand, Livia hurried over to them and embraced her sister-in-law, careful not to squash baby Elizabeth, who immediately grabbed at her hair.

Massimo watched his wife and sister's embrace, watched them exchange enthusiastic kisses, watched his wife rub a finger against his niece's chubby cheek before lifting the child into her own arms, and had to fight to keep a lid on the emotions threatening to overwhelm him.

Livia had laughed at his suggestion that they have a child.

Slowly he made his way towards them, bracing himself for the rebuke that was certain to be coming.

Madeline didn't disappoint. After the obligatory kisses, she took Elizabeth back from Livia and hitched her to her hip. 'Massimo, meet your niece, Elizabeth. Elizabeth, this is the uncle you've heard about who's been too busy saving the world to meet you.'

Were it not for the large blue eyes of his six-month-old niece staring at him with fascination, he would have sworn at his sister. 'It's been a long journey here. Can you save the harassment until I've said hello to everyone else?'

His sister smiled beadily. 'Sure. The others are in the lodge waiting for you.'

The others were, in fact, his grandfather and his army of carers, and Massimo and Madeline's parents. Tomorrow night his grandfather's surviving siblings and their spouses, children, grandchildren and great-grandchildren would either fly or sail to the island for the birthday party. It would be the first time his grandfather had seen all but one of his siblings since he'd left the island paradise, one of the remotest and smallest of all the Fijian islands, for Europe. He'd been the first Seibua to leave. In the almost seventy years since his emigration the rest of the Seibuas had, one by one, left the island of their birth too in search of better opportunities to raise their families. Most had settled on Fiji's largest island, Viti Levu. The soon-to-be renamed Seibua Island had been uninhabited for over a decade before Massimo had purchased it.

The main lodge was everything the architect had promised. Massimo had wanted a space large enough to accommodate the entire extended family, whether it was for a sit-down meal or a party, and it had been created accordingly. Dining tables lined the walls to the left, plush sofas lined the walls to the right. A bar ran the length of the far wall. The space in between was large enough for a hundred people to dance or for an army of children to skid on and scuff the expensive flooring. He estimated that tomorrow evening there would be a minimum of fifteen children there to test it out.

For now, though, it was only immediate family there and the knotted weight of expectation that came with being them. Massimo hadn't seen any of them in over a year. But Livia had, and he watched her embrace his parents as if she were the child of their loins and not a mere daughter-in-law. She had never understood where his ambivalence to his family had come from. In his wife's eyes, he'd been raised with everything she'd wanted and been denied.

Livia's childhood had been torrid; filled with violence and menace, her father murdered before she reached double digits, her mother the manager of a wedding dress shop who sold drugs for extra cash along with the white lace creations. Her mother also received a monthly payment from Don Fortunato, the mafia boss Livia's father had protected. Blood money, Livia always disdainfully referred to it as. Money had never been an issue in the Esposito home. She'd told Massimo once of going into the back storeroom of her mother's shop and finding wads of cash wrapped in elastic bands in one of the boxes that was supposed to store garter belts. She'd estimated it at half a million euros. Money that belonged to Don Fortunato, stashed away until he came to reclaim it and launder it back into the world.

It had taken more guts than Massimo could comprehend for Livia to claw her way out of that violent, narcotic-infested world. She saw his childhood as idyllic, had no comprehension of what it was like to walk rain-lashed streets with holes in the soles of her shoes or to be the butt of school tormentors' jokes because the clothes you wore were two sizes too small and threadbare. He could have coped with being the butt of all the jokes if his parents had worked hard, as his one close friend's parents had, the father holding down two jobs, the mother working school hours, but they didn't. They hadn't. His father had worked in a shoe repair shop. By mutual agreement, his mother hadn't worked since Massimo's birth.

Life was for living! his father would proudly proclaim. Not for being a slave!

What did it matter if they could only afford to eat meat once a week? Their vegetable patch grew an abundance of nutritious food!

What did it matter if they couldn't afford to buy Massimo a new calculator when his was flushed down the toilet by his school tormentors? His brain was advanced enough to be its own calculator!

His brain was advanced enough to be its own calculator out of necessity, not design. And it had been advanced enough to know that if he wanted to make anything of his life it would have to come from him alone. From the age of thirteen, he'd worked for anyone who would employ him: running errands, stacking shelves, working on market stalls, cleaning offices. You name it, he'd done it. He'd bought his own computer and a phone, the rest of the money he'd stashed away for university, which was just as well as when it had come time for him to leave home for the wonder that was higher education, his parents had not had a single cent spare to help him.

It was during his university years that he'd created the platform game that had made him his initial fortune and also brought him closer to his grandparents. They'd moved to Rome when their daughter had married Massimo's Italian father and, their apartment being much closer to his university than his parents' home, had insisted he visit regularly for home-cooked food and a comfortable bed. It was in these years that he'd learned more about his grandfather's roots and heritage.

And now he was here in the place he'd visited only in his imagination, about to be closeted with his family for the first time in two years.

His parents' eyes were alight as he approached them.

What he intended to be a sedate, functional greeting was quickly turned into a greeting worthy of Hollywood. His father ignored his outstretched hand and pulled him into an embrace that would have squeezed the life out of a weaker man, then his mother did the same. Their exuberantly delivered words were lost amidst the planting of paternal and maternal kisses all over his face.

When he was finally able to disentangle himself, he turned to greet his grandfather and found himself faltering.

The wizened man sitting in a wheelchair with an oxygen tank attached…that was his grandfather? This was Jimmy Seibua?

Getting down to his haunches, Massimo stared into the filmy eyes that had once been the darkest chocolate then gently embraced him, his heart pounding with shock and pain.

It was like embracing a skeleton.

He hid his shock with the widest smile he could conjure. From the periphery of his vision he saw Livia speaking to one of his grandfather's medical team. He would talk to them too. Soon. When he was confident he could speak without ripping their heads off.

Soon the entire family was reclining together on sofas dragged together to form a square, his grandfather wheeled over to be with them, fresh coffee, pastries and fruit brought out for them to devour.

This should be a moment of great satisfaction for him but instead Massimo felt as if he'd been hit by an articulated lorry. His chest felt tight, as if all the air had been sucked out and his lungs and heart vacuum packed. He detested small talk at the best of times but right then he could hardly move his tongue to form simple words, responding to his brother-in-law's chat with grunts and monosyllables.

At his sister's instigation, he'd arranged for them to spend the day on the yacht he'd bought for the island, sailing out to a tiny atoll twenty kilometres away. This atoll was circled by a protected coral reef even more spectacular than the one surrounding Seibua Island and which cruise liners were forbidden from visiting.

Only another forty-eight hours to go until he could leave and return to his home and work in America.

He had a feeling these were going to be the longest forty-eight hours of his life. The distance between them had never felt greater. This was his family but he'd never felt a part of it. Part of *them*. Always he'd felt like the cuckoo in the nest. If he didn't have such a strong physical resemblance to his father and the colouring of his mother, he could easily believe he'd been adopted.

The only person he'd ever felt completely at ease with had been Livia but he now knew the ease had been a dopamine-induced illusion. She was sitting on the opposite sofa chatting to Madeline with baby Elizabeth on her lap, uncaring that her hair was being pulled by a tight, pudgy fist.

His estranged wife was more comfortable with his family than he was. The woman who'd laughed at having a child with him was laughing now, pretty white teeth gleaming where the sun's rays filtered through the high windows and bathed her in their light.

It was only when their eyes met that he saw the effort

it was costing her to maintain a carefree front. When he'd walked out of his bathroom naked and found her standing there...

He'd wanted to touch her with an ache that came from the very centre of his being.

The desire he'd thought had died with their marriage had come back to life as if it had never left. Livia still breathed in his blood. She pumped through his veins in a hot, relentless motion that seeped through his every pore, making his skin feverish.

There could be no going back. She was only there because of her love for his grandfather and her affection for the rest of his family.

Massimo waited until he'd drained his coffee before getting to his feet. 'I need to stretch my legs,' he announced. 'I'll see you all on the yacht in an hour.' Without waiting for a response, he strode out of the lodge and into the blazing sun.

His chalet was the one over the bridge and he headed towards it without breaking stride. His family didn't need him to entertain them. They were already settled in and relaxed in their surroundings, already tanned and glowing. All except his grandfather...

'Massimo, will you *wait*?'

Muttering a curse under his breath, he turned his head. Livia was hurrying in his direction, her hair flowing in a stream behind her.

'Problem?' he asked tightly when she reached him.

Livia snatched a breath of air. It had been years since she'd walked so quickly. 'I was going to ask you the same thing.'

His family had all turned their questioning eyes to her when he'd left the lodge. She'd shrugged apologetically and murmured that it had been a long flight before following him out.

He grunted and set off again.

'Are you going to tell me what's on your mind?' she asked when she caught up with him. Her short legs made double his strides to keep pace.

'I'm going to call the owner of the agency.'

'What agency?'

'The one who supplied the nurses and carers who were supposed to look after my grandfather. The agency *you* used to work for.'

They both stepped onto the wooden bridge without changing pace. It felt as substantial beneath her feet as the earth itself. 'Why?'

'I chose that agency because my previous experience with them was positive. I am disgusted that they've allowed him to get into this state. He's skin and bone. When was the last time he had a shave? My grandfather has shaved every day of his adult life and now he looks like a homeless drug addict.'

They'd reached the door to their cabin but before he could open it, Livia placed a hand on his wrist.

'I tried to warn you,' she said gently when he finally met her gaze. A pulse throbbed in his jaw.

He closed his eyes then shook her hand away. 'I know his cancer is incurable,' he bit out. 'That is no excuse for allowing him to get in such a state.'

She sighed and followed him into the chalet. After closing the door, she rested her back against it and tried to think of the words to use that wouldn't add to his distress. For she was quite certain that his anger was nothing but a mask for his anguish at seeing first-hand how close to death his grandfather really was.

'He's lost so much weight because he can't handle solid food any more,' she told him quietly. 'They can't shave him as often as he would like because his skin's become too sensitive. He can only cope with them doing it once a week.'

'You would make excuses for them,' he retorted scathingly. 'The medical profession always protects its own.'

'Even if I was still on the agency's books I wouldn't make excuses for medical negligence.'

The usually soulful eyes glittered menacingly. 'You accept they've neglected him?'

'No. They have given him exceptional care. The problem is it's been so long since you last saw Jimmy that the changes are more obvious to you.'

'I knew it wouldn't take long for you to get around to *my* supposed neglect of him.'

Livia sighed again in lieu of biting her tongue and in a vain effort to temper the anger rising in her. This was a weekend for celebration, not recriminations. Massimo was the one who had to live with his conscience, not her.

'Your grandfather is very ill, Massimo, but he's as comfortable and as pain-free as he can be. He's here on the island he loves with the family he loves. *You* made this happen, all of it. Don't spoil things for him by taking your anger at his condition out on those who have done their best for him.'

His jaw tightened as she spoke. For a long time he didn't respond, just stared at her until his nostrils flared and he gave a sharp nod. 'I need to call in with the office.'

This time her sigh was one of exasperation.

'I need to answer any questions the project manager has about the analysis and data before we set sail. Okay?'

She was glad he turned his back on her and strode through to the chalet's living room, his wretched phone already in his hand. It meant he didn't see the sheen of tears that suddenly filled her eyes.

CHAPTER FIVE

LIVIA TAMPED DOWN the gulf of feelings knotting her belly and boarded the white yacht. Although dwarfed in size by the cruise ship it was moored next to, it still dazzled with elegance. After their mammoth journey to the island she would have preferred to spend the day relaxing but this was the trip Madeline had forced Massimo to concede to. Livia knew what her sister-in-law was thinking: that forcing Massimo into close quarters would stop him hiding away.

Unfortunately, Madeline hadn't reckoned on Massimo boarding the yacht with his laptop case slung over his shoulder and his phone sticking out of his shorts pocket and Livia saw her lips pull in tightly. When they set sail, Livia was the only one secretly pleased when he made his excuses and disappeared inside.

Disappointment was writ large on his family's faces.

She met Madeline's gaze and shrugged apologetically.

Barely three hours with Massimo's family and she'd already made two silent apologies for him.

Sailing at a steady pace over the calm South Pacific, it took only an hour to reach the atoll. They whiled the time away in a lazy fashion, dipping in and out of the swimming pool and chatting. The captain anchored the yacht at a distance far enough away not to cause any damage to the precious reef but close enough for them all to see the clear turquoise water teeming with brightly coloured fish and all other manner of sea life. Madeline and Raul donned their snorkelling gear and jumped in, leaving baby Elizabeth in Sera's capable hands.

Livia looked out at Madeline and Raul having the time of their lives in the water, at Sera playing happily with her granddaughter, at her father-in-law Gianni, book in one hand, large cocktail in the other, at Jimmy napping in his wheelchair in a shaded part of the deck, at the chefs cooking up a storm on the barbecue and felt a sharp pang rip through her chest.

Massimo should be there with them.

She hurried down the stairs and slipped inside in search of him.

The interior of the yacht was vast and as sleek and as elegant as the exterior and refreshingly cool after the hazy heat on deck. It took a few minutes before she found him hidden in an isolated section of the saloon, tapping away on his laptop. So engrossed was he in his work that it took a few moments before he noticed her presence.

'Lunch is almost ready,' she said briskly.

'I'll be ten minutes.'

'And then you'll turn your laptop off and leave it off?'

'I can't.'

She inhaled deeply to smother her anger. 'Your family have been looking forward to spending time with you.'

'And they will.'

'When?' she challenged. 'Tomorrow, everything will be about the party and then you go back to LA. Today is the only day when it's just us and you're missing out.

You've travelled thousands of kilometres to be here. It's not going to kill you to turn your laptop off and spend some time with your family.'

His jaw clenched, his fingers now drumming on the table rather than tapping on his laptop.

Looking at the obstinate set of Livia's jawline, Massimo knew she wouldn't give him a moment's peace until he joined the rest of them on deck.

It wasn't that he disliked spending time with his family. Not really. It was that they were all so different from him. His approach to life was alien to them. They believed he worked too hard, never understanding that it was only when he was immersed in his work that he felt at peace with himself.

It would be easier to handle these few days with them if Livia weren't there. It was hard enough dealing with his family's suffocating love without adding his estranged wife and all the intense emotions she'd drawn back out of him into the mix.

How could he find ease in her company when his attention was consumed by her every movement? She stood a good five feet from him but awareness thrummed through him, a buzz on his skin, an itch in his fingers. Her black swimsuit was designed for functionality and not for flaunting her body but still he reacted as if she were wearing the skimpiest of bikinis. The itch in his fingers became unbearable when he noticed the smudge of mascara under her left eye from where she'd dried her face after her swim. He wanted to rub the smudge away.

He breathed in deeply through his nose and nodded. 'I'll turn my laptop off and join you in ten minutes.'

She inclined her head and backed away. Just when he

thought he was rid of her she fixed him with a hard stare counteracted by a quirking at the corner of her lips. 'If you get your phone out at all while we're on this yacht, I can't promise that it won't become fish food.'

Two hours later and Livia almost wished Massimo would return to the saloon and do more work.

After they'd eaten their long lunch; barbecued fish freshly caught that morning and an array of salads, she'd gone snorkelling with Madeline and climbed back on board to find Massimo had removed his T-shirt and draped it carelessly on the back of his chair.

Trying hard to blur his magnificent physique from her sight, she wrapped her beach towel around her waist while Madeline went straight to Raul, wrapped her arms around his neck and kissed the top of his balding head. In response, he twisted in his chair and squeezed her bottom.

Livia couldn't stop her eyes from seeking Massimo, her heart throbbing as she remembered a time when they'd been as tactile and affectionate together as his sister and brother-in-law were. Her insides heated to match the warmth on her skin when she found his gaze already on her. Was he remembering those heady, care-free days too…?

His eyes pulsed before he looked away and reached for the jug of fruit cocktail. He refilled his glass then filled another and pulled out the empty chair beside him. Livia sat, accepting the drink with a murmured thanks, and tried again to blur out his naked chest. Even with the parasol raised to shade them from the worst of the heat, the sun's rays were slow-roasting them. One of Jimmy's carers had taken him inside for a nap.

Madeline pulled a bottle of sunscreen from her bag. Once she and Raul had slathered themselves in it, she passed the bottle to Livia, who rubbed the lotion over her face, covered her arms, shoulders, the top part of her chest not covered by her swimsuit and her neck. But she couldn't reach all of her back.

'Here, let me.'

Of course Massimo would offer to help. They had a watching audience, just as they'd had when they'd arrived at the lodge and he'd offered his hand to help her out of the golf buggy. His offer was for their benefit. If not for them, he would probably let her burn.

Trying valiantly to keep her features nonchalant, Livia gave the bottle to Massimo and twisted in her seat so her back was to him.

The anticipation of his touch was almost unbearable. And when it came...

Her breath caught in her throat.

Darts of awareness spread through her, memories flooding her of the first time he'd applied sunscreen to her skin. They'd been on their honeymoon in St Barts. They'd sunbathed naked, secure in their privacy. Massimo had rubbed the lotion sensually over every inch of her skin. By the time he'd rolled her onto her back and driven deep inside her, she'd been wet and aching for him. It had been the quickest she had ever achieved orgasm.

Now, he applied the lotion to her back briskly. His indifference made her heart twist with sadness but she worked hard to keep her lips curved upwards.

His hands pulled away with an abruptness that made the twist in her heart turn to an ache.

'Turn around and I'll do your back,' she ordered,

proud that her voice was as bright as she intended for their watching audience.

As he was so tall and broad, there was a lot more skin to cover than the small area of exposed flesh on her own back.

Resisting the temptation to squirt it straight onto his back and have the fleeting enjoyment of watching him squirm at the quick shock of cold on his warm skin, she placed a healthy dollop into her palm, rubbed her hands together to spread it equally between them then placed them on his shoulder blades.

He still flinched.

She worked as briskly as he had to rub the lotion into his smooth skin.

When had she last touched his back? She couldn't remember. The coldness that had entered their marriage hadn't appeared overnight. It had accumulated over time until one day there was nothing but ice where once there had been love.

She had forgotten how much pleasure she got from simply touching him. Massimo carried so much on his shoulders. She'd loved to massage his knots away and feel him relax beneath her fingers. There were knots there now beneath the pads of her fingers, at the top of his spine and around his shoulder blades. Big ones.

Livia gritted her teeth and, dragging her hands from the knotted shoulders, swept down to the base of his back and covered the last bit that needed protection from the blazing sun.

The weight on his shoulders and the knots formed by it were none of her concern.

The moment she was done she pulled her hands away with the same abruptness that he'd done with her then breathed a quick sigh of relief when the captain appeared on deck, distracting everyone's attention. It was time to sail back.

His family's natural exuberance, which Massimo had never inherited, made sailing a noisy affair. The three women were in the pool swimming with his niece, laughing and splashing, leaving him at the table with his father, grandfather and brother-in-law, answering questions as best he could about the carbon filter he was days away from testing the prototype of. He could see the effort it was taking for them to concentrate.

He couldn't help his gaze drifting to the swimming pool, his attention as attuned as it had always been to Livia's every movement.

He was also intensely aware that she'd left her phone on the table and intensely ashamed that he wanted to snatch it up, take it somewhere private and trawl through all her communications over the past four months. He wondered how she would react if he were to throw it overboard and give it the same fate she'd threatened his own phone.

As if it were aware of his attention, her phone suddenly burst into life.

His father peered at it. 'Livia, Gianluca's calling,' he called to her.

'Coming!' She scrambled out of the pool, snatching her towel as she padded to the table, but her brother's call had gone to voicemail before she reached them.

Her brow furrowed. 'Excuse me a moment. I need to call him back.'

As she climbed the stairs to the top deck, Massimo's mother got out of the pool and joined them at the table.

'How is Gianluca doing?' she asked him in an undertone, concern writ large on her face. 'I know Livia has been very worried about him.'

But he never got the chance to ask what she was talking about for Madeline had sneaked up behind him and suddenly thrust a soaking Elizabeth into his arms. 'Here you go, Massimo. You can hold Elizabeth for me.'

'Where are you going?'

'Nowhere.' She stood at the balustrade with a cackle of laughter that produced laughs from his parents and a sound that could have been laughter too from his grandfather.

With a wriggling baby thrust upon him, Massimo filed away his mother's comment about Livia's youngest sibling as something to query later. Gianluca was the only member of Livia's family he'd met. He'd turned up at their wedding looking furtive, constantly looking over his shoulder. His behaviour, Livia had later explained, was a mirror of her own when she'd first left Naples, a habit it had taken her years to break.

He hoped Gianluca hadn't finally fallen into the life Livia had escaped from and which she'd so dearly hoped he would follow her out of.

Teenage boys were pack animals. That was Livia's theory for why he hadn't attempted to escape yet. He went around the Secondigliano with his gang of friends on their scooters, chasing girls, playing video games, employed by the brutal men who ran the territory to keep watch for enemies and the police. Livia was convinced that it was a life her brother didn't want but Massimo was equally convinced that Gianluca had been as seduced by it as the rest of her family had been and that sooner or later he would be seduced into committing a crime from which there would be no going back. Livia's strength of mind and moral code were rare.

He stood his niece on his lap and stared at her cherubic face and felt the tightness in his chest loosen. This little one would be raised with security and love. She would never be exposed to the danger and violence his wife and her siblings had lived.

Huge blue eyes stared back. Unable to resist, he sniffed the top of her head. She smelled of baby.

'When are you two going to have one of those?' Raul asked with a grin.

Ice laced like a snake up Massimo's spine in an instant.

All eyes focused on him…and the presence he sensed behind him. Livia had returned from her phone call.

She sat back down, phone clutched in her hand. 'It's not the right time for us to have a child,' she said and shrugged apologetically. 'You know the hours Massimo puts into his work.'

'You would work those hours if there was a child?' his mother said, looking at him with an air of bewilderment. It was a look he'd become used to during his childhood, a physical expression that the differences between Massimo and his family were felt as keenly by them as they were by him.

'My work is important,' he pointed out cordially. He didn't expect her to understand. To his parents, work was only important in as much as it paid the bills. That hadn't stopped his parents from accepting the luxury home he'd purchased for them and for which he footed all the bills *and* the monthly sum he transferred into their bank account for everything else they could possibly need. He did the same for his sister and his grandfather and for his father's siblings and their offspring. He would have done the same for his mother's siblings if she'd had any.

He had stopped them ever having to work again—work being something none of the extended Briatores had been enamoured with either—and still his work ethic bewildered them. He provided for them all and the source of their wealth came from the technology he was creating that would, hopefully, allow baby Elizabeth, along with future generations of Briatores, to live on a planet that wasn't a raging fireball. And still they stared at him with bewilderment, unable to comprehend why he worked as hard as he did.

'I know, but…' His mother must have sensed something from his expression for her voice trailed off.

Livia had no such sensibilities. Pouring herself a glass of fruit cocktail, she said, 'Your son is a workaholic, Sera. It makes for a lonely life for me. I could not bring a child into that.'

'You could get help,' his mother suggested hopefully.

Livia shook her head. 'In America, any help would be from English speakers. I've been trying to learn but it's very hard. I had a cut on my leg last year that needed stitching and it was very stressful trying to understand the staff at the hospital.'

Talk of that incident made Massimo's guts clench uncomfortably and his gaze automatically drift down to her leg. The scar, although expertly stitched and incredibly neat, was still vivid. Livia had gone for a swim in their outdoor pool in LA. One of the pebbled tiles around its perimeter had broken away leaving a sharp edge that she had sliced her calf on when hauling herself out of the pool. He'd been at his testing facility when she'd called to tell him about it, saying only that she'd cut her leg and needed help communicating with a medical practitioner about it. He'd sent Lindy, fluent in Italian, to deal with it and translate for her.

He'd been furious when he'd returned home that night and seen the extent of the damage. Seventeen stitches, internal and external. Her reply had been the coolest he'd ever received from her—up to that point anyway— Livia saying, 'I didn't want to make a drama out of it and worry you while you were driving.' He'd stared at her quizzically. Her lips had tightened. 'I assumed you would come.'

It wasn't his fault, he told himself stubbornly. He wasn't a mind reader. He couldn't have known how bad the damage had been.

The damage it had caused to their marriage in the longer term had been far more extensive.

'Look!' His sister's exclamation cut through his moody reminiscences.

Everyone followed Madeline's pointed finger. Holding Elizabeth securely in his arms, Massimo carried her to the balustrade. Swimming beside the yacht, almost racing them, was a pod of bottlenose dolphins.

Around thirty of the beautiful mammals sped sleekly through the water, creating huge white foams with their dives. It was as if they'd come to check them out and decided to stay for a while and play.

It was one of the most incredible sights he had ever seen and it filled him with something indefinable; indefinable because it was nothing he'd ever felt before.

He looked at Livia and the awed joy on her face and experienced a fleeting gratitude that she'd forced him from his work and enabled him to enjoy this priceless moment.

Elizabeth wriggled in his arms. He tightened his hold on her to stop her falling and, as he did, Livia's blame as to their childless state came back to him and the brief lightness that had filled his chest leached back out.

Livia tried her hardest to keep a happy front going but it only got harder as time passed. Gianluca hadn't answered her returned call and he hadn't called or left a message since.

And then there was Massimo.

The excitement of the dolphins racing so joyously alongside them had waned once they'd finally swum off and the lightness she'd witnessed in his eyes had quickly waned too. Was she the only one to notice his underlying tension? She would bet the knots on his shoulders had become even tighter.

Her assumption that he would keep the reasons for his anger to himself was dispelled when they returned to the island. His family retired to their chalets for a late siesta before dinner, leaving them together on the terrace of the lodge drinking a coconut and rum creation the head bar steward had made for them.

The moment they were alone, he fixed her with hard eyes. 'Why did you say all that rubbish about a baby?'

'What rubbish?'

'You let my family believe the issue of us not having children lies with me.'

'I'm prepared to pretend that our marriage is intact but I'm not prepared to tell an outright lie.'

'You're the one who didn't want a child. Not me.'

Confused, she blinked. 'When did I say I didn't want a child?'

His jaw clenched. 'You laughed when I suggested we have one.'

'Do you mean the time you suggested we have a child to cure me of my loneliness? Is that the time you're referring to?' Of course it was. It was the only time the subject of a baby had come up since their first heady days when they'd spoken of a future that involved children. 'I laughed at the suggestion, yes, because it *was* laughable. And even if you hadn't suggested a child as a sticking plaster for my loneliness I would still have laughed and for the reasons I shared with your mother—ours was no marriage to bring a child into.'

His hand tightened perceptibly around his glass. 'You made it sound like you're a neglected wife.'

'I *was* a neglected wife,' she bit back. 'Why do you think I left you? To pretend otherwise is demeaning—'

'You're here this weekend so my grandfather can spend what is likely to be his last birthday on this earth believing everything is fine between us,' he interrupted.

'We're not going to do that by pretending that you've suddenly turned into a model husband, are we? Your grandfather isn't stupid—none of your family are, and they're not going to believe a leopard can change its spots. I visited your family on my own and made excuses for you for over a year before I left and I've been doing the same for the last four months and they have been none the wiser about the state of our marriage. When we finally come clean that we've separated, the only surprise will be that it's taken me so long to see sense.'

Livia knew she was baiting him but she didn't care. She wanted him to argue with her. She'd always wanted him to argue back but he never did. It was a circle that had only grown more vicious as their marriage limped on; her shouting, him clamming up.

True to form, Massimo's mouth clamped into a straight line. He pushed his chair back roughly and got to his feet but before he could stride away as she fully expected him to do, he turned back around and glowered at her. 'Unless you want a fight over any divorce settlement, I suggest you stick to the plan and stop putting doubts about our marriage in my family's head. I don't care what my parents or sister think but I will not have my grandfather having doubts about us.'

'If you want a fight over the settlement then I'll give you a fight,' she said, outraged at his threat, 'but I *am* sticking to the plan! You've neglected your family for so long that they think it's normal that you neglect your wife too.'

'I'm not having this argument again.'

She laughed bitterly. Her hands were shaking. 'We never argued about it. Whenever I tried to tell you how unhappy I was, you walked away from me. You never wanted to hear it.'

'You were like a stuck record.' He made crablike pinching motions with his hands. 'I'm bored, Massimo,' he mimicked. 'I'm lonely, Massimo. Why do you work such long hours, Massimo?' He dropped his hands and expelled his own bitter laugh. 'See? I *did* listen. Maybe if you'd ever paused for breath between complaints I might have felt more incentivised to come home earlier each night.'

'I only complained *because* you work such stupid hours!'

His eyes were cold. 'I didn't force you to move to America. I didn't force you to marry me. You knew the kind of man I was before we married but you thought you could change me. Instead of solving your problems for yourself you sat around the house wallowing and complaining and expecting me to fix everything for you.'

'I never wallowed!' she said, outraged. Of all the things he'd just accused her of, for some reason that was the one that immediately bit the hardest. 'And as if I would have expected you to fix anything—you aren't capable of fixing anything to do with the human heart. You've spent so much time with your machines and gadgets that your heart has turned to metal.'

He took the three steps needed to smile cruelly down at her. 'You did nothing *but* wallow. And sulk. And complain. For the first few weeks after you left I thought I'd gone deaf.'

And then his smile turned into a grimace as he turned on his heel and, parting shot delivered, strode off leaving Livia standing there feeling as if he'd just ripped her heart out.

CHAPTER SIX

MASSIMO LOCKED THE bathroom door. He didn't trust
Livia not to barge in.

He'd expected her to follow him to the chalet. Every
step had been taken with an ear braced for a fresh verbal assault.

But the assault never came.

He turned the shower on and closed his eyes to the
hot water spraying over his head.

Livia's defiant yet stricken face played in his retinas.

Guilt fisted his guts. He'd been cruel. The words had
spilled out of him as if a snake had taken possession of
his tongue.

Being here…with Livia, with his family, seeing how
close to death his grandfather really was…it was all
too much.

Hearing accusations of neglectful behaviour towards
those he loved had driven like a knife in his heart.

He'd done his best for his family. They might not see
him as much as they would like but he made up for his
lack of presence in other ways.

And he'd done his best in his marriage. That his best
did not live up to his wife's exacting standards was not
his fault. Neglect seemed to suggest that she was a child

who needed taking care of when they both knew Livia was more than capable of taking care of herself. This was the woman who'd survived the Secondigliano without being seduced by its violent glamour. This was the woman who'd discovered an affinity for nursing when the local doctor the neighbourhood gangsters visited to fix their gangland wounds recognised her coolness under pressure when one of her cousins got shot in the leg. From the age of fourteen Livia had been paid a flat fee of fifty euros a time to assist the doctor whenever required. Like Massimo, she'd stashed it away. Unlike Massimo, who'd saved his money in a box in his bedroom, never having to worry about his family stealing it from him, she'd kept her cash in a waterproof container under the vase in her father's grave. As she was the only mourner to place flowers on the grave, it was the only safe place she had for it.

She'd refused to be sucked into a life of crime. The only vice she'd picked up in her years where drugs were cheap and plentiful was cigarette smoking, which she'd quit when she'd achieved the grades needed to study nursing in Rome and taken all her cash and left the life behind her. She was as tough as nails. To suggest she needed caring for was laughable.

Finished showering, he rubbed his body with a towel then wrapped it around his waist. Bracing himself, he unlocked the door and stepped into the bedroom.

He'd been right to brace himself. Livia was sitting on the end of the bed waiting for him. But the fury he expected to be met with was nowhere to be seen. Her eyes, when he met them, were sad. The smudge of mascara was still visible.

After a moment's silence that felt strangely melancholic, she said, 'I don't want it to be like this.' It was the quietest he'd ever heard her speak.

He ran a hand through his damp hair and grimaced. 'I thought you wanted me to argue with you. Isn't that what you've always said?'

'Arguing's healthy, but this…?' Her shoulders and chest rose before slumping sharply, her gaze falling to the floor. 'I don't want us to be cruel to each other. I knew things would be difficult this weekend but…' Her voice trailed away before she slowly raised her head to meet his gaze. There was a sheen in her eyes that made his heart clench. 'This is much harder than I thought it would be.'

Massimo pressed his back against the bathroom door and closed his eyes. 'It's harder than I thought it would be too.'

'It is?'

He nodded and ground his teeth together. 'I shouldn't have said the things I said. I'm sorry.'

'I didn't know you felt like that.'

'I don't.' At her raised, disbelieving brow, he added, 'Not in the way I said it.'

'You made me sound like a fishwife.'

His lips curved involuntarily at the glimmer of humour in her tone. 'I was lashing out. Being with you…' The fleeting smile faded away. 'I can't explain how it makes me feel.'

'It just makes me feel sad,' she admitted with a whisper. Then she rubbed her eyes with the palms of her hands and took a deep breath. 'When the time is right for us to file the divorce papers, I won't be wanting a settlement.'

'I didn't mean it about fighting you. We can come to an—'

Her head shook. 'No. No settlement. You've given me enough money since we married. I've hardly spent any of it. I've enough to buy an apartment—'

'You were going to buy one when you went back to Rome,' he interrupted. 'You were supposed to let my lawyer know when you'd found somewhere.' He'd informed his lawyer and accountant that Livia would be purchasing a home in Italy in her sole name and that funds should be made available to her when she got in touch with them about it, no questions asked. He didn't care what she spent.

He'd specifically told them to go ahead without notifying him. He hadn't wanted to know when she'd made that last, permanent move out of his life for reasons he couldn't explain, not even to himself.

Massimo ran his eyes over his finances once a year when it was tax season and that was for scrutiny purposes. He would have noticed then, he supposed, that she hadn't bought herself a home.

'I've been renting my old place.' Actually buying herself a home of her own had felt too final, Livia realised. It would have been the ultimate confirmation that their marriage was over for good.

Had she been living in denial? And if so, what had she been holding out for? Miracles didn't exist. The cruel truth was that she and Massimo were wholly incompatible and she'd been a fool for believing differently. She'd known it when she'd left. It hadn't stopped her heart skipping every time her phone had buzzed only to plummet when his name didn't flash on the screen. It hadn't flashed once since their separation.

'Once everything's out in the open, I'm going to go

back to nursing,' she added, fighting back a well of tears. To cry in front of him would be the final indignity.

He rested his head back against the bathroom door with a sigh. 'You don't need to work, Liv.'

The simple shortening of her name…oh, but it made her heart *ache*. Massimo was the only person in the world who'd ever shortened her name. And then he'd stopped calling her Liv and started calling her Livia like everyone else. And then he'd stopped calling her anything.

Blinking away the tears that were still desperately trying to unleash, she sniffed delicately and gave a jerky nod. 'I need a sense of purpose. I like knowing the money in my pocket is earned by my own endeavours. I never wanted to be a kept woman.'

His throat moved before he gave his own nod. 'At least let me buy you a home like we agreed I would. The law entitles you to much more.'

And he would give it, everything the law said she was entitled to and more. If only he were as generous with his time as he was with his money…

But those were pointless thoughts to have. Massimo was who he was, just as Livia was who she was. They'd tried. They'd failed.

She just wished she could find a way to stop her heart from hurting so much.

'Thank you.' Swallowing hard to dislodge the lump in her throat, she got to her feet. 'I'll leave you to get changed. I'm going to make myself a coffee—would you like one?'

'That would be great, thank you.'

She smiled and left the bedroom and kept smiling as she made the coffee, smiling so hard that eventually the tears sucked themselves dry and her cheeks ached miserably in their place.

It didn't occur to her until she was standing under the shower an hour later that this was the first real conversation she and Massimo had had that hadn't descended to insults and recriminations in over a year.

The cloudless sky had turned deep blue, the sun a deep orange shimmering on the horizon when Livia ventured out of the chalet in search of Massimo. She found him on the wrap-around veranda drinking a bottle of beer and looking at his phone, wearing a pair of old battered jeans and a crisp white shirt, a booted foot hooked casually on his thigh.

It was the first time she'd been at the rear of their chalet and she tried hard not to let sadness fill her as she recalled poring over the architect's designs for it, imagining all the happy times she and Massimo would spend here. This chalet had been the only part of the complex Massimo had taken a real interest in. They'd chosen to build it high on the jutting mound of earth that, when the tide was low, could be walked to along a sandy pathway created by nature at its finest. This was supposed to be their own private hideaway in their private paradise. Their horseshoe swimming pool, garden and veranda were entirely hidden from prying eyes.

She hadn't been able to bring herself to think about the sleeping arrangements that night. Their chalet only had one bed. It was a huge bed but, still, it was only the one bed. She supposed she could sleep on the sofa. Massimo's long frame would never fit on it.

His eyes widened slightly when he looked up as she approached and he unhooked his foot and straightened.

The vain part of her bloomed to see his response. Although it was only a family meal they were going to have, she'd applied her make-up and done her hair with care. She'd been mortified to look in the mirror and see a huge smudge of mascara under her left eye.

But it wasn't vanity that had propelled her to make an effort. It was armoury. When she looked her best it had the effect of boosting her morale and for all the un-spoken truce they'd forged, her emotions were all over the place. She needed every piece of armour she could find to hold herself together.

Massimo turned his phone off and tried hard to temper the emotions crashing through him. Livia had dressed casually in a pair of tight white three-quarter-length trousers and a shimmering red strappy top that stopped at her midriff. On her feet were high, white strappy sandals that elongated her frame but did noth-ing to diminish her natural curves.

A lifetime ago he would have beckoned her over, put his hands on her hips and pulled her to him.

The instant awakening of his loins proved, as if it needed proving, that nothing had changed. He still wanted her with an ache he felt deep in his marrow.

Inhaling deeply through his nose, he willed the thud-ding of his heart to steady.

'You're ready?' he asked.

She nodded.

He finished his beer and got to his feet.

In silence they walked the veranda to the front of the chalet and headed to the lodge. The tide had risen in the past two hours, the sandy path now mostly submerged beneath the powerful ocean and the colourful, tropical fish that swam in it. Its gentle rhythm was soothing.

His family had beaten them to the lodge and were all sitting around a set dining table chatting noisily. One of his grandfather's carers sat discreetly in a far corner of the lodge reading a book.

The meal passed quickly. His grandfather was tired and, fed by Massimo's mother, ate only his soup before retiring for the night. Madeline and Raul quickly followed, taking an increasingly fractious Elizabeth, who'd turned her nose up at all the offerings they'd tried to tempt her with. Considering it looked like mushed vomit, Massimo didn't blame her for smacking the plastic spoon out of her mother's hand. When his brother-in-law attempted to feed her, her little face turned bright red with fury. If Massimo had been offered that excuse for food, he'd have been tempted to screw his face up and bawl too.

He was about to rise and retire to the chalet to check in on work, when his father's suggestion of a game of Scopa, the traditional Italian game played with an Italian forty-card deck, gave him pause.

His mother's hopeful gaze made his ready refusal stick on his tongue before he could vocalise it.

He didn't need to look at Livia to know she was beseeching him with her eyes to accept too. Her earlier insistence that his family wanted only to spend time with him kept ringing in his ears.

He stretched his mouth into the semblance of a smile. 'Sure.'

The beaming grins made his chest tighten.

He signalled to the barman. Soon, a bottle of bourbon, a bucket of ice and four glasses had been taken to the outside table they now sat around. Massimo and his father formed a team and sat opposite each other, the ladies playing as the opposing team. Livia sat beside his father, his mother beside Massimo. He shuffled the cards, dealt them three each and four face up on the table. The first game of Scopa began.

What began as a sop to please his parents turned into a couple of hours' mindless fun under the warm starry sky. His parents were the most laid-back, easy-going people on the planet but when it came to card games, they became ultra-competitive.

And Livia's competitive streak came out too. His wife and mother were both determined to beat their spouses and were not above cheating to achieve this. When the women were two nil down, suddenly they both found it necessary to halt the game for frequent bathroom breaks.

Soon after this mysterious onset of bladder issues, he spotted his mother furtively pulling something out of her handbag, which, when she was challenged, turned out to be a king with a value of ten points. Rather than display any shame, his mother giggled. Livia though…her throaty cackle of laughter filled his ears and suddenly he was thrown back to his sister's wedding and the first time he'd heard it.

It was a sound that speared him.

Firmly dragging his mind away from that fateful first meeting, he confiscated the card but then found he couldn't stop his own burst of laughter when, barely a minute later, Livia stood to use the bathroom for the fourth time and two high-value cards slipped out of her top.

'Shameless,' he chided with a stern shake of his head.

'All's fair in love and war,' she replied, a gleam in her eye he hadn't seen for so long that suddenly he could

fight the swelling emotions no more, body blows of longing and pain ravaging him.

He couldn't tear his gaze from her.

In the beat of a moment her amusement vanished and
her dark brown eyes were swirling with more emotion
than there were stars in the sky.

Hardly single-digit seconds passed as their stares remained fixed on each other but those seconds contained
so much weight he felt its compression on his chest. He
knew with a bone-deep certainty that she was thinking
about their first meeting too and that the memory lanced
her as deeply as it did him.

Then Livia turned her gaze from him.

'I really do need to use the bathroom,' she murmured,
reaching down to pick up the illicit cards and placing
them on the table.

In the plush ladies' room, Livia put her hands on the
sink and dragged air into her lungs.

For a moment there her heart had felt so full of so
many emotions that it had felt as if it could burst out of
her chest.

Teaming up with Sera against their husbands had
been so wickedly joyful that for a while she had forgotten that she and Massimo were estranged and preparing for a divorce.

For a short, glorious time, it had been like slipping on
a pair of shoes that transported them to their early days
when there had been as much fun in their marriage as
there had been desire and love.

She had adored making Massimo laugh. He was such
a serious person that to see his face light up had brought
her more joy than anything. Laughter had been in short

supply in her childhood so to discover this side of herself with him had been joyful in its own right.

Like the smiles she'd been unable to form in the four months since she'd left him, laughter had become a distant memory too. Until tonight.

Back outside in the warm evening air, she found the cards had been put away and the glasses empty. Sera and Gianni got to their feet as she approached the table and both apologised for having to call it a night. They were tired and needed to get some sleep.

Kissing them both goodnight, Livia poured herself another bourbon and watched them walk away.

The silence they left behind was stark. Apart from the white noise in her ears.

'I suppose we should go to our chalet too,' she said, avoiding Massimo's stare.

They'd spent a whole day travelling between time zones quickly followed by a day out at sea. All of this, when added to her frazzled nerves brought about by being with him again, was a recipe for exhaustion. Yet she felt anything but tired.

When he didn't answer, she stared up at the sky. The stars were in abundance that night, twinkling like gold diamonds in the vast blackness. She'd thought the sky in LA was big but here, on this island, it seemed to stretch for ever.

'I'll sleep on the sofa,' she added into the silence.

'No. You take the bed.' She felt his eyes on her. 'I've work I need to get on with.'

'The sofa's too small for you, and you can't work all night.' But he could. She knew that. He'd worked through the night on many occasions.

'I'll work for a few hours then sleep on the hammock.'

'We have a hammock?' That was the first she'd heard of it.

'I'm surprised you didn't notice it earlier. It's on the veranda by the outside table.'

'I probably didn't register it,' she murmured, taking a hasty sip of her bourbon.

She wouldn't have noticed any hammock because when she'd stepped out onto the veranda her eyes had been too consumed by Massimo to register anything else.

They finished their drinks and, as silently as they'd made the walk from their chalet to the lodge, walked the return journey together. The incoming tide now lapped the beach noisily, so deep beneath the bridge that if this had been her first sight of the island she would never have believed it could ebb back far enough for a sandy pathway to open up between the main island and their private peninsula.

But as much as she tried to distract herself with their surroundings she couldn't block out Massimo's lean frame striding beside her.

When they reached their chalet, he picked up the briefcase he'd left on their dining table.

Everything about this chalet was supposed to be theirs. Everything had been designed to their exact instructions; a love nest they'd imagined themselves escaping to whenever time allowed, designed and dreamed up before Livia had realised time would never allow it. For Massimo, time existed only for work.

He stared at her for a moment before his chest rose sharply. 'I'll work on the veranda. Sleep well.'

Her goodnight to him came out as a whisper.

He closed the door quietly behind him.

* * *

Massimo powered his laptop but, other than reply to a few urgent emails, found he didn't have the concentration to work.

Sighing heavily, he ran his fingers through his hair and closed his eyes.

It felt as if he'd slipped into a time loop, taken back to the days when he'd worked from the sprawling building that homed Briatore Technologies and found his concentration fighting a war with himself. Livia had taken back possession of his mind. She'd been all he could think of then. She was all he could think of now.

It didn't matter, he told himself grimly. One more full day and night and then that would be it for them. She would live her life in Italy and he would live his in LA.

Thinking he could do with another drink before attempting to sleep in the hammock he'd instructed be erected when he'd remembered the chalet he would share with his estranged wife had only one bed, he padded quietly back inside. Before he could switch the light on and head to the bar, he noticed a slant of light coming from beneath the closed bedroom door.

His heart fisted.

He'd left her over an hour ago, plenty of time for her to do her night-time beauty routine and fall asleep. Was she reading?

Was she wearing the cream pyjamas that managed to be both modest and yet revealing…?

He stepped closer to the bedroom door, his ears craning when he heard her voice. She was talking to someone.

A lover?

Hating himself yet unable to stop, he put his ear to the door. The wooden barrier muffled her words.

She laughed. It sounded pained. And then she said something distinguishable even through the muffling.

'Please. I love you.'

CHAPTER SEVEN

NIGHTMARES HAD PLAGUED Livia's life as far back as she could remember but it was rare for them to pepper her sleep over a whole night. After a night of exactly that and feeling distinctly unrefreshed, she showered and dressed quickly, choosing a black bikini, mid-thigh-length denim shorts and a loose white top.

Years of practice had allowed her to switch her mind off from her brother's problems—she would never have slept a wink if she hadn't—but last night his problems had been too great to stop her from worrying.

She had a feeling that even without Gianluca's issues overshadowing everything, she would still have had problems sleeping. She had never successfully learned to switch her mind off from her husband.

Their bed had been everything they'd been promised, like sleeping on a supportive cloud. Having never shared it with Massimo, she'd assumed she'd be all right sleeping in it alone but her twitchy body had betrayed her. This was a bed designed for lovers, chosen when divorce hadn't entered her head.

Before leaving the chalet she checked her phone, hoping Gianluca had messaged as he'd promised he would. Her chest loosened a fraction to see his simple message on the screen telling her he was fine and that nothing had happened.

The message did nothing to quell the sick dread curdling in her stomach.

Out on the veranda she wasn't surprised to find Massimo awake, dressed in the same clothes he'd worn the previous evening, and drinking a cup of coffee at the table. He must have made it while she'd been showering.

He would have heard the shower. He would have known she was awake. He hadn't thought to make her a coffee too.

It hurt that he hadn't thought of her, especially since she'd made him a coffee barely twelve hours ago. It had been an attempt at a peace offering she'd assumed— wrongly—that he'd accepted.

Her attention was caught by the hammock behind him swinging between the low roof of the chalet and one of the palm trees.

How had she not noticed it before?

Pushing petty thoughts of coffee aside, she inclined her head towards the hammock. 'How did you find sleeping on that?'

He shrugged in answer.

'I don't mind sleeping on it tonight.'

'No need,' he answered sardonically. 'It was fine.'

'But it doesn't seem fair...'

'I said no need,' he said through what sounded like gritted teeth before rising to his feet. 'I'm going to take a shower.'

Her eyes narrowed. Since when did Massimo wake up in such an obviously foul mood? She had a strong inkling his ire was directed at her, although she couldn't think what she'd done to cause it. 'Suit yourself. I'm going to make a coffee. I would offer you one but seeing as you've already taken care of yourself, I won't bother.'

His smile was as cutting as his tone had been. 'Good.'

Despite her much shorter legs, Livia made it to the chalet ahead of him.

Inside, he strode past her and into the bedroom, closing the door firmly behind him.

She scowled at the door and wished she had laser eyes that could cut through it and zap him.

She hoped he regretted suggesting the main bathroom be adjacent to where they slept.

In the small yet eye-wateringly expensive kitchen area, she opened a cupboard door, removed a glass mug then closed it with a slam. One small spoonful of sugar was thrown into the mug before she snatched an espresso pod and rammed it into the machine, then punched the button to get it working.

Alone in the bathroom, Massimo looked at the beauty paraphernalia left higgledy-piggledy all over the ledge and rammed his hands into his pockets to prevent them sweeping the entire lot onto the floor.

From the sounds of banging coming from the kitchen area, Livia was having more trouble controlling her own temper. But then, she always had.

His fury, he recognised in a dim, grim fashion, should be aimed at himself.

Until he'd heard her utter words of love to another, he'd never believed in his heart that she'd found someone else. The confirmation that she had a lover had come as a bigger blow than he'd ever imagined it could.

Seeing her in the flesh for the first time since hearing that confirmation had lanced him; a different pain from the constant ache he'd learned to live with since she'd left him. This pain went far deeper.

How could he go on pretending all was well in their marriage knowing another man had kissed those lips, knowing her pretty hands had touched another's body?

Was it for her lover that she'd cut her hair and added colour to it?

Nausea roiled deep in his stomach and he stripped his clothes off and threw them onto the floor, kicking his jeans for good measure.

Knowing that volatile emotions were usually his wife's domain only increased his temper.

Setting the temperature to cold, he stood under the frigid water for as long as he could bear it. It did little to temper the violent emotions churning in him.

After donning shorts and a T-shirt in his private dressing room—at least he was spared having to dress surrounded by Livia's clothing—he stepped back into the bedroom and this time was unable to stop his eyes falling to the neatly made bed.

It was a habit he'd never been able to break her out of. In LA she'd insisted on making it herself even though his housekeeping team would go into their bedroom later on and remake it to hotel standards.

The tightness in his lungs loosened a little.

He shouldn't take his unfathomable jealousy out on Livia. She had done nothing wrong. Their marriage was over.

But his calm rationale flew out of the window when he went back into the main living area and found her slumped on the sofa, her feet on the coffee table, ankles hooked together, fingers flying on the screen of her phone, concentration etched on her face. An empty glass mug lay on a coaster only inches from her bare feet.

More contact with her lover? he wondered bleakly.

She didn't look at him but a mutinous expression he recognised formed on her face. 'Are you going to tell me what I've done to upset you?'

'You haven't done anything,' he answered stiffly.

She made a pft sound he recognised. It had become a familiar sound in the months leading up to her leaving him.

'I didn't sleep well,' he confessed, attempting a less hostile tone.

'You said you'd been fine on the hammock.'

'It wasn't the hammock. I couldn't switch my mind off.' This much was the truth. How could he sleep when his mind tortured him with images of his wife with another man?

Now her eyes did rise to meet his. He saw suspicion in the dark brown depths. After long moments, she sighed and put her phone down on the coffee table. 'Okay,' she said with a shrug.

Massimo was an insomniac, Livia reminded herself. Switching his mind off enough to sleep was a battle he'd fought his entire life.

But never, not even when they'd been in the midst of their cold war, had he woken in such an obviously foul temper. She didn't believe for a minute that it was lack of sleep causing his current mood but experience had taught her the futility of trying to get him to open up.

Her phone vibrated and bounced on the table. Snatching it up, she read the message that had pinged in and sighed again.

'Problem?' Massimo asked.

Even though she could feel the animosity in his politely delivered question and even though his bad mood had perversely put her in a bad mood too, the growing panic in her belly needed an outlet.

She rubbed her eyes with the palms of her hands and looked back at him. 'Gianluca.'

A furrow grooved in his brow. 'What's happened?'

'Don Fortunato's requested a meeting with him.' She didn't need to tell him what that meant. She had spared him nothing about the world she'd grown up in. The meeting could only mean one thing—that Gianluca would be invited to 'prove' himself. If he proved himself successfully then he would become one of Don Fortunato's trusted foot soldiers, a marked step up from his current role as a watcher.

The groove deepened. 'Requested? So he hasn't met with him yet?'

'Not yet, no. He's been summoned to his home this evening.' If Gianluca wanted the life Don Fortunato was offering, this would be a summons he'd been hoping for. Their father's loyalty and death had marked all the Esposito children as foot soldiers of the future. Now it was Gianluca's turn to prove himself a man.

'What's he going to do?'

'I don't know.' She pinched the bridge of her nose and tried to calm her rabid thoughts. Pasquale had been summoned for this same meeting within days of his sixteenth birthday. Livia had lost him that night. Gianluca's immaturity must have been noted for he'd been given an extra two years before his summons. It felt as if she'd spent these two years doing nothing but beg him to take the lifeline she was offering and escape.

If he went ahead and met Don Fortunato tonight,

there would be no escape. Whatever he was tasked to do would be much more than dipping a toe in their criminal world.

'I've offered him money and I've already got a room set up for him at my apartment. He wants to leave but he's scared.' And she was scared too; far more frightened for her baby brother than she had ever been for herself.

'When did he tell you this?'

'Last night. He called when I was in bed.'

'Last night?' he clarified. There was an expression on his face, a flickering she couldn't interpret.

She nodded heavily. 'He's always known this day would come but inside he always thought it would be tomorrow. He's been happy roving around with his friends on their stupid scooters and chasing girls... How cruel is fate that the day it comes I'm on the other side of the world and unable to help him?'

All the plans she'd made to help him flee were worthless. She was too far away. Gianluca was technically an adult but emotionally he was still a child. She didn't know if he had the strength to break away without her own strength to encourage and sustain him.

She watched Massimo stride to the kitchen area and pull two glass mugs out of the cupboard.

'How did you escape, Livia?' he asked thoughtfully, placing both mugs in the coffee machine.

'You know how. I took my money and jumped on a train and never looked back.'

He put a large pod in the machine and pressed the button. 'You did that without help?'

'You know I did but I wasn't in his position.'

'Has Gianluca saved any money?'

'No.' Saving was an alien concept to her brother.

'I've offered to transfer him the money for his ticket out but he's scared to take it. He knows they're watching him.'

Frustration burned deeply enough for her to want to scream. Gianluca looked up to her. If she were in Italy she would be right there, her hand extended, a source of strength and a physical reminder that it was possible to leave and possible to build a good life outside the Secondigliano.

'Are you sure he wants to leave?'

'*Yes.* The summons has frightened him.' She managed a twisted smile then twisted her fingers together to stop herself biting the horrible gel stuff off her nails. 'I think my baby brother has grown up overnight.'

He stirred their coffees and carried them over, handing one to her.

Strangely, the hostility that had been shooting off him had gone.

He sat opposite her. 'Let me speak to him.'

'You? What for?'

'I can help.'

'How? You're as far away from him as I am.'

'But I have resources at my disposal that you don't. Have you heard of Felipe Lorenzi?'

She shook her head.

'He's ex-Spanish Special Forces and now runs his own security business protecting high-profile people. He only employs other ex-special forces. They're the best at what they do and used to dangerous situations. They can get him out safely.'

She stared at him dumbly. She'd confided in Massimo only because her fears for her brother had grown so large she'd felt as if she would explode if she kept them contained a minute longer. She hadn't expected him to offer help. It hadn't crossed her mind.

'You would do that?' she whispered. She hardly dared allow hope to fight through the fear. If they could get Gianluca out before his meeting with Don Fortunato, before he was tasked with something that would cross the line for ever and before he was made privy to the secrets that would put a mark on his head, then there was a good chance he would be left in peace.

He reached into his pocket and pulled out his phone. 'Leave it with me. By the time of my grandfather's party tonight, your brother will be out of the Secondigliano and free.'

Having Livia's brother to concentrate on and the preparations for the party that evening to oversee helped the day pass quickly. It kept Massimo's mind occupied. It stopped him having to think of the relief that had almost doubled him over to learn his wife hadn't been exchanging endearments with a lover.

She'd been talking to her brother.

But this only caused a shadow to form on his relief because he knew he had no right feeling relief. He had no business feeling what he'd felt.

Knowing how he should feel and behave did nothing to stop the twisting ache that had burrowed in his guts and set up home in his short time on the island. He had to get a grip on it. One day in the future Livia would find a new lover who could give her the happiness she deserved, a man who could give her the attention and time she needed.

He couldn't imagine meeting anyone for himself. A casual lover, possibly, if his body ever became receptive to a woman who wasn't his wife. He would certainly never marry again. Or have children. Before he'd met Livia he'd never even thought of having children. The subject had completely passed by his radar.

Her pointed remark that theirs had been no marriage to bring a child into had hit a nerve with its truth. He would be as lousy a father as he'd been a husband.

Before he could switch his mind away from his latest bout of acidic ruminations and call his PA for a business update, he spotted two figures approaching in the distance. Livia was returning from her walk with his grandfather. They'd gone for an exploration of the island that had been his grandfather's home together. She was the only member of the family Massimo felt comfortable for his grandfather to spend time alone with. If there was an emergency she would know exactly what to do.

Whatever his conflicting feelings towards his estranged wife, he would never deny that she was an exceptional nurse who'd cared for his grandfather with a devotion that had allowed the entire family to sleep at night. Her return to nursing would be other cancer sufferers' gain.

He failed to stop his heart blooming as she neared him. His blood stirred too, thickening the closer she came. She'd removed her T-shirt and tied it around her waist, exposing her bikini-clad breasts, which swayed gently as she walked towards him pushing the wheelchair. Her hair, normally worn loose, had been pulled into a high ponytail, no doubt to counter the heat coming from the blazing sun. Her golden skin had darkened in their short time on the island and it suited her beautifully.

His grandfather had fallen asleep. She adjusted the

parasol above him then gave Massimo a cautious smile. 'Any news?'

He looked at his watch. 'One hour.'

Felipe's wife, Francesca, was about to go into labour with their second child so his right-hand man, Seb, was coordinating events. Seb had been confident they could get Gianluca out without anyone noticing their presence. But this depended on Gianluca following the plan and being in the right place at the right time without changing his mind.

If Gianluca had half the strength of mind his sister had, then everything would go well.

If was a big word and Massimo had his doubts. He hoped for Livia's sake that Gianluca went through with it. He didn't like to think of her devastation if the opposite happened.

She would cope though. That was one thing he didn't doubt. Livia was a tough cookie. The life she'd lived, the life they were now trying to remove her brother from, had made her that way.

This was the first time since he'd met her, though, that the reality of her childhood had seeped into their life together. Her childhood had always been stories narrated from the safety and comfort of their bed, fables completely removed from his own existence. He'd appreciated intellectually what an awful life it had been for her but this was the first time he'd really *felt* it. It was as if her fear had transplanted like ice in his heart.

'As soon as I have word, I will let you know,' he promised. Gianluca had been instructed to turn his phone off in case it had a tracker in it. Massimo had already organised a replacement one for him.

'Thank you.' Her lips pulled together before her chest and shoulders rose then fell sharply. 'Whatever happens... thank you.'

His own chest inflated at this simple, sincere gratitude. He hadn't offered assistance out of any form of altruism. Livia had needed help and he'd been in a position to provide it...

He'd never seen fear on her face before. He defied any man in his position not to offer their help too.

It struck him then that in the whole of their marriage she had never asked for or needed his help for anything of importance. Not once. All she'd ever wanted from him was the one thing he'd been unable to give. His time.

Her shoulders rose again. 'I'm going to find one of Jimmy's carers and get them to put him to bed, then I'll be back out to help...if you want it?'

As she spoke, a golf buggy delivering the first batch of workers for the evening's party emerged from the thick forest. There was much to oversee to ensure the event went perfectly. His family had offered help earlier but he'd refused, told them to enjoy their last full day on the island. This was something he'd wanted to do himself. His last gift to his grandfather.

About to give the same refusal to Livia, he found his tongue forming words of its own accord. 'If you haven't anything better to do.'

Her smile this time was wide. 'Only sunbathing, which bores me.'

She wheeled his grandfather away.

He closed his eyes and breathed deeply, telling himself he'd accepted her offer so as to give her something to distract herself with while they waited for news on her brother.

The acid burning in his guts exposed that for the lie it was.

Livia, her head upside down, dried her hair on a low setting and tried to pretend she wasn't keeping an ear out for Massimo. He'd sent her back to their chalet over an hour ago saying he'd join her shortly. The party was due to start in thirty minutes and he still needed to shower and dress. This was cutting it fine even for the man who could get himself ready in ten minutes flat.

Together, they'd supervised the arrival of the vast volume of staff employed for the evening, the exquisite finger buffet the army of chefs had spent the day preparing, the decoration of the interior and exterior of the lodge, the quantities and varieties of drink, made sure the extra chalets some of the guests were staying in for the night were ready, and fielded a constant flow of calls.

During all this, Massimo had kept her updated on Gianluca. As of three hours ago her brother was in a hotel two hundred miles from Naples. Tomorrow he'd be moved from the hotel to her rented apartment.

Knowing her brother was safe and had turned his back on the life she too had fought so hard to escape from had left her dizzy with relief. Every part of her felt the relief, her lungs looser, her limbs stronger, her shoulders lighter. She could hardly wait to get back to Rome and smother him.

Massimo's help in extracting Gianluca...

She'd learned at much too young an age that to get through life she could only rely on herself. Self-reliance had been so inured in her that it had never occurred to her to ask for help. She'd always managed alone.

It was the first time anyone had ever removed a burden from her shoulders and her heart swelled in gratitude for it.

Maybe Gianluca would have found the nerve to leave on his own that day with nothing but a transfer of money from her and the promise of her apartment but there was no doubt that Massimo taking control of the situation had given Gianluca the final injection of courage he needed. *He'd* been the one to talk Gianluca round.

When Gianluca had called her from the hotel, he'd been relieved to be out but torn at all he was leaving behind. She understood those feelings. They were the same emotions she'd lived through. As dangerous an environment as the Secondigliano was, it was where their family and friends were. It was their home. Starting over was never easy.

Leaving Massimo had been harder than leaving her family. She'd never felt an atom of relief at leaving him, only overwhelming pain. The future without him had never appeared bright, only bleak.

There had been times that day when she'd found herself staring at him with a heart so full she'd felt the individual heavy beats vibrating through her body.

There had been times, too, when she'd had to turn her face away from him and blink back hot tears at all they had lost. Today, working together harmoniously, supporting each other, teasing each other, laughing... it was like being thrown back to the early days of their marriage.

Why had they thrown it away?

When she'd finished drying her hair, she heard yet another small plane flying low over the cabin. More guests arriving. Unfortunately—or fortunately, depending on your perspective of paradise being spoilt by a mile-long runway—the island only had the capacity to admit small aircraft, so half the guests were being flown in as the staff had been: tag-team-style. The remaining guests were sailing to the island on Massimo's yacht.

She'd just finished applying her lipstick when the bedroom door opened and Massimo's reflection appeared in the mirror.

She stared at him, her chest filling so hard and so quickly that it pushed the air from her lungs.

She cleared her throat and turned around to face him properly, trying desperately hard to mask the turbulence raging beneath her skin. 'I was about to send a search party out for you.'

Caramel eyes glittered. His throat moved a number of times before he responded with a gruff, 'I had a work call I needed to take care of. Give me ten minutes?'

She nodded.

He strode to the bathroom door and turned the handle.

As he pushed it open, he suddenly stopped and turned back to face her. His throat moved again. 'You look beautiful.'

CHAPTER EIGHT

THE SETTING SUN bathed the lodge in a warm golden glow. The glow bounced off the delicate lights that adorned the exterior of the lodge and the high trees nestled around it, creating a sight that made Livia sigh with pleasure. The abundance of flowering shrubs filled the air with exotic scents that seemed more pronounced than usual to her sensitised state.

The lodge's huge double doors were open. Music and chattering voices echoed out of it like a friendly greeting.

She walked in step with Massimo, heartbreakingly gorgeous in a black tuxedo and a black tie she doubted would stay around his neck for any length of time. In thirteen minutes flat he'd showered, dressed and trimmed his beard. He'd even tamed his thick black hair.

From the moment they'd closed their chalet door behind them, the urge to take his hand had been all-consuming. It swung by his hip as he made his graceful long strides. All she had to do was stretch her fingers…

Temptation was taken away when they entered the lodge. They were welcomed by a sea of happy faces all dressed in their finest clothes, embraces and smacking kisses flowing free and fast.

Madeline pounced at the earliest opportunity. 'Come

with me and introduce yourself to anyone you've never met before,' she hissed in Livia's ear. 'Everyone seems to know my name but I have no idea who lots of them are and I don't want to embarrass myself or them by saying so.'

Laughing, Livia happily stepped into the throng and introduced herself to the strangers, making sure to repeat their names for Madeline's benefit. A handful were Jimmy's old childhood friends, people who had once called this island home, others soldiers he'd befriended during his voluntary deployment in the Second World War. In all, there were ninety guests celebrating Jimmy's birthday with him. The language barrier between herself and the native English speakers was easy to overcome, she found, by simply placing her hand to her chest and reciting her name. After that, Madeline would take over and translate.

Getting everyone to the island for the party had been a logistical nightmare but the look on Jimmy's face proved all the effort Massimo had made and the vast expense had been worth it. Currently talking to an old school-friend who was in his own wheelchair and had his own carer in attendance, Jimmy was smiling from ear to ear.

Livia's heart swelled with love for the elderly man whose home she had entered as his nurse and left as his granddaughter-in-law. He had an inherent kindness and a decency about him that had shone through from their first meeting, qualities inherent in his daughter and granddaughter too. This was the kind of family Livia had longed for as a child. A family where you felt safe and cocooned in love. There had been love of a sort in the Esposito home but it was a hard love, the kind that came with conditions.

Her gaze drifted to Jimmy's grandson and some-how her heart swelled even more. Massimo was on his haunches chatting to a frail great-aunt. Massimo was different from the rest of his family in more ways than she could count but he had their decency. He had an un-limited quota of generosity running through his veins. All this, the purchase of the island, the building of the entire complex…all of that had been achieved by Mas-simo so Jimmy could spend his final birthday in the place of his birth.

The island would also be Jimmy's legacy. The staff employed to work full-time on the resort doubled as war-dens for the nature reserve. Jimmy's offspring and his siblings' offspring would enjoy this paradise for genera-tions to come. All of it courtesy of Massimo.

Massimo tried to concentrate on what his great-aunt, a woman he'd never met before, was saying to him. Her heavily accented English flew like a burr from her mouth. Her gratitude towards Massimo for arranging the party and ensuring she got to see her youngest brother for the first time in almost seventy years touched him. He imagined her as a young girl playing with his grand-father and their other siblings, the last generation of Seibuas to live, work and play here before their way of life had become unsustainable.

But it wasn't her accent that made it hard for him to concentrate. His lack of concentration was down to his wife.

She always looked beautiful but tonight… Beauty did not do her justice. He had to fight his eyes' desire to keep seeking her out but somehow he was always fully aware of exactly where she was. Right then, she was at the buffet table with his father.

The mid-thigh-length strappy black sequined dress she wore with its plunging neckline, the gold locket she wore around her neck, the gold hooped earrings that gleamed through the locks of her hair...

Everything about her glittered.

The Livia he'd first met had come back to life. The confident, gregarious woman with the throaty, dirty laugh, the woman who'd never found language to be a barrier for communication, she was here, radiating with the joy of life.

And why shouldn't she radiate in it? Life for Livia had been a hard-fought battle.

Where had this woman gone in those awful cold months before she'd left him?

He knew her brother's escape had something to do with her carefree mood but there had to be a greater explanation than that.

Suddenly her stance shifted and her eyes fell on him.

That feeling of being punch-drunk hit him again.

He had no idea how long they stared at each other. He barely recalled his last few minutes of conversation with his great-aunt either.

In need of a drink, he was manoeuvring his way around small children dancing vigorously, when his grandfather caught his eye and beckoned him over.

Massimo squatted to the same level as his wheelchair and took his frail hands into his own. It was like touching tissue paper. 'Are you enjoying the party, *Nonno*?'

'You have made an old man very happy. Thank you.'

Massimo would never get used to the raspiness of his

grandfather's voice. He squeezed the frail hands gently. 'My pleasure.'

The filmy eyes that had once been the same colour as Massimo's held his and the old gleam in them returned. 'What does an old man have to do to get a bourbon here?'

'I thought you'd been advised against drinking alcohol?'

'What does advice matter when you're dying?'

Massimo winced.

His grandfather twisted his hands so he was the one holding Massimo's. He leaned closer to him. 'I'm not afraid of death, Massimo. I've had a good life. All the people here remind me how good it's been. I've *lived*, and the short time I have left, I want to live that too.'

There was no guile in his grandfather's stare but Massimo had the strong impression the elderly man was trying to tell him something.

He kissed the bald head and wished he knew the words to tell his grandfather how much he meant to him.

By the time he returned with his grandfather's drink, a crowd had gathered around him. Not wanting to be snared in a large group and forced to make more small talk, he decided an upgrade from the beer he'd been drinking was in order and went back to the bar to order himself a large bourbon.

He was on his second when Livia sidled up to him.

'Hiding away?' she asked.

'Taking a breather.'

Dark brown eyes studied him, a combination of sympathy and amusement in them. Livia knew well how social situations made him feel.

She caught the barman's attention and ordered herself a bourbon too. 'This is a great party.'

'People are enjoying it?'

'Very much.' She nudged him with her elbow and pointed at one of the sofas. Two of the small children he'd almost tripped over earlier were fast asleep on it. A third, who'd gone a pale green colour, was eating a large scoop of ice cream, utter determination etched on her face. 'Someone needs to get that girl a sick bag.'

He laughed and was immediately thrown back to his sister's wedding again.

He'd approached Livia at the bar. She'd said something inane that had made him laugh. He wished he could remember what it was but it had slipped away the moment she'd said it, his attention too transfixed on her for words to stick.

She'd blown him away.

Those same feelings...

Had they ever really left him?

The music had slowed in tempo. The dance floor had filled, the children making way for the adults.

'We should dance,' he murmured.

Her chest rose, head tilted, teeth grazing over her bottom lip. 'I suppose we should...for appearances' sake.'

He breathed deeply and slowly held his hand out.

Equally slowly, she stretched hers out to meet his. The pads of her fingers pressed into his palm. Tingles shot through his skin. His fingers closed over them.

On the crowded dance floor, he placed his hands loosely on her hips. Her hands rested lightly on his shoulders. A delicate waft of her perfume filtered through his airwaves.

He clenched his jaw and purposely kept his gaze focused above her head.

They moved slowly in tempo with the music, their bodies a whisper away from touching...

'When did you take your tie off?' Livia murmured when she couldn't take the tension that had sprung between them any longer.

She'd been trying very hard not to breathe. Every inhalation sent Massimo's familiar musky heat and the citrus undertones of his cologne darting into her airwaves. Her skin vibrated with awareness, her senses uncoiling, tiny springs straining towards the man whose hands hardly touched her hips. She could feel the weight in them though, piercing through her skin.

Caramel eyes slowly drifted down to meet her gaze.

The music beating around them reduced to a burr.

The breath of space between them closed. The tips of her breasts brushed against the top of his flat stomach. The weight of his hands increased in pressure.

Heat pulsed deep in her pelvis.

Her hands crept without conscious thought over his shoulder blades. Heart beating hard, her fingers found his neck...her palms pressed against it.

His right hand caressed slowly up her back. She shivered at the darts of sensation rippling through her.

Distantly, she was aware the song they were dancing to had finished.

His left hand drew across her lower back and gradually pulled her so close their bodies became flush.

Her cheek pressed into his shoulder. She could feel the heavy thuds of his heart. They matched the beats of hers.

His mouth pressed into the top of her head. The warmth of his ragged breath whispered in the strands of her hair. Her lungs had stopped functioning. Not a hitch of air went into them.

A finger brushed a lock of her hair.

She closed her eyes.

The lock was caught and wound in his fingers.

She turned her cheek and pressed her mouth to his throat...

A body slammed into them. Words, foreign to her drumming ears but unmistakably words of apology, were gabbled.

They pulled apart.

There was a flash of bewilderment in Massimo's eyes she knew must be mirrored in hers before he blinked it away.

A song famous at parties all around the world was now playing. The floor was packed with bodies all joining in with the accompanying dance. Even the passed-out children had woken up to join in with it.

And she'd been oblivious. They both had.

The rest of the party passed in a blur, as if she'd been sucked into a time warp that had her in Massimo's arms on the crowded dance floor one minute, the next following him into their chalet. Had they even spoken since they'd left the dance floor?

Vague images flashed in Livia's mind. Jimmy, ably assisted by all the children under the age of ten blowing out the ninety candles on his cake. The exchange of goodbye kisses.

After the noise of the party, the silence in their chalet was deafening.

She stared at Massimo with a thundering heart and tried to think of something, anything to say to cut through this tension-filled silence but her brain seemed to have been infected with a fever.

His chest rose before he nodded his head in a decisive manner. 'I'll brush my teeth and leave you to sleep.'

Every inch of her body screamed in protest.

She managed to incline her head.

He turned and disappeared into the bedroom.

Massimo brushed his teeth vigorously, as if the bristles could brush away the longing raging through him.

One dance with Livia had smashed through his defences.

One touch of her hand had set his pulses racing.

One look in her eyes had set his heart pounding.

One press of her body against his had set the arousal he'd been suppressing by a thread off in an unstoppable flow that denial had no longer been able to contain.

He could still feel her lips against his throat. That one brush had marked him. His body still buzzed from the thrills that had been unleashed in that one short dance.

He wanted her with an ache that burned. He'd never *stopped* wanting her.

Done with his teeth, he slapped cold water over his face then stared hard at his reflection.

He was going to leave this bathroom, walk calmly through the bedroom, wish Livia a good night then go outside and sleep on the hammock.

He would not linger. He would not engage in conversation. He would not touch her.

To do any of these things would prise open the lid of the box they had both hammered shut. Their marriage was over for damn good reasons. In the morning they would say goodbye and fly to separate continents. The ripping of his heart at this thought meant nothing but an acknowledgement of his own failure. For a man who had succeeded on his own merits at everything he'd attempted in life, failure was a hard thing to tolerate. Their marriage had been a failure and much of that had been down to him. It was bound to sit uncomfortably.

He patted his damp face dry, shoved the towel back on the rail and moved purposefully out of the bathroom, through the bedroom that had been designed to be theirs, and through to the main living area...

Livia was in the kitchen area, her back to the counter, glass of water clasped tightly in her hand.

Their eyes met.

His heart squeezed unbearably but his steps did not falter.

'Sleep well,' he muttered as he continued to the door.

Only when he'd closed the door behind him did he pause for breath.

He closed his eyes and filled his lungs with resolve...

But he could still feel her eyes on him.

He fisted a hand and punched it into the palm of the other.

He tried to set off again. His legs and feet refused to cooperate.

Livia stared at the closed door for so long her eyes became fuzzy.

There was a cramping in her chest that made every breath she took an effort.

She wanted to run out after him and beg him to come back inside. She wanted to wrap her arms around him and kiss him; his mouth, his face, his neck, his chest, every inch of him.

She wanted his arms around her. She wanted to feel

the intense pleasure that had cemented the love they had once found together.

Deep in her soul she knew she would never find what they'd had with anyone else. It wasn't possible for a heart to love as deeply as hers had loved Massimo and move on without leaving a part of it with him.

And he had loved her too. He *had*. Self-preservation had had her denying his love but being with him again had unleashed the memories she'd suppressed about all the good times they'd had.

Those good times had been the best of her life.

She'd *had* to focus on the bad times that had destroyed them because to remember the good times would have been to remind herself in multicolour detail of all they had thrown away.

Resolve suddenly took her in its grip, pulling her out of the paralysis that had kept her immobile in her desperate thoughts.

Shoving her undrunk glass of water on the counter, she kicked her shoes off and put one bare foot in front of the other…

Without any warning the door flew open.

Massimo filled the doorway, breathing heavily through his nose, his hair dishevelled, caramel eyes pulsing.

There was a moment of stillness. Only a moment but it stretched and pulled like an invisible band looping around them, pulling tighter and tighter until the binds became too great and, feet moving in sync, they closed the distance between them.

Livia drank in the face she had never stopped dreaming about. Everything inside her had cramped. Except for her heart. That felt as if a hummingbird had nestled in it.

The throat she had unthinkingly kissed moved. The top three buttons of his shirt were undone. The dinner jacket he'd worn to the party had long been discarded with the tie that had adorned his neck.

This was Massimo; heartbreakingly handsome yet unkempt, lacking in vanity and dismissive of his own beauty. Yet he had made her feel feminine and beautiful. He had made her feel as if she were the only woman on this earth.

The look reflecting back at her now...

It made all those old feelings come roaring back to life.

The electrified air between them swirled as his hand inched to hers. Fingers locked together. Slowly, he lifted their hands to his chest as, equally slowly, his other hand touched her hair. Using the backs of his fingers, he stroked the strands.

How could hair feel alive? she wondered dimly, shivering as sensation tingled from the top of her head and spread through her heated veins.

Their entwined fingers tightened.

The hand in her hair dived through the locks and gently traced the rim of her ear.

Her legs weakened.

The hand at her ear slowly skimmed down the side of her neck. The hummingbird in her heart was trying to beat its way out. It almost succeeded when the eyes her gaze was locked on drew closer and closer, the lids closing, and the wide, firm mouth she had once believed she would kiss for ever brushed against her aching lips.

CHAPTER NINE

MASSIMO, EYES CLOSED, rested his mouth against the softest lips in creation and breathed Livia in.

He felt her quiver. The nails of the fingers entwined in his dug into his hand.

Emotions were erupting through him, so many it was impossible to pinpoint one and say *this* was what he was feeling.

The only certainty he could find was that this was where he needed to be.

He needed Livia's touch like a fish needed water.

And he needed to touch her like a drowning man needed air.

A tempest raged inside him, a storm crashing onto the drowning man.

Livia was the air he needed. She was on his mind with every breath he took.

The thunder of his heart vibrated through his bones. When she placed her small hand on the top of his chest he knew she must be able to feel it too.

He could feel her heartbeat through their tightly wound hands.

The fingers splayed on her soft neck drifted back up to spear her hair. He hadn't realised that he'd been afraid the changes she'd made to her hair would have changed its texture until relief had coursed through him on the dance floor to find it had the same silky feel.

He'd been as helpless not to touch her then as he was not to touch her now.

Livia was more than air. She was the fire in his heart, the water in his veins, the earth that kept him grounded.

Their lips moved slowly together, fused mouths parting, the kiss deepening.

Her sweet breath curled into his senses.

Their entwined hands released. Arms wrapped tightly around each other, bodies crushed together, tongues danced as the desire he had fought since she had stepped into the cabin of his private jet was finally set free.

A million tastes and scents and sensations filled Livia's starved senses. Being wrapped so tightly in Massimo's arms and being kissed so deeply and passionately was awakening the last parts of her she had kept locked away.

He'd torn the last of her barriers down but the feelings erupting in her were too heady, too familiar and too wondrous to be frightening.

If she were to be cast away on a desert island and allowed to choose only one person to join her on it, there was no question of who she would choose. Massimo. He was scarred on her heart and etched in her soul.

She didn't want to think of what she was doing—what they were doing. She needed this too much. Needed him too much.

Only now, as she drowned in the heady delights of his touch, did she understand how starved she'd been since she'd left him and how slowly time had crawled in those awful dark days.

To feel the crash of their hearts pounding so violently together through their embracing bodies...

Everything inside her bloomed wide open and light poured in.

Her stomach swooped as he lifted her into his arms.

He'd carried her like this on their wedding night, she remembered dreamily, pressing her mouth against his neck and inhaling the Massimo scent that had always made her stomach swoop all on its own.

There was such tenderness in the way he laid her down on the bed that the light that had poured inside her sparkled and glimmered through her skin and veins.

His hooded eyes glimmered too.

She could feel his hunger as keenly as she felt her own.

Gently he brushed away the locks of hair that had fallen across her face.

No words were spoken between them. No words were necessary.

She raised her hand and palmed his cheek. The bristles of his beard grazed against her skin.

Their mouths locked together.

The hand palming his cheek slipped around his neck, her other hand sliding around his waist, pulling him down so she could feel his solid weight on her. She needed to feel that brief crush of her lungs before he shifted to release the weight, needed the assurance that she hadn't fallen into a dream.

She couldn't bear it if this was nothing but a dream. She'd suffered too many dreams in those dark days where they would be making love only for her to wake to the cold reality of a lonely bed.

There had been nightmares too, ones where he'd found someone else. One in particular had stayed with her for days. She'd been walking down the street when she'd spotted Massimo walking arm in arm with a faceless woman. She'd run after them but couldn't catch them, screaming his name as loudly as she could but no sound coming out. She'd awoken from it with a start, tears soaking into her pillow and her heart cold with a fear a hundred times worse than she'd felt in the nightmares from her childhood.

Being with him like this, here, now, evoked only warmth in her soaring heart.

She was flying.

For now, tomorrow didn't exist.

There was only now.

His hands stroked down the sides of her breasts and down to her hips where he gathered the skirt of her dress and hitched it to her waist, his mouth raining kisses over her face, her hands scratching into his scalp. They only broke away so her dress could be pulled over her head and discarded.

She saw the pulse in his eyes as he dragged his stare over her body, naked save for the skimpy black knickers she wore.

Heat flooded her with an intensity that stole her breath when he dipped his head and kissed her breasts in turn, and now it was his shirt she was scratching at, grasping to untuck it.

Every part of Livia's body had been etched in Massimo's memory but he stared at her feeling as if he were seeing it all for the first time.

His memory had played tricks on him. He'd forgotten how damned sexy she was, how perfect she was.

He'd forgotten the way her legs writhed when she was hungry for him and to see them doing that now…

He kissed her breasts again, with more savagery than the first tender kisses he'd placed on them. He'd forgotten, too, how much she loved him lavishing attention on them. She was as receptive to his touch as he was to hers, the perfect fusion that had so blown his mind the first time they'd made love and every time after.

He moved down to her belly, divesting himself of his shirt as he went, then gripped her knickers in his fingers and pulled them down her legs to land in the pile their other clothing had formed. Working quickly, he removed the last of his own clothing too.

He could smell the musky heat of her excitement…

There was not a single thing about Livia that didn't set his blood aflame.

He kissed her thighs, digging his fingers into the pliant flesh, then ran his tongue between the soft mound of dark hair between her parted legs.

There was a clenching in his heart. Fresh memories assailed him of the first time he'd shaved her bikini line for her and trimmed the hair. She'd been about to make an appointment at a salon when he'd suggested with a wolfish gleam that he do it for her. Her eyes had pulsed with agreement.

It had been sexy. It had been fun. The trust she had bestowed in him had blown his mind as much as everything else they had shared. After that first time they'd adopted their own language for it. It had always ended with wild lovemaking.

Her bikini line now was smooth but the rest was as nature intended. It looked to him that she hadn't bothered with it since she'd left him. For a woman who always liked to feel her best as well as look her best, right down to always wearing matching underwear that no one other than him would see, this told him everything he needed to know.

Livia hadn't been with anyone since they'd parted.

No other man had buried his face between her legs and experienced her uninhibited wild responses, the soft moans and pleas…

No other man had teased her to orgasm with his tongue alone.

He *knew* he had no right to feel such relief at this. But he did.

Livia was *his*. Just as he was hers.

Gripping her hips, he snaked his tongue back up her petite, curvy body, inhaling her skin, tasting it, nipping it, the primal eruption that had so consumed him the first time they'd made love stronger than it had ever been.

She belonged to *him*. And he belonged to her. He would always belong to her.

Elbows resting either side of her face, he gazed down in wonder. The same ragged-breath wonder reflected right back at him.

Why had he let her go? How could he have let this beautiful, sassy woman walk away without a fight?

With a groan, he plundered her plump, delectable mouth. Her arms looped around his neck and she arched her back so her breasts crushed against his chest as they devoured each other with a hungry desperation. Her legs hooked around his thighs, encouraging him, and he drove inside her in one long thrust.

The relief at being in Livia's tight, slick heat was such

that he had to screw his eyes shut and drag in a breath lest he lose control immediately.

But, damn, a man could happily die like this.

Livia's head had gone. She'd lost control of her sanity when Massimo had brought her to orgasm using nothing but his tongue and now, with him sheathed so tightly inside her, the sensations were too incredible to do anything but cling tightly to him and soar in the heavenliness they were creating together.

The hummingbird that had nestled in her heart had broken free and she was flying high in the sky, reaching for the stars.

They made love with abandon, Massimo driving into her with fury tempered by tenderness, wet kisses, bites on necks, nails digging into skin, nothing existing but this moment, them, together, the fire that had always blazed so brightly between them reignited but now burning with the blue flame of desperation.

For the first time ever she found herself fighting release. She didn't want this to end. She wanted these wonderful feelings to last for ever.

From the concentration carved on Massimo's face and the pained desire she caught every time she looked in his eyes, he was fighting the same battle.

Squeezing her eyes shut tight, she pressed her mouth into his neck and fought the growing sensations pulsating deep inside her pelvis. But it was like fighting against the tide. The pleasure was just too much...

She forgot all about fighting when the pulsations turned into an eruption that spread through her like a rippling wave. All she could do was tighten her hold on him and submit to the waves carrying her as high as the soaring hummingbird of her heart.

* * *

Livia opened her eyes with a start and immediately rolled over to check Massimo was still there. She'd fallen asleep in his arms but at some point after drifting off she must have disentangled herself.

The night was still dark but hazy light filtered in from the moon and stars. She swallowed back her relief to find his solid form lying peacefully beside her, facing her on his side. His chest rose and fell steadily.

She inched closer and covered his hand, then gently brought it up over the mattress to her lips. She razed the lightest of kisses against his knuckles and soaked in every detail of his sleeping face.

Something sharp and painful filled her chest. The hummingbird had nestled back into her heart. If Massimo opened his eyes he would see its thrumming wings beating through her skin.

She swallowed again and tried to regain control of her suddenly erratic breathing.

She pressed her mouth back against his knuckles. His fingers twitched.

Feeling herself in desperate need of air, she released his hand and slipped out of the bed. She wrapped her robe around her naked body and padded out of the bedroom.

At the back of their chalet, down the steps of their veranda, was their private garden and swimming pool. Livia sank onto a sunlounger by the pool and stared at the sun peeking over the horizon.

The cusp of a new day was showing its face but for Livia this cusp was the beginning of the end. This was the day she would say goodbye to Massimo for good...

The realisation hit her like a cold slap.

She didn't want to say goodbye.

Her feelings for Massimo were as strong as they'd ever been and the feelings he'd had for her were still there too. He'd shown it with every look, every touch and every kiss.

Why had they let that love go? Why hadn't they fought for it? The love they had once shared had been *everything*.

Massimo had slipped away from her. That was the truth. It had been so gradual that to begin with she'd only sensed it. That was what had brought her fears and insecurities out and deepened her loneliness and homesickness. Everything had escalated from that.

She talked too much but he didn't talk enough. Not about the things that were important.

That needed to change.

She looked up at the brightening sky and breathed in the warm, fragrant air. The chirrup of awakening birds sounded all around her, a joyful sound that sparked hope in her heart.

Where there was life there was hope.

What they had was worth fighting for. All she had to do was make Massimo see that too.

Filling her lungs with resolve, Livia walked back into the chalet.

If she had any chance of saving their marriage, she needed her phone, which was in the bedroom.

She pushed the door open quietly.

Massimo lifted his head. He'd woken to an empty bed. He'd registered this little fact before his eyes had opened, an emptiness where warmth should be.

He breathed a little easier to see Livia's silhouette in the doorway.

'Are you okay?' he asked, his voice croaky from sleep. He had no idea what time it was other than it was early.

It was the deepest sleep he'd had in…since she'd left him.

She stared at him for the longest time before a smile curved over her beautiful face and she released the robe wrapped around her.

'I needed some air,' she said as she padded to the bed.

He pulled the sheets back and held his arms out for her, his body responding automatically to her unashamed nudity.

His desire for her was the one thing he'd never been able to turn off.

She nestled into his embrace.

He closed his eyes and breathed into her hair, his chest swelling. For long silent moments they did nothing but lie entwined together.

This would be the last time he held her like this.

'Why did you get spearheads added to your tattoo?' she murmured, tracing it gently with her finger before kissing it. 'I thought it was finished.'

'I thought it was finished too.'

His tattoo hadn't been finished but their marriage was.

He tightened the embrace. Regrets swirled in the air around them but it was too late for regrets. However good it felt to spend one last night with Livia, they were better off apart. They both knew that. You couldn't play on broken strings. The strings that had bound them together hadn't merely broken; they'd been irrevocably severed.

Whatever desire-driven thoughts had consumed him when they'd been making love didn't change the fact that he was better on his own. He worked better and functioned better.

Their lips found each other and the hunger that had always left him feeling starving when he was without her reared back to life.

They could have this, he thought dimly as she sank onto his length, her hair falling onto his face.

One last moment of bliss together before they said goodbye for good.

CHAPTER TEN

AFTER A LATE breakfast in the lodge, it was time to say goodbye. The guests who'd stayed the night left first until it was only Massimo, his immediate family and his grandfather's care team left.

Heart heavy, Massimo walked with them to the jetty where the cruise liner awaited. This return journey would be much shorter than the outward one. They were sailing to Viti Levu and flying to Rome from there on a private jet he'd chartered for them. After two months away from their homes, his family was looking forward to their return to Italy.

Unspoken between them all was his grandfather's health. It was the reason they were flying back. Jimmy had reserved all his energy for this stay on his birth land and his party. A two-month sail might be too late for him to have his last request of dying in his home met.

Madeline wrapped her arms around him and looked up at him with an unusually serious expression. 'Come home soon, Massimo. Please?'

Instead of the usual vague response he gave to these kinds of requests, Massimo found himself kissing his sister's cheek. 'I'll try.'

She tightened her hold. 'Try harder. We miss you.'

For the first time he found himself thinking that he *would* try.

Something had shifted in him. For all his dread at being cooped up on an island with his family, the weekend had gone much better than he'd anticipated. The more time he'd spent with them, the easier he'd found it. There had been an acceptance he'd never felt before. Or was it that he now looked at his family with fresh eyes?

Gazing over his sister's head, he saw his mother fussing with his grandfather's wheelchair. His mother loved to fuss. She was never happier than when doing things for those she loved, whether it was ironing shirts to within an inch of their lives or slaving over steaming bowls of simple home-cooked food to fill their bellies with. His father was the same too.

An old memory surfaced: sleeping on his sister's bedroom floor while his father had made a bed and wardrobe for Massimo's room. All the materials were old, reclaimed stuff but his father had made the entire lot himself right down to painting them in a colour of Massimo's choosing.

That had been his first practical exposure to the idea that something could start out as one thing and then be turned into something completely different.

Just as he was thinking that he'd finally found the root of his love of engineering and science, another memory surfaced, of the time his father found an old bicycle at a central rubbish-collection point. He'd brought it home, serviced it and painted it. By the time he presented it to Massimo—a gift for him to run his errands on—the bike looked brand new.

A wave of affection washed through him and he embraced his parents tighter than he usually did. For all the resentment he'd once felt at growing up poor, he'd never had to sleep with one ear alert to danger. He'd never had to worry about his sister being seduced into a life of crime.

After a cuddle with his niece, it was time to say goodbye to his grandfather. He sent a silent prayer that this would not be for the last time.

He watched them sail away with a weighted heart and a lump in his throat.

Beside him stood Livia, waving vigorously at his departing family.

However hard he tried to blur her from his vision she remained solid. Beautiful.

The lump that felt like granite in his throat grew. He felt all disjointed.

Abruptly, he turned on his heel and strode back down the jetty, scanning the sky for signs of the Cessna, which had taken the last of the party guests to Viti Levu and should be back by now to take Massimo and Livia to Nadi International Airport where his flight crew were waiting for them.

'Massimo?'

He closed his eyes and drew in a breath, slowing his pace enough for Livia to catch up with him.

The last thing he wanted was a long, protracted goodbye with his wife. He had enough tumultuous feelings ripping through him.

'Are you okay?'

'Yes.'

'You've hardly spoken to me since we got out of bed. Do you regret last night?'

That was Livia. Straight to the point, as always.

'I don't regret it. I just don't see any point in talking about it.'

'We spent the night making love. I would say that gives us lots to talk about.'

That was Livia too, always so keen to discuss *feelings*, as if feelings mattered a damn.

'Last night…' He closed his eyes again and sucked in another breath, fighting the heat that spread through his veins to remember how incredible it had been. 'I'm not saying it was a mistake but, with hindsight, it shouldn't have happened.'

'Why not?'

'We're getting divorced, Liv. I know we're going to wait for my grandfather to…' He couldn't vocalise the words. They were waiting for his grandfather to die before they went ahead with the legalities. 'It won't be long,' he finished. He didn't know if it was his grandfather's imminent death or the final severance of their marriage that caused his heart to constrict.

Dark brown eyes held his. 'Don't you have doubts?'

'Doubts?'

'About whether we're doing the right thing.'

'None.'

She flinched but didn't drop her stare. 'I do.'

'How can you have doubts?' he asked incredulously. 'This was your idea. You left *me*.'

Her slim shoulders rose. Her lips drew together before she said, 'I want to try again.'

His heart made a giant lurch. He took a step back and stared hard at her. 'One night of sex doesn't mend a broken marriage and our marriage *was* broken.'

'But we never tried to fix it. We were always too busy arguing…' She held her hands in the air. '*I* was always too busy arguing. You refused to argue. It doesn't matter who did what, the truth is we never sat down and talked and tried to find a way to fix things. We just gave up.'

'Some things can't be fixed. Our marriage is one of them and you were right to leave me. I'm sorry if last night has caused you to have doubts but—'

'Last night made me see the truth. We gave up too easily.'

'It changed nothing for me.'

Her burst of laughter sounded hollow. 'You *liar*.'

'I can't be the husband you want me to be.'

'You don't know what I want.'

'You screamed it in my face every day.'

'Then maybe you should have listened.'

'I'm not going to rehash old wounds.' He put his hand out, palm facing her; a visual sign to back up his words that he wanted this conversation to end. 'You wanted a divorce and I accepted it. It is the right thing for us to do. I'm going back to America and you're going back to Italy. That's it. Over.'

He started walking again.

'I *knew* you'd run away as soon as I brought the subject up.'

Ignoring her, he continued, craning his head to the sky again for sign of the plane. It should have been here thirty minutes ago.

'It's not coming.'

He stopped in his tracks.

'The plane. You keep looking out for it. It's not coming back today.'

Livia folded her arms across her chest and braced herself.

When he turned to look at her, his face was dark. 'What have you done?'

'I've cancelled the Cessna until tomorrow. We need to talk.'

'No, we need to go home. I have work and you have your brother waiting for you. I thought you were keen to see him and convince him that he's done the right thing in leaving.'

'He's safe,' she countered, 'and as long as he's got a gaming thing to play on and a mountain of food to eat, which he has, he won't be going anywhere. To save you time making wasted phone calls, I might as well confess that I've sent your flight crew on a sailing trip on your yacht. Even if you manage to get another Cessna to take you from the island to the mainland, you'll find it hard to leave Fiji itself.'

'What the...?' He swore loudly.

Bad language didn't faze her. She'd grown up in a home where every other word was punctuated with a curse.

His jaw clenching hard enough to snap, he pulled his phone out of his back pocket. 'I don't know what game you think you're playing but it won't work. My crew take orders from me, not from you.'

'When we married you told all your staff, flight crew included, that they were to take my orders as seriously as they took yours. Have you changed those orders?'

If looks could kill she would be dead on the ground beneath her.

'Call them if you want but you'll find they're already on the yacht drinking the champagne I ordered for them. They won't be fit to fly.' Massimo might be the undisputed brains in their marriage but when it came to planning, Livia could beat anyone. If she had any chance of getting him to stay on the island a little longer, she had to cut off all his options to leave.

Glaring at her, he punched his fingers against the screen of his phone. 'I shall charter another plane to take me home. You can stay here and rot.'

'You think you'll be able to charter a plane today? You'll be lucky to get one for tomorrow.'

'I'll take my chances.' He put his phone to his ear. A moment later he swiped it with another curse.

'If you were calling Lindy then I've already spoken to her. It's Saturday in Los Angeles…' The time difference had taken a while for Livia to get her head around but thankfully she'd found it worked in her favour. 'She's taking her daughter out for the day and keeping her phone switched off.'

'Lindy was never given instructions to obey you.'

'I asked her a favour and she agreed. It's her own private time so she's not in breach of her contract with you.'

There was a long pause of venom-filled silence.

Livia held her breath.

Then he smiled. His eyes remained blocks of ice. 'I don't need Lindy to charter a plane for me and I don't need her to book me into a hotel for the night if you're right that it's too short notice for me to charter a plane. You lose.'

'No, *we* lose,' she called to his retreating back. 'One extra day, Massimo, that's all I'm asking for. Call the flight company and have another Cessna flown in to take you off the island and check into a hotel while you wait for your flight crew to get back from their trip, or stay here with me and see if we can try and fix this marriage.'

'I am not willing to waste my energy fixing something that's beyond repair.'

'How can you say that when you've dedicated your working life on solutions for the greatest problems facing this earth that people said were beyond repair?'

'Those are problems that can be fixed by science and engineering. Our problems are fundamental.'

'I thought that about us too but now—'

Suddenly he stopped and spun round. If she hadn't stopped walking too she would have careered into him.

'But now, *nothing*. What you have done is deplorable. I need to be back at the facility first thing Monday. We have the prototype to test...'

'Why does it have to be you?' She strove to keep her voice steady but could feel the all too familiar anger rising. 'You employ four thousand people. Are you telling me not one of them can test the prototype for you? Why can't the project manager do it?' It was an argument she'd made countless times about all the different aspects of his business.

'It's a controlled environment that I need to oversee.' It was a variation of an answer he'd given countless times too.

'The only controlled environment is your heart,' she finally snapped.

His face contorted. 'I don't have to listen to this.'

'Oh, yes, you do. If you hadn't noticed, you're stuck on an island with me. There's nowhere for you to escape unless you pay someone to get you out.' Seeing he was about to walk away again, she grabbed hold of his wrist and took a deep breath to calm her rising temper and tremulous heart. The heavy thud of his pulse against her fingers gave her the courage to continue. 'Please, Massimo, give me this one day. The Cessna's scheduled to pick us up in the morning. When it gets here, if you still want us to go our separate ways then I'll accept it but if I ever meant anything to you, and if our marriage ever meant anything to you, please, give us this chance.'

Her tight chest loosened a fraction to see a softening in the icy gaze boring into her.

He dropped his gaze to her hand and gently prised her fingers from his wrist.

'Seeing as the options you've left me mean I'm going to be a day late getting home, I need to make some calls.'

'You'll stay?' She hardly dared to hope.

He met her stare again, his expression now inscrutable. 'I'll stay but only because of the situation you've engineered. I'm not staying for us. I have no wish to be cruel but I'm not cut out for marriage. It took our marriage for me to see that.'

Massimo, sitting on the veranda at the back of the chalet, ended his final call and rubbed his fingers over his head. The testing on the prototype he'd spent the last year working on had been put back twenty-four hours, the first time he'd ever deferred anything to do with work. Livia had smashed his carefully planned schedule on its head.

Why was she doing this? Revenge for all the late nights he'd spent in his facility? This devious streak was a side of her he'd never seen before.

Surely she wasn't serious about them trying again? After everything they'd been through and everything they'd put each other through, she wanted to patch their marriage back up? The idea was ludicrous.

They *had* tried, for two long years. He couldn't make her happy then so why did she think he could make her happy now?

He pushed away the thought that the first year of their marriage had been the best of his life. That was easily explained by the high levels of dopamine and other hormones induced by great sex.

He should never have made love to her last night. That was what had brought all this stupid, devious behaviour from her on. The hormones released by their lovemaking had messed with his head too but in the bright light of day the fog his brain had succumbed to had cleared and he could see with clarity again.

He hoped his blunt parting words had given her some much-needed clarity too.

A burst of frustration shot through him and, without thinking, he threw his phone onto the veranda's terracotta tiles. If not for the protective case around it, it would have shattered.

Scowling at the phone as if it were its own fault that it was on the ground, he got off his chair and reached down to pick it back up. As his fingers closed around it a pair of bare feet with pretty painted toenails appeared before him. Attached to the feet was a pair of smooth, bare legs, a scar running along the calf of one, attached to a curvy body wrapped in a sheer pale blue sarong beneath which Livia was very obviously naked. Her newly cut and highlighted chestnut hair was piled high on top of her head, locks spilling over a large pair of aviator shades.

He straightened, his foul mood deepening at the spark of response that flashed through his loins and darkening to see the bucket she carried under her arm, which had a bottle of champagne in it, and the two champagne flutes she held by the stems.

Seemingly oblivious to her presence being unwelcome, she placed everything carefully on the table without speaking and poured the champagne into the flutes. Then she had a large drink from one and removed her shades. Her eyes didn't even flicker at him.

Still not speaking, she then turned around and walked to the steps that led down to their private garden and pool. Before going down the steps, she paused.

He held his breath.

The sarong dropped to the ground.

He clamped his lips tightly together to smother the groan that formed in his throat.

What was she playing at now?

Whatever it was, he would not play along.

But he could not tear his eyes from the nymph-like form.

Her naked bottom swayed gently as she made her way slowly…seductively…down the steps to the thick, green lawn. When she reached the pool she dipped a toe in the water, then entered the pool, wading into it from the wide, gently sloping steps in the arch of the shallow end until she was waist deep. And then she began to swim, a slow breaststroke.

There was no suppressing the groan from his throat at the first frog kick of her legs.

Livia swam to the end of the pool and stopped. The water being only chest deep here, she pressed her hands together on the pool's ledge, rested her chin on them and stared out at the softly rippling waves of the ocean lapping only metres from the edge of the private garden and enjoyed the feel of the sun baking her skin.

Massimo's reaction to her entrapping him on the island hadn't surprised her but it had still hurt. But, whatever he'd said about not being cut out for marriage, she wasn't about to raise a white flag and admit defeat. She knew he still had feelings for her. She just had to break down his barriers for him to see that, with a little compromise and a lot of effort, they could have the life together they'd once dreamed of.

The barriers she'd erected to protect herself had been demolished in one blissful night. What did she have to lose?

Being here this weekend, with the man she loved and with the family she wished she could have had for her own… It had brought back everything she'd wanted for them, everything they'd had at the beginning of their marriage. Gentle teasing. Mutual support. Fun. Laughter. Love.

If she failed, at least she could look herself in the eye and say she'd tried. At least she'd be able to move on rather than being stuck in the awful limbo she'd spent the past four months existing in.

She sensed movement behind her before she heard it. Her heart began to thud but she didn't move, not even when the water rippled around her.

CHAPTER ELEVEN

MASSIMO FELT AS if he'd been drugged.

He'd kept his gaze fixed on Livia, telling himself again and again that he wouldn't play her game.

He'd still been telling himself that when he'd stripped his clothes off.

He'd still been telling himself that when he'd stepped into the water and swum to her.

She made no effort to acknowledge him, not even when he stood behind her.

His hands working of their own volition, he reached into her hair and pulled the pin holding it together out.

Her right shoulder made the smallest of movements but she still didn't acknowledge him.

Her hair tumbled down.

He smoothed it with his hands then pressed his nose into the fragrant silk while dragging his fingers down her back and then sliding them around her waist. 'Why did you cut it?' he murmured.

She leaned back into him with a soft sigh and moved her hands to slide them over his arms. Her nails scratched through the fine hairs of his forearms as her bottom wriggled provocatively against his arousal.

He slid his hand over her ribcage and cupped a

weighty breast. His blood had thickened so much that even his heart felt sluggish within the heavy beats.

The small hands pulled away from his arms and reached up behind her shoulders, her fingers groping for him. And then she twisted around to face him.

Her breasts brushed against his chest, her abdomen pressed against his arousal, her hands cupped his neck.

Colour heightened her face, the dark eyes black with desire, the plump lips parted…

Those lips…

Mouths fused together in a kiss of hard, passionate savagery as the desire between them unleashed like a coil springing free from its tight box.

This was how it had always been between them, he thought, in the hazy recess of his mind. One touch had always been enough to ignite the torch that blazed so brightly between them.

Gripping her hips, he lifted her from the water to place her bottom onto the pool's ledge, parted her legs with his thighs, and thrust straight inside her welcoming heat.

She gasped into his mouth then kissed him even harder.

His fingers digging into her hips, her fingers digging into his neck and scalp, mouths clashing together, he drove in and out of her, fast, furious, thrusting as deep as he could go, pain and pleasure driving them on and on to a climax that had her crying his name and Massimo finding himself separating from his body in a wash of brilliant colour.

It took a long time to come back to himself.

He barely remembered climbing out of the pool and collapsing into an entwined heap of naked limbs on the soft lawn. The afternoon sun above blazed down on them, its heat tempered by the breeze coming from the ocean.

'We should get some sunscreen on you,' he muttered.

Her lips pressed into his neck before she clambered upright and got to her feet. 'Don't go anywhere. I'll be back in a minute.'

When she'd disappeared from view, he rolled onto his back and stretched his limbs with a long sigh.

Slinging an arm across his forehead, he closed his eyes. There was a lethargy within him. His heart still thumped heavily.

He should get up and put his clothes back on before Livia came back with the sunscreen.

He knew what he *should* do. The trouble was his lethargic limbs refused to cooperate, just as his limbs had refused his mind's instructions not to play her sensual game in the pool.

His body had been Livia's slave from the moment they'd met.

He wanted to be angry with her for using her sexuality as a weapon against him but he couldn't. He understood what she was doing. His anger was directed at himself.

When she returned wearing her sarong and carrying two full flutes of champagne whilst also balancing the sunscreen and a couple of beach towels under her arm, he rolled onto his side and propped himself on his elbow.

'Livia, I'm sorry...'

'But this doesn't change anything?' she finished for him with a raised brow. She put the champagne and towels on the poolside table and removed her sarong.

'It's okay, Massimo,' she said as she spread the sarong out like a blanket on the lawn. 'Sometimes great sex is just that—great sex. Could you do my back for me, please?'

Livia sat with her legs stretched out on the sarong and waited for him to join her on it.

Massimo, she had discovered early on in their relationship, opened up more easily after sex, when his defences were down in the wave of euphoria that followed it.

She knew stripping naked and seducing him visually could be considered as fighting dirty but there was no shame in seducing her own husband. They both took great pleasure from making love. If she could go back in time and do one thing differently it would be to stop herself turning her back on him in the last months of their marriage. Without sex to keep the intimacy between them alive, the glue that had held them together had disintegrated. There had been nothing left.

But sex wasn't all a marriage could or should be and intimacy came in many forms.

She leaned forward, hugging her knees when he put his hands filled with sunscreen on her back.

Unlike when he'd worked the screen into her skin briskly on the yacht, he took his time. His touch was soothing. She closed her eyes to savour the sensation.

'What did I do to turn you away from me?' she asked quietly.

His hands paused in their work. 'I don't know what you mean.'

'Yes, you do. You turned away from me, Massimo. You stopped caring. Even if tomorrow you decide everything's still over for us, I need to know because the not knowing's killing me.'

Massimo clenched his jaw and breathed in deeply.

What was the point in discussing something that wouldn't make the slightest difference to anything? But she'd steered it so he had no choice. If she'd shouted her demands as she'd always done, he would happily walk away, as he always used to. But she was using temperance. Using the closeness of sex.

He rubbed the sunscreen into her lower back and forced his mind to disassociate from the soft skin beneath his fingers. 'You didn't do anything. We're just not suited. My work is my life. There isn't the space for anything more.'

'You didn't think that when we got together.'

'My feelings for you took me by surprise.' They'd floored him. 'I let those feelings guide me instead of sitting down and thinking them through rationally. You and I have a rare chemistry but, when you boil it down, it's nothing but adrenaline, dopamine, oxytocin, serotonin...'

'Do not reduce my feelings to a chemistry lesson.' An edge crept into her voice.

Good. The dopamine currently flowing through her needed to be extinguished.

'All the effects of desire and what we think of as love can be reduced to a chemical level,' he explained levelly. 'The overwhelming feelings we experience at the start of a relationship are a surge of chemical reactions but those chemicals are raised to unsustainable levels. Eventually they lessen, which is what happened to us.'

'Nice try at deflection but what happened to us is that you turned away from me.' She leaned forward and traced her finger along the scar on her leg. 'This cut was when I really felt it. You didn't care that I was injured.'

'I did care but you told me it wasn't anything seri-ous.' But his first instinct had been to grab his keys and speed straight to her. That had been the day after he'd realised how far behind they were on the carbon filter project because of basic errors *he'd* made. The first er-rors he'd made in his entire career. The day after he'd woken Livia from a nightmare and held her trembling body tightly to him and found himself developing his own cold sweat at how badly he'd wanted to dive into her head and rip out the terrors that plagued her.

That had been the moment he'd understood what a dreadful mistake he'd made.

The fun, sexy marriage he'd envisaged for them had become an all-consuming sickness in his blood. Livia had taken full possession of his mind as well as his body.

He'd *had* to back away. Before he lost everything.

If she had given him the space he needed things might have been very different but she hadn't and a gulf had opened between them that had only solidified how wrong they were for each other.

'I didn't want to worry you because I thought you would drive to me,' she said wistfully. 'When we first married, I slipped and bumped my head one evening. Do you remember that? It wasn't anything serious but you stayed home the next day to keep an eye on me. You were worried about concussion even though I'm a nurse and told you there was nothing to worry about. Less than a year later you sent your PA to drive me to hospital with a gashed leg.'

He'd sent his PA after first having to prise his car keys from his own hands to drop them in Lindy's palm.

He shifted away from Livia's smooth, golden back and got to his feet. 'Do you have any idea how much work I missed in the first year of our marriage and how behind we got because of it?' He snatched up one of the beach towels she'd left on the poolside table. 'This carbon filter we're about to test should have been ready months ago.'

'That's because you have to micromanage everything.'

He secured the towel around his waist. 'It's my company.'

Her eyes found his. If she felt at a disadvantage remaining naked while he'd covered himself, she didn't show it. 'You employ some of the world's biggest brains. If you can't trust their skills and judgement then what does that say? It says you're either a control freak or you need to employ people who you do trust.'

'No, it says I take my responsibilities seriously.'

'You're in the position where you can allow others who are equally responsible and qualified to share the burden. You choose not to. You use the excuse of your work to cut yourself off from everyone who loves you and you still haven't explained why you cut yourself away from me. We were *happy*, Massimo. We were. And then we had nothing and I need to understand why and, please, for the love of God, don't explain it to me as a scientific formula. I get that we're nothing but atoms and dust but we're also conscious beings who feel and love and dream.'

Feeling in better control of himself, he took a seat at the poolside table and drank his champagne in one deep swallow. Bourbon would have numbed the agitation growing in his stomach much better but this would do.

He had to make her understand. Whatever delusions Livia had allowed herself to believe, he needed to dispel them. Since she'd left him, his world had reverted to its prior orderly calm. His time was where it needed to be—with his business. His mind was clutter-free. The stupid errors that had crept into his work were relegated to history. His wife would soon be relegated to history too. Everything would be as it should be.

'It's just the way I am. I was always different from the rest of my family.' Damn but he really could do with a bourbon. 'They didn't care if the clothes they wore were fraying at the seams or if there wasn't the money available to fix things that broke but I did. They think love alone can fix everything when in reality only hard work achieves anything. I love them in my own way but I never felt as if I belonged and I never wanted to settle for making do. I didn't set out to be rich but I did set out to be well off enough that I would never want for anything.'

Livia pounced on his choice of words. 'You love them in your own way? That implies you're aware of feeling love on something other than a chemical level.'

His eyes narrowed. 'You're twisting my words against me.'

'No, I'm pointing out your hypocrisy. You know perfectly well that love, however it is formed, is real but you're using science as an excuse to deny that what you and I had was real. I never had shoes with holes or clothes that didn't fit but, given the choice, I would have suffered that than live through my childhood. My father was always generous with his money and gave me everything I asked for but I was terrified of him.'

There was the barest flicker in the shuttered caramel eyes but it was enough for the faint hope in her heart to continue beating. 'Whenever he hugged me, all I felt was his gun digging into my chest from his pocket. When he was killed, I was upset because he was my father but I never grieved him like the rest of my family did because the bogeyman of my early childhood *was* my father. My mother was hardly ever there and when she was she would be high or drunk. I practically raised Gianluca—I was the one who took him to school every day and helped him with his homework and made sure he had a hot meal at night.

'Your parents are decent, law-abiding, loving people.' If she was going to fight, she might as well fight on his family's behalf too. But it wasn't just a fight for herself or for the Briatores. She was fighting for Massimo, for him to wake up and see all the joy of love and family that he was denying himself. She got to her feet and gathered the sarong as she continued, 'They could have worked longer hours or taken additional jobs to give you everything you wanted but they made the choice to be there for you whenever you needed them and I wish I could make you see how priceless that was.'

'From your perspective, anyone else's childhood would be priceless.'

'Maybe,' she conceded, wrapping the sarong around her. 'But we're talking about our own, not anyone else's. You are very different from your family but there are similarities. You have their generosity but yours is given in material ways where theirs is given in time.'

His fingers curved on the table but his eyes remained fixed on her. 'I cannot un-live my childhood just because yours was, on a sliding scale, much worse. It made me who I am. It taught me that anything I wanted or needed, I had to get by myself. My parents loved me, yes, but their love didn't change the reality of us being poor. It didn't solve anything. You could be right. I could be a control freak. But everything I have has been achieved by my own endeavours. Science is logical and it's real. It's where I feel most comfortable. It's where I belong but to do my best work, I need my mind to be free from clutter.'

It took her a moment to process the implication of what he'd just said. 'Are you calling me *clutter*?'

His response was unapologetic. 'You became a distraction. You demanded my attention when I needed to be focused.'

'All I ever *demanded* was your time.' Try as she might, she couldn't hide the rising anger. 'Since when is it a crime to want to spend time with your own husband?'

'That is my point perfectly encapsulated. I cannot produce my best work when I'm constantly worrying about you. I need to be free to focus without limits, not clock-watching, not worrying about you being lonely at home, not thinking I need to drive home because you're waiting for me with your dinner going cold.'

'My food wouldn't have gone cold if you'd bothered to let me know you were going to be late,' she retorted.

'That was never intentional.'

'And now you're contradicting yourself again. If it wasn't intentional you wouldn't have worried about it.'

Over the still air, Massimo's ringtone suddenly played out. He looked from Livia to the table on the veranda and back to her.

She gritted her teeth. 'Please. Leave it.'

But of course he wouldn't leave it. It might be *important*. Far more important than her and their marriage.

He strode away without a backwards glance.

She suspected bitterly that he would have cut their conversation short to answer it even if it were a cold caller.

Massimo had set himself up in a shaded part of the veranda, laptop open before him and his phone wedged to his ear. Furious with his retreat from their conversation and his deliberate immersion back into his work, Livia knew she needed to create a little distance between them before she snatched his phone off him and chucked it into the ocean. Doing that would only make things worse. If they could get any worse.

Of the many stories Jimmy had told her about his childhood on this island, the one that had fed Livia's imagination the most had been tales of the Seibua children playing in the naturally formed freshwater pool hidden in the thick forest. When she'd taken Jimmy for an exploration of the island, he'd pointed in the direction of its location and it was with that in mind, and conscious that the sun would soon begin its descent, that she set off.

By the time she passed the lodge, her fury had dimmed a little, enough for her to pass a message to Massimo through one of the staff members of where she was going. Just in case he missed her. Which he wouldn't, a knowledge that curdled her belly with bitter misery.

Her head streamed their conversation continually as she reached the red mangrove saplings planted at the edge of the shore; it echoed as she made her way inland past the black mangroves, which Massimo had explained were protection against the shallow flooding that occurred at high tide, still burred in her ears as she strode upwards to the white mangroves and onwards to the butterwoods until she reached the island's natural forest.

The pathway the Seibua children had taken had disappeared long ago but she'd walked in as straight a direction as she could and she was sure she would find it. If not, she'd go back.

Here, under the natural canopy of trees, the vegetation was dense with colourful wildlife and rich with sound. The heat was stifling but she didn't care. Large red-chested sociable parrots chattered noisily in squeaks and whistles, other less visible birds adding to the wonderful cacophony. None of them seemed bothered by her presence.

Soon, just as Jimmy had described, the canopy began to thin until she was standing in a small, sandy clearing centred around a startlingly clear pool of water no bigger than their private swimming pool. It was like stepping into a magical fairy tale.

She stood still for a moment to inhale the fresher air and enjoy the feel of the light wind on her face. At the water's edge two coconut palms stood tall and proud, their fronds dancing to the breeze's rhythm.

The last of her anger left her as she noticed the distinctive red heads and bright green bodies of Fiji Parrotfinches bathing happily in the pool. She wouldn't be surprised if a couple of deer and rabbits appeared and began communicating with her.

Livia removed her sandals and sat carefully on the stony wall encasing the pool. The Fiji Parrotfinches were not prepared to tolerate this and flew off back into the surrounding forest, leaving her in silence.

Her thoughts weren't silent though. They were screaming their rising desperation and panic in her ears.

Foolishly, she'd hoped Massimo would at least consider giving their marriage another try. The happiness they'd once shared...that had been *real*.

Why hadn't she fought sooner? There had been so much to fight for but they had both let it descend into cold acrimony. She bore as much responsibility for this as Massimo. Livia knew how to fight. Fighting was one thing she excelled at. She could shout and scream and stamp her feet but she hadn't done the most important thing, which was to listen. When he'd asked for space and peace she'd taken it personally. She'd allowed her insecurities and fears to take root. Instead of giving him what he'd asked for she'd pushed even harder.

Exhaustion washed through her. What did all this even matter? How could she fight for a marriage when her husband didn't see anything worth saving? He'd had a taste of life without her and found it preferable.

Oh, God, the *pain* that ripped through her. And then the panic. It was all there in her battered, frightened heart as the depth of her love finally screamed unfiltered to the surface.

Massimo was the love of her life. How could she ever sleep again if he slipped away for good? How could she ever breathe properly?

The tears that had threatened to unleash since she'd woken in his arms filled her eyes. She no longer had the strength to hold them back.

Hugging her knees to her chest, Livia bowed her head and wept.

CHAPTER TWELVE

THE SKY HAD turned golden when Massimo disappeared under the canopy of trees.

He hadn't planned to go in search of Livia. He'd fixed the business problem that had cropped up and had intended to keep working but the silence Livia had left when she'd slipped away without a word had been louder than the ocean. It had deafened him. Every time he'd looked at his laptop, nothing had penetrated his brain.

The disjointed feelings had returned with a vengeance.

He'd decided a brisk walk on the fine white sandy beach was in order but he'd barely taken ten paces when one of his workers had rushed up to tell him Livia had gone off in search of the freshwater pool in the forest.

He'd shrugged the message off and walked another ten paces when an image of Livia lost and alone in the forest had formed in his head. He'd performed an abrupt about-turn.

Mercifully, the worker knew exactly where the pool was located.

The forest canopy cast everything in shadow and he increased his pace, praying he was heading in the right direction and not meandering from the route.

How long had she been here? She'd walked away from their chalet a couple of hours ago. Had she even found the pool? The island was small but the forest was dense and large enough to lose yourself in.

Perspiration clung to his skin when he finally found the clearing but he didn't know if it was from the heat or the fear that had gripped his heart. The sky had turned a deeper orange in his time in the forest. There was little daylight left.

He exhaled a long breath of relief to see her there. She was sitting with her feet in the pool gazing down into the water.

On legs that felt strangely unsteady, he stepped over and crouched beside her.

Other than a long, defeated sigh, she made no reaction to his presence.

He followed her gaze to peer into the still, clear water. He couldn't see what had captivated her attention so greatly.

Long moments passed before she turned her face to him.

He sucked in a shocked breath.

Even under the fading light he could see the puffiness of her red eyes. Her cheeks and neck were blotchy.

'Have you been crying?' he asked in a hoarse voice.

Eyes dark with misery met his. Her pretty nose wriggled, her chin wobbled and her shoulders shook before her face crumpled and tears fell like a waterfall down her face.

Massimo froze.

Not once in the entirety of their marriage had he seen his wife cry.

A tiny fissure cracked in his heart.

Working on autopilot, he twisted round to take her into his arms and held her tightly. She clung to him, sobbing into his chest, her hot tears soaking his T-shirt.

Something hot and sharp stabbed the back of his eyes and he blinked violently to clear it.

'Tell me what the matter is,' he urged, kissing the top of her head and strengthening his hold around her. Livia's vulnerability was something he'd always sensed rather than seen, something she'd always striven to mask. To witness her like this, with all her barriers and defences stripped away...

The fissure in his heart splintered into a thousand crevices all filling with an emotion so painful it felt as if his insides were splitting into pieces.

Her shoulders shook and she slowly raised her face to look at him. There was a despairing quality when she whispered his name before the ghost of a smile flittered on her tear-drenched lips. 'For such a clever man you can be incredibly stupid.'

He never got the chance to ask what she meant for her lips found his and he was pulled into a kiss of such hungry desperation that his senses responded before his brain could stop it.

Desperation had formed in his own skin too, an agonising ache of need for the woman whose tears hurt him in a place he'd never known existed.

In a crush of arms they tumbled to the sandy ground. There was no attempt or need for seduction or foreplay, that hungry ache to be as one all-consuming. Deep inside him breathed a wish to crawl into Livia's skin and rip out every demon that had filled his beautiful, strong wife with such desolation.

Together, their hands tugged frantically at his shorts

and her bikini bottoms, anguished passion there in every touch and every kiss.

They clung to each other as he drove deep inside her, their mouths crushed together, bodies fused tightly. There was a hopeless urgency in their lovemaking he had never experienced before and it flowed through them both, every soft moan of pleasure from her mouth a cry, every gasp a sob, a feeling in his soul that his world was on the verge of collapse, all of it combining to heighten the pleasure and shadow it with despair.

Only the despair racked him when it was over and the heady sensations had seeped away from him.

But his heart still thumped painfully when he pulled away from her and covered his face.

This had to stop.

They were over. *Over.*

Why prolong the pain? Hadn't they hurt each other enough?

Long moments passed in heavy silence before he rolled onto his side and got to his feet. Pulling his shorts on, he muttered, 'It's getting dark. We should get back.'

She didn't answer, simply rearranged her clothing and ran her fingers through her hair. As she did so, he noticed something that made him pause, perplexed. One of her nails was missing…

He snatched at the diversion from all the weight crushing him. 'What happened to your nail?'

She shrugged. 'It fell off.'

'They're false?'

She nodded.

He had no idea why this disturbed him so much. 'Since when do you wear false nails?'

More to the point, since when did she *bite* her nails?

Livia had always taken pride in her nails. Even when she'd worked as a nurse and been forced to keep them short for practical reasons they'd been buffed and polished. This nail was so short and ragged the nail bed was exposed.

She shrugged again. 'They needed doing.'

Shrugging the subject away with the same indifference she'd dismissed it with, Massimo reached into his pocket for his phone and turned the torch app on. It was bright enough to lead them back through the forest in relative safety but, all the same, he made sure to keep Livia close to him as they headed back along the route he'd taken to reach her, resisting the urge to take her hand.

No more touching her. He would dine alone and sleep in a cabin far from her. Far from the temptation he'd proven himself incapable of resisting.

But those tears…

Where had they come from? Surely she hadn't been crying about them?

It disturbed him to recall how close he'd come to tears too. He hadn't cried since he was a small child.

When they emerged from the forest and into the young mangroves, the first stars had emerged in the night sky.

Livia looked up at them and wished their shining brilliance could penetrate Massimo's heart and make him see that what they had could shine with that same brilliance too.

The incoming tide had covered most of the beach and she sat on the stone wall that acted as a barrier and looked up again at the vast night sky.

She had no idea what the time was.

Time was slipping away from her as fast as Massimo was.

Her fight to save them was a fight she was losing. She could feel it in her soul.

She could still taste their lovemaking on her lips but here he was now, sitting beside her at a distance that meant she would have to stretch her arm out to touch him.

'Did you know I fell in love with your family before I fell in love with you?' she said into the still air. 'Before I met them, I was stone inside. I'd had to fight and work for everything I had, escaping the Secondigliano, getting into nursing, supporting myself through my degree…even getting my placement in oncology so I could be a cancer nurse was a battle. Keeping myself detached while not losing my compassion for my patients and their families was a constant fight.'

She'd worked hard and fought her entire life. But her marriage? She'd thrown that away with hardly a whimper and now she feared she'd left it too late to repair it.

He shifted, stretching his legs out. The lapping tide drew in inches from his toes.

'Your grandfather was the first patient I ever became attached to. His home was so *warm*. All those photos of you all everywhere…' She sighed to remember the feelings being in that home had brought about in her. Jimmy had been her third private placement after she'd been head-hunted by the agency to work as a private oncology nurse. 'I was used to family members dropping in for regular short visits with the other placements, but your family were always there. They fed him, watched television with him, read to him. They lifted his spirits better than any medicine. The love they all had for each other opened my eyes to what a family should be like: built on love and support and just being there for each other. I wanted that so badly I could taste it. And then I met you...'

She clasped her hands together, remembering how it had felt to lie naked and cocooned in Massimo's arms that first night, the beat of his strong heart thudding against her... Nothing had ever felt more right in her life.

It made her soul weep to think she might never feel that rightness again.

'I fell so *hard* for you,' she whispered. 'When you proposed, I imagined a family life like the one your family had. I imagined babies and lots of visits to and from your parents. I assumed your detachment from them was a result of you being a single man living on the other side of the ocean and that once we were married you would want to spend more time with them. It took me a long time to realise that my assumptions had been delusional.' She filled her lungs with the fresh salty air. 'I could have coped with all that if you hadn't started detaching yourself from *me*. It scared me, Massimo. I could feel you slipping away and I didn't know how to bring you back and I made everything worse with my reaction to it all. I knew you didn't respond well to confrontation but I still kept on confronting you because that's the only way I knew to deal with things. Growing up was a survival of the fittest. If someone upset you, you confronted them. You learned to never show weakness. To back down made you weak and made you a target. I try so hard not to be that woman any more.'

Those confrontational traits had become her default position, a cycle she hadn't known how to break out of.

'You have two ears and one mouth for a reason,' Massimo had once said to her on one of the rare times she'd been able to spark a reaction out of him.

Those were words she'd carried every day since she'd left him.

She'd stopped supporting him in his work. She'd become *resentful* of his work. All the wonderful qualities she'd fallen in love with…she'd forgotten them because he'd hidden them away. He'd turned into a recluse from her and she in turn had become a shrill person she despised.

Fresh tears welled behind her eyes.

She let them fall.

There was nothing to hide any more. This was her, stripped bare of the things she always kept locked away from him, the vulnerabilities she'd hidden as she'd always hidden them since she was too young to even know what vulnerability meant.

'I remember us going to that technology awards ceremony you were guest of honour at. I got talking to one of the other trophy wives…'

'You were *never* a trophy wife,' he interrupted tightly.

'Not to begin with but that's how I felt in the second year. The wife I was talking to asked me how many lovers you'd had since we'd married. You should have seen her face when I said none. She thought I was delusional. All rich men have lovers. But not you. I never doubted you. Even when you spent nights in your office rather than come home to me, I never once had suspicions you were seeing other women. It would have been easier to compete with a flesh and blood woman but your mistress was always your business and I grew resentful towards it. I hate myself for walking away and not fighting harder for us. I hate that I became so needy and resentful. We could have the marriage we once dreamed about but we both have to want it and work at it.'

Massimo had never felt the thuds of his heart as clearly as he did right then. The crash they made in his ears reverberated with the distant crash of waves and sluiced through his entire being.

'But that's the problem,' he said harshly. 'I don't want it. We did try, Liv, but it wasn't enough then and it wouldn't be enough now. You might not want to hear about our marriage being reduced to a scientific formula but everything that drove us to marry in the first place was because of the heightened chemicals overpowering our rationality. What you're feeling now is a reignition of those chemicals brought about by—'

'Don't you *dare*,' she interrupted with a tearful edge. 'Don't tell me what I feel. I *know* what I feel. I love you. I'm well aware that the early days of a relationship are driven by heightened emotions and hormones—that's what normal people call the honeymoon period—but for you to keep reducing the love we shared to science is an insult to every memory we created together. If you simply stopped loving me, at least have the guts to say so.'

Nausea swirled violently inside him. 'I don't know if what I felt for you was love or not. I don't know if it was real. The feelings I had for you were the strongest I have ever felt but you must see that even if it was love, it doesn't solve anything. The problems we had would still be there eating away at us.'

'I don't see that. Not if we're both prepared to work at it.' The hitch in her voice made his heart contract but he made himself stay focused and strong.

This was for the best. One day, when the intensity of

everything they'd shared these last few days had subsided, she would see that too.

'I'm afraid that I do see it like that,' he said in as even a voice as he could manage. 'I'm not prepared to return to a marriage that's a proven failure. I'm not prepared to put myself through that again. It isn't worth it.'

There was a moment of silence until, without any warning, she jumped off the wall and waded out into the ocean until she was standing thigh high in the water. The moon had risen, bathing her in a silvery glow.

'Do you know what I don't understand?' Her voice carried through the breeze and the waves. 'How you can work so hard to save the world we live in when you've no intention of enjoying anything it has to offer. And I don't see or understand how you can put your mind to *anything* and make it succeed when you won't put a fraction of that energy into saving our marriage.'

'A marriage is not a business.'

'You're right. A marriage involves feelings. A business won't care for you when you're sick or lonely.' She rolled her neck and turned. Treading slowly through the water, she seemed to become magnified as she neared him.

The expression on her face sent coldness snaking up his spine and through his veins.

'You might not think our love *worth* it or know if it was real or not but I do. My love was real. I left you and I fell to pieces. I don't know what was worse—living with the ghost you'd become or living without you. Being apart from you felt like I'd had my heart ripped out. Every day was a battle just to get out of bed. I have no idea how I kept the charade going when I visited your family or Gianluca.' As she spoke, her voice grew steadily colder to match the expression on her face. 'I don't care what you think about your feelings for me but don't you ever lie to yourself that my love for you was anything but pure. You were my whole world. I gave up everything to be with you but I wasn't even worth fighting for, was I? You just breathed a great sigh of relief to be rid of me and got on with your life. My God, I've been *pathetic*.'

She took a step back and brought the hand with the missing nail to her face and stared at it as if she were seeing it for the first time before looking back at him. 'I'm no better than my mother. She would sit at the kitchen table late at night biting her nails while she waited for my father to come home.'

Massimo had seen many emotions from Livia in their time together but this was the first time she'd ever looked at him with contempt.

'And you're no better than my father.'

As insults went, that was the worst she could have thrown at him. A hot cauldron of anger rose in him. 'Do not compare me to that man.'

'His work, if you can call it that, came first in his life, just as yours does.'

Rising to his feet, Massimo flexed his hands and leaned forward to speak right into her face. 'Your father was killed in a gangland shooting. That was his work. You dare compare it to mine? My work has the potential to save the world from catastrophe!'

'And that's all that matters to you,' she spat back but still in the same controlled voice. 'Your work. At least my father loved his family.'

'Love?' He burst into a roar of incredulous laughter. 'You were terrified of him!'

'I was terrified because he was a monster but even monsters can love their family. He loved us and he wasn't afraid to show it but you... You shut out everyone who loves you. You want to know why I cut my hair?' She turned and parted her hair at the back of her scalp.

His heart throbbing madly, his guts cramped, confounded and disjointed that his temper was fraying at the seams while Livia had hers under such tight control, he blinked rapidly and leaned forward to see what she was showing him. Even with only the moon and the stars to illuminate them, he could see the exposed section she'd parted contained a small bald patch.

'Stress-induced alopecia,' she explained tightly, releasing her hair as she looked back at him. 'I had it cut and layered to cover it when I had my nails done last week because my pride couldn't bear for you to look at me and think I'd suffered in any way without you. I was trying to prove to myself, too, that I was over you and now I know I am because all the love I had for you... you've just killed it.'

His nausea had returned with a vengeance. 'Livia...'

'I don't want to hear any more of your excuses.' Her eyes blazed with a hardness he'd never seen before, a look he instinctively knew she hadn't given since leaving Naples. 'I'm not *prepared*...' she dragged the word out with a sneer '...to waste another atom of energy on a man who refuses to give me an inch of what he devotes to his business. Enjoy the rest of your life—I hope you and your business are very happy together.'

The footprints she made in the sand as she walked away with her head held high were covered by foaming ocean within moments of being created.

CHAPTER THIRTEEN

THE RETURN JOURNEY was harder than the outbound journey had been. Livia had debated the idea of making her own way back to Italy but reluctantly decided against it. It would take twice as long as it would to fly with Massimo and she wanted to be at home with her brother.

She had walked away from him with her head held high and kept her own company since, her emotions veering from humiliation to anger and back again. The only emotion she wouldn't allow herself was despair.

Her anger was directed only at herself.

She *had* been pathetic. Not only in her marriage but in the aftermath, after she'd walked away. When she should have reclaimed her life and moved on, she'd become stuck in purgatory, unable to sever the emotional ties that had kept her bound to Massimo.

They were severed now.

Their only communication since her disastrous attempt at reconciliation had been a text message from him that morning informing her they would be leaving the island in ten minutes.

She'd spent the night in Madeline's chalet. She neither knew nor cared where Massimo had slept.

During the short flight on the Cessna to Nadi airport, she'd refused to look at him and rebuffed his few attempts at conversation. When they'd boarded his jet, she'd taken her original seat, stuck her earphones in and selected the most mindless movie she could find.

The moment they were in the air, she'd put the physical barrier around her seat up. It went perfectly with the metaphorical barrier she'd erected.

The one good thing about this return journey was that Massimo would only be travelling as far as LA with her. She had no doubt he would go straight to his precious facility.

When one of the cabin crew asked if she would like something to eat she readily accepted and forced the warm baguette filled with smoked cheese and prosciutto into her cramped stomach.

She would never allow her feelings to prevent her from eating ever again.

She had no idea if Massimo ate. She refused to look.

She still refused to look at him when they landed in LA, even when he hovered by her seat as if trying to get her attention.

'Take care of yourself,' he muttered after she'd ignored him for as long as he could tolerate.

And then he was gone.

She didn't expel a breath until he'd left the cabin.

The baguette she'd eaten felt as if it wanted to expel itself out of her system. She held it down and left the plane too, escorted by a hefty security guard to a private lounge. She didn't have to worry about bumping into Massimo. He would already be in his car.

But he wasn't in his car.

Livia's heart came to a shuddering halt when the lounge door opened a few minutes later and Massimo stood at the threshold looking paler than she'd ever seen him.

She knew what was wrong before he spoke, her heart already aching for him before the words came out.

'My grandfather had a bad turn on the flight home. They don't think he's going to make it.'

The only illumination in the room Massimo sat in came from the machines hooked to his grandfather's weakening body. The incessant beeping from them grated in his head like nails on a chalkboard.

He'd shifted the armchair as close to the bed as he could get it. His parents were sleeping in a spare room down the corridor. The medical team were resting in the adjoining room. His sister had gone home for the night, making Massimo promise to call her if anything changed.

Nothing had changed in the two days his grandfather had been home. Nothing apart from his steadily weakening heart.

Jimmy Seibua was dying. But he was dying in the home he loved. His bedroom had been turned into its own hospital room with everything needed to keep him comfortable and pain-free until nature finally took its course.

The door opened.

He didn't need to look to know it was Livia. He would know her movements blindfolded.

'Hot chocolate,' she said softly.

He took one of the steaming cups from her with a muted thanks.

She placed her own cup on a ledge before pulling a thermometer from the dedicated medical cupboard and running it gently over his grandfather's forehead. After logging the reading and checking the equipment he was hooked to, she pulled the other armchair closer and sat beside Massimo. 'He's comfortable. That's the most important thing.'

Massimo nodded.

In the two days they'd been holed up in his grandfather's home, Livia had left only once, a short trip to her apartment on the other side of the city to check in on her brother.

He could never put into words how grateful he was to have her there. Her calm, compassionate presence soothed his family's nerves.

It soothed his nerves too. She could easily save her compassion for the rest of his family and pretend he didn't exist but she didn't.

'How are you doing?' she asked quietly.

He shrugged. He didn't know how he was doing. He felt battered from the inside.

'Have you eaten?'

'I'm not hungry.'

Her small hand rested on his and gave a gentle squeeze. It lasted only seconds but it spread a little warmth into his cold veins.

He had to stop himself from reaching over to snatch her hand back and keep it tucked in his.

She stayed with him for the next hour. They didn't speak but it was a companionable silence. When she whispered that she was going to try and get a few hours' sleep, the warmth she'd brought into the room left with her.

Time dragged on. The clock on the wall ticked slowly. The first hint of daylight seeped through the curtains.

Needing to stretch his legs, Massimo got to his feet and walked to his grandfather's dressing table. His mother had placed a dozen framed photos on it for him, his grandparents' wedding photo taking pride of place. Massimo picked it up and smiled sadly at the two beaming faces. How young they had been. How happy. And how in love. They'd met during his grandfather's deployment in the Second World War. His grandmother, who'd come from a wealthy English family, had worked for a secret government agency during that period. She'd kept those secrets for all her life. The only concrete facts Massimo knew were that they had met and fallen in love. His grandfather had left his home on the other side of the world permanently to marry her. Her parents, dismayed that she'd fallen for a man with skin they considered too dark, had disowned her. Massimo's grandparents had never allowed their subsequent poverty to get them down. They'd got on with life as best they could, raising a daughter, Sera, who was their pride and joy. When Sera married the Italian Gianni Briatore, they hadn't hesitated to follow her to Italy and make it their home.

He tried to imagine the challenges they'd faced. A mixed race couple in a time when mixed race marriages were frowned upon and in a time when most of the world was reeling from unimaginable horrors. Yet they had remained strong. Their love had endured. He didn't think it a coincidence that his grandfather was first diagnosed with cancer within a year of his grandmother's death.

His hand trembled as he placed the frame back on the dresser. His knuckles brushed the picture next to it, the one photo he'd spent two days blurring from his vision. This time, he picked it up.

It was his own wedding photo. He and Livia were in the centre, his parents to his left, his sister and grandfather to Livia's right.

If smiles could be converted into energy, Livia's could have powered a small country.

Massimo's own joy was there too on his beaming face. The camera didn't show that Livia's hand had been squeezing his bottom when the photo was taken.

Their wedding day had been the happiest of his life.

His grandfather coughed.

Abandoning the photo, Massimo hurried to his side and took his hand.

His grandfather's eyes were open. He coughed again. And then he smiled.

The love behind that smile could have fuelled the same country as Livia's and it filled Massimo's chest and spread through his veins.

He returned the smile.

He didn't notice the tear that had leaked from his eye until it rolled down his chin and landed on their joined hands.

The filmy eyes closed and his grandfather drifted back to sleep.

He never woke up again.

Three hours later, with the family he loved at his side, Jimmy Seibua took his last breath.

Livia switched the dishwasher on and dried her hands absently on the front of her black trousers, wishing there were something else she could do but there wasn't a single mark left to wipe down. She'd scrubbed the kitchen so hard it gleamed.

She felt heartsick to her core.

She'd sat with her brother during the full Requiem mass for Jimmy. Gianluca had held her hand and kept her supplied with tissues. She was so proud of him and grateful for his support but she couldn't stop her heart from wishing it were Massimo's hand she'd been holding.

Stupid heart. One day it would catch up with her brain and let him go for good. All the resolutions she'd made had been destroyed before she'd had a chance to put them into practice.

But what else could she have done? Massimo's family had wanted her there while they'd nursed Jimmy in his final days. She'd wanted to be there too, with the old man who'd given her the most precious gift she could have received. A family.

The wake was being held in a marquee in the garden of Sera and Gianni's home. Caterers had been brought in for the refreshments, allowing family and friends to drink and reminisce his memory unhindered.

After an hour of it, Livia had needed to escape and slipped into the house to hide in the kitchen. Massimo's immediate family knew now they were getting divorced. He'd told them shortly after Jimmy's death. All had privately told her that their marriage was their own business but, divorce or not, she would always be family to them.

She wished that could be true and wished that when she said goodbye to them all later it wouldn't be for the last time.

She needed a clean break. There was no way she could move forward with her life if Massimo's family remained a central part of it. She would be permanently reminded of all she had lost.

She hoped they understood. She hoped they could forgive her.

'What are you doing?'

She turned her head to find Massimo at the kitchen door, his brow creased. His suit looked slightly baggy. Unsurprisingly, Massimo had lost weight. Livia doubted he'd eaten a full meal since they'd left the island.

She supposed he would go back to LA tonight. She was surprised he hadn't gone back after Jimmy's death and returned for the funeral. He'd stayed with his parents. She didn't think she was imagining the growing closeness between them. She could only hope it was a closeness that lasted.

'Cleaning up.'

'You didn't have to do that.'

She shrugged and stared at the floor. It hurt too much to look at him. 'I wanted to.'

Massimo closed the door and stood with his back to it. 'I want to thank you.'

'For what?'

'Everything you did for my grandfather and for all the support you've given my family.'

She raised her shoulders. It wasn't a shrug but he knew what she was trying to convey. That she didn't want or expect thanks. It was something she'd done because it was the right thing to do and because she couldn't not do it.

He wondered if she had any idea what a difference she'd made this last week.

Their last conversation before his grandfather had been taken ill…he'd hurt her so badly. She'd put her heart and her pride on the line for them to have a future together and he'd thrown it back at her and denounced the love they'd shared as anything worth fighting for.

And yet here she was, still there, still giving the support he'd once taken for granted. Because he had taken it for granted. He'd become so damned frightened of his own feelings that he'd forgotten how good it had felt to go home and unload what was on his mind to her receptive ears and to lie in her arms and feel her massage the tension from his head and his shoulders. The errors he'd made… They hadn't been Livia's fault. They'd been his alone. But he'd punished her for them.

He'd pushed her away and shut her out one cold retreat at a time when he should have wrapped his arms around her and told her he loved her every single day.

After the funeral service, she'd joined the line of mourners waiting their turn to give their personal embrace to Massimo, his sister and their parents. She should have been by his side.

If she'd been at his side and he'd had her strength to lean on he would have found it easier to endure. He'd found everything easier to endure with Livia by his side. He'd forgotten that too.

'When are you going home?' she asked, breaking the silence.

'Tonight.'

'What's happened with the prototype?'

'Nothing. I've deferred the testing again until I get back.'

The raise of her shoulder seemed to indicate something different from her first raise but this was a shrug he couldn't interpret.

'Come back with me.' The words left his mouth before he could stop them.

Her eyes shot up to meet his. 'What?'

He rested the back of his head against the door as everything suddenly became clear. 'Come back with me. To Los Angeles.'

She just stared at him, lips parted but no sound coming out.

'Those things I said on the island. I didn't mean them...'

'They sounded convincing to me.'

'I love you.' And as he said the words aloud he felt a physical shift inside him.

'No!' Her voice ricocheted through the kitchen like a bullet.

'Livia—'

'I don't want to hear it.' She pressed her hands to her ears then finally met his eye. The pain reflecting back at him almost tore him in two. 'And I don't want to be the salve for your grief.'

'It's not about my grief.' How had he been so *blind*? 'I've been...'

'I don't want to hear another word of your lies.' Her shoulders rose in shudders and her throat moved before she turned away to take her bag from the counter. 'It's too late. I don't believe you. And even if I did, the answer would still be no. I could never trust my heart with you again.' She slung the strap of her bag over her shoulder and stood before him. When her eyes met his this time, they were devoid of emotion. 'I need to go.'

Something cold scratched deep in his throat.

He'd never fully recognised the love that had always reflected back at him until now that it was gone.

He moved to one side to let her pass.

She walked out of the kitchen without looking back. When he could no longer hear her footsteps and all that remained was the lightest linger of her fragrance, his knees finally gave way and he sank to the floor.

Head clasped in his hands, he breathed in deeply, calling himself every name under the sun until he could hold it back no longer and punched the nearest cabinet.

The crack it made echoed through the walls closing in around him.

He brought his hand to his face. Blood poured from his knuckles but he felt no pain.

The only pain came from the bleeding in his heart.

His grandfather's words at his party about having lived… Finally he understood them.

For the first time since he'd been a small child, Massimo wept.

He understood *everything*.

He understood that the blood in his veins never pumped as hard as it did when he was with Livia. She brought him to life. She had brought him back to his family. She had brought joy and love to his cold heart. She had lit the way and pulled him out of the darkness he hadn't realised he'd become lost in.

He understood, finally, that he could live in the warmth of her love or die in the cold of that darkness.

Livia hauled the shopping bags into the ground-floor apartment and closed the door with her bottom, craning her ears for the sound of the gaming console. Since she'd returned to her apartment after Jimmy's funeral two weeks ago, the sound of fast cars racing had become the background music of her life. She never complained about it. She needed the noise to drown the sound of her tortured thoughts.

Today, though, the apartment was quiet.

'Gianluca?' she called.

Her brother appeared as she was putting the bags on the side.

'Guess what?' he said, grinning and waving his phone in that goofy way of his.

'What?'

He looked as proud as a strutting peacock. 'Massimo's giving me a job.'

The name landed like a cold sharp shock against her face, just as it did every time Gianluca uttered it. She took a moment to compose herself. 'A job? Working for him? You're moving to America?'

His grin widened. 'You're not getting rid of me that easily. He's opening his European headquarters in Rome and has offered me a job on the security team.'

'He's opening headquarters *here*?'

Gianluca had the grace to look sheepish. 'He told me his plans the night of Jimmy's funeral after you'd gone but said not to say anything until everything was confirmed.'

So desperate had Livia been to get away from Massimo that she'd left the wake without her brother. Gianluca hadn't cared that she'd forgotten him. He'd had a great time getting drunk on bourbon with Massimo.

'You were told not to tell me?'

The sheepish expression morphed into the same confusion as she knew she must be showing. 'He didn't say not to tell you specifically. Just said it was best to keep it quiet until he'd bought the premises and knew for certain it would go ahead.' The confusion turned into beaming pride. 'And I kept my mouth shut exactly as he asked.'

'You certainly did. A job in security?' That was quite a step for an eighteen-year-old who'd never held down a job and had left school with only minimal qualifications. She had to practically crack her skin to get a smile to form. 'This is wonderful news. Congratulations. I didn't realise the two of you had kept in touch,' she added casually.

She should have guessed though. Since Massimo had brought in the team to help Gianluca escape the Secondigliano without reprisals, her brother had developed a serious case of hero worship.

Hearing him go on and on about how marvellous her estranged husband was... It was frustrating, to put it mildly. But she had the sense to reason with herself that if her brother was going to hero-worship anyone and use them as a base to model himself on, better it be Massimo than one of the men who had terrorised their lives.

'He's going to pay for me to take some courses too, so I can build on my qualifications. He said if I work hard, I could one day run his security for him.'

'This is wonderful,' she repeated. And it was. Truly. Livia had tried very hard not to be concerned that her brother hadn't been actively looking for work, telling herself he needed time to get used to this new life in a new city without the safety net of their family and his friends. She'd planned to give him a month to settle in before broaching the subject, when all along Massimo had already decided to give him a chance.

That was a big thing for him to do, she acknowledged. He knew full well what a handful Gianluca could be.

Handful or not, she'd been glad to have him around, and not only because it meant he was safe. His playful puppy-like ways were a welcome distraction from the painful ache in her frozen heart.

She dug into one of the shopping bags, pulled out the fresh tagliatelle she'd purchased and threw it at him.

He caught it easily.

'Put the water on and get this cooked. There's ricotta and spinach in the other bag. I'm going back to the shop to buy a bottle of prosecco. We need to celebrate!'

She hurried out of the apartment, Gianluca's protests that he didn't know how to cook pasta a distant ringing in her ears.

As soon as the door shut behind her, her smile dropped.

She walked down the street, her mind in a whirl.

Massimo was opening a headquarters here? In the city she lived in? The city he'd actively avoided throughout their marriage?

He'd once mooted the idea of opening a headquarters in London but that had been over a year ago, a throwaway musing of an idea. He hadn't mentioned it when they'd been in Fiji…

She firmly pushed the thought of Fiji from her mind. Every time a memory from it flashed through her, the nausea that seemed to have become a constant presence in her stomach swirled harder. It swirled now, strong enough to make her giddy.

As she passed a steakhouse, a customer opened its doors, unleashing the aromas being cooked within. Smells she would normally find tempting swirled through Livia's airways, increasing the nausea.

Suddenly fearing she really was going to be sick, she rested one hand against a wall, the other to her roiling stomach and forced as much air as she could into her lungs.

It seemed to take an age to pass.

When she finally felt capable of continuing, she looked up, but instead of her gaze fixing on the shop she was heading for, it landed on the neon-green cross on the other side of the street.

She didn't even realise she was staring at it until a small child walked into her. The mother, who was pushing a pram with a tiny baby in it, apologised but her words sounded like an echo in Livia's ears.

Thoughts of prosecco all but forgotten, she crossed the busy road and entered the pharmacy.

She'd stopped taking her pill when she'd left Massimo. They hadn't used protection when they were in Fiji. The thought hadn't even occurred to her, not even when she'd cuddled baby Elizabeth or when they'd had that angry conversation about babies.

Why had that been? She'd taken her pill religiously throughout their marriage. She'd wanted a baby with Massimo but it had been something they'd both agreed was for the future. And then their marriage had become so cold that it would have been cruel to bring a baby into it.

Two minutes later she walked out, a pregnancy test tucked in her bag.

Twenty minutes after that she was back in her apartment and in the bathroom, having given Gianluca the cash to go out and buy them food—he'd burnt the tagliatelle—and prosecco.

But he would have to drink the prosecco himself.

The test was unambiguous. She was pregnant.

Her head swimming, she did the only thing that made sense. She reached into her bag for her phone and called Massimo.

He answered on the third ring. 'Liv?'

Just hearing his voice made her heart clench and tears fill her eyes.

She squeezed them shut.

'Livia? Are you there? Is something wrong?'

She could hardly hear her own dull voice over the roar in her ears. 'I'm pregnant.'

CHAPTER FOURTEEN

THE SUDDEN PEAL of the doorbell only added to the pounding in Livia's head.

'If it's for me, I'm not in,' she shouted to her brother, who was playing on his games console in the living room.

Mercifully, Gianluca was a selfish teenager and had been oblivious to there being anything wrong with her when he'd returned with their takeaway. He'd also been oblivious when she'd eaten only half of her portion, using her lack of appetite as an opportunity to consume more food for himself, and oblivious to there being anything out of the ordinary when she'd announced immediately after eating that she was going to get an early night.

The bell rang again.

Grabbing her pillow, she pulled it over her head and burrowed deeper under the covers.

She would wallow for one night, she'd decided. Discovering she was pregnant was an exceptional circumstance that merited wallowing.

But...

For all the fear an unexpected pregnancy had brought there had also been the first flutterings of excitement.

Deciding that suffocating herself was probably bad for the baby, she removed the pillow and put it back under her head and stared at the ceiling.

She put a tentative hand up her nightshirt and pressed it against her belly. It didn't feel any different but a tiny life form was growing in there. A life created by her and Massimo.

Massimo...

She closed her eyes.

She couldn't decide if fate was being cruel or kind. When she'd finally found the strength to move forward with her life it played this most magical of tricks on her. She would never be free of him now.

She'd struggled to move on as it was. She'd kept a smile on her face, used iron willpower to stop herself biting her nails and gone through the motions of reclaiming her life but the wrench in her heart hadn't even started to heal yet.

She lived in hope rather than expectation.

She lived with an ache that left her always feeling cold. The sun could shine as hard as it wanted but she never felt it any more.

A knock on her bedroom door interrupted her wallowing.

She sat up, expecting Gianluca's face to appear and the request of money to be given.

But it wasn't her skinny brother who walked into her bedroom.

She blinked a number of times, certain she must be imagining the towering figure standing there, dressed in snug black jeans, a black T-shirt and a tan leather jacket. Her immediate impression was that he hadn't shaved since his grandfather's funeral.

She had to clear her throat to get any words out. 'What are you doing here?'

Massimo closed the door and gazed at the woman he loved sitting like a princess in her bed. He soaked in every detail of the face he'd missed so much.

'You didn't think I would take the news of you being pregnant and not come straight to you?'

Her brow creased in confusion. 'Do you have a time portal? I only told you two hours ago?'

'I would have been here sooner but I couldn't find my car keys and I'd already sent my driver home for the night. I walked.'

'You were already in Rome?'

'I never left.'

Now her whole face creased.

He grinned and removed his jacket, draping it over her dressing-table chair without taking his eyes from her. God, it felt so good seeing her. Knowing he was in the same city as Livia but unable to reach out to her had almost killed him. He took a step towards her. 'I've bought a house here.'

She shrank back as if afraid he was going to touch her. 'Since when?'

'The sale went through yesterday. I was going to wait a little longer for a few of the other pieces to fall into place before I came to you.'

The wariness in her eyes almost killed him too. 'Came to me for what?'

'To see what else it would take for you to believe that I do love you and that you can trust your heart with me.'

Since his epiphany at his grandfather's funeral, he'd done a lot of thinking.

Everything Livia had said about him was true. He

did shut people out. Livia was the only person he'd ever let in but the moment he'd felt her get too close, the moment his heart had truly opened for her, he'd slammed it back shut and pushed her away.

He'd got so used to doing everything for himself, to relying only on himself that he'd convinced himself that it was the only way to be. He'd got so used to everything he touched turning into gold that when he'd made the first basic errors of his career he'd automatically blamed Livia for them, forgetting that he was only human.

She'd brought such joy into his life and, fool that he was, he'd turned his back on that joy and turned his back on her.

He'd pushed his parents away too. He'd been a condescending, arrogant bastard about the choices they'd made. They'd chosen family over money and he'd been too blind to appreciate the sacrifices they'd made so he could have that security. He'd taken their love for granted. He'd never had to walk his sister to school or cook her meals as Livia had done for Gianluca. He'd never slept with a weapon under his pillow out of fear. The threadbare clothes he'd been so ashamed to wear had always been lovingly repaired, the holes in his shoes fixed until the shoes could be replaced. He'd been so focused on creating his own future that he'd never taken the time to appreciate all the things he'd had right there. Love. Security. An abundance of affection. All the things that when added together made life worth living.

He'd been blind about everything.

But Livia had seen everything clearly.

He didn't blame her for dismissing his half-formed declaration of love.

Along with all his thinking he'd done a lot of doing.

The path to bringing her back into his life had been clear. He'd needed to rebuild her trust with actions rather than words.

Her shoulders rose before she brought her knees up and wrapped her arms around them. 'Not this again,' she whispered. 'I told you, it's too late. I've moved on.'

'Nature doesn't think so or you wouldn't be pregnant.'

'Nature is a joke.'

'A wonderful joke.'

She rested her chin on her knees. 'You're happy?'

'That we're having a baby together? Liv, there is only one thing that could make me happier than I feel at this moment but I will get to that shortly. Why didn't you tell me you'd come off the pill?'

Colour flamed her cheeks. 'I didn't think.'

'And I didn't think to ask if you were still on it.' He pulled his T-shirt over his head.

'What are you doing?' she asked, alarm in her voice but something different in her eyes.

'Showing you something.' Dropping the T-shirt on the floor, he kicked his boots off and climbed onto the bed. Then he leaned forward to take her rigid hand and placed it on his left bicep. Eyes holding hers, he said, 'The spearheads on this tattoo… One of the meanings for it is willpower. I had it done to remind myself to remain strong. I needed that reminder when you left me otherwise I would have chased after you and begged you to come back to me.'

He moved her hand so it rested on his chest above his beating heart. 'I married you because the madness of my attraction to you compelled me to. I knew my feelings for you ran deep and I assumed what I felt for you was love but I didn't know it could grow deeper. I didn't know my feelings for you would take root in my soul and that you would become my reason for breathing. You challenged me on so many levels I didn't know where I ended and you began. When you left me I felt as if I'd been freed from madness itself. I threw myself back into my work a liberated man and I would have worked myself into an early grave rather than stop for a minute and open myself to the pain beating right here in this cold, shrivelled heart that losing you caused.'

He reached for her hair with his free hand and ran his fingers down the silky locks he loved so much. 'I'm sorry for pushing you away. I'm sorry for shutting you out. I'm sorry for throwing your love back at you and demeaning everything we meant to each other. I'm sorry for every minute of hurt I caused you.'

She opened her mouth but he put a finger to her lips.

'I'm sorry for doing nothing when I knew how miserable you were in LA.'

'Don't,' she whispered, turning her cheek. 'My loneliness was my fault too. I should have gone out and had English lessons and taken art classes or something.'

'Art classes?'

She shrugged. 'Something that got me out of the house. Something that stopped me being dependent on you for my happiness.'

That reminded him of something he'd meant to ask her on the island. 'Have you had English lessons since we separated?'

'I started an online course. I didn't get very far. My head wasn't in the right place for new information to sink into it.'

He rubbed his thumb along her cheekbone, his heart swelling. 'There was a lot I could have done to make your life easier and if you come back to me, I swear things will be different. I'm moving back to Italy.'

Her eyes found his again. There was a glimmer of something in them that gave him hope.

'Everything you said before we left the island was right, including what you said about my relationship with my family,' he said quietly. 'How can I build a proper relationship with them if I'm living on the other side of the ocean?'

'Is that why you're opening a base here in Rome?'

He nodded and slid his hands down her cheeks to cup her face. 'Partly. But mostly for you. Your life is here and my life is with you…if you'll let me back in it. That's all I want. To be with you. It took losing you for me to see how much I need you.'

A tear spilled out and rolled down her cheek and over his hand. 'You said that about our marriage. That you hadn't realised how unsuited you were to marriage until you married me.'

'I said a lot of things. I believed a lot of things.'

'So why should I believe you now?' Livia wanted to believe him more desperately than she had ever wanted to believe anything but she was frightened. Her heart had been wrung too many times to bloom properly any more.

'Because now my head is clear. I want to make our marriage work more than I have ever wanted anything and I'm willing to do whatever it takes for it. You're my priority, now and for ever…you and our baby.' He could hardly believe he was going to be a father. 'I was waiting for confirmation of the sale of my house in LA before I came to you…' He gave a rueful smile. 'Your news about the pregnancy brought me to you a few days earlier than I anticipated. I wanted to be able to look you in the eye and give you categorical proof that you're more important to me than anything else. The house I've bought here in Rome is in your name.' Another rueful smile. 'I'm hoping you will let me share it with you. If not, it's yours to keep. I'll still need a base in LA but I'm hoping you'll come with me and choose a house for us to share there. A house you're comfortable in, in a neighbourhood you can feel at home in. There's a lot that I'm hoping for but whatever happens from this point forward is up to you.'

'And what if I say no?'

He closed his eyes and inhaled deeply through his nose. 'Then I will have only myself to blame and I will have to be content with having a child with you even if I can't be your husband. All I would ask is that you allow me to be a proper father to it.'

Livia blinked back the fresh tears blurring her vision so she could look at him properly.

Ringing from the soulful caramel eyes was nothing but sincerity.

Her heart thumped and expanded.

'Let me get a few things straight,' she said slowly. 'In the last two weeks you've bought me a house, bought new business premises here in Rome, offered my delinquent brother a job and put your house up for sale in LA. Have I missed anything?'

'I think that's everything.'

'And you've done all this for me?'

He shifted forward and pressed the tip of his nose to hers. 'You're my life, Livia. Everything I have is yours.'

Her heart expanding a little more, she nudged her face a little closer to place the softest of kisses to his lips. 'I need you to promise me something.'

'Anything.'

Her hands crept onto his shoulders. 'Don't ever push me away again.'

'Never.' Now he placed the softest of kisses to her lips. 'Does this mean…?'

She hooked her hands around his neck. The blooming in her heart was growing with every breath she took. Staring deep into his eyes, she smiled. 'It means yes. To everything.'

The eyes staring back at her were searching. 'Do you think you can ever love me again?'

She kissed him once more and kept her mouth there, breathing him in, filling her lungs and her senses with the taste and scent she'd believed she would never enjoy again. She moved her lips away long enough to say, 'Massimo, you are etched in my heart. I've loved you since the day I met you and I will love you until the day I die.'

'You're etched on my heart too. And my soul. There is only you.'

And with those words her blooming heart swelled and reached out to join with his for ever.

A long while later, naked and replete in each other's arms, Massimo suddenly pulled himself out of the light sleep he'd fallen into.

With everything that had happened that evening, the full, wonderful magnitude of their situation finally hit him. 'We're having a baby.'

Livia giggled softly and kissed his chest. 'Yes, we are!'

'Have I told you recently how much I love you?'

'Not recently enough.'

He told her. And then he showed her.

EPILOGUE

LIVIA STOOD AT the front of the chalet's veranda, her hands on the wooden balustrade, and watched in awe at the rain lashing down. From her vantage point, she could see the main part of Seibua Island and all the surrounding ocean.

In the distance, she spotted one of the staff running through the rain in exaggerated leaps and grinned. If baby Sera weren't sleeping in her crib, Livia would be out there running a dance through it too. Massimo thought her a little bit mad for loving the rainy season so much but for her it was perfect. It unleashed Seibua Island's scents so that even the dullest of them filled the air with their potency and made the landscape a glimmering sheen of verdant brilliance. The rainbows that came when the sun blazed through the rain were the most glorious sight. She hoped one appeared soon.

The buzzing of her phone distracted her from her rainbow watch and she pulled it out of her shorts pocket, rolling her eyes at yet another of her brother's joke messages. She quickly fired a message back telling him he should be working and got an indignant reply that it was early morning in Rome and even the birds weren't awake yet. Smiling widely, she put her phone back in her pocket and resumed her position on the veranda.

While she scanned in all directions, she saw her mother-in-law poke her head out of her chalet door and laughed when she immediately whipped it back in.

In truth, it wasn't only Massimo who thought her a little mad for her love of the rain. His entire family thought the same. None of them understood how magical she found it, how without it there would be no rainbows and none of the glorious colour that now filled her life.

She remembered reading something once, how without the dark we wouldn't see the stars. That was how she felt about the rain.

She laughed again when she saw Jimmy make his escape from the lodge to go dancing in it as he'd watched her do numerous times. He saw her looking and waved wildly.

She waved back, waving harder when Massimo, who'd been caught in the lodge when the downpour started, came out to join their three-year-old son, his bemusement obvious even from the distance that separated them.

Her heart swelled to see him scoop their son into his arms and swing him around. She didn't need to be close to hear Jimmy's squeal of laughter. It was a sound locked in her memory bank.

And then her heart swelled enough to burst when, right above their dancing heads, the clouds parted and the multicoloured arc appeared in all its glory.

It appeared to be shining just for them.

* * * * *

CINDERELLA'S SCANDALOUS SECRET

MELANIE MILBURNE

CHAPTER ONE

THE PENTHOUSE IN the grand old Edinburgh hotel was the last room on Isla's shift. The irony didn't escape her that she was now cleaning penthouses rather than occupying them.

She knocked on the door and called out, 'Housekeeping.' When there was no answer she swiped her pass key, opened the door and brought her cleaning trolley inside.

It was like stepping into another world—a world she had once briefly visited and fooled herself she could belong to… Had it only been five months ago?

Isla placed a protective hand over the slight swell of her abdomen, where the soft flutter of tiny developing limbs moving in their sac of amniotic fluid reminded her that in another four months her life would change yet again.

For ever.

Isla closed the door of the suite, tried too to close the door on her thoughts, but they lingered, floating around her head like black crows circling above a carcass. The carcass of her short but passionate relationship with her baby's father.

Rafe Angeliri, who didn't even know he was going to be a father.

'Relationship' was probably too generous a word to describe what she had experienced with Rafe. A fling. An affair. Two months of madness. Magical, mind-altering, body-fizzing madness. Two months where she had forgotten who she was, where she came from, what she represented. They had met in a bar and in under an hour she had ended up in bed with him. Her first ever one-night stand—except it hadn't been a one-night stand because Rafe had asked to see her again. And again. And again. And within a few days they were enmeshed in a passionate relationship she hadn't wanted to end.

But it had.

She had made it end.

Isla swept her gaze over the plush furnishings of the suite. During her fling with Rafe, spending a night in a luxury room such as this had become the norm. Sleeping between one thousand thread Egyptian cotton sheets, sipping French champagne from sparkling crystal flutes, eating at Michelin starred restaurants, wearing designer clothes and shoes and glittering jewellery that cost more than a car. Going to charity balls and opera and theatre shows and premiere red carpet events dressed like a supermodel instead of a foster kid from the wrong side of the tracks.

Trailer trash, tarted up to look like royalty.

The penthouse had been slept in the night before—the bed was rumpled on one side, the covers thrown back over the mattress in a way that snagged on her memory like a rose thorn on silk. Even the air smelled faintly familiar—a subtle blend of bergamot and citrus that made the skin on Isla's arms lift in a tide of goosebumps, the hairs on her scalp tightening, tingling, tensing at the roots. The room seemed to have a strange energy, as if the presence of a strong personality had recently disturbed the air particles and they hadn't quite yet recovered.

Isla gave herself a concussion-inducing mental slap, strode to the bed and stripped the linen off like a magician ripping a tablecloth from under a full setting of crockery. She had work to do and she couldn't allow her imagination to get the better of her. She had made her own metaphorical bed and she was happy to lie on it.

Alone.

Telling Rafe about her pregnancy had never been an option. How could it be? She couldn't risk him pressuring her into a termination. Couldn't risk him rejecting her *and* the baby. She had experienced repeated rejections throughout her childhood. Even her own father had sent her back to foster care for others to raise. How could she risk Rafe sending her away? She couldn't risk him offering to marry her out of a sense of duty. She knew first-hand how duty-motivated marriages worked out—with unwanted, unloved, unnurtured kids ending up in long-term foster care.

Isla remade the bed with the fresh linen from the trolley, stretching it over the mattress and straightening it to perfection, plumping up the pillows and neatly arranging them, along with the navy-blue scatter cushions and throw rug for the end of the bed. She stepped back to admire her handiwork when the door of the suite opened behind her.

Isla turned to face the guest with her best apologetic housemaid smile in place. 'I'm sorry. I'm not quite fin…'

Her smile faded along with her apology and her heart leapt like a ping-pong ball and lodged high and tight in her throat. She couldn't find her voice, couldn't stop her heart from thudding against her chest wall like it was trying to punch its way out. *Bumph. Bumph. Bumph.* Her skin tightened all over her body, pulling away from her skeleton in panic. She ran her eyes over her baby's father before she could stop herself, her gaze drawn to him by a force the passage of time hadn't changed. There should be a law against looking so good, so fit and healthy and virile. So very irresistible.

Unlike her, Rafe Angeliri hadn't changed in the three months since she had seen him last. His dark blue designer business suit and crisp white shirt paid homage to the superior athletic build it covered. Long muscled legs, broad chest and toned arms and an abdomen so hard and flat you could have cracked open a coconut. The open neck of his shirt revealed the tanned column of his throat and a tiny glimpse of masculine black chest hair. Aftershave-model-handsome, tall and lean with a clean-shaven, take-no-prisoners jaw, he commanded a room just by entering it. His slightly wavy black hair was neither long nor short but somewhere stylishly in between, brushed back from his intelligent forehead and curling against the edges of his shirt collar. The loosely casual hairstyle belied the relentless drive and meticulous focus of his personality.

However, his hazel eyes were even more cynical and there were vertical lines running down each side of his mouth that hadn't been there before.

But there was one other difference Isla detected before he quickly masked it—shock. It rippled across his features, sharpened his gaze, froze his movements until he was as still as a marble statue. But only for a microsecond. He had always had far better self-control than anyone she knew, certainly better than her, and yet she had always prided herself on her ability to mask her feelings. How else had she survived all those childhood foster home placements with perfect strangers?

'Isla.' Rafe gave a nod that somehow managed to be both formal and insulting. 'To what do I owe the pleasure of finding you waiting beside my bed?'

Isla stepped away from the bed as if it had suddenly burst into flames. Being anywhere near a bed when Rafe was within touching distance was a bad idea. A very tempting but bad, bad, *bad* idea. They had spent more time in bed than out of it during their short and volatile fling. Sex had brought them together in a thunderclap of attraction at their first meeting in a bar—an explosion of lust that had sent shockwaves through her entire body. She hadn't really enjoyed sex until she experienced it with Rafe. It had been out of this world sex and even now she could feel the memories of it coursing through her body. Little pulses and tingles in her flesh—the flesh he had awakened with his lips and tongue, as if being in the same room as him triggered her body into remembering, longing, *wanting*.

Isla snatched up some fresh towels from her trolley, desperate to hide the slight bulge of her belly. No one was going to be cracking coconuts on her abdomen any time soon. She had never had a particularly flat stomach, which made her hope Rafe wouldn't notice the slight change in it now. It had always surprised her that he had found her so attractive. She was nothing like the super-slim and glamorous women he normally dated. She was desperate to occupy her hands in case they were tempted to slap that imperious look off his too-handsome face. Or worse—pull his head down to crash his mouth against hers to make her forget everything but the heat and fire of his masterful, mesmerising, bone-melting kiss.

'I work at this hotel. Now, if you'll let me finish your room, I'll get out of your way and—'

'I thought you were going back to London to resume your Fine Arts degree?' A frown tugged at his brow, his green and brown flecked gaze holding hers with the force of a searchlight. 'Wasn't that the plan?'

'I… I changed my mind.' Isla swung away and strode into the bathroom with the towels. She placed the new ones on the towel racks and then gathered up the damp ones, bundling them against her body like a barrier. Her plans had changed as soon as she found out she was pregnant.

Everything had changed.

Rafe followed her into the palatial bathroom, his presence shrinking it to the size of a tissue box. Isla caught a glimpse of herself in the mirror over the twin basins and inwardly groaned. She had never been more conscious of her lack of make-up, the dark circles under her eyes, the lankness of her red-gold hair under her housemaid's cap. Or the secret swell of her belly beneath her housemaid's white frilly apron. Was he comparing her to his latest lover? She had seen photos of him with numerous women in the time since she had brought their relationship to an end. She wondered if it had been deliberate on his part—to be seen out and about with as many women as possible as an *I'll show you how quickly I can move on from you* slap to her ego. After all, Isla had been the one to end their fling, which clearly wasn't something he was used to. Women were queuing up to be with him, not rushing to leave.

'That was rather sudden, was it not?' His voice contained a note of scepticism that matched the piercing focus of his gaze. 'I thought you liked living in London?'

Isla sucked in her tummy to her backbone. She straightened the toiletries on the marble counter for something to do with her hands, annoyed they weren't as steady as she would have liked. 'I felt ready for a change of scene. Anyway, I could no longer afford living in London.'

His top lip curled and his glittering eyes pulsated with barely controlled anger. 'Is there someone else? Is that why you called time on us?'

Isla met his gaze in the mirror, her stomach freefalling at the bitterness shining in his eyes. 'Us? We weren't an "us" and you know it. It was a fling, that's all, and I wanted it to end.'

'Liar.' The word came out like a bullet. Hard. Direct. Bullseye. 'At least have the decency to be honest with me.'

Honest? How could she be honest about anything about herself? About her background. About her shame. It didn't matter if she was wearing haute couture or hand-me-downs, the shame burned like a flame inside her. 'There's no one else. I told you in my note— I simply wanted out.'

Finding out she was carrying Rafe's baby had thrown Isla into a terrifying world of uncertainty. The thought of him rejecting her, throwing her and their baby out of his life like her father had done to her had been too painful. She couldn't think of any way she could tell him about her pregnancy that wouldn't cause irreversible destruction in his life. She hadn't known him long enough or well enough to trust he wouldn't try and pressure her into having an abortion. Not that she would have allowed him or anyone to do that. She had enough doubts about her own mothering ability. She had been in and out of foster care since she was seven; her memories of her own mother were patchy at best, painful at worst. What sort of mother would *she* make? It was a constant nagging toothache type of worry that kept her awake at night. The doubts and fears throbbed on the inside of her skull like minia-ture hammers.

'Ah, yes. Your note.' There was a disparaging bite to Rafe's tone.

Isla forced herself to hold his searing gaze. She put on her game face, the one she had perfected over the years. The face that had helped her survive yet another placement with strangers. The mask of cool indiffer-ence that belied the churning, burning, yearning emo-tions fighting for room in her chest.

'You're the one who needs to be honest. You're only angry because I was the one to leave you. But you would've called time sooner rather than later. None of your flings last longer than a month at the most. I was already on borrowed time.'

A muscle worked in the lower quadrant of his jaw, his eyes still brewing and boiling with bitterness. 'Couldn't you have waited until I got home from New York to speak to me face to face? Or is that why you didn't come with me on that trip while I negotiated that deal? Because you'd always planned to leave while I was away. You didn't want to risk having me try to change your mind.'

Isla pressed her lips together, struggling to keep her own temper in check. She had known how important that deal was to him. The biggest of his career. The man he was negotiating the deal with was a deeply religious family man who might not have signed off on the deal if news broke about Rafe's pregnant lover with the salacious background. She had started to feel nauseous just before he'd suggested she come with him to New York. Thinking at first it was a mild stomach bug, she had decided to stay at his villa in Sicily while he went abroad. She had gone everywhere else with him during their two months together, slotting into his life without giving too much thought as to why she shouldn't be subsuming her life so readily, so recklessly into his. But then a wriggling worm of suspicion about the possibility of pregnancy had tunnelled into her brain to such a degree it was all she *could* think about. She'd had to know one way or the other. And she'd wanted to be alone when she did. She hadn't wanted him finding her with a test wand in her hand, or finding her bent over the toilet heaving her insides out.

Once she'd seen the test was positive, she'd known what she had to do.

End it.

End their fling and get the hell out of his life before more harm was done. Because she would have brought him harm. Great harm. Harm from which there would be no easy recovery. The Pandora's Box of her past would have created havoc and mayhem in his well-to-do circles. The New York deal would have been compromised—the deal he had worked on for months and months. One leaked photo of her in lingerie, dancing in that sleazy gentlemen's supper club, and Rafe's desire to chair a prominent children's charity would be destroyed. Future business deals of his would be jeopardised from the stain of her background.

Isla had pictured the headlines—*Exotic dancer pregnant with billionaire Italian hotelier Raffaele Angeliri's love-child!* He would not have come back from that easily, if at all. Scandals stuck to high-profile people, sometimes for the rest of their lives. She couldn't do it to him; she couldn't do it to their child. To have it surrounded by shame from the moment it was born, even *before* it was born.

Isla raised her chin and chilled her gaze to freezing. 'You wouldn't have been able to change my mind.'

His eyes went to her mouth and then back to her gaze. 'Are you sure about that, *cara*?' His voice was a deep gravelly burr that was as wickedly sensual as a slow stroke of one of his hands between her legs. And his smouldering gaze threatened to scorch her eyes out of her head and leave two smoking black holes in their place.

Isla swung away from the marble counter, grabbing the used towels from the rack. She had to get away from him before she did or said something she would regret. Like, *Guess what I'm hiding underneath this apron? Your baby.* Of course, a part of her—a huge part—believed he had a right to know he was to become a father. And if she had come from a similar background to his she would have told him upfront—no question about it.

But they came from different worlds and there was

no way she could see to bridge the deep chasm that divided her world from his.

'Leave that.' He gestured with his hand at the towels she was carrying, a frown etched between his eyes. 'Why are you cleaning hotel rooms? Surely you could have picked work more in line with your artistic aspirations?'

Isla kept the towels against her body. She needed whatever armour she could use against his disturbingly potent presence. Damp towels were hardly going to cut it, but still. 'I'm working for a friend, helping her out. She runs a cleaning agency—Leave It to Layla and Co. You might have heard of it?' She knew she was rambling, sounding as flustered as she felt. It annoyed her to be so on edge because she had always prided herself on her acting ability. Hadn't she spent most of her life pretending to be someone she wasn't?

Rafe's gaze was unwavering. 'I haven't but I'll keep the name in mind. I'm thinking about buying this hotel. That's why I'm staying here under an assumed name to see how things work behind the scenes.'

'Don't you have enough hotels by now?' Isla didn't hold back on the sarcasm in her tone. 'I mean, you nailed that New York deal, didn't you? One of your biggest, right?'

If he was proud of his achievements he didn't show it in his expression. She might as well have been commenting on how many shirts and ties he'd collected since their breakup. One side of his mouth lifted in a smile that wasn't quite a smile. 'Nice to know you've been taking a keen interest in my business affairs.'

Argh. Why had she made it sound as if she was poring over the newspapers for every little snippet of information about him? Isla affected a bored expression to make up for lost ground, moving past him to go back to the main part of the suite. 'Look, I really need to finish this suite. My shift ends in a few minutes.'

He caught one of her arms on her way past, his fingers a deceptively gentle bracelet around the fine bones of her wrist. Her skin reacted to his touch, every nerve standing up to take notice—remembering, wanting, needing. 'Stay and have a drink with me.' His voice had dropped to that same low deep burr that made the base of her spine fizz like thousands of bubbles in top shelf champagne.

'No can do.' Isla pulled her wrist away, pointedly rubbing at her skin. 'I have another engagement.' The lie slipped so easily from her lips, but then she had a Master's degree in face-saving deceit.

Something moved at the back of his gaze as quick as a camera shutter click. Disappointment? Pain? Anger? She couldn't quite tell. 'I'm sure they won't mind waiting.'

Isla lifted her chin, locking her defiant gaze on his. She could feel the tug-of-war between their two strong wills prickling and pulsing in the air like soundwaves. The push and pull of their personalities had more or less defined their whirlwind fling. 'You can't force me to do anything any more, Rafe.'

His eyebrows lifted ever so slightly above his hazel eyes. And his cynical half-smile was back. 'When did I ever force you, *cara mia*? You were with me all the way, *si*?' His voice was so low and deep it sounded like it was coming through the floorboards. Deep enough to strike a chord in the secret core of her being, reverberating like the sound of a struck tuning fork.

Isla tried to block the storm of erotic memories that flooded her brain. Memories of her limbs entangled with his, her body singing with delight and satiation and super-heightened sensuality. The taste of him, the musky scent of their coupling in the air, the feel of his hands lazily stroking the flank of her thigh, so close to the pounding heart of her need. She drew in a sharp breath and went back to her trolley, grasping the handle to stop herself from touching him. Surely she was immune to him by now? She hadn't felt a flicker of lust for anyone since they'd broken up.

She wondered if she ever would again.

'I have to go.' Isla pushed the trolley towards the door but before she could get any distance his voice stalled her.

'One drink. In the bar downstairs. I promise I won't keep you long.' A tiny pause and he added, 'Please, *cara*?'

Isla should have walked out without saying another word but something in the quality of his tone stopped her. If she refused it would make her look churlish. After all, she had been the one to end their relationship. If anyone should be feeling churlish it should be him. She had left a note at his home rather than tell him face to face. The most telling thing about their breakup was that she'd only received one phone call from him where he'd left a stinging voicemail. One final call that had allowed him to vent his anger and thus confirming to her she had done the right thing. If he had truly cared about her, wouldn't he have called multiple times? Wouldn't he have done everything in his power to find her? To meet with her in person and beg her to come back to him. Except men like Rafe Angeliri didn't beg. They didn't have to. Women never left him in the first place. They were the ones who begged to stay.

But spending time with Rafe was dangerous for her now. Dangerous on so many levels. She was only just starting to show her pregnancy; her bump was still in that *is-she-or-isn't-she?* phase. A quick drink might be just enough contact to assure him she had well and truly moved on with her life. Moved on from *him*. Surely she owed him a few more minutes of her time? He was the father of her baby, even if she'd vowed never to let him know it. She would look upon having a quick drink with him as a fact-finding mission. She needed to know what his plans were so she could adjust her own. If he was going to spend time here in Edinburgh then she would have to leave. To disappear and hope he wouldn't come looking for her.

Isla turned to face Rafe, her heart and mind still at war. When had she ever been able to resist him? A big fat never. Which was why she had to be careful around him now. 'Okay. One drink.'

Once the door closed behind Isla, Rafe let out a breath he hadn't realised he'd been holding. Five months had passed and he still couldn't be in the same room as her without wanting her. The lust hit him like a sucker punch. Seeing her standing beside his bed had brought back so many memories. Memories he had never been able to erase from his mind, much less his body. It was as if Isla McBain had imprinted herself on his flesh. No one else could satisfy the burning, aching need she aroused. He had dated other women since but each time he had thought about sleeping with them something had made him pull back. He was turning into a damn monk and he had to sort it out so he could move on with his life.

Move on from *her*.

Rafe was annoyed at himself for still being bitter about their breakup. But usually it was him who called time on his relationships. He was the one who set the agenda and changed it when it suited him. It had been a new experience—an uncomfortable experience— to have Isla leave him, especially when he was out of town working on the biggest and most important deal of his career. And especially when he had taken her home to Sicily—the first lover he had ever taken to his private sanctuary.

His villa in Sicily was normally out of bounds for casual lovers. It blurred the boundaries to have lovers sleep over too many times, but for once he had relaxed his guard. He had taken Isla there for weeks on end, cancelled important work meetings just so he could spend time with her without the press documenting every moment. Something about their relationship had made him want to keep it out of the public eye. Not because he didn't like being with her but because he did. A lot. A lot more than he had enjoyed being with other lovers.

But somehow he had read her wrong and that bothered him. Big time. What niggled him the most was that he suspected she had waited until he was preoccupied with that deal so she could maximise the impact.

Coming home to an empty villa and a note from Isla propped up on the mantelpiece had blindsided him. And if there was one thing he detested more than anything else it was being blindsided. Hadn't his duplicitous father set the bar for blindsiding? With his father's two families operating simultaneously—two wives, two families, who each thought they were Tino Angeliri's entire world until Rafe had discovered the truth when he was thirteen. A phone call from one of his father's staff had changed everything. Revealed everything. When his father had been critically injured in a car crash while away on business, the staff member had felt compelled to inform Rafe and his mother of Tino's life-threatening injuries. But when he and his mother flew to Florence to be by Tino's bedside they discovered Tino already had visitors. Four of them. His other family. His wife and two sons. His father's first family. His father's *official* family. His father's other life. Rafe had stood by the hospital bed and recounted every one of his father's blatant lies. Years and years of bold-faced blatant lies.

Rafe was his father's dirty little secret. His illegitimate son.

Coming home to that damn *Dear John* letter from Isla had enraged Rafe so much he had torn it into confetti-like shreds. It had reminded him of walking into that Florence hospital when everything he believed about himself and his family was found to be false. A pack of lies. Secrets and lies. He hadn't realised he was capable of such anger until it hit him in sickening, gut-shredding waves. Why hadn't he seen it coming? Surely there must have been a sign. Or had Isla deliberately misled him, lulling him into a false sense of security just as his father had done for all those years? Pretending, lying, misleading—the three deadly sins of any relationship.

He had called Isla as soon as he'd read the note and left a message. It wasn't a message he was particularly proud of, but he was not one to hand out second chances. She hadn't called him back and, in a way, he had been glad. Clean breaks were always to be advised. But nothing about their breakup felt clean to him. It felt rough around the edges, torn instead of neatly cut, ripped and raw instead of resolved.

Rafe paced the floor of the penthouse until he was sure he would wear his way through the carpet to the suite below. Something was off about her now. Her body language, her averted gaze, her caginess. Why had Isla had given up her Fine Arts degree and moved back to Scotland? She had been so passionate about her art and had said how much she enjoyed living in London. He had seen some of her drawings and he'd been amazed at her talent. What had made her turn her back on her dreams and work for a friend in a job that didn't maximise her creativity? Had something happened in the time since their breakup? Something that had poisoned her artistic aspirations. But what?

He turned and looked at the neatly made bed, picturing her in it with her slim limbs wrapped around his. He let out a filthy curse and swung away, his guts twisting and tangling in disgust. Disgust at himself for allowing her to *still* get under his skin.

Isla was by far the feistiest and most fascinating woman he had ever been involved with and he couldn't help wondering if that was why no one else since had measured up. He had found Isla's quick wit and hair-trigger temper entertaining as well as frustrating. So few people stood up to him. So few women treated him as an equal instead of a meal ticket.

Isla had been different. She had made it virtually impossible for him to be satisfied by anyone else. He had enjoyed their heated debates, enjoyed how all their fights were settled between the sheets. He'd enjoyed goading her to get a rise out of her just so he could have her quaking and shuddering in his arms.

She looked the same but different somehow. Her figure was still slim but some of her curves had ripened, making him ache to touch her, to feel her, to smell and taste her. Her breasts were a little fuller. *Dio.* He had to stop thinking about her gorgeous breasts. How soft they felt in his hands, under his lips and tongue. How it felt to have her moving, thrashing beneath him as he took her screaming all the way to paradise.

The new energy that surrounded her now intrigued him. Her gaze blazing with defiance one minute and skittering away from his the next. Her skin paling and then flushing, her body turned away when before it had always turned towards him like a compass point finding true north.

Isla's rejection was like a scabbed-over sore. Seeing her again had ripped off the scab and left the wound smarting, stinging, festering. He had to expunge her from his system so he could finally move forward. One drink with her and he would walk away without a backward glance. He owed it to himself to leave what they'd shared in the past where it belonged.

It was over and the sooner he accepted it the better.

CHAPTER TWO

ISLA CHANGED OUT of her work uniform and back into her street clothes. Gone were the designer threads Rafe had bought her. She had left everything behind, wanting no reminders of their fling—other than the one she carried within her body. These days she wore practical and cheap off-the-peg casual outfits.

She stepped into her black leggings and pulled on her long-sleeved jersey top, but rather than disguise her shape, her clothes drew attention to it. She stroked her hand over the bulge of her belly. Surely the baby hadn't grown in the last few minutes? She pulled the garment away from her abdomen but as soon as she let it go it lovingly draped across her body as if to say, *Look at my baby bump!*

Isla picked up her jacket even though it was a little warm to wear it inside. She fed her arms through the sleeves and tied the waist ties around her middle. She glanced at herself again in the changing room mirror, doing her best to ignore the niggling of her conscience over the lengths she was going to in order to keep her pregnancy concealed from Rafe.

She took out her small make-up kit from her tote bag and did what she could to freshen up her features.

Concealer—her new best friend—was first, followed by a tinted moisturiser and some strategically placed eyeshadow to bring out the blue in her eyes. She followed that up with bronzer, highlighter, lip-gloss and a decent coat of mascara, a part of her wondering why she was going to so much trouble. But, in a way, make-up was another form of armour and, God knew, she needed a heck of a lot of armour around Rafe Angeliri.

Isla released the ties of her jacket and skimmed her hand over her belly again. Was it her imagination or was her baby more active than usual? She was so used to calling it her baby but it was Rafe's baby too. The prod from her conscience was like the stab of a dart to the heart. *Rafe's baby.* Of course, he had a right to know. Hadn't she always believed that to be the case? His New York deal was finalised now, so why shouldn't she tell him about the baby? There was a risk he might reject the child, but she wouldn't insist on his involvement if he didn't wish it.

The thought of her baby being rejected by Rafe made her heart tighten. The last thing she wanted for her child was a reluctant father. Isla had experienced one of those and look how *that* had turned out. Rejection. It might as well have been her middle name instead of Rebecca. Years and years in and out of foster homes, never belonging to anyone, never being chosen for an open adoption. Never feeling loved.

No. Her baby deserved better and she would do everything in her power to give her child the best upbringing she could, with or without Rafe's support.

Isla drew in a shuddering breath and retied her jacket around her waist. She would look for an opportunity to tell him during their catch-up drink rather than dump it on him straight away. She knew that much about him—he didn't like surprises.

The hotel bar was downstairs on a mezzanine level and Isla walked in with a tight band of tension around her head and her stomach like a nest of agitated ants. Rafe was seated in a quiet corner on one of two burgundy-coloured leather chesterfield tub chairs and, as if he sensed the precise moment she arrived, he looked up from his phone and locked gazes with her. A zap of awareness shot through her body. They might as well have been the only people in the bar—the only people on the planet. The only people in the universe. She couldn't look away if she tried. Her gaze was tethered by his, her body under his command as if he had programmed her to his particular coordinates.

He was still wearing the dark blue business suit and white shirt but he had since put on a silver and black striped tie. That small gesture had a strange effect on her, momentarily ambushing her feelings. Feminist she might be, but she had always admired his attention to the old-fashioned manners of dating. During their fling, she hadn't opened a single car door for herself. He had always walked on the road side of the footpath…he had never sat down before she was seated. It was so starkly different from the way other men in her past life had treated her and she had lapped it up, enjoying every moment of feeling like someone of value.

Rafe rose from the chair as she approached, his gaze sweeping over her in an assessing manner. 'You look very beautiful but I quite liked you in that sexy housemaid outfit.' His voice had a rough edge and his rich Italian accent seemed even more pronounced.

Isla had always been a sucker for his accent. She

had worked on her regional Scottish accent for years, doing all she could to rid herself of any trace of her chaotic and underprivileged childhood. These days, no one would ever guess she hadn't been educated at an exclusive fee-paying Edinburgh school and that was the way she wanted it.

Isla gave him a stiff-lipped, no-teeth smile and, finally tearing her gaze away, sat in the chair beside his, placing her tote bag on the floor next to her chair. 'I hope there isn't a policy about hotel cleaning staff fraternising with guests but here goes.'

'If there is any issue I will deal with it,' Rafe said and then frowned. 'Don't you want to take off your coat? It's warm in here.'

'No. Not yet.' Isla couldn't meet his gaze and picked up the cocktails menu and pretended an avid interest in the selection.

'What would you like to drink?' Rafe signalled the drinks waiter.

'Something soft—lemonade.'

His ink-black eyebrows rose. 'What about some champagne? Or a cocktail? You used to love—'

'You know that saying: when life hands you lemons?' Isla sent him a wry look and leaned forward to place the cocktail menu back on the table between them. 'Suffice it to say, I've developed quite a taste for lemonade.'

Rafe gave the order for drinks to the waiter, who had just then approached, and once the young man had left Rafe turned back to study Isla's expression for a long moment. 'You don't seem yourself. Does my company distress you that much?'

Isla could feel the heat crawling into her cheeks and

right now the last thing she needed was more warmth on her person. Her jacket was making her feel as if she were sitting in a sauna. 'It was quite a shock running into you like that while I was doing your room. I... I haven't quite recovered.' She was pleased with her response. It sounded reasonable and it was more or less the truth. She would probably *never* recover.

'Yes, indeed it was.'

The silence contained an undertow of tension that tugged at Isla's already fraught nerves.

The waiter came over with their drinks, setting them down in front of them and discreetly melting away.

Rafe watched Isla take a generous sip of her lemonade with a slight frown between his eyes as if he couldn't quite understand why she wasn't sipping a Bellini instead. The lemonade was cold and sweet but it did nothing to reduce the tide of colour she could feel in her cheeks. Beads of perspiration formed under her hairline and between her shoulder blades but the thought of removing her jacket and letting her body deliver the message for her was suddenly too daunting.

Isla put her glass back on the table and forced herself to meet his gaze. 'Why are you looking at me like that?'

'You're not happy.' It was a statement, not a question.

Isla pushed a strand of sticky hair back off her face, uncomfortable with his probing scrutiny. Uncomfortable that he could see things she had fought so hard to conceal. 'I hardly see why that is any business of yours.'

'I could have made you happy, *cara*.' The pitch of his voice lowered to a low growl of bitterness.

She crossed one leg over the other and moved her

top foot up and down in jerky movements. 'How? By dressing me up like some sort of doll? A toy you played with only when the fancy took you. No thanks.'

A brooding frown entered his gaze. 'I told you how important that deal was to me. Bruno Romano was a nightmare to negotiate a coffee date with, let alone a hotel chain that size. I'm sorry if you read that as neglect.'

Isla picked up her glass of lemonade again, the ice cubes rattling against the glass betraying her nervousness in Rafe's presence. She had to find a way to tell him about the baby, but how? Meeting him like this was crazy, but hadn't she always been a little crazy where he was concerned? Her feelings for him were so confusing. There were times when she didn't even like him and yet her body adored him. Her body craved him like a powerful drug. Damn it, her body even *recognised* him. She could feel the tingles and fizzes moving through her flesh just by sitting within reach of him, every cell of her body vibrating.

She took another sip of her lemonade. 'So, why are you interested in this hotel? I didn't realise Scotland was on your radar.'

'It wasn't until I met you. You awakened my interest.' Rafe lifted his small dram of whisky to his mouth and took a measured sip, savouring the taste for a moment before he swallowed. Isla couldn't tear her gaze away from the up and down movement of his tanned throat, her eyes drifting to the dark stubble around his mouth and jaw. She tightened her hand around her glass, remembering how it felt to run her fingertips over that sexy regrowth, remembering the way it felt grazing against the soft skin of her breasts. On her inner thighs…

She glanced at him again with her making-polite-conversation expression in place. 'So, are you going to buy it?'

He cradled the whisky glass in two hands, his long strong fingers overlapping. That was another thing she remembered—how those clever fingers could wreak such havoc on her senses when they got down to business on her body. His gaze tethered hers in a lock that made her inner core contract like the tightening of a small fist. 'I like what I've seen so far.' Somehow, she didn't think he was still talking about the hotel.

Isla released a shuddery breath and took another sip of her lemonade, acutely conscious of his probing gaze. She was too warm from still wearing her jacket, or maybe it was being within touching distance of the man who had scorched every inch of her body with his touch.

Rafe leaned forward and put his whisky glass on the small table between their chairs and then sat back, his hands resting on his thighs. 'Tell me why you quit your Fine Arts degree.'

Isla shrugged one shoulder and rolled one of her ankles to burn off restless energy. *You should have told him by now.* Her conscience was jabbing at her but she couldn't work up the courage. 'I lost interest after I came back to the UK. I'd already missed half of one semester by staying in Italy with you. I only planned on going for a two-week sketching holiday if you remember.'

'But you could have made it up, surely?'

'I couldn't be bothered.' She looked into the contents

of her glass rather than hold his gaze. 'It was a pipe dream to think I could make a career out of painting portraits. I decided it wasn't worth the effort of trying.'

His frown deepened. 'But surely cleaning hotel rooms isn't going to satisfy you long-term?'

Pride stiffened Isla's shoulders and sharpened her gaze. 'Careful, Rafe. Your privileged upbringing is showing. Anyway, my friend Layla has made a career out of it—or is starting to.'

'But you're an artist, not a businesswoman.'

Isla affected a laugh. 'You make it sound like you know me. You don't.'

'I know you well enough to know you will not be satisfied unless you express your creativity.' Rafe leaned forward so his forearms were resting on his thighs, his gaze trained intently on hers. 'I have a proposition for you. Business, not personal.'

Isla raised her brows. 'Oh? Let me guess… You want me to paint your portrait?'

He gave a twisted smile. 'No. My grandmother, actually. My mother's mother. She's about to turn ninety. She's difficult to please. I don't think she's liked a single thing I've bought for her. But I thought a portrait would make a nice birthday present for her.'

Isla chewed at one side of her mouth. How ironic her first ever commission offer came from Rafe. Of course, she couldn't accept. But the thought of the money he might be prepared to pay her gave her pause. Why would he want to commission *her*, though? Did he think he could talk her into another fling with him? But, even so, she couldn't help feeling intrigued about his family. He had rarely mentioned anything about his background and she'd been deliberately evasive about hers. They had somehow come to a tacit agreement to leave the topic of families alone.

'Surely there are other artists, much more established artists, you could commission?' she asked.

'I want you.' His eyes glittered with something that seemed to suggest it wasn't just her artistic ability he was solely interested in.

The thought of resuming their affair was strangely exciting. Thrilling and exciting and dangerous.

But completely and utterly out of the question.

Isla leaned forward to put her drink on the table and began to rise from her chair. 'I'm sorry. I'm not available.'

Rafe placed a hand on her knee before she could stand, locking his gaze with hers. 'Think about it, Isla. You can name your price.'

She was close enough to him to smell his citrus-based aftershave. Close enough to see the flecks of brown and green in his eyes that made his irises look kaleidoscopic. The warm press of his hand on her knee sent a wave of heat straight to her core, stirring wickedly erotic memories in her flesh.

The air seemed to vibrate with energy. Sexual energy so powerful she could feel its *tug-tug-tug* on her insides, reminding her of the wickedly erotic delights she had experienced in his arms. Delights she had not been able to erase from her memory. They were seared into her brain and body so that every time he was within reach of her, her flesh tingled and prickled with excitement.

Isla knew she had to put a stop to this. Right here. Right now. She couldn't agree to spending time with Rafe—not under any circumstances. He'd said she could name her price but wouldn't *she* be paying the biggest price in the end? She pushed his hand off her knee. 'Rafe, there's something I need to tell you...'

'What?'

She brought her gaze to his and swallowed against the restriction in her throat. 'The reason I left you so abruptly...' *Oh, God, why was this so difficult?* 'I was scared about how you'd react and I—'

A frown carved into his forehead. 'Did you cheat on me? Tell me, Isla. Were you unfaithful?' His tone contained more hurt than anger. It seemed to bruise the atmosphere like mottled clouds.

Isla had a strange desire to laugh at the absurdity of the notion of her being unfaithful. He was the most amazing, exciting, thrilling lover and she had missed him every day since. And probably would for the rest of her life. No one would ever rise above the benchmark he had set. 'No, of course not. No, it wasn't anything like that.'

'Then what was it?'

She took a deep breath and slowly released it. 'I'm... pregnant.'

He looked at her blankly as if he hadn't registered what she'd said.

'Rafe, I'm having a baby.' She undid the ties from around her waist, gradually revealing the swell of her abdomen. His eyebrows drew together as realisation slowly dawned on his features, leaching him of colour, stiffening every muscle on his face.

'You're...*pregnant*?' His voice sounded nothing like his. Locked. Tight. Strangled. His Adam's apple bobbing up and down, a host of emotions flickering over his face—shock, horror, anger. And, yes, hurt. Waves of it rippling like an eddying tide.

Isla pressed her hands together in her lap. *Here it comes. The rejection.* Cold dripped into her stomach, the icy shards slicing at her insides. *I'm so sorry, little baby. This is all my fault.* 'I didn't want to tell you because—'

He opened and closed his mouth a couple of times as if his voice had momentarily deserted him. 'Is it… mine?'

'I…' Her voice deserted her for a moment as the pain of his question hit home. Of course, he had every right to ask but it hurt to think he thought her capable of such betrayal. She might not have been honest with him about her background but she would never cheat on a partner. It went against her moral code.

His eyes drilled into hers. 'Answer the question, damn it.'

Isla gave a single nod. 'Yes. Of course, it is. I'm sorry I didn't tell you before—'

Rafe shot to his feet like his chair had exploded. 'Wait—I'm not having this discussion in a freaking wine bar. Upstairs. Now.' His voice had that commanding edge that never failed to put her back up like a cornered cat.

'I don't think that's a good idea right now—'

'You will do as I say. You owe me that, surely?' His mouth was pulled so tight his lips were almost bloodless, his eyes flashing with livid sparks of anger.

Isla put up her chin. 'You can tell me to get out of your life here. You don't need me to go up to your room.'

He flinched as if she had struck him. 'Is that how poorly you think of me?'

Isla no longer knew what to think. He wasn't acting the way she'd expected. He was angry, yes, but for some reason she sensed he was angrier with himself than with her. She didn't want to create a scene in a public place so gave in with as little grace as possible, not wanting him to think he could boss her around like one of his employees. She rose from her chair like a sulky teenager being sent to her room, her mouth set in a stubborn line. She hoisted her tote bag strap onto her shoulder and sent him a mutinous glare. 'You can cool it with the caveman routine. You should know by now it doesn't work with me.'

'Nothing seems to work with you, does it?' Rafe's tone was so cutting it shredded her already frayed nerves like a sword slashing satin ribbons. He led her to the private elevator that went to his penthouse, his fingers firmly cupping her elbow. He stabbed at the call button, his expression thunderous, but underneath that dark brooding tension Isla could see tiny flickers of hurt. And it shamed her. She hadn't thought in any detail about how he would feel if he ever found out about the pregnancy. Or at least she had tried *not* to think about it. She had been too concerned about protecting him from her past, protecting herself from the shame of it being splashed over every newspaper or online news or gossip outlet. She had fooled herself into thinking Rafe would be better off not knowing about his love-child—that it was easier for her to disappear than to risk him demanding she marry him or insist she have an abortion.

The elevator trip to the penthouse was conducted in a silence so thick Isla could feel it pressing against her like a dense invisible fog. Every breath she took in caught at the back of her throat, every second that passed heightened the tension in her body until she thought she would snap. The mirrored walls reflected Rafe's demeanour—the tension rippling across his features as if he was recalling every moment of their fling and wondering how it had come to this point.

'Rafe, I—' she began.

'Wait until we are inside.' His tone was as commanding as a drill sergeant and the elevator doors whooshed open as if they too were frightened to disobey his orders.

Isla followed him into the penthouse, the door closing behind him with a resounding *kerplunk* that set her stomach churning fast enough to make butter. She let her bag drop to the floor with a thump, her legs feeling so feeble that they might go from beneath her. Tension was building behind her eyes and she worried she might be getting another one of the debilitating headaches that had plagued her during early pregnancy.

He came to where she was standing, his gaze focused, direct, searching. 'So, let me get this straight. You knew you were pregnant *before* you left?'

Isla drew in a shaky breath. 'Yes…'

His own inward breath sounded sharp and painful and he swallowed a couple of times, the tanned column of his throat moving up and down in an almost convulsive manner. 'How did it happen?'

'The usual way…'

He made an impatient sound in his throat. 'You told me you were on the Pill and I always used condoms. You can't get much safer than that.' His gaze sharpened with accusation. 'Unless you *lied* to me?'

'I was on the Pill but I might have compromised its

effectiveness that weekend we went to Paris. I got a stomach bug, if you remember? And you didn't always use a condom.' She lifted her chin and forced herself to hold his gaze. 'We made love in the shower a couple of times without.'

Something passed through his gaze, as if he was recalling those passionate lovemaking sessions in intimate detail like replaying an erotic film. Images of them locked together with steamy shower water cascading over their rocking bodies. Images of him with his mouth sucking on her breast or her sucking on him, drawing his essence from him until he groaned out loud, his legs buckling at the knees. Or her with her hands flat against the marble walls of the shower with him driving into her from behind, her cries of earth-shattering pleasure filling the air. The warm cascading water. The slick press of their bodies. The need. The need. The need. The explosion of release that left them both gasping under the spray of the shower...

'And do you have a good reason for not telling me you were pregnant before now?' His voice sounded as intimidating as a headmaster admonishing a recalcitrant student, but his eyes still pulsed with waves of hurt.

Isla hugged her arms around her middle, trying to keep control of her escalating emotions. 'I was worried you might pressure me into having a termination and—'

His frown was so deep it closed the space between his eyes. 'Do you really think I would do something like that? For God's sake, Isla. Surely you know me better than that?' His ragged tone contained deep notes of anguish along with the chord of anger.

Guilt rained down on her like hail, making her huddle further into herself, her gaze lowered from his. Had she made a mistake? Had she seriously misjudged him? Would it have been better to be honest with him from the outset? Hindsight was all very well, but she had thought she was doing the right thing at the time. The shock of finding out she was pregnant had thrown her completely. In her panicked state, it had felt safer to leave than have him send her away.

Hadn't she been sent away too many times in her childhood to count?

'I didn't know what to think,' Isla said, slowly raising her gaze back to his. 'I wasn't prepared to hang around long enough to risk you doing something radical like asking me to marry you or—'

'Well, at least you do know that much about me, because that's exactly what I plan to do.' The stridency in his voice was matched by the glint of determination in his gaze. 'I'm not having any child of mine grow up illegitimate. I want it to have my name and my protection. I can't—won't—accept any other alternative. We will be married as soon as it can be arranged.'

Isla's mouth dropped open and her stomach turned over. 'You can't be serious? We're practically strangers who—'

'We spent two months living and sleeping together. That's hardly what I'd call the action of strangers. We've made a child together. That's not something that I can approach in a casual manner. Formalising our relationship is the next step. The only step.' He walked over to the minibar and took out a bottle of mineral water, holding it up. 'Drink?'

Isla nodded; her mouth was so dry it felt like she

had been licking the plush carpet at her feet. 'I can't marry you, Rafe. I *won't* marry you.'

'You can and you will.' His mouth had a stubborn set to it, his eyes now as hard as lichen-covered stones. 'I am not taking no for an answer.' He unscrewed the top of the mineral water with a loud hiss of released effervescence and poured it into two glasses and then turned back to hand her one.

Isla took the glass from him with a hand that was visibly trembling. 'Rafe…be sensible about this. Marriage between us would never work.'

Lingerie waitress weds Sicilian hotel billionaire? How would she cope with the shame of her past splashed over every paper and news outlet?

'We will make it work for the sake of our child.' His jaw was set in an intractable line. 'How far along are you? Are you feeling well?' His tone softened a fraction, his eyes losing their hard glitter to be replaced by a shadow of concern. 'I'm sorry, I should have asked earlier.'

Isla put her glass down on a nearby table and then placed a hand on her small baby bump. 'I am now… I was more or less constantly sick for a couple of months. I'm five months into the pregnancy. I'm due around Christmas.'

His eyes went to where her hand was resting, his throat moving up and down over another swallow. He stepped closer, coming to stand in front of her. 'Can you feel the baby moving?'

'I started feeling it moving around the sixteen-week mark. Here—' She reached for his hand and laid it on the swell of her abdomen, watching his face as their baby gave tiny kicks. 'Can you feel it kicking? There—feel that?'

Rafe was standing so close she could see the dark and generous spray of stubble around his mouth and jaw. She could smell the sharp notes of citrus in his aftershave, redolent of sun-warmed lemons. She could feel the magnetic pull of his body making her ache to close the small distance to mesh her body to his—thigh to thigh, pelvis to pelvis. Why couldn't she be immune to him? Why did her body have to betray her? Could he sense the storm of hungry need he caused in her flesh? A need he had awakened.

His gaze softened in wonder as the baby moved against the press of his hand. 'That's amazing…' His voice became husky. 'Do you know the sex?'

'No. I didn't want to find out until the birth.'

The baby quietened and Rafe removed his hand and stepped back, his expression hardening once more. 'Were you *ever* going to tell me?' The note of accusation in his voice was sobering.

Isla moved to a little distance away so he wouldn't see how much she ached for him to hold her, to comfort her, to reassure her. *I was only trying to protect you.* The words were assembled like soldiers on the back of her tongue but she couldn't give the command for them to march forward. What good would it do? The less he knew about her reasons for not telling him the better. 'I decided it was better for both of us if I just quietly disappeared from your life.'

'*You* decided.' He spat the words out like bullets. 'You had no right to decide for *me*.' He thumped his fist against his chest for emphasis. 'I had a right to know I was to become a father. And my child has a right to know me. To have me in its life.' He swung away with a muttered curse, his hand scraping through the thickness of his hair so roughly she was surprised some of it didn't come out at the roots. He turned back and glared at her. 'For God's sake, Isla. Do you know how it feels for me to find out like this?'

Isla bit her lip, the tension in her head now feeling like needles poking into the back of her eyeballs. 'Look, I know it must be upsetting but—'

'Upsetting?' He gave a rough humourless laugh. 'Now that's an understatement. You denied me knowledge of my child. You planned to keep my child away from me indefinitely. Don't you think I have the right to be a little upset?'

Isla closed her eyes and pinched the bridge of her nose, trying to quell the stabbing pain behind her eyes. 'I was worried you would do exactly what you're doing. Barking commands at me as if I have no will of my own.' She dropped her hand from her face and sent him a defiant look. 'I will not marry you just because you insist on it. Lots of couples have babies together without marrying. And yes, even couples who are no longer together.'

His eyes clashed with hers in a battle she fought not to lose, but in the end, Isla was the first to look away. She couldn't cope with him when she was feeling so fragile. She couldn't cope with him, full stop. He was too commanding. Too directive. Too everything.

'You will marry me, Isla.' His voice had a steely thread that sent a chill rolling down her spine like a runaway ice cube. 'For, believe me, you might not like the alternative. If there were to be a custody battle between us, I can assure you I will win it.'

The pain behind Isla's eyes intensified to a piercing drill that felt like it was burrowing deep into her brain. *Oh, God. Oh, God. Oh, God.* He was threatening to take her baby off her once it was born? He would be able to do it too. It wouldn't take too much digging into her background to cast doubt on her suitability as a mother. Those topless photos she'd stupidly been talked into doing for her 'portfolio', for instance. Who would ever believe she hadn't done them willingly? That she had been duped into making those shamelessly provocative poses, never realising how they might come back to haunt her. The photos alone might not be enough in a court of law to take her baby off her, but the thought of having those lewd photos out in public, splashed over newspapers and gossip magazines, was too much to bear.

Rafe's veiled threat only confirmed why she hadn't told him she was pregnant in the first place. He could be coldly ruthless when he needed to be. How else had he accumulated the amount of wealth he owned?

Her vision became blurred and the room began to tilt and sway as if gravity had been removed. She reached out her hand for the nearest solid object to stabilise herself but misjudged the distance. Her hand patted at mid-air and then a tide of nausea swept over her in an icy wave that prickled her scalp and sent pins and needles to her fingertips.

'Isla?'

She was vaguely conscious of Rafe's concerned tone but she couldn't get her voice to do anything much past a mumble. And then she folded like a ragdoll and slumped to the floor and everything faded to black…

* * *

Rafe rushed to Isla's slumped figure on the floor, his heart thumping in dread. 'Isla? Are you okay?' He was shocked at her pallid complexion—shocked and shamed that he had caused her to drop down in a faint.

He put her in the recovery position and then took her pulse, finding it more or less normal. A tornado of guilt assailed him, hammering into him with the force of knockout blows. He brushed the hair back from her clammy forehead, willing her to open her eyes. 'Come on, *cara*. Talk to me.'

What sort of man had he become in the last hour? It was unforgivable to harangue a pregnant woman into a state of collapse. Sweat broke out over his own forehead, remorse like bitter bile in his mouth. He was disgusted with himself, furious he had been so intent on communicating his ire that he hadn't considered her mental and physical state. She was pregnant, for God's sake—with *his* child.

He realised with a jolt of remorse that he hadn't even asked her how she felt about being pregnant. Whether or not the news had pleased her or shocked her. Had she considered other options? He would not have criticised her for considering a termination. He would not have criticised her for having one because he firmly believed it was a woman's choice what she did with her body. But there was a place deep inside his heart that felt relieved she hadn't chosen that path. *He was going to be a father.* It was still hard to get his head around but the evidence had kicked against his hand only minutes ago. 'Come on, *mio piccolo*. Talk to me.'

Isla slowly opened her eyes and groaned. 'My head aches…'

Rafe gently placed his palm on her forehead. 'I'll call an ambulance. I need to get you to hospital.' He reached for his phone in his trouser pocket but she placed a hand on his arm.

'No, please don't. It's just a tension headache. I've been getting them now and again. I don't need to go to hospital… I think it's because my blood sugar is a bit low.'

He helped her into a sitting position, cradling her around the shoulders with his arm, his other hand gently stroking the red-gold curls of her hair off her forehead. 'When did you last have something to eat?'

She gave a weary-sounding sigh. 'I don't know…a few hours ago. I skipped lunch as I was running late and—'

'Right, well, that makes me all the more determined you're coming back with me to Italy,' Rafe said. 'You have to think about the baby. You can't go skipping meals and working long hours in a physically demanding job. Not when I can more than adequately provide for you.'

Isla gave him one of her combative looks but it didn't have its normal heat and fire. 'Must you be so bull-headed? I've told you I don't want to marry you.'

Rafe bit back a retort about her obeying his orders. He would raise the issue of marriage when she wasn't feeling so poorly. But he wasn't giving up. It wasn't in his nature to step back from a decision he'd made. He would never countenance walking away from his own flesh and blood. His own child. 'Let's leave the topic of marriage for later. For now, I'd like to see you with a bit more colour in your cheeks.' He brushed his fingers against the pale creaminess of her cheek. 'Do you think you can stand up? I'll help you to the bed so you can lie down for a bit. And I'll organise some food for you from Room Service.'

She looked like she was going to argue the point, but then sighed again and took hold of his proffered hand and he helped her into a standing position. She glanced up at him briefly, her teeth sinking into the fullness of her lower lip. 'I'm sorry for being such a nuisance...'

'Don't apologise,' Rafe said, leading her to the bed with his arm around her waist. 'I'm the one who should be apologising.'

Not just for upsetting her but for getting her pregnant. It took two to tango and how well they had tangoed. They had created a new life and it was up to him to make sure that new life was protected from now on. Protected and nurtured and provided for in every way a decent father could.

It still shocked him how slow he had been to realise Isla's condition. Why hadn't he noticed her slightly swollen tummy when he had first encountered her in his suite? Her uniform with its frilly apron had covered it reasonably well, so too the way she'd used towels and the trolley to hide her tell-tale shape. His only excuse for not noticing was that pregnancy had been the last thing on his mind when he'd found her in his room, standing next to his bed. He had been too intent on staring at her gorgeous mouth and breasts, recalling all the times he had sought pleasure from them.

Even now, with his arm around her waist, his body reacted to her closeness. Even the most casual touch produced a torrent of need within him. He had never experienced such fiery physical chemistry with anyone else. Her body fitted so perfectly against him as if they were two pieces of a complicated puzzle. He could smell the light flowery fragrance of her perfume and it evoked a host of memories—both good and bad. He had smelt that perfume for weeks in his villa after she'd left him. It had haunted him, tortured him.

Rafe helped Isla onto the bed and gently drew the cashmere throw rug over her curled up form. She looked so young and vulnerable and it sent another wave of guilt thrashing and crashing through him. Now was not the time for bitter recriminations and accusations. She clearly needed rest and better nutrition and it was up to him as her baby's father to provide it—regularly and consistently.

Her baby's father.

How strange to say those words. To have them applied to him. He had not thought of fatherhood in any detail before. It was something he'd thought he might look into one day in the future, but it certainly hadn't been on his to-do-soon list. His own father had not been the best role model, although in the early days his father had made Rafe feel special and loved. But then, at the age of thirteen, he'd found out that was nothing but a lie.

Rafe picked up the phone on the bedside table and ordered a nutritious meal and freshly squeezed fruit juice. Once the meal was ordered, he put the phone back in its cradle and sat on the edge of the bed next to Isla, taking one of her hands, and began stroking his thumb over the back of her hand. 'It shouldn't be too long. Do you want a mineral water or lemonade or something in the meantime?'

She opened her eyes and met his gaze. 'Why haven't you insisted on a paternity test?'

Rafe was ashamed to admit he had thought of doing exactly that, but something had stopped him. He wasn't one to hand out his trust too easily but, for some reason, he knew on a cellular level she was telling the truth. 'I figured I didn't need to confirm the baby is mine. You wouldn't have gone to so much trouble to avoid telling me if it was someone else's.'

Her gaze drifted to their joined hands, her teeth doing that lip-nibbling thing that always made him want to kiss her lip back into its soft, ripe shape. 'I won't stop you getting one if you want one.'

He gave her fingers a gentle squeeze. 'It won't be necessary.' He waited a beat before asking, 'When did you first suspect you were pregnant?'

'Just before you went to New York. I thought it was another stomach bug like in Paris, but then I realised I was a few days late…'

'It must have come as a shock.'

She glanced at him again, worry clouding her beautiful periwinkle-blue eyes. 'I was shocked and terrified. I didn't know what to do. Where to turn…'

If only she had turned to him. Why hadn't she? But he was reluctant to drill her with questions that might upset her in her current state. 'Did you consider…ending the pregnancy?'

She pulled her hand out of his as if his touch burned her. 'No. I'm sorry if you think I should've got rid of it but I couldn't. I have no problem with other women choosing that option but I didn't feel it was the right choice for me.'

Rafe took her hand again, holding it gently within his. 'I'm glad you didn't have a termination.' His voice came out rusty as he thought about the tiny life they had created. It felt surreal to be talking about a baby and yet it seemed the most natural thing in the world. Their baby. Created out of passion unlike any other he had experienced. It might not be love in the truest sense but surely it counted for something.

She looked at him with wide eyes. 'You are?'

Rafe stroked the back of her hand with his thumb. 'Like you, I believe it's a woman's choice what to do with her body but, while I can't deny I'm shocked at the news and still getting my head around becoming a father, I'm glad you chose to go ahead with the pregnancy. We will be good parents to our child, *cara*.'

A flicker of something passed through her gaze before it fell away from his. 'I'm sorry you found out the way you did.' Her forehead puckered in a frown. 'I should have told you at the beginning but I didn't feel I could take the risk.'

Rafe placed a finger over her lips to halt her speech. 'Hush now. You're supposed to be resting. What's done is done. It won't help either of us move forward if we keep rehashing the past. It's time to think of the future. The baby's future and ours.'

He lifted his finger from her petal-soft mouth, fighting to stop himself leaning down and covering her lips with his own. The fierce hunger he'd always felt for her was as stunning now as it had been in the beginning, when he had first locked gazes with her across a crowded bar. His blood heated to boiling, racing through his veins at rocket-force speed. He could feel the stirring of his groin—the hard swell of his flesh an erotic reminder of the heart-racing pleasure he had experienced so many times with her. Two months of phenomenal sex. Sizzling hot sex that he hadn't forgotten. He hadn't been able to erase it from his mind or his body. It had left echoes in his flesh he felt to this day. Being near her sent him into a frenzy of longing. It was all he could do to stop himself drawing her into his arms and reminding her of the red-hot passion they had shared.

But he had to ignore it. The baby was what mattered now. Rafe needed Isla to marry him so he could nurture and provide for their child. He just had to convince her to accept his proposal.

And convince her he would.

CHAPTER THREE

A SHORT TIME later Isla was propped up with pillows on Rafe's king-sized bed, the soft cashmere throw rug covering her legs, waiting for the meal he had ordered to arrive. The doorbell sounded in the suite and Rafe opened the door and the young male waiter—whom Isla had met once or twice in the staff quarters—brought in the Room Service silver service trolley. The waiter's brows rose when he saw Isla but, before she could explain why she was currently lying on a guest's bed, Rafe handed the young man a ridiculously generous tip and informed him that his fiancée would no longer be working for the hotel.

'But I haven't agreed to—' Isla began.

'Congratulations.' The young man beamed and pocketed the money. 'Thank you, sir. Much appreciated. I hope you enjoy your stay.'

'I'm already enjoying it immensely.' Rafe's tone contained a satirical note that set Isla's teeth on edge.

Once the waiter had gone, Isla glowered at Rafe as he bent over her to place the tray of delicious food across her lap. '*Fiancée?* Did you listen to a word I said before about not marrying you?'

Once the tray was secure across her lap, Rafe sat

on the edge of the bed beside her stretched out legs. 'I was only thinking of your reputation, *cara*. Do you want the staff of this hotel to gossip about the housemaid who leapt into bed with a guest? Becoming my fiancée offers you an element of respectability, does it not?'

He had made a good point but Isla didn't want to admit it. 'They'll gossip regardless. But that was your intention, wasn't it? Our supposed engagement will be all over the hotel and God knows how many social media platforms within minutes.'

'Good. It will save me making a formal announcement. Gossip works faster anyway.'

Isla ignored the food and kept glaring at him. 'I'm not going to be bullied into marrying you, Rafe. You might be used to getting your way in the business world but you won't get your way with me.'

One of his dark brows arched up and a glint appeared in his eyes. 'From memory, it only took me forty-two minutes to get you from the bar and into my bed the first day we met.'

Isla could feel the hot bloom of colour spreading across her cheeks. 'It won't happen again.'

He leaned closer to brush a lazy finger over the pool of pink in her cheek. 'Are you sure about that, *tesoro mio*? Remember how good we were together.' His low deep voice with its edge of huskiness was doing serious damage to her resolve. 'So explosive, *si*?'

Isla suppressed a shiver. She remembered all too well. She had never orgasmed with a partner before Rafe. She had not enjoyed sex the way it was meant to be enjoyed until his touch set her aflame. She wondered now if she would ever be able to make love with anyone else. The thought of doing it with anyone else made her flesh crawl. 'Look, I know you want to do the honourable thing and all that, but really, Rafe, marriage is going to ridiculous extremes. We can still co-parent without—'

'I want my child to have my name and my protection,' Rafe said. 'I want him or her to live under my roof so I can be involved in every aspect of its upbringing. Part-time parenthood is not an option.'

Isla pushed the tray away to the other side of the bed, her appetite completely deserting her. She swung her legs over the side of the bed and stood. 'I don't want to talk about it. Not now.' She moved over to the windows to stand with her back to him, her arms crossed over her chest. The sunshine had faded and a bank of ominous-looking clouds had drifted in from Arthur's Seat, making the dark fortress of Edinburgh Castle look all the more forbidding.

'Will you at least come back to Sicily with me? Think of it as a holiday. Let me take care of you and the baby and then you can make your final decision in a few weeks.' Rafe's voice had lost its commanding edge and it made it so much harder for her to think of a valid reason why she shouldn't go with him.

What did she have to lose by going with him? Just for a week or two until she began to feel a little stronger. Life had been a constant struggle since she'd left him. It had been hard trying to work and cope with gruelling nausea and the fatigue common in early pregnancy. If it hadn't been for her friend Layla helping her out with casual cleaning work at this hotel, Isla didn't know what she would have done. It wasn't as if she had a family network to call on to support her.

There was no one.

Or at least no one she *wanted* looking after her.

Isla turned to meet his gaze with her sceptical one. 'But will you accept my final decision?'

His expression gave no clue to what he was thinking or feeling. 'I will respect your decision once I am sure you're in the right frame of mind and healthy enough to make it.' He rose from the edge of the bed and picked up the tray and placed it on a nearby table. 'Now, eat this meal while I make the arrangements. We will leave tomorrow. Don't worry about packing—most of your things are still at my villa.'

Isla frowned. 'But…but why?'

'You didn't leave a return address. I decided to wait until I heard from you.'

'You weren't tempted to throw them all out?'

He gave her a wry smile. 'Oh, I was tempted. But I thought it would be much more satisfying to have you pick them up in person.'

Isla woke from a deep and refreshing nap to find herself alone in the penthouse. She got off the bed and stretched, feeling immensely relieved that all remnants of her headache had gone. For a moment she wondered if she should leave the hotel while she had the chance. Disappear before things got even more complicated. Remove herself from the temptation of Rafe's company. The temptation of his touch. But was running away again going to change anything? She was having his baby and he had a right to be involved in its upbringing. He had expressed a desire to be involved and she had to honour that.

But going to Sicily with him was a big step. A dangerous step, but the thought of continuing to work in a job she wasn't truly cut out for made her feel even more conflicted than spending a couple of weeks at Rafe's villa. Besides, she knew Layla had only given her the part-time work as a personal favour. She wouldn't be able to continue working much longer into the pregnancy anyway.

Isla fished her phone out of her tote bag and dialled Layla's number and briefly explained the situation.

'Seriously? You're going back to Sicily with him?' Layla's voice rose in shock. 'But I thought you said you never wanted to see him again?'

Isla sighed. 'Yes, well, it seems I might have misjudged him a bit. He sounds really keen about the baby and is insisting on marrying me. Not that I've agreed to it or anything. How could I, given the difference in our backgrounds?'

'Marriage? Gosh, that's a bit extreme, isn't it?' Layla said.

'Those were exactly my words,' Isla said. 'He doesn't love me and the last thing I want to do is marry someone who doesn't love me. But I'm only going with him to Sicily for a short holiday. I figure I owe him that at the very least.'

'But your background might not be an issue for him. Have you thought of telling him about it? About the photos too?'

'I can't do either. I can't risk him looking at me like I'm something he wants to scrape off the bottom of his handmade Italian leather shoes.'

'Mmm, I hear you.' Layla sighed. 'But what if he

doesn't? What if he doesn't care what happened in your past? You were with him two months without anyone finding out. Why would marrying him be any different?'

'We flew under the radar when it was just a fling,' Isla said. 'Can you imagine what press interest an announcement of our engagement would bring? He's one of Italy's most eligible bachelors. Everyone, and I mean everyone, will want to know everything they can about the woman he chooses as his bride.'

'But is it wise to go to Sicily with him? I mean, you seem to have zero willpower when it comes to that man. He was your first and only one-night stand, remember? You. The girl who has to date someone like five times before you even think about kissing them, let alone sleeping with them.'

Isla was glad their phone call wasn't a video one as she could feel heat creeping into her cheeks. 'That's rich coming from the girl who doesn't even go as far as kissing a man before she rejects him out of hand.'

'You know my reasons for that,' Layla said. 'You've seen my limp and the scars on my leg. Men today have such weak stomachs.'

'One day you'll meet a man who doesn't even notice your limp and scars.'

Layla snorted. 'I stopped believing in fairy tales a long time ago. Anyway, we're not talking about me. We're talking about you. I'm worried you're going to get hurt all over again.'

'I know what I'm doing this time around. I'm not going to do anything rash.'

'Maybe on some level you do love him but don't want to admit it.'

Her feelings about Rafe were confusing to say the

least. She wouldn't go as far as saying she was in love with him, but neither could she understand why her attraction to him was so powerful and irresistible. 'I'm not in love with him. In lust, maybe, but that's not enough to build a marriage on.'

'I don't know about that,' Layla said. 'It's a damn good start. Besides, a marriage of convenience can often turn into something else. It happens.'

'I thought you stopped reading fairy tales?'

'Touché,' Layla said with a little laugh. 'But seriously, Isla, you should give it some thought. You've made a baby together. It would be wonderful to be able to bring up the baby in a stable and secure home, unlike what we had growing up. And you could do a lot worse than Rafael Angeliri.'

'I know, but it's a big step and I need more time to think about it.'

Rafe had come crashing back into her life, making her feel things she didn't want to feel. The closer she got to him, the more dangerous it became. Lust often masqueraded as love and vice versa. Loving someone was too dangerous. It gave them the power to hurt you. To leave you. To reject you. She couldn't allow herself to experience the emotional devastation of her childhood all over again.

'Does he want to sleep with you?' Layla asked. 'I mean, did you get that vibe?'

'He's a hot-blooded thirty-five-year-old man. Of course, I got that vibe, but I'm going to do my best to resist him.'

'Good luck with that.'

Isla had a feeling she was going to need more than luck. She was going to need a flipping miracle.

* * *

When Rafe came back to the penthouse, Isla was standing looking out at the view of Edinburgh Castle and the Princes Street Gardens below. She turned when he came in but it was hard to read her expression.

'Weren't you worried I might do a runner?' she asked.

He shrugged one shoulder. 'I would have found you without too much trouble. Hotel management have your address.' He held up the small travel bag he was carrying. 'I took the liberty of going to your flat and picking up a few of your things. Your landlady was most obliging when I told her we are a couple.'

Her eyebrows snapped together in a frown. 'You did *what*?' Her hands balled into fists at her sides. 'You had no right to—'

'As your baby's father, I have the right to make sure your health and safety is my top priority,' Rafe said, placing the bag on the luggage rack. 'I've arranged a flight in the morning. You can spend the night here with me.'

'I'm not sleeping in that bed with you.' Her voice vibrated with fury and her eyes flashed blue streaks of lightning. 'You can't make me.'

'As much as I would love to prove you wrong, *cara*, on this occasion I will gladly relinquish my place in the bed and sleep on the sofa. You need your rest before we travel tomorrow.'

She continued to glower at him like her eyes were heat lamps. 'I want to make something perfectly clear. I'm only going to Sicily with you to rest and recuperate. Not to resume our…our fling.'

'Fine, but you will need to share my bed at my villa

because I don't want my staff speculating on our relationship,' Rafe said. 'You will be there as my fiancée. That is one thing I will not compromise on. You are no longer a casual lover. You are the mother of my soon-to-be-born child.'

Her shoulders stiffened and her lips flattened. 'You think I won't be able to help myself, don't you? You think once I lie down next to you I'll be crawling all over you begging you to make love to me.'

That was exactly what Rafe thought. Trouble was, he was exactly the same. She might pretend to be immune to him but he knew her too well to buy it. And as for his own immunity to her? He had none. He was as aware of her as he had ever been—maybe even more so. 'The decision as to whether or not we resume our physical relationship will be entirely up to you.'

She spun away so her back was towards him, her arms wrapped around her body. 'How many lovers have you had since I left? Or have you lost count?' Her voice had a hoarse quality as if the question had come out against her will.

Rafe didn't see any reason to lie. 'None.'

Isla swung back around to face him, her expression etched in puzzlement. 'None? But I saw pictures of you with…' Her words and her gaze dropped away, her teeth savaging her lower lip.

He gave a rueful smile. 'I went on dates, yes. But I didn't sleep with anyone.'

Her gaze crept back up to meet his. 'But why not?'

'It didn't feel appropriate until I worked out what went wrong with us.'

A frown crinkled her smooth forehead like tiny creases in silk. 'But you've had plenty of breakups before ours. Do you normally take a time-out between flings to reflect on what went wrong?'

'Not usually, but then again I'm normally the one to end a fling and I always know exactly why I've ended it.' Mostly out of boredom and disinterest. The novelty and excitement having worn off. But it hadn't with Isla. Not one little bit.

A spark of her old feistiness lit her gaze. 'So that rankled, did it? That I got in first.'

It rankled far more than Rafe cared to admit. 'If it hadn't been for the pregnancy, would you have ended our fling when you did?'

Her eyes drifted out of reach of his and her hands made a business of straightening her clothes over her body. 'Your track record isn't great with relationships, Rafe. But then, nor is mine. We would have bored each other sooner rather than later.'

'You didn't show any signs of boredom. I haven't had a more enthusiastic lover.'

Her cheeks were tinged with a delicate shade of pink. 'It was just sex.'

'Was it?' Rafe had had plenty of 'just sex' and it had felt nothing like what they had shared during those passionate two months.

Isla moved a little further away as if she didn't trust herself around him. Rafe didn't trust himself either and had to keep a firm lid on his self-control, because all he wanted to do was prove to her how good they were together. To remind her of the scorching-hot passion that flowed so naturally between them. He could feel the pulse of it now. The crackling energy in the air tightening the atmosphere.

She flicked him a cutting glance, raising her chin in

an imperious fashion. 'You only want me now because you can't have me. I've become a challenge to you.'

'And you're only resisting because we both know if I came over there and kissed you I would have you on that bed and naked within two minutes flat.'

Her gaze stayed locked on his but he could see the effort it cost her. Her body gave a tiny shudder as if she was remembering every time they had landed on a bed in a hot tangle of naked limbs. 'Don't even think about it.' Her voice sounded breathless and uneven. Her gaze slipped to his mouth, as if mentally recalling how it felt to have his lips crushed to hers.

Rafe was desperately trying not to think about it. He was getting hot and hard being in the same room as her. He had never kissed a more responsive mouth. He could still recall the pillow softness of her lips against his, the sweet milky vanilla and honey taste of her mouth, the heat and fire of her playful tongue.

Before he could stop himself, he closed the distance in slow measured strides, giving her plenty of time to move away if she wanted to. But she stayed statue-still, the ink-black circles of her pupils flaring the closer he got. Her slim throat moving up and down over a swallow, her tongue snaking out to moisten her lips. He took a handful of her luxuriant red-gold hair, watching as she momentarily closed her eyes like a cat anticipating the next sensual stroke of its master's hand. 'Tell me you don't like me touching you like this, *tesoro*.' He traced the outline of her mouth with a lazy fingertip, delighting in the way her lips parted with a soft gasp of need.

She placed her hands flat against his chest, her touch as searing as a brand, and he had to fight not to haul her closer to imprint his body on hers from pelvis to pelvis. Her fingers curled into the fabric of his shirt and she moved a fraction nearer as if compelled by a force outside of her control. The same force that was drawing his body to her like a metal filing to a magnet. He sucked in a breath as her hips came into contact with his. The blood surging to his groin, swelling, stiffening, extending. How he had missed her! Missed the feel of her supple body against him, responding to him, needing him as much as he needed her. The feverish desire rippled through him in hot waves, shooting electrifying darts around his body. He slid a hand to the base of her spine, the lush curves of her bottom so close to the edge of his hand it made it tingle. He couldn't take his eyes off her mouth. Her lips were naturally cherry-red, the top lip as full as the lower one and pushed up slightly in a cupid's bow.

'If you kiss me it will only complicate things...' Her voice was just shy of a whisper.

Rafe slid his other hand along the creamy curve of her cheek, her skin petal-soft against his palm. The need was thrumming deeply inside him like the background hum of a microwave. 'That doesn't sound like a no. I want to hear you say it. Tell me you don't want me to kiss you.'

Her eyes were luminous, shining with the same need he could feel barrelling through his body. 'Why are you doing this?' Her eyes flicked from his mouth to his gaze and back again.

Because I still want you. Rafe's hand moved in a slow glide from the base of her spine to the back of her head, sinking into the silky softness of her cloud of curls, his fingers massaging her scalp the way she had loved so much in the past. 'What am I doing, *cara*? Hmm?'

'You're making me want you.'

'And that's a bad thing?' Rafe asked, meshing his gaze with hers, his body so hard with need it made thinking difficult. He was going on instinct—primal instinct that drove his blood through his veins at breakneck speed. Swelling his tissues into a hotbed of longing that called on every bit of willpower he possessed to keep in control. Had he ever wanted a woman more than Isla? It was like a tornado in his body, rampaging through him until he could think of nothing but sinking, plunging into her tight wet warmth.

She pressed her lips together so firmly they went from red to white. But as soon as she released them they flooded with blood and he ached to cover them with his own. 'I've spent the last three months trying to forget about you, Rafe.'

Rafe sent a finger along the underside of her cheek to the base of her chin. 'Were you successful?'

Her eyelashes came down to half-mast, her hands leaving the front of his shirt to pull his head down so his mouth was within a breath of hers. 'No. Damn you. Not at all.'

He had dreamed of this moment for the last three empty and lonely months. It was all the invitation he needed. He closed the distance between their mouths and let the fireworks begin.

Isla had told herself she was prepared for Rafe to kiss her. He'd kissed her so many times before so she should have known what to expect. But as soon as his mouth came down on hers an explosion erupted in her body. Desires and needs she had almost forgotten about leapt to life like embers stirred into dancing flames and shooting and darting sparks. His lips moved against hers in a drugging kiss, slow and sensual, his hard lower body pressed against hers in such an erotic contact it made her legs unsteady. Electric pulses shot from her mouth to her pelvis, his masterful kiss tingling every cell of her flesh into throbbing life.

He deepened the kiss with a commanding stroke of his tongue against the seam of her mouth, and she opened to him like a flower opening to the first hot blast of spring sunshine. How had she survived months without this magical madness rushing through her body? How had she survived the feel of his arms around her body, holding her as if he never wanted to let her go? She wound her arms around his neck, desperate to keep his mouth clamped to hers. Desperate to feel alive again. Desperate to feel the storm of ferocious attraction pounding from his mouth to hers.

No one kissed her like Rafe did. His kiss was like a potent drug she had lived too long without. Now she had tasted his lips again, she was addicted all over again. Powerfully, dangerously addicted. His lips continued their sensual exploration, his tongue dancing with hers with such exquisite and mesmerising choreography it caused a swooping sensation in her stomach. Isla pressed herself closer, more than a little shocked at the sounds of pleasure and encouragement she was making but unable to stop herself. She wanted this. She wanted *him*. She had never stopped wanting him.

His hand came up to cradle one side of her face, the other pressing in the small of her back, holding her close against his growing erection. Feeling the extension of his body, his unmistakable desire for her, feeling *him*, ramped up her own need until she was practically grinding her pelvis against him to get closer.

His hand slid up to her hair, his fingers splayed at first and then clutching at the strands with just the right amount of tension. The sort of tension that made every hair on her head shiver at the roots, every cell in her body shudder in reaction and her self-control roll over and play dead. How could she resist this man? How could she resist the feelings he and he alone evoked in her? Passion hot and strong and irresistible. Passion that made her forget about everything but the biological need of their bodies. The passionate need to unite their bodies in the most primal way of all to trigger a tumultuous storm of blissful release.

Suddenly the kiss was over.

Rafe pulled away from her as if a director on a movie set had suddenly called 'cut'. His expression was masked, although his eyes were bright and his pupils wide as bottomless black pools. 'So, at least that's something that hasn't changed.' The was a note of triumph in his voice that made her wish she hadn't been so responsive. So transparent. So wanton. *Again*. Why did she have zero resistance to him? Why?

Isla moved a few steps away, swishing her hair over one shoulder in a gesture of nonchalance she was nowhere near feeling. 'What time are we leaving tomorrow?' A subject change was her only way of restoring some of her dignity. She couldn't help feeling he had engineered that little kissing session to prove he had the upper hand when it came to self-control. But hadn't she always been out of her league where he was concerned? He was sophisticated and suave and she was riddled with shameful secrets.

'Mid-morning. I've allowed some time for you to sleep in.'

She sent him a spearing glance. 'Alone?'

A dark gleam entered his gaze. 'I will leave that up to you to decide.'

CHAPTER FOUR

ISLA WOKE EARLY the next morning to find the space beside her in the bed hadn't been slept in. The sheets were smooth and crease-free, the pillows showing no indentation of Rafe's head ever having rested there. Had he gone out? She had been so tired she hadn't registered any sound of him coming or going in the suite once she'd closed her eyes the night before.

She got out of bed and padded out to the sitting room of the suite and found Rafe asleep in one of the sofa chairs, his long legs stretched out in front of him and crossed at the ankles. He looked a bit worse for wear—his shirt was open to the middle of his chest and crumpled and half out of one side of his trousers. His jaw was richly peppered with dark regrowth and his hair was tousled as if his hands had gone through it a few times. There was a book, open and face down on the floor, as if it had tumbled from his lap while he had drifted off to sleep.

Isla was reluctant to disturb him but she felt a twinge of guilt that he had spent the night sleeping in a chair rather than share the bed with her. His gallantry was not only unexpected but strangely touching.

He suddenly opened his eyes as if he sensed her

looking at him. He uncrossed his ankles and pulled his legs back closer to the chair and ran a hand over his face, the sound of his palm moving across his stubble loud in the silence.

'How did you sleep?' He smothered a yawn and stood and stretched his lower back by placing his hands on his hips and leaning backwards slightly, not quite disguising a wince.

'Clearly a bit better than you,' Isla said. 'Why didn't you come to bed?'

He dropped his hands back by his sides and gave her a rueful smile that made something in her chest ping. 'I didn't trust myself to keep my hands off you.'

Isla felt betraying warmth spreading through her cheeks so bent to pick up his book rather than encounter his gaze. She hadn't trusted herself not to drift into old habits—reaching for him in the middle of the night, snuggling up against his back, her arms around his waist, her legs entangling with his. Her hands exploring his... She snapped the book closed and placed it on the nearest surface. 'I'm sorry you had such an uncomfortable night. I was so tired I probably wouldn't have noticed if you had joined me.'

'Wouldn't you?' His eyes met hers in a challenging lock that made her inner core contract.

The silence seemed to buzz with a host of erotic memories.

Isla couldn't stop her gaze from drifting to his mouth, her tongue sneaking out to moisten her suddenly parchment-dry lips. She was aware of him following the betraying movement, his eyes darkly hooded, the subtle change in his breathing signalling his own attraction. She brought her gaze back up to his. 'You don't strike me as the sort of man to touch a woman when she's expressly told you not to.' Her tone fell a little short of starchy schoolmistress and leaned more towards *I want you to kiss me.*

Rafe came over to her and tucked a wayward cork-screw curl back behind her ear. His touch was light and tender and it made every cell in her body cry out for more. He knew all her pleasure spots, all her erogenous zones, all her vulnerabilities. All her needs. And how pathetic her self-control. 'I would find it a lot easier not to touch you if I didn't think you wanted me. But you do, don't you, *cara*? You haven't forgotten how good we were together, *sì*?'

His hand cupped her cheek as if he were cradling a ripe peach he was trying not to bruise, his thumb moving back and forth in a slow caress. Isla couldn't disguise her delicate shiver of reaction in time. She placed her hand on his wrist, fully intending to push him away, but instead her fingers curled around the tanned strength of his arm. His skin was warm and the black masculine hairs on his wrist tickled against her skin. His eyes were as dark and mysterious as a deep forest, flecks of leaf litter brown and lichen green fringed with ink-black lashes framed by prominent eyebrows above.

'This is like a game to you, isn't it?' Her voice didn't come out quite as reproving as she would have liked.

'The fact that you're carrying my child is not a game to me, Isla.' His tone had a deep note of gravitas and a frown pulled at his forehead. 'Nor is the fact that we still feel something for each other.'

This time she managed to summon enough will-power to step back from him. She folded her arms across her body, sending him a cool stare. 'If I wasn't pregnant and we'd run into each other again, would you have offered me what you're offering now?'

Something flickered at the back of his gaze. He gave a rough-edged sigh and pushed a hand through the thickness of his hair. 'An affair maybe, but probably not marriage.'

'So, I was fling material but not wife material.' Isla didn't say it as a question but as a statement. A confirmation of all she believed about herself. Beliefs that had been reinforced throughout her childhood.

You're not good enough.

'Marriage wasn't something I was actively seeking,' Rafe said. 'But things are different now.'

'But I'm not different. I'm the same person I was five months ago.'

His eyes cruised over her abdomen. 'Not quite the same, *mio piccolo*. You are pregnant with my child. That is a game-changer.'

A few hours later, they arrived at Rafe's Liberty style villa situated in the borough of Mondello in Sicily, the site of a popular white sand beach. In spite of her travel weariness and conflicted feelings about coming with Rafe to his home, Isla couldn't help feeling thrilled to be back where she had spent some of the happiest weeks of her life. Their time together here had shown her a world she had never been part of before. A world she had barely realised existed. Not just the glamour and riches he took for granted, but the sensual world of his lovemaking. She had spent her days sketching and painting or exploring the sites while Rafe worked, and then in the evenings he had devoted his entire attention to her. And the last couple of weeks Rafe hadn't worked at all. He'd cancelled all his engagements and spent the whole time with her. No one had ever made her feel so special, so desired, so fulfilled.

However, the sensual idyll had been slightly tainted for her by the presence of Rafe's housekeeper, Concetta. Isla had never been able to relate to the older woman, who seemed to wear a perpetual frown of disapproval but, interestingly, only when Rafe wasn't around. Isla found her sly and surly and sneering but Rafe would never hear a bad word about her. Isla had tried to talk to him a couple of times about his housekeeper's behaviour towards her but he'd always laughed off her concerns and told her Concetta was old-school Sicilian—a little guarded and formal with newcomers. On reflection, Isla wondered if he couldn't be bothered back then to do anything about Concetta's behaviour because he knew his relationship with her had an end point, as all his relationships had in the past.

How would the housekeeper take the news of Isla's pregnancy? Had Rafe told her? And how would she react to the news of Rafe's intention to marry the mother of his child?

'Do you still have Concetta working for you?' Isla asked once they had entered the refreshingly cool foyer of the villa.

'*Sì*, I am still here. He hasn't fired me yet but who knows?' the housekeeper said, approaching from further inside the villa. Concetta was a spritely woman in her late fifties who moved as quickly and efficiently as her acerbic tongue. She had black button eyes and weathered features and wiry salt and pepper hair pulled back tightly into a bun at the back of her head. Isla had

never seen a hair out of place on the housekeeper's head
and suspected not one strand would dare to escape its
rigid confines. Concetta was dressed all in black and
her deep frown reminded Isla of a pernickety schoolmistress about to dress down a recalcitrant pupil. And
eagerly looking forward to it.

'It's nice to see you again,' Isla said, trying to inject
some authenticity into her tone.

'Hmph.' Concetta swept her gaze over Isla's swollen belly, her thin lips pursing. She swung her gaze to
Rafe. 'Are you sure it's yours?'

Rafe's mouth tightened and he spoke to the housekeeper in a rich Sicilian dialect that Isla couldn't understand. But the message was loud and clear, for Concetta
raised her eyebrows and, with another insolent flash of
her gaze at Isla, turned and stalked out in the direction
of the kitchen, further inside the villa. Even the sound
of her retreating footsteps seemed to contain an insulting rhythm. I. Will. Get. You. For. This.

'I'm sorry,' Rafe said, turning back to Isla. 'Concetta can be a bit difficult but she'll soften up over time.
Our news has been a shock to her, that's all.'

Isla arched a sceptical eyebrow. 'And you want to
marry me? Seriously? I can't see her accepting me as
your wife any time soon. She's never liked me. Not that
you listened when I tried to tell you how awful she was
to me at times. I can only imagine what juicy insults
she'll save for me when you're not around.'

His expression hardened and he closed the front
door with a definitive *clunk*. 'She will have to accept
you or find some other employment.'

Isla folded her arms and cocked her head. 'Tell me
something... Was she rude to all your other lovers?

No wonder your relationships only lasted a matter of a week or two.'

Rafe's gaze shifted away and he shrugged off his lightweight jacket and hung it on a black wrought iron coat stand. 'I haven't brought anyone here before you. I mostly hooked up when I was away on business. It made it less…complicated.'

Isla stared at him in shock. 'What? No one? No one at all?'

He turned with an unreadable expression on his face. 'This is my home. My private sanctuary. I don't like sharing it with strangers.'

'Nor, apparently, does your housekeeper.' Isla's tone was deliberately wry to disguise how unsettled she was by his revelation about his past. What did it mean? Why had he brought *her* here? What had it been about her that had made him relax his rules and have her stay for almost two months as his live-in lover?

An enigmatic smile suddenly tilted one side of his mouth. 'I know what you're thinking.'

Isla did her best to keep her expression neutral. 'Oh? Do tell.'

He came to stand in front of her, close enough to tuck a wayward curl back behind her ear. His touch sent a wave of shuddery longing through her and it was all she could do to stand there as still as one of the marble statues in the grand foyer. His hazel eyes roamed her features, lingering for a pulsing moment on her mouth. The atmosphere became charged with electricity—a pulsing energy that made every pore of her skin lift in heightened awareness.

'You're wondering why I brought you here, *si*? Why you and no one else.' His voice was low and deep, a gravel and honey combo that made the base of her spine tingle like fine sand was trickling between her vertebrae.

Isla glanced at his mouth and disguised a swallow. His fingers found another tendril of hair but this time he wound it around his finger, gently tethering her to him. A silken bond that made her scalp prickle with delight and her inner core tug and tighten.

'I know one thing for sure—it wasn't because you fell madly in love with me.' She aimed for a light tone but somehow ended up sounding bitter.

A small frown tugged at his forehead and he slowly unwound her hair from his finger, tucking it behind her ear as he had done previously. 'No. It wasn't that... But then you weren't in love with me, or has that changed in the last few months?'

Isla screened her expression with cool indifference. An indifference she was not so sure she felt. Had ever felt. She wouldn't go as far as saying she was in love with him—it was too threatening to lower her guard to that degree. Loving someone gave them the power to hurt you and hadn't she been hurt enough? 'Of course not. No offence or anything. I'm sure plenty of women before me have fallen deeply in love with you and paid the price for doing so.'

His eyes moved back and forth between each of hers as if looking for something screened behind her gaze. 'One of the reasons I brought you here was to avoid the press. I wanted to enjoy being with you without a bunch of cameras following us all the time.'

'And the other reason?'

He gave another mercurial half-smile. 'Put it down to a moment of weakness on my part.' He stepped back from her and picked up her bag he'd brought in earlier. 'You should rest for a bit. It's been a long day.'

Isla followed him to the master bedroom, a strange sense of déjà vu assailing her as she entered the suite. She could recall in intricate detail the first time she had come into this bedroom with him. And the explosive passion they had shared on that massive bed moments later. She sent Rafe a surreptitious glance to see if he was showing any signs of being affected by memories of the past but his expression was inscrutable. So impersonally inscrutable he could have been a butler showing a low-status houseguest to their room.

The room contained the light but intoxicating citrus notes of his aftershave and the smell of freshly laundered bedlinen. The windows overlooking the estate were open, the sheer silk curtains billowing like sails.

'Are you cold? I can close these if you'd like.' Rafe gestured to the windows.

'I'm fine. Leave them open. It's nice to have some fresh air after being on the plane.' Isla placed her tote bag on a velvet chair, doing her best to keep her eyes away from the bed.

'I'll get Concetta to bring you up some refreshment.'

She swung back around to look at him. 'Please don't. I'd… I'd like to be alone for a while.' Her gaze fell away and she bit down on her lower lip. The last thing she needed right now was a hail of insults from Rafe's unfriendly housekeeper. Her emotions were all over the place as it was. Coming back here had stirred them into a writhing nest of anguish.

She was uncertain of how she should handle Rafe's proposal. Uncertain of her place in his life, even if she *had* a place in his life other than as the mother of his child. A child he might well be able to take off her if he put his mind to it. She didn't belong in his world and coming back here only reinforced it. She was a fish so far out of the safety of water she was choking, gasping. It would be foolish of her to let her guard down. She had let her guard down in the past and ended up bitterly disappointed each and every time. After her mother died, she'd hoped her father would claim her but he had handed her back into the foster system as soon as he could. Then there was the disappointment of family after family showing an interest in her, meetings arranged and then suddenly cancelled. Her hopes shattered time and time again. Even her past two boyfriends—men she'd thought she had a future with— had dumped her without ceremony.

Was she cursed always to have people leave her?

Rafe came over to her and took both her hands in his. His gaze softened and his hands gently squeezed hers. 'Are you feeling unwell? Nauseous?'

Isla kept her gaze averted, looking instead at her hands encased in the warm strong shelter of his. 'No. Just…tired.' Overwhelmed. Out of place. Worried. Vulnerable.

He nudged up her chin with his finger to mesh his gaze with hers. 'I know this is a big step for you, coming back here with me. But we have to focus on what's best for the baby. *Our* baby.'

Isla slipped out of his hold and put some distance between them, her arms going around her middle. 'Your housekeeper doesn't even think it is your baby.'

Rafe let out a rough-edged sigh and rubbed a hand over his face. 'Do you want me to get rid of her? Is that what you want? To dismiss her and find someone else? Concetta has only ever worked for me. Her life hasn't been easy. She was married to a brute of a man who left her penniless after she finally worked up the courage to leave him. She has no other skills.'

There was a part of Isla that wanted exactly that— for him to terminate the housekeeper's employment right then and there. But there was another part of her that knew how it felt to be dismissed from a much-needed job for speaking her mind too freely. Knew how it felt to be let go. Dismissed. Rejected. 'No. That's not what I want,' Isla said, turning her back to him. 'I can stand up for myself. I've had to do it most of my life. God knows no one else was going to do it for me.'

Rafe came up behind her and placed his hands on the tops of her shoulders and turned her to face him. His expression was etched in a frown. 'What was your family's reaction to the news of your pregnancy? Were they happy for you?'

Ah, the sticky web we weave...

Isla went to duck out of his hold but his grip tightened on her shoulders.

'No,' he said, his frown deepening. 'Don't run away. Talk to me.'

Isla couldn't meet his gaze and focused on the tanned column of his throat instead. 'I don't have a family. My mother died of alcohol poisoning when I was seven. I was handed to my father, who'd been divorced from my mother since I was five, but he didn't keep me for long. I spent the rest of my childhood in foster care.'

The sound of Rafe's sharply indrawn breath brought

her gaze back up to his. 'Why didn't you tell me before?' he asked. 'Why give me the impression you had a normal childhood?'

This time Isla was successful in extricating herself from his hold. She cupped her elbows in her crossed over hands, keeping her expression guarded. 'Because it was easier than explaining. You didn't talk about your family either and I was okay with that. We were having a fling, Rafe. Not promising to share our lives for ever.'

'Was anything you told me about yourself true? Anything at all?'

Isla sat on the end of the bed before her legs gave way out of sheer exhaustion. Emotional exhaustion more than anything. The only person who knew about her childhood was her friend Layla because they had met in foster care. But Layla had been lucky enough to be claimed by her great-aunt, who took her to live with her at her place of employment as housekeeper for a wealthy Scottish family. 'I'm sorry but I don't like talking about my background. I try to forget it as much as possible.'

He came to hunker down in front of her, one of his hands coming to rest on her knee. 'What did you think I was going to say if you had told me?'

Isla affected a light ironic laugh. 'I can tell you one thing—you wouldn't have invited me back here to live with you for two months. You date supermodels and starlets, not girls from a Scottish slum.'

His eyes searched hers for a moment. 'You seriously think I wouldn't have become involved with you because of your background? You think I'm that much of a snob?'

Isla inched up her chin, pride her only reliable armour. 'Why would you? We have nothing in common. You grew up with money. I grew up in poverty. You have a mother and a father and siblings. I have no one.'

A shadow of something passed over his face and he got to his feet like he had suddenly morphed into a tired old man. He pushed a hand through his hair, leaving deep finger comb marks. It seemed an age before he spoke.

'My father's wife is not my mother. And my brothers are only half-siblings. My mother died when I was fourteen. She was my father's mistress.'

Isla's eyes rounded. 'But everything I've read in the press about your background—'

'Was fabricated by my father to whitewash his reputation,' Rafe said with an unmistakable note of bitterness in his tone. 'He kept his two lives separate until he had an almost fatal car accident when I was thirteen. We didn't question why he was always travelling for business—it was his job. He provided for us, took us on nice holidays, showered us with gifts. We didn't even question why he couldn't spend Christmas with us every year. There was always a crisis he had to attend to, staffing problems or whatever that only he could fix. When it looked like he might not make it through the night, someone from his company phoned my mother and we rushed to the hospital to find him surrounded by his family. His first family. His *official* family.'

Isla rose from the bed and went to him, touching him on the forearm. 'It must have been awful finding out like that.'

'It was.' The two words were as sharp and brutal as slash marks on tender flesh.

Her arm fell away from his. 'You said your mother died when you were fourteen. Did you live with your father and his...other family after that?'

A cruel smile twisted his mouth. 'No. I was sent to boarding school. In England. Far enough away so I didn't disturb my father's happy little nest.'

'It can't have been too happy a nest if your father felt the need to have a mistress for all those years,' Isla said, frowning.

'My father's wife came from money. Lots of money. A divorce was out of the question. She gave him an ultimatum once he recovered from the accident—ditch his mistress and keep his distance from me. So he did.'

'What? He dumped you both just like that?' Isla snapped her fingers for effect.

Rafe's eyes were as hard and cold as marble. 'His company would have collapsed without Elena's steady injection of funds. Money was always going to win over sentiment with my father.'

'Have you any contact with him now?'

'Minimal.' Rafe straightened one of the original artworks on the wall with a minuscule adjustment. He turned to look at her and added, 'It's funny, but my father and his wife find it far less distasteful to include me in their happy family game now I have become one of the wealthiest men in Sicily.'

'I don't know how you can have anything to do with them after the way you and your mum were treated,' Isla said.

'My half-brothers are decent men. It's not their fault our father is a weak man whose primary motivation is greed.'

'But you loved him once? Your father, I mean.'

Rafe's mouth turned down at the corners and another shadow passed over his face. 'I idolised him. He was my hero, the person I most looked up to. For years I modelled myself on him.' He made a harsh sound of disgust at the back of his throat. 'But everything he told me was lies.'

And Isla had done the same. Guilt crawled over her like a spreading stain and she could feel its hot colour blooming in her cheeks. She had lied by omission rather than blatantly telling mistruths. She was still doing it, withholding information—for how could she tell him about the photos? The shameful shots of her in that gentleman's bar. Her young nubile body flagrantly exposed. Photos that would be circulated for large sums of money if she were ever to marry Rafe. She knew how much he hated the intrusion of the press. Trailer trash to marry one of Sicily's richest men? Of course, it would cause a storm of avid interest. Rafe's housekeeper wouldn't be the only person in his life who would be throwing nasty insults at her—the whole world would do so.

'I'm sorry you've had such a difficult time,' Isla said. 'But you must feel some sense of satisfaction that you made it on your own?'

A fleeting smile touched his mouth. 'Like you, *si*?'

She gave one of her pretend laughs. 'I've hardly made it, Rafe. I haven't touched a paintbrush in three months.'

'Then we will have to do something about that. I have organised for us to visit my grandmother in a couple of days. She lives in Marsala, about eighty kilometres from here.'

'You didn't mention anything about her when I was here last. Why?'

His expression became shuttered. 'My *nonna* is old-school, like Concetta. She disapproves of casual relationships. She's been waiting for years for me to settle down. The time is right now for you to meet her as my fiancée.'

There was that annoying F word again. Fiancée. And what was his old-school *nonna* going to think of Isla's topless photos if they were to go public? It didn't bear thinking about.

'I haven't said I was going to marry you, Rafe.'

He pulled back the bed covers and patted the bed, his gaze giving nothing away. 'Have a rest now, *cara*. I insist. You look tired and a little flushed.'

Isla slipped off her shoes and lay down on the cloud-soft bed and he pulled the cool sheet back over her, leaning down to press a soft-as-air kiss to the middle of her forehead. The surprising tenderness of the kiss made her wonder if somewhere deep inside him he actually cared a little for her. Not just for the baby she was carrying but for *her*. Was she being foolish to hope? Hadn't she learned her lesson by now about harbouring vain hopes? He was a good man, a caring man, with perhaps more sensitivity than she had given him credit for in the past. Surely his treatment of his housekeeper proved that he had a heart. But would he ever open it enough to welcome Isla in?

He was almost to the door before she found her voice. 'Rafe?'

He turned to look at her. 'Yes?'

Isla chewed at her lower lip. 'But what if, like Concetta, your grandmother doesn't accept me?'

A determined light appeared in his green and brown gaze. 'Once you are wearing my ring, she will accept you. Concetta too. Now rest.'

If only he knew how far from acceptable she felt.

CHAPTER FIVE

RAFE SAT IN his study at his desk and flicked his gold pen back and forth. He had business matters to see to—emails to send, documents to sign, deals to negotiate—but for once in his life he didn't feel like working. He felt like walking back upstairs and joining Isla in his bed.

That was where he wanted to be right now. With his arms around her, kissing her until she moaned, touching her until she begged. Burying himself in her sweet hot warmth and forgetting about everything but how good they were together.

Better than good—the best.

He should be angry with her for not telling him about her background. He should be feeling blindsided and betrayed, but somehow he wasn't. Instead, he felt compassion for her. Deep compassion. The circumstances of her childhood were terrible and it pained him she hadn't felt comfortable telling him when they were having a fling.

Bringing her back here to his villa had opened up a vault of memories. A vault he had kept tightly locked. When she'd left him three months ago, he had ruthlessly disciplined himself *not* to think about their time together. Every time his mind would drift to the scent of her skin, the softness of her mouth, the creamy perfection of her breasts, he would throw himself into work or do a punishing, muscle-burning workout. He hadn't allowed himself to dwell on what he was missing. Not just the hot sex and lively conversations—he'd had plenty of hot sex and lively conversations before. It was Isla he'd missed. Her smile, her tinkling bell-like laugh, her silken touch on his skin.

Dio, her touch on his skin. He ached to feel it again. Ached and throbbed to bury himself in her and send them both to paradise.

Concetta had questioned on numerous occasions why he insisted on keeping Isla's things in the walk-in wardrobe but he had expressly forbidden his housekeeper to remove them. Every time he went to his wardrobe and was confronted with Isla's clothes it was a form of self-torture. Things he had bought her. It was inconsistent of him to keep them there, as he'd been trying *not* to think about her, and yet he had kept them there to remind himself of his failure to read the signs on their relationship. Failure was a word he loathed and nothing reeked of abject failure more than to be blindsided in a relationship. Her presence in his villa had changed the atmosphere from the moment she had stepped over the threshold.

And it had changed it again now.

Rafe tossed his pen aside and rose to go to the windows that looked out over the stunning white sand–fringed beach of Mondello below. His villa, with its private gardens and infinity pool overlooking the ocean, was his castle. His fortress. The home he wished his mother had lived long enough to see. To enjoy with him. Years of her life had been spent living a lie and it churned his guts to think of all the things she'd done without because his father had kept her in limbo, feeding her empty promises year after year. Unlike Rafe, his mother had always known about Tino Angeliri's wife but had put up with being his mistress because she had loved him so much. And Rafe had loved him too. Deeply. And he had thought his father loved him but that was another lie. For a time, Rafe had been angry at his mother for not telling him the truth about his father earlier, but over time he'd come to realise she had only wanted to protect him.

Rafe and his mother had lived in a nice enough apartment—paid for by his father—but the one thing his mother had longed for was a garden. So Rafe had spent a veritable fortune on the garden here to honour her wish. Years of living out of his various hotels had made him appreciate this private sanctuary all the more. He had a handful of staff but mostly he was here alone.

But not now.

Isla was here and he wanted her to stay. Indefinitely. They would be parents in four months' time. He wanted his child to experience what he hadn't—legitimacy. Yes, it was old-fashioned of him in this day and age to insist on the formality of marriage. But he would settle for nothing less. He would not have Isla referred to as his mistress. He would not have his child called a love-child. He would not have his child called a bastard. He would not be a part-time parent like his father. He and Isla would be a family and he would do everything in his power to make it work.

Rafe opened the window and the salty tang of the sea breeze wafted past his nostrils. It had shocked him to find out Isla had grown up without a loving family, especially when she'd hinted at the opposite. But, looking back with the benefit of hindsight, there had been clues if he had taken the time to notice them. Isla had never called anyone on her phone in his presence. And no one had called her, apart from her friend Layla.

Not that he could talk. He didn't call his father or stepmother or half-brothers and only sent a text for birthdays. The only family member he called occasionally was his grandmother, because she was his last link to his mother. But even that relationship was tricky to handle. The shame of having a daughter 'living in sin' and having an illegitimate son by her married lover had caused a rift between his grandmother and his mother that had meant Rafe hadn't met his *nonna* until after his mother's death. It was hardly the way to build a close family bond.

Rafe sighed and turned away from the window and rubbed a hand over the back of his tense neck. Maybe there was something fatalistic about the way he and Isla had met in that bar in Rome. Perhaps they had recognised something in each other—a sense of isolation. A sense of not really belonging to anyone. He had noticed her the moment he'd walked into the bar. She'd been sitting in a quiet corner with a sketchpad on her lap, her beautiful features frowning with concentration as she drew a sketch of one of the patrons. The likeness was astonishing and Rafe had struck up a conversation and…well, the rest was smoking-hot history as they say. One drink and forty-two minutes later he had her back at his hotel and in his bed. The sex had been so phenomenal he had—uncharacteristically for him— impulsively asked her to come with him on a business trip to Paris. After Paris, for the next month he took her everywhere with him: Berlin, Zurich, Prague, Vienna, Amsterdam, Athens and Copenhagen.

And then, even more uncharacteristic of him—home to Sicily.

But, if he were honest with himself, it wasn't just the sex that had made him spirit her away to his private sanctuary. He'd wanted her to himself. The more time he'd spent with her, the more he'd realised she was different from his other casual lovers. He had taken lovers on business trips and holidays before but by the end of the trip he couldn't wait to end the fling.

But not with Isla.

He had wanted one month with her, then two, and then without notice she'd gone.

Rafe sat back down at his desk, a frown pulling at his brow. Had it been the difference in their backgrounds that had made her bolt as soon as she'd discovered she was pregnant? He clenched his right hand into a fist until his knuckles whitened. Why hadn't he tried harder to find her? Why had he allowed his pride to get in the way? He had wasted three months of valuable time, and if he hadn't by chance run into her he might never have found out about his child. And who could blame her for wanting to keep quiet about the pregnancy? He had made it clear their fling was temporary. He had made no promises. He had made no commitment other than to insist their fling was to be exclusive for its duration.

Marriage was the only way to make it up to her. The security of a formal relationship in which to bring up their child was the way forward.

The *only* way forward.

* * *

Isla woke from a surprisingly refreshing nap and sat up and pushed her tousled hair away from her face. The bright afternoon light had faded to the pastel hues of sunset, giving the room a muted and calming glow. She tossed the sheet covering her to one side and got to her feet, waiting for a moment to make sure she wasn't feeling faint. Once she was sure she was feeling fine, she went to the luxuriously appointed bathroom and did what she could to freshen up. She toyed with the idea of a shower but didn't want to chance Rafe coming in on her. Even glancing at the shower recess made something in her belly flutter. The erotic memories of what he had done to her in there flooded her brain and sent a wave of longing through her body.

She came back out to the bedroom and glanced in the direction of the walk-in wardrobe. Had he really kept all of her things? She had only taken the things she had brought with her on her trip abroad. Everything he had bought her she had left behind. She hadn't wanted any accusations of gold-digging cast her way by either him or his surly housekeeper.

She slid back the pocket doors and entered the wardrobe and something tripped in her stomach. Her clothes were neatly hanging on the opposite side to his. Her shoes arranged in tidy rows, the jewellery he'd bought her in the drawer of the glass-topped cabinet. She trailed her fingers along the row of silk and chiffon and satin articles of clothing. She opened one of the drawers below the jewellery display cabinet and found all the sexy lingerie she had once worn for him—exquisite lace and satin in an array of colours: black, red, midnight blue, hot pink and virginal white.

Isla picked up a dark blue silk and lace-trimmed camisole and matching knickers, running the gorgeous fabric through her fingers, mentally recalling the way Rafe had removed them from her body inch by inch, leaving a blazing trail of searing kisses on her exposed and quivering in anticipation flesh. She shivered and put the camisole and knickers back and shut the drawer with a snap.

But it wasn't so easy to lock away the memories of his touch.

Isla heard the door of the bedroom opening and she came out of the wardrobe to see Rafe coming into the suite carrying a long tall glass of freshly squeezed orange juice. She suddenly felt embarrassed to be found checking out the left-behind loot, so to speak. 'I'm not sure any of those things will fit me for too much longer.'

He set the juice down on the bedside table. 'Then I will buy you things that will.'

'You don't have to do that. I can buy my own clothes.' A remnant of pride sharpened her tone.

Rafe came over to her and took her hands in his. 'Did you get out of the wrong side of the bed?'

Isla pushed her lips forward in a pout. 'Not the wrong side—the wrong bed.'

His jaw tightened as if he was grinding his molars. 'I want you in my bed, Isla. It's where you belong.' The unmistakable note of authority in his voice made her all the more determined to defy him. To prove she still had some willpower where he was concerned. Some, not a lot. But some.

Her chin came up to a combative height and a surge of energy coursed through her. 'You think we can simply pick up where we left off? Get real, Rafe.'

His hands released hers to hold her by the hips instead. Isla knew she should try and get out of his hold but somehow her willpower had completely deserted her. His touch was like fire even through the layers of her clothes.

'I'll tell you what's real. This.' He brought his mouth down to just a breath away from hers. 'You can feel it, can't you?'

Isla couldn't stop her body from moving closer to his—as though it was programmed like a mobile robot going back to base for a much-needed charge. The hot hard heat of his arousal and the yearning ache of her pelvis coming into contact sent a zapping bolt of electricity through her body. Her mouth was suddenly fused to his but she didn't know who had closed the final distance. It didn't matter. All that mattered was the feeling of his lips moving with such masterful expertise on her own, feeling the commanding thrust of his tongue calling hers into sensual play. Feeling the need spiralling through her flesh, lighting up all her erogenous zones into a state of anticipatory awareness.

Isla wound her arms around his neck, her hands grasping handfuls of his hair in case he changed his mind and stepped away. She would *die* if he stepped away. A desperate moan of approval escaped her lips and she pressed closer, rubbing up against his erection, the urge to have him inside her so intense it was overwhelming.

His mouth continued its bone-melting exploration, his lips soft one minute, hard and insistent the next. His tongue darted and danced with hers in an erotic choreography that made her legs weaken, her spine tingle, her heart race. The slight graze of his stubble on her face as he changed position stirred her senses into overdrive. He took her lower lip between the gentle press of his teeth—a sexy nip and tug that sent a shower of fizzing fireworks to her core.

Isla took his lower lip between her teeth, tugging and releasing and then salving it with a slow sweep of her tongue. He shuddered and made a rough sound at the back of his throat and pulled her hard against him, one of his hands firm on the base of her spine.

'You make me crazy for you without even trying.' Rafe's voice had a desperate edge and his mouth came back down and covered hers in a searing kiss that made her need for him pummel harder through her body.

One of his hands glided underneath her top to gently cup her breast and she groaned in delight. Her breasts were even more sensitive than three months ago but her flesh recognised his touch and responded with excited fervour. He deftly unclipped her bra and brought his mouth down her naked breast, his tongue like the expert stroke of an artist's brush across her skin, around her tightly budded nipple, along the underside and back again. It was torture and yet tantalising, every nerve in her breast dancing in frenzied excitement, her inner core liquefying into molten heat.

Isla's hands went to the waistband of his trousers, fumbling with the fastening in her haste to uncover him. She needed to touch him. To taste him. To torture him the way he was torturing her. But he moved her hand away and walked her backwards to the bed, laying her down and coming down beside her, his hand continuing its frisson-inducing glide over her naked breast.

'I want you…' She was shocked at how desperate she sounded but was beyond caring. She didn't need her pride right now—what she needed was pleasure. Mind-blowing pleasure that only he could deliver. 'Please, Rafe. *Please*...' She writhed as he brought his hand to her mound, cupping her through her clothes with just enough pressure to make her arch her spine.

'Are you sure you want this?' His voice was calm and even and yet she could see the naked desire glittering in his gaze.

'Yes. A thousand times yes. You know I want you. You want me too.' Isla pulled his head down so he would kiss her again.

He covered her mouth in a long, spine-tingling kiss, his hand going under her elastic-waisted skirt and to her knickers. He peeled them down and she bucked and writhed so she could be rid of them. She wanted no barriers between their bodies. She needed him *now*. His fingers explored her feminine folds, caressing and teasing her into throbbing excitement. She was so close. So close. *So desperately close...*

Rafe moved down her body, placing his mouth where his fingers had been caressing, using his tongue to send her over the edge into oblivion. The sensations rippled through her sensitive flesh and Isla was swept up into a cataclysmic orgasm that seemed to involve every muscle and sinew in her body. She arched, she writhed, she bucked under the exquisite ministrations of his tongue. She cried out loud—whimpering, breathless cries as her flesh rippled and ricocheted with intense pleasure.

She came back to her senses with a shuddering sigh, her eyes seeking Rafe's with sudden shyness. 'You certainly haven't lost your touch.' She reached for his hand and interlaced her fingers with his, but she sensed a guardedness in him. A pulling away even though they were holding hands, his lazy smile at odds with the mask-like expression in his gaze.

'Nor you,' he said, leaning forward to press a light kiss to her forehead.

Isla frowned in confusion, doubts creeping in like shadows under a door. Why wasn't he continuing? Why wasn't he as desperate for release as she had been just moments ago? Or was he trying to prove a point? She was the one who needed him more than he needed her. 'Aren't you going to finish—?'

'Not right now.' He moved off the bed with athletic grace, standing beside it to look down at her. If he had constructed a brick wall between them it couldn't have been any more obvious that he was done here. Done with *her*. 'Concetta will have dinner ready shortly. Why don't you shower and change and I'll meet you downstairs?'

Isla launched herself off the bed, scrabbling at her clothes to put them in some sort of order. 'Why don't you stop telling me what to do?' she shot back, stung by his rejection. Stung with the pain of being discarded like a plaything that had lost its appeal.

A line of tension rippled along the length of his jaw and turned his eyes to stone. 'I am merely trying to do the right thing by you, Isla. You've had a long and exhausting day.'

'Is it my pregnancy that's a turn-off for you? You're feeling a little squeamish about making love to—'

'No.'

'Then what? Five months ago we would have been onto our second orgasm by now.' Possibly her third or fourth.

Rafe tucked his shirt back into his trousers and then raked his hand through his hair. 'We rushed into our relationship in the past. I'd like to take things a little more slowly this time around.'

Isla let out an unladylike curse. 'Why? So you can make me fall in love with you so I won't be able to say no to your offer of marriage? Not going to happen, buddy. No flipping way.' She spun away and stalked to the bathroom, furious with him—furious with herself for not resisting him. She slammed the door and leaned back against it. Why had she fallen into his arms like a wanton, desperate woman? She had gone up in flames and he had been in total control, not once being tempted beyond his endurance. What did that say about their relationship? It said it was out of balance. The power dynamic put her at a distinct disadvantage.

But hadn't it always?

His world. Her world. And never the twain shall meet.

But their worlds had collided with the conception of a child. A baby who could bridge the chasm as nothing else could. Could she settle for such a compromise when all her life she had wanted to be loved for herself?

Rafe knocked on the bathroom door. 'Isla. Open up.' His tone contained a warning note.

'Go away.' Isla glared at her reflection, ashamed of herself for being so weak. 'I *hate* you.'

His mocking laugh made her want to throw every cosmetic jar on the marble bathroom counter at the door. Smash. Smash. Smash. Then she would write a rude word all over the mirror in red lipstick and on the snowy white towels—every single one of them. She clenched her hands into fists, fighting the urge to scream with frustration, but instead a broken sob came from nowhere and she bent her head and clasped her face in her hands, her shoulders shaking with the effort of keeping her emotions in check.

The door suddenly clicked open and Rafe stepped inside the bathroom. He took her by the shoulders and turned her into his broad chest, stroking the back of her head and making gentle soothing noises that totally disarmed her.

'Shh, *mio piccolo*. I didn't mean to upset you. There now…'

Isla breathed in the citrus and spice scent of him, her face pressed against the steady thumping of his heart. His other arm was around her waist, holding her as securely as an iron band. 'Sorry about this…' Her voice was muffled by her face buried in the front of his shirt.

'Don't apologise. I'm the one at fault.'

Isla eased back a little and sniffed, not quite able to meet his gaze. 'It's hormones—it must be. I… I never cry normally.'

Rafe reached behind her to pluck a tissue out of the box on the marble counter and, lifting her chin with his finger, gently mopped beneath her streaming eyes, his expression so warm with concern it made her want to cry all over again. 'A lot has happened in a short time. Your life has been completely overturned. And I hold myself entirely responsible for it. Forgive me for upsetting you, *tesoro*. It was not my intention.'

He handed her another tissue and Isla blew her nose and, easing out of his hold, turned to look at her reddened complexion in the mirror. 'Argh. That's why I never cry. What a mess.'

Rafe met her gaze in the mirror and smiled and

stroked his hand down from the back of her neck to the base of her spine. 'Personally, I don't think you've ever looked more beautiful.'

Isla turned from the counter and faced him, somehow her hands ending up resting on the hard plane of his chest. 'Would you mind if I gave dinner a miss? I don't feel like going downstairs tonight...'

He brushed a stray curl away from her face. 'I'll bring you something up on a tray. How does that sound?'

'It sounds perfect.'

CHAPTER SIX

RAFE CAME BACK upstairs with a meal on a tray, after giving his housekeeper the rest of the evening off, but when he entered the bedroom Isla was sound asleep. She was curled up on her side, the red-gold cloud of her hair spread out over the pillow, one hand resting on the swell of her belly, the other lying under her cheek. He was in two minds whether to wake her or not. She needed her rest but she needed food too.

And he needed to keep his hands off her.

But he wanted her with an ache that wouldn't go away. Touching her earlier had stirred his desire into a throbbing beat that barrelled through his body even now. He had called on every bit of willpower he possessed, and then some, to keep his desire in check. He didn't want to be blinded by lust, so blinded he got caught out a second time.

He was determined to take things slowly this time.

Slowly but surely, that was his plan.

The future was what he was focused on—their future as a family. He had to show her she had a place in his life as his wife and partner and mother of their child.

A permanent place.

Rafe placed the tray on the bedside table with as little noise as possible. He sat on the edge of the bed beside her curled-up legs and pressed his hands hard against his thighs to stop himself from touching her.

Let her sleep. Let her sleep. Let her sleep. He chanted the words in his mind but to no avail. He found himself brushing a corkscrew curl away from her face and her periwinkle blue eyes opened and met his.

She gave a self-conscious smile and pushed herself up into a sitting position. 'I must have fallen asleep...' She glanced at the fragrant array of food on the bedside table and a little frown tugged at her forehead. 'Gosh. That seems a lot of food for one person...'

'You're not one person at the moment,' Rafe said, placing the tray across her lap. 'You need to feed the baby that's growing inside you.'

Her gaze shifted but her frown didn't go away and her teeth sank into her lower lip. 'Rafe...'

'Eat first. We can talk later.'

He handed her the cutlery and her gaze slowly crept up to meet his. 'I just wanted to thank you for earlier. You've been so kind and I've been a bit of an ungrateful cow towards you.'

Rafe brushed back another stray strand of hair off her face, tucking it behind the neat creamy shell of her ear. 'This isn't an easy time for either of us. You more than me. But I'm confident we can make this work. We have to. We have a child in common and he or she has to be the priority going forward.'

Isla's frown crept back between her eyebrows and she began to pick at the food. 'Have you ever changed your mind once it's made up?' she asked after a moment.

'Not often.'

She gave him the side eye. 'Were you this stubborn as a child?'

'Always. I drove my mother nuts.'

'I can well believe it.' She picked up a plump juicy strawberry from the fruit plate on the tray and bit into it with her small white teeth.

Rafe wanted to suck the juice off her luscious lips right then and there and had to freeze every muscle in his body to stop from doing it. Desire rippled through him in waves, heating his flesh, hardening him to stone.

'Why are you looking at me like that?' Isla asked, wiping her fingers on the linen napkin.

'How am I looking at you?'

A faint blush crept into her cheeks and she swept her tongue across her lips. 'You know how.'

Rafe picked up a strawberry from the plate and held it close to her mouth. 'I like watching you eat.' He liked watching her, full stop. She could be watching paint dry and he would still find it fascinating to observe her.

She took a small bite of the strawberry, chewed, swallowed and licked her lips. 'Doesn't it make you hungry?'

He kept his gaze locked on hers. 'Ravenous.'

A glimmer of mischief sparked in her gaze and she took the half-eaten strawberry from his hand and held it against his mouth. 'Why don't you have a bite?'

There was something deeply erotic about placing his lips where hers had been just moments earlier. He bit into the soft flesh and the sweet flavour burst in his mouth. 'Mmm... Delicious.'

She picked up another strawberry but, before she could bring it to his mouth, he took her wrist in a gentle but firm hold. He didn't want strawberries. He wanted her. The strawberry dropped out of her hand with a soft little thump that sounded loud in the silence. The tip of her tongue came out to lick her lips and her pupils flared as his head came down so his mouth could meet hers.

The sweetness of the strawberry had nothing on the sweetness of Isla's mouth. Rafe lost himself in the softness of her lips, the playful dance of her tongue as it met the entry of his. The fire of lust licked along his flesh like tongues of flame, his blood surging south with the force of a nuclear missile. His hands went around her, drawing her closer so he could deepen the kiss even further. The meal tray rattled between them and he released her and lifted his mouth off hers with a muttered curse. He removed the tray from across her lap and set it back on the bedside table.

He came back to take her face in both his hands, desire thrumming through him like rapid drum beats. 'Now, where was I?' he asked with a smile.

Isla placed her hands on his wrists, pulling them down from her face, a shadow passing through her gaze. 'Is this going to be like last time? You holding back just to prove a point?'

Rafe frowned and gathered her hands in his in a gentle hold. Her comment was a timely reminder that he was moving too fast. His willpower had its limits and tempting it beyond its endurance was not such a great idea until their relationship was on more secure footing. 'It's not going to be like last time because we're not doing this until you're wearing my engagement ring. I've organised for us to select one tomorrow.'

No way was he introducing her to his *nonna* without a ring on her finger.

Her eyebrows rose. 'Isn't that a little old-fashioned of you all of a sudden? What happened to the man who took me back to his hotel room and got me naked in under an hour?'

Forty-two minutes. And during each one of them Rafe's body had been humming and thrumming with lust. The moment he'd laid eyes on her he'd wanted her. It had never happened that way with another woman before. Sure, he'd had plenty of casual encounters in his time, but he couldn't remember one that had captivated him from the very moment their gazes met. Engaging in conversation with her had only reinforced his determination to have her. And knowing she had felt exactly the same way had made it one of the most exciting encounters of his life. *The* most exciting.

'Patience, *cara*. We have the rest of our lives together.'

Isla pulled her hands out of his hold and folded them across her chest, glowering at him. 'You're so confident I'm going to fall in with your plans. But I have a mind of my own, Rafe. I told you before—I will not be bullied into marriage. Marriage is for people who love each other and want to spend the rest of their lives together.'

Rafe rose from the bed and stuffed his hands in the pockets of his trousers. He figured it was better to put them there than reach for her and show how love was not necessary when it came to the chemistry they shared. 'The romantic love you're talking about is largely a fantasy. It doesn't last. So many supposedly madly-in-love couples end up divorcing after a couple of years together. We have a much better chance of making it work because we're starting with realistic expectations and the right motivation to do the best thing for our child.'

'What has made you so cynical about love? Did some woman in your past break your heart?'

Rafe gave a short laugh at the thought of himself falling in love. He hadn't even come close. He hadn't allowed himself to. Loving someone blinded you and left you vulnerable. He had loved his father and look how that had turned out. The father he had loved and modelled himself on had been nothing but a lying, cheating fraud. There was no way he ever wanted to feel that level of disappointment and devastation again. 'No. I've never been in love. I've just seen what being in love looks like and what it does to people when it ends.'

Isla uncrossed her arms and rested her hands on the swell of her belly, a frown still etched on her forehead. 'But surely for a percentage of people it doesn't end. It lasts for a lifetime.'

'Maybe, but there are no guarantees.' He took his hands out of his pockets and moved to collect the tray from the bedside table. 'Are you done with this?'

'Yes. I've had enough.'

Rafe picked up the tray and turned to look at her again. 'I don't want you to think I'm completely without feeling, Isla. I care about you and the baby. You do know that, *si*?'

Her eyes flicked away from his. 'I'm not asking you to fall in love with me.'

'Are you not?'

Her gaze met his but it was as if there was a screen

up. 'Men like you don't fall in love with women like me. Not outside fairy tales, that is.'

'Now who's sounding cynical?' Rafe said, softening it with a smile. 'Is there anything else I can get you? Another juice or tea or—'

'I'm fine. Please don't fuss. I'm not ill—just pregnant.' Her tone had an edge of irritation that made him wonder if it was masking hurt. But he didn't feel comfortable making promises he couldn't deliver on. Love was a no-go zone for him and he had good reasons for it. It was an emotion he didn't trust.

Could never trust again.

Once Rafe left the bedroom Isla lay back against the pillows with a heavy sigh. She wasn't sure why she kept pushing him on the subject of love. It would be a disaster if she fell in love with him. An unmitigated disaster, because her background would make it all but impossible for him to love her back. Rafe was a proud and intensely private man. The disclosure of her lurid past would destroy any hope of a future together. How could anyone in their right mind, herself included, think she was good enough for someone like Rafe? Like him, she had never fallen in love before, but a secret part of her dreamed of doing so. To be in a relationship with her partner, who openly expressed the same love she felt for him.

But how could she allow herself to hope Rafe would be that partner?

But the more he talked about marriage and bringing up their baby together, the more tempting it became. She didn't relish being a single parent. Her mother had struggled to cope with the demands of a small child, especially once Isla's father had left. Their marriage had only come about because of her mother's pregnancy with her and it had been a mistake from the get-go. Her father had been an immature man-child himself, no way ready to take on the responsibilities of parenthood. When the marriage folded, Isla's mother had dropped into a cycle of self-medication with prescription drugs and alcohol. Isla had far too many distressing memories of gnawing hunger while her mother slept off yet another hangover. Shivering with cold when there wasn't enough money to pay the heating bills. Shouts and slaps and sarcastic put-downs when her mother had run out of her drug or drink of choice, blaming Isla for the train wreck of her life. Then, after her mother's death and her father's subsequent rejection, Isla had spent her childhood being passed around foster homes, never belonging, never fitting in, never feeling loved.

A marriage between her and Rafe might not have any of the financial hardship of her parents' marriage but it would still be a duty-bound contract, not a love-bound one.

Could she risk it for the sake of their child?

The following day Rafe took Isla to a jewellery designer he knew in Palermo, where the designer escorted them to a private room and brought out an array of exquisite rings for her inspection. Isla knew she should have put her foot down earlier that morning about Rafe's insistence on buying a ring but somehow found herself going along with his plans. Perhaps wearing his ring would stop his housekeeper from eyeing her with undisguised distaste. Besides, they were due to visit his grandmother that afternoon and she knew it would be easier to meet the old lady wearing Rafe's ring than without.

The designer left them alone with a selection of rings and Isla's gaze homed in on a simple mosaic setting, the tiny individual facets glittering brilliantly as each caught the light. It wasn't the biggest ring in the selection and it was set along more traditional lines but she loved it on sight.

'May I have this one?' Isla pointed to it.

'This one?' Rafe lifted it out of its velvet home and took her left hand. 'Let's see if it fits.' It slid over her finger as if it had been made specially for her. He smiled. 'It suits you.'

Isla tilted her hand this way and that to watch the diamonds glinting. 'It's beautiful…' She glanced up at him and added, 'I hope it's not too frightfully expensive. There aren't any price tags and—'

'It's not a problem.'

Isla immediately felt gauche for mentioning price tags. Of course, Rafe didn't have to worry about price tags. He could afford any ring in the store—*every* ring when it came to that. She waited to one side while he paid for the ring on his credit card and then, once he was done, he came to take her hand and led her out of the shop.

'Thank you,' Isla said. 'It's a gorgeous ring.'

'I've ordered a wedding ring to match. Pablo is going to work on it straight away.'

It was on the tip of her tongue to tell him not to bother ordering a wedding ring but something stopped her. Would it be a mistake to marry him? He was the father of her child and would love and provide for it and not shirk parental responsibility like her father had done. Marriage to Rafe would offer her and the baby the sort of financial security she could only dream of. Money wasn't everything, and it certainly wasn't the best motivation for marrying someone, but to never have to worry about providing for her child was a big inducement, one she found increasingly hard to resist.

'I'm thinking a small wedding with just close friends and immediate family,' Rafe said on the way back to the car. 'I have a dress designer in mind but if you have someone you'd rather use then feel free.'

'I don't have any family to speak of,' Isla said. 'And I would only want Layla and a couple of other friends as bridesmaids.' She waited a beat and added, 'How soon are you thinking?'

He glanced at the swell of her abdomen. 'Two weeks.'

Her eyes rounded to the size of dishes. Satellite dishes. 'Are you crazy? No one can organise a wedding *that* quickly.'

A glint appeared in his hazel gaze. 'Watch me.'

CHAPTER SEVEN

AFTER A LIGHT lunch at a café they had dined in previously, Rafe drove the seventy-odd kilometres to the historic coastal town of Marsala in western Sicily, made famous for its fortified wine and ancient ruins. Isla hadn't visited it when she was involved with Rafe a few months ago but had read about the Stagnone Nature Reserve with its salt pans and migratory birds.

Lucia Bavetta's small but beautiful villa was situated not far from the main square of Marsala. A demure housekeeper in her late sixties called Maria opened the door, exchanged a few words with Rafe, smiled briefly at Isla before leading them inside and then melted away like a shadow. Rafe put his arm around Isla's waist and led her to where the old lady was waiting in grand style in the salon.

The well-preserved old-world furnishings gave the room a time capsule atmosphere that made Isla feel distinctly out of place. There were some concessions to modernity—the old lady was sitting in a recliner chair, surrounded by books and newspapers, a tablet and television remote control and a phone set, giving the impression she spent most of her time residing there. There was a walking frame parked nearby and the room had clear pathways between the furniture for ease of passage. There was an elderly tortoiseshell cat curled up asleep on a nearby sofa. It was so still that at first Isla thought it was a taxidermy model, but then it opened one slitted golden eye, made a croaky *miaow* and then went back to sleep.

Lucia's black button eyes coolly assessed Isla's abdomen even before Rafe could make the introductions. 'So, you have brought your latest mistress to meet me.'

'Isla is not my mistress, Nonna. She is my fiancée.' Rafe's tone was firm, his arm around Isla's waist protective.

The old lady raised her chin, her dentures clacking in disapproval. 'When is the wedding? Sooner rather than later, one would hope.'

'Saturday fortnight,' Rafe said. 'I'd like you to be there.'

Lucia grunted noncommittally and waved an imperious hand towards the sofa opposite her chair. 'Sit. But mind Taddeo there. It's straining my neck looking up at you both.'

Once they had sat side by side on the sofa next to the sleeping cat, the old lady turned her attention to Isla. 'My grandson tells me you're an artist. Are you any good?'

'Erm… I'm not sure I'm the right person to answer that,' Isla said, gently stroking the elderly cat, which set off a round of audible purring.

'She's very good,' Rafe said, holding Isla's hand against his muscle-packed thigh. 'I've asked her to paint your portrait in time for your ninetieth birthday. She would need you to do a few sittings for her.'

Lucia made a self-deprecating noise. 'That's all I do, day in and day out—sit. My legs won't do what I want them to do any more. I fall over even when there's nothing to fall over.'

'It must be very frustrating for you,' Isla said.

Lucia glanced at Taddeo, who had now rolled onto his side so Isla could stroke his belly. Her gaze came back to Isla's. 'How many sittings would you need?'

'Two or three to start with,' Isla said. 'I can take photos to work from as well, but I like spending time with the subject of a portrait. It's when I observe their mannerisms or micro-expressions that define their character.'

The old lady folded her hands in her lap as if she had come to a decision. 'When would you like to start?'

Isla didn't like to say she had already started. From the moment she'd walked in she'd been taking in the details of the old lady's personality. Lucia Bavetta presented as a starchy and critical old-school woman who didn't suffer fools gladly, and yet Isla could see traces of the much softer girl and young woman she had once been before the vicissitudes of life had toughened her up. 'I could take some preliminary photos with my phone today and then make a time to come back for a more formal sitting.'

The old lady's bird-like eyes narrowed. 'Don't you have a wedding to plan?'

'Erm…it's not going to be a big affair—' Isla began.

'I've got it in hand,' Rafe said. 'Working on your portrait will be a nice distraction for Isla. Won't it, *cara*?'

Isla smiled a weak smile. 'A distraction right now would be good.'

* * *

They ended up staying longer than Rafe expected but his *nonna* insisted on serving refreshments that her housekeeper and long-time companion, Maria, had prepared. But, given he had a surprise in store for Isla that was being prepared back at the villa while they were out, it suited him to dawdle a little over coffee and cake.

Once they'd said their farewells, Rafe led Isla back out to his car. 'That went well, I thought. She likes you.'

Isla swung her gaze to him in surprise. 'You think so?'

'You liked her cat and it liked you. You're in, as far as Nonna is concerned. "Love me, love my arthritic flea-bitten cat" is her credo.'

She gave a visible shudder and rubbed her hands up and down her upper arms. 'Does it have fleas?'

He laughed and gently brushed his bent knuckles against her cheek. 'Only teasing. There isn't a flea in the world who'd have the courage to enter Nonna's villa, much less reside on her precious cat's body.'

Isla's smile made something in his chest loosen. 'I like your grandmother. She's a straight shooter but has a softer side she takes great pain to keep hidden.'

A family trait? Rafe brushed the thought aside. He had no problem with showing his softer side when the occasion demanded it but there was no way he was going to allow feelings to cloud his judgement—or at least not again.

Rafe opened the passenger door for her and pulled down the seat belt once she was seated. 'Thank you for being patient with her. That could have gone very badly.'

Once they were on their way, Isla swivelled in her

seat to look at him. 'Was your mother like your grand-mother? In temperament, I mean.'

Rafe sometimes found it hard to think of his mother without feeling a sharp stab of pain at how her life had turned out. Estranged from her own mother, strung along for years by a man who'd claimed to love her but who wouldn't give up his meal ticket marriage for her, only to die of cancer the year after she had been rejected by the man she loved. 'Not in temperament, no. She was *too* soft. Gave too much of herself to other people—my father in particular.'

'Did your father love her, do you think?'

He gave a bark of cynical laughter. 'My father is incapable of loving anyone but himself.' He sighed and continued, 'My mother wanted a different life but didn't have the courage to fight for it. She went along with my father's empty promises for years, hoping he would one day leave his dead marriage and formalise their relationship.' His fingers tightened on the steering wheel. 'She did it for me. Like most mothers, she wanted the best for me even if it meant sacrifice on her part. But she didn't live long enough to see her wishes fulfilled.' He forcibly relaxed his grip and added, 'Nor will she get to meet her grandchild.' He glanced at Isla but she was chewing her lip as if deep in thought. Or deep in worry. Was she comparing his mother's situation with their current one? Seeing similarities that were not really there?

He reached for her hand and placed it on his thigh. 'Stop worrying, I am not like my father. I've made a promise to you and our child. I won't break it.'

She gave a fleeting movement of her lips that almost passed as a smile. 'What was her name?'

'Gabriella.'

'If we have a girl we could name her after your mother if you like.'

Rafe glanced at her again, his heart suddenly feeling as if it had slipped from its moorings. Her gaze was warm and soft with compassion and he realised with a jolt that his mother would have adored her. His mother would have admired her for her strength and courage, for her ability to speak her mind. 'You wouldn't mind?'

Her smile was like a flash of sunshine on a cloudy day. 'Of course not. It's a gorgeous name—although we might have a boy.' Her smile dimmed and she removed her hand from his thigh. 'I don't suppose you want to name him after your father?'

Rafe gave her the side eye. 'No.'

There was a silence, broken only by the sound of the car tyres passing over the road.

He glanced at Isla. 'Your mother won't get to meet her grandchild either.'

She looked down at her hands, where her fingers were fiddling with her engagement ring. 'No, but that's probably a good thing. She wasn't a born nurturer. If she hadn't got pregnant with me, I don't think she would have ever had kids.'

Rafe hated to think of what Isla must have endured as a child for her to end up in long-term foster care. She deserved so much better. *So* much better. And he would do everything in his power to make sure she got it to make up for all she had missed out on. Her revelations about her background made him realise what an amazing strength and resilience she had. No wonder he had felt so drawn to her from the moment they'd met. His background was no way as difficult as hers but it had left its mark. 'I have no doubt you'll be a wonderful mother in spite of not having a good role model. Besides, you will have me to support you every step of the way.'

Her gaze met his briefly before flicking away again. 'My father once told me my mother trapped him by deliberately getting pregnant.' Her voice was toneless, stripped bare of emotion, and yet he could feel it throbbing just beneath the surface. 'He married her out of a sense of duty and because of family pressure, but he never loved her or me, when it came to that.'

Rafe reached for her hand and brought it to his chest, laying it against his heart. No wonder she was baulking at his proposal. But he would make sure she had every reason to feel secure. 'No one is pressuring me to marry you, Isla. I want you to be my wife and I want us to bring up our child together. Deep down, I think you want it too. Over time, the love we have for our child will only strengthen the bond between us.'

There was another small silence.

'I'm sorry I didn't tell you straight away about the pregnancy,' Isla said. 'In hindsight, it looks so selfish of me but I really thought I was doing the right thing under the circumstances.'

Rafe gave her hand a gentle squeeze and brought it up to his lips, pressing a kiss to her bent knuckles. 'You have to learn to trust me, *tesoro mio*. Now, I have a surprise for you. It will be waiting for you when we get home.'

Home. Isla wondered if she would ever look upon Rafe's villa as her home, especially with his guard dog housekeeper Concetta on site. But when they returned to the villa there was no sign of the housekeeper.

Rafe took Isla's hand and led her to one of the downstairs rooms overlooking the garden and water feature. He opened the door and waved his hand for her to precede him. She stepped inside the room and gasped when she saw the array of art materials, including an easel, worktable and drop sheet covering the parquet flooring. He had even had a small sink installed so she could wash her brushes without leaving the room. 'Oh, Rafe, it's amazing. How on earth did you do all this?' She swung around to look at him. 'Thank you so much.'

He smiled. 'I thought it best to give you a room downstairs, given your pregnancy. I don't want you climbing up and down those stairs too much. If I've forgotten anything or you need any other supplies, write me a list and I'll get them for you.'

Isla picked up one of the top-notch brushes and ran her fingers through the soft bristles. He was assuming she would be here right to the end of her pregnancy and beyond. She wanted to be angry with him for railroading her into formalising their relationship, but how could she feel anything but grateful for the way he was handling the situation? She realised she *wanted* to stay with him. To be married to him and provide a safe haven for their child, even if it meant she was a little short-changed on the thing she wanted most of all—love. She glanced at him. 'Everything's wonderful. I could never afford brushes like this. I can't wait to get started on your grandmother's portrait.' She put the brush down and came over to him. 'I don't know how to thank you.'

He brushed a strand of hair away from her face, his eyes dark and smouldering. 'A kiss will be enough.'

Isla stepped up on tiptoe and, linking her arms around his neck, planted her lips on his. For a moment she thought he wasn't going to respond, but then the heat from his lips seeped into hers and suddenly their mouths were pressing against each other in the hungry drive for deeper contact. Lips parted, tongues partnered, desire leapt and danced like roaring flames.

Rafe's arms went around her and hauled her closer, her pelvis pressed against his growing hardness. The intimate contact sent her senses into a tailspin, the need for his possession so rapid, so sudden, so overwhelming it swept through her like an unstoppable tidal wave.

He groaned at the back of his throat and pressed her harder against his erection, the desperation in his kiss matching hers. Her tongue played with his in little cat and mouse movements that escalated the passion flaring between them.

One of his hands came to her breast, cupping it through her clothes, but it wasn't enough. She wanted skin-on-skin. She ached and burned for his intimate touch. 'Please, Rafe, touch me.' Her voice came out breathless and laced with longing.

He found the zipper at the back of her dress and slid it down until the dress was in a puddle at her feet. Isla stepped out of the circle of fabric, feeling no shame at being in just bra and knickers with her ripening belly on show.

His eyes devoured her shape, his hand caressing the mound of her abdomen in a worshipful fashion. 'You're so beautiful, so curvy and gorgeous I can hardly stand it.' His tone was rough around the edges, his gaze burning with incendiary heat.

'Make love to me.' It was part demand, part plea but she was beyond caring how she came across. Need was gripping her so hard it was close to pain.

He framed her face with his hands, breathing deeply. 'I'm not making love to you on a drop sheet on the floor. We'll finish this upstairs in bed.'

Shame suddenly found Isla like a spotlight homing in on a target. Rafe was still fully dressed and here she was, standing in her underwear like a desperate wanton practically begging him to make love to her. It was yet another reminder of the power imbalance between them. He wanted her but far less than she wanted him. She pulled out of his hold and turned to snatch up her dress off the floor. 'Why do you always *do* that?' Her voice was so sharp it could have sliced through concrete.

Rafe frowned. 'Do what?'

Isla stepped back into her dress and worked the zipper up as far as she could. 'I remember a time when nothing would have stopped you making love to me, no matter where we were.'

He came over to her and reached for her hand but she whipped it out of reach. '*Cara*, what's wrong? Why are you being so tetchy? I'm simply thinking of you.'

She bit her lip and turned her back, annoyed at how close to tears she was. That would be the ultimate humiliation—to end up in floods of tears again. 'I know you don't want me as much as I want you, but you don't have to rub it in every flipping chance you get.'

He came up behind her and placed his hands on the tops of her shoulders, slowly turning her to face him. His expression was still etched in a frown. 'You think I don't *want* you? Why do you think there's been no one since you left?' His voice was rough with an emotion she couldn't name. 'I want you so badly it gnaws at me night and day. Every day since you left it's tortured me.'

Isla swallowed. 'Really?'

His frown faded and he gave a lopsided smile, his hands coming up to cradle each side of her face. 'No one turns me on like you do.' He pressed a kiss to her mouth, once, twice, three times. 'But I'm worried about hurting you or the baby.'

'You won't hurt me, Rafe,' Isla said, winding her arms around his waist. 'It's perfectly fine to have sex when you're pregnant. In fact, the hormones right now are making me crazy for you.' It touched her that he had only been thinking of her and the baby, putting his own desire on hold for her sake and that of their child. It made her feel ashamed for jumping to the conclusion that he didn't want her as much as she wanted him. And the thought of him being celibate all this time made her feel even more special. The magic they had shared had left an impression on him that he hadn't wanted to erase by sleeping with someone else. She didn't have the words to describe how much that meant to her.

The most recent memory of a woman's touch on him was hers and hers alone.

He dropped another kiss on her lips and then he gathered her up in his arms.

'Eek! What are you doing? I'm way too heavy,' Isla protested.

His hazel gaze smouldered with desire. 'I'm taking you upstairs to bed. Any further objections?'

Isla looped her arms around his neck and smiled. 'Not a single one.'

A short time later Rafe lowered Isla until her feet touched the floor of the master bedroom, sliding her body down the hard length of his. Every inch of the journey down his body set her senses on fire. He held her against him, one firm arm around her waist and his other hand gently cupping the side of her face. His eyes were as dark as a forest—earthy brown and leafy green and shadow black, with glints of desire as brilliant as slivers of sunlight. 'Are you sure about this?' A battle played out in his gravel and treacle tone—a battle between desire and concern.

Isla placed her hands on either side of his face, her need for him a pulsing ache between her thighs. Her appreciation of his tenderness about her condition made it all but impossible to remember why she had hated him. How could she hate such a man? A man who made her feel such magical sensations. Who made her feel alive in a way she had never felt before. 'I want this. I want *you*. Now.'

He lowered his head and covered her mouth with his, the movement of his lips slow and drugging at first, but then the intensity changed like a switch had been turned. Heat exploded between their mouths, their tongues colliding in passion, hot streaks of longing firing through her like arrows of flame.

Isla's hands went to the waistband of his trousers, desperate to hold him, to feel the heat and power of him. To feel his blood pounding for *her*. Only for her.

But he held her off by walking her back towards the bed, sliding down the zip on her dress, his warm firm hand caressing her naked back in one long, smooth stroke that made every nerve sit up and take notice.

His smouldering gaze threatened to incinerate the wallpaper off the walls, his touch on her body creating an inferno of lust. 'Let's not rush this. I want to savour every moment.' His deep voice was another stroke down the length of her shivering spine. Low and deep and seductive.

'I want to rush. I was ready half an hour ago. Stop torturing me, damn it.' Isla set to work on his shirt, tugging it out of his waistband and doing her best to undo the buttons, which were not cooperating with her haste-driven fingers.

Rafe laid his hand over hers, stilling its frenzied movements. 'That was our mistake in the past. We rushed headlong into an affair and didn't take the time to get to know one another first. I want things to be different now. I want to know you in every sense of the word.'

A tremor of shame rippled through Isla. The portfolio of saucy photos flashed through her mind. He didn't need to know *everything* about her. There were some things that were best left in the shadows. She couldn't allow him to ever find out about her chequered past. Would do everything in her power to prevent it. She found it hard to hold his gaze and looked at his mouth instead. 'Kiss me, Rafe.'

He bumped up her chin with his finger, meshing his gaze with hers. 'I want to make this work. Us, I mean. Our marriage. And it can only work if we work together.'

She traced his mouth with her finger. 'I want it to work too.' Her voice came out whisper-soft. 'More than anything.'

His gaze intensified. 'You won't regret it, *cara mio*. I'll make sure of it.' His mouth came back down and sealed hers in a kiss that reignited the flames of need in her body.

Her arms went around his neck, her lower body pressed against the hardened heat of his, her mouth moving in unison with his. He deepened the kiss with a slow and deliberate glide of his tongue, calling hers into a playful dance that had distinctly erotic overtones. Need pooled hot between her thighs, her legs feeling like the bones had dissolved.

Rafe laid her on the bed in just her knickers and bra and trailed his hands down the length of her legs to remove her shoes, the sound of them thudding one by one to the floor heralding what was to come. His glittering gaze held hers in a sensual lock that made her inner core pulse with longing. He stood at the end of the bed and shrugged off his shirt, kicked off his shoes and tugged off his socks. He stood with the proud bulge of his erection lovingly contoured by his dark briefs.

'Aren't you going to take those off?' Isla's voice was husky.

His eyes roamed over the curves of her breasts, still encased in her bra. 'You go first.'

She sat up and pulled one strap over her shoulder, then the other one in a slow striptease that made his eyes flare with heat. She kept her gaze locked on his while she reached behind her back for the hook fastening, releasing the bra and tossing it to one side, her naked flesh exposed to the feasting of his hungry gaze.

'And the rest.' His voice had a note of commanding authority that made the back of her knees tingle like sand trickling through an hourglass. No one else's voice could have such a potent effect on her. No one else could render her to such a quivering mess of need.

Isla peeled her knickers down her thighs, past her knees and over her ankles, tossing them in the same direction as her bra. Her body in all its lush ripeness was exposed to his gaze but, instead of feeling uncertain or shy, she felt empowered. His child was growing in her womb, a product of the passion they had shared. A passion that was as unstoppable as the rising and setting of the sun. And just as hot.

Rafe stepped out of his briefs and came to her on the bed, his hand resting on the swell of her abdomen, his eyes holding hers. 'You are so damn beautiful. So sexy it takes my breath away.'

Isla placed her hand over his, her own breathing a little chaotic. 'You won't hurt me or the baby, Rafe. I want you inside me. I want to feel you. I've missed you so much.'

'I've missed you too.' He leaned down and spoke the words against her mouth, then joined her on the bed, drawing her into the circle of his arms.

Isla caressed the hard length of him, moving her fingers up and down his shaft in the way she knew he loved. The agony and the ecstasy were played out on his darkly handsome features—little flinches of muscles and flutters of eyelids a sign of his enjoyment at her touch. She smothered a groan and covered her mouth with his, the meeting of their tongues sending an arrow of need straight to her core.

He moved from her mouth down her neck, taking

his time over each delicate scaffold of her clavicles, his tongue leaving a trail of fire in its wake. He moved closer and closer to her breasts, his slow pace both pleasure and torture. Then finally, *finally* his mouth came to her breasts and subjected them to a sizzling caress of teasing lips and gently tugging teeth. Her nipples peaked to tight buds, her sensitive flesh relishing the stroking glide of his tongue. He left her breasts to work down her body, over the mound of her belly and down the other side to the heart of her.

Isla placed a hand on his shoulder. 'Wait. I want you inside me. Please, Rafe, don't make me beg.'

He gave her a look so hot it made the base of her spine tingle. 'I want you too. You have no idea how much.'

She reached for him again, stroking the silk and steel of his body. 'I think I do.' Touching him stirred her own need into overdrive. Every throb and pulse of his blood found an echo in her own body. An erotic drum beat that was as old as time.

He made a growling sound of pleasure and settled between her thighs, adjusting his limbs to make sure she wasn't taking too much of his weight. 'Tell me if I'm going too fast or too deep or—oh, *Dio...*' His words were cut off by another deep guttural groan as she lifted her pelvis to welcome him. His body entered hers in a silken thrust that sent Isla into a spiral of delight, her body wrapping around him as tight as the grab of a fist.

She wouldn't let him slow his pace. She arched up to meet each downward movement of his body, gripping him by the buttocks to hold him to where she needed him most. The need for release was screaming through her sensitised flesh, a need so urgent, so intense it overtook every rational thought. She was almost to the edge of oblivion, so desperately, agonisingly close, her breath coming in gasps, her body straining for that final blessed friction. *So close. So close. So close.* It was a chant in her head in time with the throbbing need in her body.

Rafe slipped a hand between their bodies, caressing the swollen heart of her, and finally she flew off into the stratosphere. Waves of pleasure rolled through her, leaving her spinning in a whirlpool of sensation that emptied her mind of everything but a total sense of bliss.

Within moments of her release, Rafe followed with his own and Isla held him through each shuddering second, delighting in the knowledge she had evoked such ecstasy for him. That was what had marked their fling from the moment it started. Making love with Rafe was a mutually satisfying experience that seemed to get better and better the longer they'd stayed together.

Rafe propped himself up on one elbow, his other hand idly stroking the curve of her hip. 'For the past three months I wondered if I'd imagined how good we were together.'

Isla tiptoed her fingers up and down his sternum. 'I'm glad there's been no one else.'

He captured her hand and brought it up to his lips, his eyes dark and lustrous with erotic promise. 'Me too.'

CHAPTER EIGHT

ISLA WOKE FROM a deep sleep an hour or so later to find the bed empty beside her. She decided not to be disappointed Rafe hadn't stayed with her. He was a busy man with a global empire to run. She couldn't expect him to put his career on hold for days or months on end for her. Besides, once they were married, they would have to establish some sort of routine to live together harmoniously. His reason for marrying her might not tick all the romantic fantasy boxes but since when had she bought into the happy ever after fairy tale? Nothing about her life so far had any hint of fairy tale about it.

Life had been one long struggle to survive against the odds.

Isla laid her hand on the swell of her belly, feeling the tiny movements of little feet and elbows inside her womb. At least her baby would not have to face the same relentless struggles. Her baby would be protected from neglect and lack of nurture. It would be surrounded by love from both its parents.

And, no matter what happened between her and Rafe, she knew he would always do the right thing for their child. Always.

Isla had a shower and coiled her still damp hair into a makeshift knot on top of her head. Her hand went to her make-up kit but then she decided against it. Rafe hadn't mentioned going out and the only person she would possibly encounter apart from him was Concetta. She knew there would be no pleasing Rafe's housekeeper unless she packed her bags and left.

Isla made her way downstairs to the studio Rafe had set up for her. She sat at the workstation and began some preliminary sketches of his grandmother, now and again referring to the photos on her phone. She lost track of time until her lower back started to protest. She got up from the table, placed both hands at the base of her spine and stretched backwards.

The door opened and Concetta stood there with a tray carrying a pot of tea and a slice of cake. 'The *signor* told me to bring this to you.' Her tone dripped with resentment, her black button eyes hard.

'Thank you, Concetta. That was kind of you.' Isla cleared some space on the worktable and summoned up a smile. 'Did you make the cake yourself?'

'But of course.' The housekeeper placed the tray on the table with a thud and a little clatter of the crockery. 'No packaged food is served in this house.'

Isla could feel the older woman's disapproval like a chilly fog that had entered the room with her. 'For some people, packaged food is a luxury. Or at least it was for me, growing up.' She didn't know why she had revealed that little snippet of information about herself or why she added, 'And sometimes there wasn't even that.' But maybe it was because she suspected Concetta had always seen through her to the scared and lonely child she had once been. Which was why Isla hadn't tried to make more of an effort to get on with her. The housekeeper saw too much. Sensed too much. Knew too much.

The housekeeper's stiff posture softened—her shoulders going down a notch, her tight mouth relaxing slightly. She glanced at the sketches. 'So, you have met the *signor*'s grandmother.'

'Yes, I like her. She's feisty and opinionated but I felt drawn to her in spite of that.' Isla wished she could say the same for Concetta.

Concetta picked up one of the sketches and examined it for a moment. Something passed over her weathered features—tiny flickering shadows as if a painful memory had been triggered. She put the sketch back down and met Isla's gaze. 'If I give you a photograph of someone, can you draw a portrait for me?' There was a different quality to the housekeeper's voice—a softer, more hesitant quality.

'Of course. But it would be great if the person could sit for me for an hour or—'

'Not possible.' The housekeeper's tone was sharp enough to sever steel.

Isla blinked. 'Okay. The photo will have to do then.'

Concetta worked her jaw a couple of times, as if searching for the right words to use. '*Grazie, signorina.* I will bring it tomorrow.' She turned and walked out without another word, closing the studio door with a resounding click.

Isla sighed and, turning back to the tray set in front of her, poured the tea into the cup and took a refreshing sip. It was too soon to tell if the housekeeper was softening in her icy stance towards her, but not too soon to hope.

* * *

Rafe had been fighting with himself to give Isla some space in her studio. He'd had to tear himself away earlier before he was tempted to spend the rest of the day in bed with her. But his own work had lost its appeal and all he wanted to do was be with her, getting to know her better, peeling back the intriguing layers of her personality. For a hard-nosed workaholic, the change in his motivation was as surprising as it was a little disconcerting. He realised he felt happy for the first time in years. He realised he was starting to relax. He could even feel less tension in his neck and shoulders.

Yes, *relax*—that word he had erased from his vocabulary.

Rafe found Isla working in the studio. The remains of the afternoon tea he had instructed his housekeeper to take to her were sitting to one side. Isla's head was bent over a sketch, the quick-fire movements of her pencil across the sketchpad never failing to impress him. She glanced up as he came in and smiled and something in his stomach toppled over. Would he ever get blasé about her smile and the light in her eyes? Her skin was make-up-free, her curly hair half up and half down in a red-gold cloud about her head. She was wearing dove-grey leggings and an oversized white shirt that skimmed her curves in all the right places. His groin twitched as the memory of her touch rippled through him. He only had to be in the same room as her and it caused a storm in his flesh.

'You look hard at work.' He came over to inspect what she was doing but it wasn't a sketch of his grandmother she was working on but one of him. She had drawn him sleeping, covered at the waist by a sheet that clung to his contours like a drape across a marble statue. He had never seen himself asleep before and it felt strange that she had captured that period of vulnerability. 'It's a good likeness.'

Isla placed another piece of sketch paper over it, her cheeks a faint shade of pink. 'It's just a flash sketch from memory.'

He stood behind her, lifted some of her fragrant hair off the back of her neck and planted a soft kiss to her skin. 'I have a charity dinner to attend in Paris next week. I've been invited to chair one of my favourite children's charities. It's a huge honour and I'd like you to be with me—it will be an excellent way to introduce you in public as my wife-to-be.'

Her body visibly tensed under the gentle press of his hands resting on her shoulders. 'I... I thought we were staying here until...until the wedding?'

He turned her around on the swivelling chair to face him. Her periwinkle blue eyes were troubled, her teeth sinking into the softness of her bottom lip. 'You've attended public dinners with me in the past. What's the problem with doing so now? Especially as you're wearing my ring.'

She glanced down at the glittering diamond ring on her left hand, before coming back to meet his gaze. 'No one knew who I was before. I was just one of your casual lovers.' A shadow passed through her eyes. 'I'm not sure I can handle the press attention. It's...daunting.'

Rafe gently squeezed her shoulders. 'It is daunting but I'll be with you. I'll do everything in my power to protect you. You know that, surely?'

Isla slipped off the chair and from under his hold,

moving behind the worktable as if in need of a barricade. Her arms were tight around her body, her eyes flicking out of reach of his. 'Why don't you go alone? I can stay here and work on your grandmother's portrait as well as rest.'

Rafe wondered what was causing her to react so negatively to a trip abroad. 'Isn't Paris one of your favourite places in the world? What's the sudden aversion to going there with me?'

She sucked in a breath, unfolded her arms and steepled her fingers over her nose and mouth. She closed her eyes in a wincing movement, then lowered her hands from her face to glance at him, the colour in her cheeks darkening to crimson. 'Rafe…there's something I need to tell you. I… I was hoping I wouldn't have to but—'

Rafe's stomach pitched. 'What?' His guts roiled with the possibilities. The horrendous unthinkable possibilities. Another man in the background? Was she already married? His chest was suddenly so tight he couldn't take a breath. *Mio Dio, don't let her be already married to someone else.*

She bit her lip again. 'A long time ago… I made a stupid error of judgement. I was desperate for employment and agreed to work in a…in a—' she swallowed and did that little wincing eye movement again '…a gentlemen's club.'

Rafe's scalp prickled. There were clubs and there were clubs. Some were waiting list exclusive. Some were sleazy. Had someone abused her? Hurt her? Sexually harassed her or worse? The thought of anyone touching her inappropriately sent a wave of fury through his body. '*Cara*, if anyone hurt or threatened you in any way then there are avenues to press charges. I can help you seek justice and—'

Isla bent her head to her chest and sighed, her hands gripping the edge of the worktable. 'I was a lingerie waitress, Rafe. I served businessmen drinks in my underwear.' Her tone was as flat and listless as if she were confessing to an unconscionable crime.

Rafe came over to her and took her stiff little hands in his, stroking the backs of them with his thumbs. 'Look at me, Isla. It's in the past. Lots of people loathe their first job. Not everyone has the luxury of choosing a job that looks good on their CV.'

Her gaze slowly crept up to his, shadows of worry still swimming in their blue depths. 'You don't understand... I agreed to have photos taken.' She gave a gulping swallow and continued. 'A portfolio of photos, some of them topless. I don't know why I agreed to it. I was naïve and too frightened I might not keep the job if I didn't do what the boss said. I was in arrears with my rent, I hadn't eaten for three days, and I was so worried I just did what he said. I've regretted it ever since.'

Rafe wasn't one to resort to violence, but right then he wanted to find the man and rearrange his face so that even the world's best reconstructive facial maxillary surgeon would throw their hands up in defeat. He wanted to find those photos and tear them up and force feed them down the sleazy creep's throat. He wanted justice. He wanted Isla to feel safe. He wanted to protect her so she never had to worry again. Ever. It reminded him of his father's scandal and the impact it had on him as a young teenager. The shame that clung to him like sticky mud. It had taken a lot of strength and willpower and growing a thick skin to move beyond it.

Rafe pulled Isla against his chest and stroked the back of her silky head. 'I'm disgusted with that man for exploiting you. Disgusted and appalled. But I won't allow you to run yourself down because of the sleazy actions of some lowlife creep.' He held her away from him to meet her gaze. 'Where are the photos now? Does he still have them? Has he blackmailed you or made any threats to—'

'No, nothing overt but he hinted at it when I left the job after he came on to me.' Her expression was a landscape of pain, regret and lingering shame. 'He wouldn't have deleted them. And they'll never go away if he puts them online.' Fear and defeated resignation coloured her voice.

Rafe's insides twisted into knots that felt as big as tree stumps. 'I want to fix this for you. I *will* fix this for you.' His hands tightened on hers in determination.

'You can't fix this, Rafe.' Tears welled in her eyes and her voice caught and she pulled out of his hold, putting distance between them again. 'You can't fix me. I'm a liability. I have a target on my back and as soon as you announce you're going to marry me, I know what will happen. Those photos will be on every platform, bringing shame and humiliation to me but also to you.'

An ice-cold trickle of realisation went through his mind. 'Is that why you left me the way you did three months ago? Because of *this*?'

Regret and pride flickered across her expression and through her eyes. 'I panicked when I suspected I was pregnant. You were negotiating that huge deal in New York. I knew how important it was to you and I didn't want to be responsible for jeopardising it. You'd told me a little about Bruno Romano, how conservative he was. I thought it was best if I just disappeared out of your life. Easier for you. Easier for me. But then you found me in that Edinburgh hotel and here we are.'

Rafe speared his fingers through his hair with a hand that was visibly shaking. Emotions he had no name for, no time for, rose in him like a foaming, boiling liquid. He didn't know whether to be angry at himself, or sad for her that she had felt she had to keep the knowledge of the pregnancy to herself. That she had trusted him so little. That somehow his career-driven focus had made it impossible for her to tell him.

That *he* had caused her to run away.

He went to her and gathered her close, hugging her, reassuring her with soothing strokes of his hand on her slim back and murmurings of comfort while he tried to get his emotions in order. If he hadn't run into her at that hotel in Scotland, he might never have known about his child. His gut tightened with an invisible fist. He might never have known his own flesh and blood. And the child would have known nothing of him. It was painful to accept he was partly, if not fully, responsible for her decision to keep quiet.

He had set the rules for their fling.

He had insisted on short-term.

He had made her no promises of a future with him.

He had held her close physically but at arm's length emotionally. He had cordoned off his feelings because he never wanted to give someone the power to hurt him, and yet he had hurt her and himself in the process.

And even more distressing—potentially hurt their child.

Rafe eased her back from him to mesh his gaze with hers. 'I don't know how to make it up to you. It pains me to think you felt you had no other choice but to leave the way you did. But we can put that behind us now. We have to put it behind us and move forward.'

She gave him a world-weary smile tinged with sadness. 'You're being very generous about this. But if I had told you at the time, do you think you would have been as understanding?'

Rafe's conscience was having a tug-of-war. He liked to think he would have been generous and accepting but how could he be so sure? He might have created even more harm by refusing to believe the baby was his or by insisting on a paternity test on the spot, offering her a conditional relationship on the result. Guilt crept over him like a dark accusing shadow, colouring, questioning everything he had once believed about himself. He hoped he was better than that imagined version of himself.

Hoped, but suspected he wasn't.

'Thing is… I'm not sure.' Somehow, he got his voice past the tightness in his throat. 'One thing I do know for sure—I would not have turned my back on my own flesh and blood.'

'Once you'd established it *was* your flesh and blood, which you still haven't insisted upon doing. Why?'

Rafe released her and stepped away, dragging his hand down his face. 'Is that what you want me to do? Insist on black and white proof?'

Something flickered in her gaze. 'I just thought most men would insist on knowing one way or the other, given we were only having a fling.'

'I like to think I'm not most men,' Rafe said with a

little grunt. 'I insisted on us being exclusive and I had no reason to believe you betrayed my trust. I still have no reason to believe it.'

Her bottom lip quivered and tears shone in her eyes. 'Thank you.'

Rafe held out his hands. 'Come here.' She stepped forward and placed her hands in his and he pulled her back into the circle of his arms, resting his chin on the top of her head. He breathed in the flowery scent of her, wondering if he would ever walk by a vine of jasmine again without thinking of her. He had to make their relationship work. He had to make up for his mistakes and mishandling of the situation. He couldn't guarantee the press wouldn't have a shame-fest if those photos ever surfaced but he would do everything in his power to prevent it.

Everything.

CHAPTER NINE

A few days later Isla was still trying to get her head around the fact that Rafe now knew her scandalous secret. But she had felt compelled to bring it out in the open when he'd mentioned the charity dinner in Paris. She'd figured it was far better for him to be prepared for the fallout if there was one than to be caught off-guard. It had been a risk telling him, yet he had surprised her by showing amazing compassion and comfort. And since she had disclosed her secret he had been particularly tender and attentive towards her.

But, with the wedding date looming, it was still hard for Isla to be totally confident she was doing the right thing by marrying him. Even as she was fitted for a wedding dress with an exclusive Italian designer, a ghost hand of doubt tapped her on the shoulder. *He doesn't love you.* It was impossible to escape from that one tripwire in their relationship. She could wear the most beautiful wedding dress, have the most wonderful ceremony and honeymoon, and yet, without the assurance of those three little words, what did she really have?

A marriage founded on duty, not love.

A marriage between two people who could never be equals.

Isla went to the kitchen in search of a cool drink, where she encountered Concetta preparing the evening meal. The housekeeper had maintained her distance since their conversation in the studio, and Isla wondered if she had changed her mind about bringing her a photo for her to work from.

'Can I help you with anything?' Isla said to test the waters. 'I'm not much of a cook but I can set the table or arrange some flowers.'

Concetta wiped her hands on her apron, her expression guarded. 'Signor Angeliri pays me to cook. I do not need help doing my job.'

Isla perched on one of the stools next to the large centre island, deciding for once not to be daunted by the housekeeper's attitude. 'Weren't you going to bring me a photo to work from? Or have you changed your mind?'

Concetta picked up a carrot and began scraping the skin off in swift movements. 'You have the wedding to see to first. It can wait.' She picked up another carrot and stripped it as well.

'Who's the photo of?'

The housekeeper's hands stilled for a brief moment, the muscles around her mouth tightening. 'My daughter.' Her voice lost its sharp edge and her gaze softened.

'Oh, lovely. What's her name?'

Concetta blinked a couple of times and swallowed. 'Her name was Marietta.'

Was? A prickle of alarm crept across Isla's scalp like the march of tiny ants. Could the housekeeper's choice of word simply be a language issue? English was not her native tongue and it was all too easy to misuse words. Or could it mean her daughter was no longer alive? 'I'm sorry if this sounds intrusive but did you mean—' Isla began.

'She is dead.' The words were delivered in a toneless voice that belied the host of emotions flickering across the older woman's face.

'Oh, Concetta… I'm so terribly sorry. I can only imagine the pain you've gone through—still going through.'

Concetta wiped across her eyes with her forearm and then continued preparing the vegetables. 'It was a long time ago but the pain never goes away.'

'How old was Marietta when she…?'

'Four. She had not even started school.' Her lower lip trembled and she pressed her mouth flat to control it. 'She caught a…a disease. I am not sure how to say in English. Mena…meni…'

'Meningitis?'

'That is the one' She shook her head sadly. 'My husband started to drink after we lost her. It changed him. We were not able to have any other children—I had an emergency hyster…whatever it is in English, after her birth.'

'Hysterectomy?'

'Sì.' She sighed and picked up a courgette and sliced off the top and the tail. 'My future died with her. I will never see her married, never hold my own grandchild. There is no end to the pain of losing a child.'

Isla blinked back her own tears and reached across the workbench for the housekeeper's hand, squeezing it in comfort. 'I'm so sorry.' No wonder the older woman was so prickly and unfriendly. She was suffering unimaginable sadness.

Concetta looked down at their joined hands and,

after the briefest of pauses, laid her own on top of Isla's. *'Grazie.'* She gave a back-to-business flicker of a smile and moved to the other side of the kitchen where she had laid her purse and keys. She opened the purse and took out a small photograph, brought it back and handed it to Isla.

Isla looked at the image of a dark-haired smiling child and her heart gave a painful spasm. The little girl was wearing a pretty pink dress and had a matching bow in her hair. 'She's gorgeous, Concetta. Absolutely gorgeous.' She glanced at the housekeeper. 'Do you have other copies of this? I don't want to take the only one off you.'

'I have made many copies. It is my favourite picture of her. She was so excited about going to a birthday party.' Concetta's expression was etched with sadness. 'The friend whose party she went to is married now with children of her own.' She gave a wistful sigh. 'But I only have memories.'

'I will enjoy doing her portrait for you. It will be an honour.'

'It can wait until after the wedding. A bride has many things to see to.'

Isla lowered her gaze a fraction. 'Yes, well, Rafe is doing most of the organising. I just have to show up on the day.' She couldn't quite remove the dejection in her tone.

'Do not marry him if you do not love him.'

Isla met the housekeeper's frowning gaze. 'But that's the problem, you see. I *do* love him but he doesn't love me. Not in the way you'd expect a man to love someone they're about to marry.' It was a relief to finally admit how she felt but she wasn't sure if she had chosen the right person to confess it to.

Loving Rafe had crept up on her, or maybe it had been there all the time as her friend Layla had suggested. Now that she recognised the emotion for what it was, she realised it had been there right from the start. As soon as she'd met him she had felt a seismic shift in her body. It had been like two planets colliding and she hadn't been the same since. And not just because of the pregnancy. She had lied to herself, convincing herself she didn't really like him other than sexually. But he was exactly the sort of man she had dreamt of finding—strong, self-sufficient, hard-working, trustworthy and honourable. She knew deep down he was capable of love; she just didn't know if he was capable of loving her. The armour around her heart had been gradually dismantled by each one of his smiles, his touches, his kisses, his compassionate acceptance of her background and the shame of her past.

Concetta wiped her hands on a tea towel. 'Love can grow over time. Do not underestimate him. He is not like his father. He is a good man.'

Isla gave a half-smile. 'I know he is. A wonderful man who has so many amazing qualities.'

But he doesn't love me.

How long could she live on the hope he might one day do so?

Rafe and Isla were having dinner out on the terrace that evening. The weather was perfect for alfresco dining and Concetta had accepted Isla's help in setting up the table with a large scented candle and some flowers from the garden.

Rafe picked up his water glass, having thoughtfully decided to refrain from drinking alcohol during the rest of her pregnancy—a gesture Isla found incredibly touching. 'You seem preoccupied tonight, *cara*. And you haven't eaten much. Are you not feeling well?'

Isla put down the fork she'd been using to shift her food about her plate without getting much to her mouth. 'I was thinking about Concetta.'

He frowned and put his glass back down on the table. 'Has she been difficult again? I'll have a word with her. I know she can be touchy but she hasn't had the easiest life.'

'I know. She told me today about her daughter, Marietta.' Isla's eyes watered up just by saying the wee girl's name. 'She gave me a photo of her so I can do a portrait. Did you know about Marietta? I wish you'd told me earlier. I would have made more of an effort to get on with Concetta. The loss of a child is the worst possible experience.'

His expression was rueful. 'Yes, perhaps I should have told you. But she's a very private person and she doesn't like talking about it. I'm surprised she told you, actually.'

'Yes, well, we didn't get off to the best start but that was probably more my fault than hers,' Isla said. 'I guess I didn't try too hard back then because I knew I was only going to be a temporary fixture in your life.'

He rolled his thumb over the diamond ring on her hand. 'But you're not now.' His gaze was warm, his tone deep and reassuring. But not reassuring enough for her lingering doubts.

Isla turned his hand over and traced her finger down the middle of his palm. 'This charity dinner next week...' She looked up to meet his gaze. 'Aren't you worried about the effect it will have on the people closest to you if those photos were to surface?'

He curled his fingers around hers, his expression grim. 'There aren't too many people particularly close to me so it won't matter what people think.'

'What about your grandmother? Aren't you close to her?'

He released her hand and leaned back in his chair, his features set in intractable lines. 'You have to remember I didn't meet her until I was a teenager. Nonna refused to have anything to do with my mother because she was a married man's mistress. Her lifestyle clashed with Nonna's strict religious beliefs. When my father dumped my mother, Nonna still refused to have any contact with her.'

'It seems stubbornness is a genetic trait in your family.'

He gave a grunt of assent and picked up his water glass and drank a mouthful before placing it back on the table. 'That and pride. My mother discovered she had cancer a few months after my father deserted her. She kept the knowledge to herself, refusing treatment that could have saved her. I think she just gave up because she felt so rejected and ashamed of what her life had become. And because she was too proud to beg to be taken back into the arms of her family.'

Isla frowned in empathy. 'Oh, that's awful, Rafe. And how terrible for you. You must have felt so alone when she died.'

He gave a crooked movement of his lips that wasn't anything near a smile. 'I made the choice back then to make my own way in life and rely on no one.'

'Is that why you've only ever had short-term relationships?'

Rafe rested one forearm on the table and draped the other arm over the back of his chair—a casual pose that was at odds with the shadows in his eyes. 'It worked back then but I'm ready to settle down now.'

'But only because of my pregnancy. Not because you fell madly in love.' Isla couldn't quite remove the note of despondency in her voice.

His gaze searched hers with an intensity she found distinctly uncomfortable. It was as if he could see *I love you* written across her eyeballs, even though she desperately tried to hide it.

'Isla.' His tone reminded her of a lecturer about to deliver an important message. 'How many gossip magazines have you seen featuring big celebrity weddings? The couples all claim to be madly in love but half, if not most, end in divorce. What happened to the once-in-a-lifetime love they were raving about? Did it die or wasn't it there in the first place?' His mouth twisted in a cynical grimace. 'I tend to believe the latter.'

Isla placed her napkin on the table for something to do with her hands. 'So…you don't believe there's such a thing as romantic love? Love that lasts for ever. Not for anyone?'

'Maybe for a few lucky people. But you'll usually find one person loves more than the other, and there's your problem right there—almost certain heartbreak.'

'Like your mother?'

He gave a grim nod. 'She gave up everything for my father but he kept her dangling on a string for years and then cut the string. She could have had a different life. A more satisfying and fulfilling one.'

Isla could see why he was so cynical about love but it didn't stop her hoping he might change his mind and experience it for himself with her. Was it too much to ask that he fall in love with her? The woman he was marrying in two weeks, the mother of his child? 'At least she had you,' she said. 'You must have given her much joy and she would be so proud of you now.'

Rafe smiled and pushed back his chair and stood. 'Why don't you go up and prepare for bed? Concetta will clear this when she comes first thing in the morning.'

Isla rose from her chair and began to gather the plates. 'I can do it now. It won't take me long.'

His gaze smouldered with a promise that made her shiver in anticipation. 'I'd much rather you save your energy for what I have planned for you.'

Rafe might not claim to love her but his desire for her was unmistakable. A desire that had been there right from the beginning, from the first moment their eyes had met. It gave Isla hope that out of his desire would come a love that defied the odds, love that blossomed and grew deep and secure roots into their future as a family.

CHAPTER TEN

A FEW MINUTES later Isla turned her back to Rafe in the master suite for him to unzip her dress. He lowered the zip but an inch at a time, planting a soft kiss to each knob of her spine. She shivered in reaction, her need for him already sending her pulse skyrocketing. Her dress slipped from her shoulders and then from around her hips, landing in a pool at her feet. Rafe unhooked her bra and turned her to face him, his eyes feasting on the ripeness of her curves.

'Your body is getting more and more beautiful. I had no idea pregnancy could be so sexy.' His voice was thick with lust, his hands reaching for her breasts, cradling them, touching them with exquisite expertise.

Isla's legs were trembling from the assault on her senses. She felt drunk on his touch, dizzy with longing. She gave a wry smile. 'I might not look so sexy to you in a few weeks' time.'

He cupped her face in his hands and pressed a firm kiss to her lips. 'You will always be sexy to me. I have never had a more exciting lover. You stir in me desires I didn't even know I had.'

His words created a warm glow through her body. 'I'll let you in on a secret.'

His hands stilled on her hips. 'Another one?'

Isla smiled and wound her arms around his neck, pressing her naked breasts against his chest. 'Not *that* kind of secret. I've never been able to orgasm with a partner before. Only with you.'

He frowned. 'Really? Why didn't you tell me before now?'

She shrugged one shoulder and began to undo the buttons on his shirt. 'Too embarrassed, I guess.'

He placed his hands over her hands working on his buttons, a frown still creasing his forehead. 'You have no need to be embarrassed, *cara*. Ever. Not with me.'

Isla gave a rueful smile and looked at their joined hands. 'I thought I was hopeless at sex but now I realise I didn't have the right chemistry with other people.'

'How many people?' His expression was dark and brooding, as if he was sickened by the thought of her with other men.

Isla raised her brows. 'I hope you're not going to go all double standards on me. You've had plenty of lovers. Why shouldn't I?' Not that she'd had anywhere near 'plenty'. Her number of lovers didn't even go into double figures.

His mouth tightened for a moment and then he let out a breath, his hands going to rest on her hips. 'You're right. I have no right to be jealous.'

Isla gave him a teasing smile. 'You're jealous? You're actually admitting it?'

A dull flush appeared high on his aristocratic cheekbones but his expression was still brooding. 'I hate the thought of other men touching you the way I touch you.' His voice was a deep growl that made her insides quiver.

She pressed a soft kiss to his tight mouth and smiled. 'Stop glowering at me. I've only had two lovers and neither of them were as amazing as you.'

His hands on her hips drew her closer, the ridge of his erection sending a shockwave of need through her entire body. 'What's wrong with those men that they didn't satisfy you? You're the most responsive lover I've ever had.'

She planted another kiss on his lips. 'They weren't you—that's what was wrong.'

He returned the kiss with a low deep groan, his tongue thrusting between her lips to tangle with hers in a sexy duel that sent fireworks fizzing and whizzing in her blood. She felt his sensual excitement running through him, the probe of his aroused flesh and the erotic flickers of his tongue in her mouth making her inner core clench.

Isla continued to undo the buttons on his shirt, leaving a kiss on each part of his chest as she uncovered it. She peeled his shirt away from his shoulders and set to work on the fastening on his trousers. His eyes darkened with desire and he sucked in a breath as her fingers skated teasingly over the hard ridge of his arousal. She lowered herself in front of him, uncovering him so she could tease him with her lips and tongue. His fingers dug into her scalp as if he thought his legs would go from under him without her support. His groans and heavy breathing were a delight to her and she continued her sensual exploration of him, enjoying the power it gave her to reduce him to the same level of longing as he had done to her. *This* was the balance of power she craved—to know he wanted her as much as he wanted his next breath.

He pulled away from her with a desperate groan. 'Stop. I can't take any more. I want to be inside you.'

His words sent a hot, pebbly shiver over her flesh. She took his hand and got to her feet, leading him to the bed, taking off her knickers as she went. Rafe kicked his trousers and shoes to one side and tugged off his socks and came down beside her on the bed.

His mouth went to her breast, kissing, stroking, teasing her nipples into tight and aching peaks. He moved down her body, leaving a blistering trail along her flesh until she was gasping out loud and writhing to get closer, to have him where she most wanted him.

'I want to taste you.' His voice was rough with desire, his warm breath skating over her lower body to claim his prize.

Isla grasped him by the hair. 'No. I want you inside me. Now.'

He gave her a devilish grin. 'Say please.'

'Please, Rafe. Make love to me. Please, please, please.'

'With pleasure.' He came back up to position himself over her, his legs entangled with hers. He drove into her centre with a guttural groan, his movements fast, feverish, frantic. She was with him all the way, welcoming each thrust with a gasp of pleasure. Isla gripped his taut buttocks, holding him to her, desperate for release as the sensations rioted through her body in hot pulsing waves.

With the merest coaxing of his fingers on her swollen centre she was off and flying, her entire body thrashing with a cataclysmic release. Within moments, Rafe followed with his own deep and gravelly groan of desperation, his body shuddering as the ripples of pleasure went through him.

Isla held him against her, stroking her hands over his back and shoulders, delighting in the spray of goosebumps that peppered his flesh. *She* had done this to him. Brought him undone with her touch, with her body—with her love.

How could she call it having sex now? It was making love. Isla had been making love with him from the start. That was why sex had been so awkward with other people. She hadn't been able to give all of herself, to feel comfortable enough to express herself physically. She had needed the connection to be deeper, stronger, more meaningful than just two bodies getting it on.

And what stronger and more meaningful connection could there be other than love?

Rafe propped himself up on one elbow, his other hand idly playing with her hair. 'I thought of you every day after you left.' His voice had a sombre note that matched his thoughtful frown. 'Every single day. And night.' His mouth twisted into a self-deprecating smile. 'I was angry at you but over time I realised I was really angry at myself.'

Isla stroked away the crevasse of his frown between his eyebrows. 'Why?'

He captured her hand and brought it to his mouth and kissed each of her fingertips, his gaze holding hers. 'I hadn't met anyone like you before. Someone who wasn't in awe of my money or what gifts I bought you or places I took you. I liked that about you. It impressed me and, believe me, I'm hard to impress.' His frown came back and he continued, 'I was angry because…it…it *hurt* to lose you.' A flicker of something passed over his face as if saying the word 'hurt' had caused him further pain. 'I hadn't felt like that before. I didn't allow myself to get invested in relationships where it could even be a possibility. I didn't take those sorts of risks.'

Isla gently pulled her hand out of his and sent her fingers on a journey down the length of his richly stubbled jaw. 'But you did with me.' Her voice was barely above a whisper, her hopes barely above water. Was he about to tell her he loved her?

He leaned down and pressed a soft-as-air kiss to her mouth. 'You should come with a warning. Take care when handling.' His tone was mildly teasing, his eyes dark and shining.

Isla circled his mouth with her finger. 'So should you.'

The teasing light went out of his eyes and his frown came back. 'I worry about how much your life has changed because of this—' he placed his hand on the mound of her belly '—our child. You're the one who's had to make the most adjustments so far and that will likely continue.'

She placed her hand over the top of his and tentatively smiled. 'But you'll be with me every step of the way, right?'

His hand came up and cradled one side of her face, his expression grave. 'Never doubt it, *cara mio.*'

Why then was she still doubting? Not that he wouldn't support her during the rest of the pregnancy and beyond. But what about love? What about the special emotion two people felt for each other that would last a lifetime?

The special emotion she felt for him and had done so from the first moment she'd met him.

For ever love.

Isla wondered if she should risk telling him how she felt. But telling someone how she felt had always ended badly when she was a child, so over the years she had taught herself not to reveal and not to feel. Telling the first foster parents how much she loved them had been her first mistake. She had been moved within days to another home, to live with more strangers. Kind strangers who had also over time evoked such feelings of gratitude in Isla that she had told them she loved them too.

And she'd been moved again.

And again.

And again.

Her adult self knew it was the system. Kids didn't always stay long in any one place due to other needy kids needing urgent placements, but as a child it had felt like she was unlovable.

Rafe sent a lazy finger between her eyebrows and down the bridge of her nose. 'What's that frown for, hmm?'

Isla circled her fingers around his wrist, pulling his hand down from her face. 'I need the bathroom... Sorry.' She wasn't ready to tell him. She couldn't tell him and risk being rejected.

Or worse—being reminded she was unlovable.

He rolled aside and got off the bed, holding a hand out to her, his features etched in lines of concern. 'Are you feeling unwell?'

Isla ignored his hand and pushed herself off the bed, sending a hand through the wild mess of her hair. 'I'm fine, Rafe. I just really need to pee.'

And I need to be alone to get my dangerously tempted-to-confess-all tongue back under control.

The bathroom door closed with a snick of the lock that somehow felt to Rafe like a slap to the face. He scraped a hand through his hair and turned back to look at the rumpled bed. He leaned down and straightened the covers and wished he could just as easily straighten his tangled thoughts. Why had he told her he'd felt hurt when she'd left? *Hurt?* No, hurt was an emotion he never allowed himself to feel. Another word he had deleted from his vocabulary. He made sure he didn't care enough to be hurt by anyone.

But somehow, in the afterglow of good sex, he had revealed things about himself he revealed to no one.

Half the time, not even to himself.

Making love with Isla had a strange effect on him and had done so from the start. In the moments after orgasm, when his body was relaxed and satiated, a guard lowered inside him. The locked vault around his heart developed a small fissure, letting in a tiny sliver of light. It was in that brief window of time he *felt* vulnerable.

There, he had confessed to feeling the dreaded V word.

Vulnerable.

It didn't last long—he didn't allow it to, but the thought of that feeling lurking, waiting for another chance to catch him off-guard, was incredibly disquieting.

A few days later, Isla and Rafe flew to Paris for his charity dinner and he settled her into his penthouse at his hotel in the exclusive and gentrified Saint Germain. He had organised for her to have her hair and beauty treatments done in advance and spent a fortune on a new dress for her that would accommodate her baby bump. The glorious royal blue satin shoulderless dress draped her figure in all the right places, and Isla couldn't help thinking even Cinderella would have been envious.

And yet, now she was in Paris with Rafe, Isla sensed a clock ticking on a time bomb. As soon as the news spread about their impending wedding, as it would surely do after a high-profile event such as this, her private shame had a very real possibility of being exposed to every critical and judging eye. The impact on Rafe and his reputation couldn't be underestimated. Not to mention the impact on her.

Isla sat at the mirror in front of the dressing table in the penthouse, putting the last touches to her make-up, waiting for Rafe to come back to collect her for the ball. He had been called away to speak to his hotel manager downstairs but assured her he would be only a few minutes.

The penthouse door opened and she heard the distinctive sound of Rafe's footsteps approaching the bedroom and, when he arrived, met his eyes in the mirror. 'Everything all right with your manager?'

'*Sì.* All good.' He smiled and took out a flattish rectangular velvet jewellery box from inside his tuxedo jacket pocket. 'I have something for you.'

Isla stood from the dressing table stool and gave him a mock-stern look. 'You didn't really need to speak to your manager at all, did you?'

His smile became a grin and he handed her the box. 'I had to ask him to unlock the safe for me.'

Isla took the box from him, flicked the tiny brass catch open and lifted the lid to reveal a glittering sapphire and diamond necklace and matching droplet earrings. 'Oh, my goodness. They're beyond beautiful—they're absolutely stunning.'

'Like their new owner.' His voice dropped in pitch to a deep rough burr that made her spine feel tingly.

Cinderella, eat your heart out. How could Isla feel anything but beautiful wearing such exquisite jewels? She trailed her index finger over the sparkling diamonds and densely blue sapphires. 'I'm almost too afraid to wear them in case I lose them.'

'Don't worry. I insured them three months ago.'

Isla glanced up at him in puzzlement. 'You bought these before? *Before* I... I left?'

Something came down at the back of his gaze with the speed of a camera shutter click. He gave a loose one-shoulder shrug that was at odds with the sudden tightness of his mouth. 'What of it? It's just a gift I bought when I was in New York.'

Just a gift? A pretty expensive gift to Isla's reckoning. To anyone's reckoning. What did it mean? She looked down at the gorgeous jewels and swallowed. 'I don't know what to say...'

'Thank you will be perfectly adequate.' His tone had a sharp edge that brought her gaze back up to his.

'Oh, Rafe...' she said, touching him on the arm. 'It's the most beautiful gift I've ever received. Thank you so much. I'm sorry I wasn't there when you brought it back from New York. No wonder you were so angry with me.'

He let out a long slow breath. 'It wasn't about that.' He took the box from her. 'Here—let me put them on you. Turn around.'

Isla turned her back to him, her skin lifting in a delicate shiver as his fingers touched her skin in the process of fastening the necklace around her neck. The sapphires made her blue eyes pop and she had never felt more beautiful or bewildered. He had bought her gifts before, many gifts that were expensive and gorgeous, but something about this gift was different. She was no jewellery-valuer but this ensemble was clearly worth a fortune.

And he had bought it for her months ago.

Rafe handed her the earrings one at a time, waiting as she inserted them into her earlobes. His hands came to rest on the tops of her shoulders and he smiled. 'They suit you.'

Isla crossed her right arm over her body to place her hand over one of his, meshing her gaze with his. 'Thank you. I will always treasure them, no matter what.'

He bent his head to drop a kiss to the back of her neck. 'We'd better get going, otherwise I'll be tempted to see what you're wearing under that dress.'

Isla laughed. 'Not very much.'

His eyes smouldered with molten heat and he stroked his hand over one of her bottom cheeks. 'That's what I thought.'

CHAPTER ELEVEN

THE BALL WAS being held in a grand hotel on the seventh arrondissement with spectacular views of the Eiffel Tower and the city beyond. Rafe led Isla into the hotel past the throng of the press but the rapid fire of cameras going off was distinctly off-putting. How was she supposed to act calm and poised and comfortable when she didn't belong in Rafe's world?

His world was one of high finance, exotic destinations, glamorous events and even more glamorous people.

Her world was one of salacious secrets and cringeworthy shame.

A journalist approached and asked, 'Rafael Angeliri, we have heard rumours that the beautiful woman beside you is soon to be your wife. Is that true?'

Rafe's arm gathered Isla close to his side. 'Yes, it is true. We are marrying next weekend in Sicily.'

Isla swallowed and painted a smile on her lips and tried to look as if she was used to having forty cameras aimed in her direction. The journalist glanced at Isla's abdomen and asked, 'We have also heard congratulations are in order for another happy event. Do you have anything to say on that?'

'Isla and I are delighted to be having our first child in December,' Rafe said. 'Now, if you'll excuse us, we have a function to attend.'

Several other journalists vied for Rafe's attention but he led Isla inside the hotel with a firm arm around her. Once they were safely inside and away from most of the crowd of guests waiting to enter the ballroom, he took her hand and kissed the backs of her fingers, holding her gaze with his. 'That wasn't so bad, was it?'

Isla gave a weak smile. 'I seriously think I need to attend press-handling classes.'

He squeezed her hand. 'They're just ordinary people trying to do their job. There will be official photos later but for now try and relax and enjoy the evening.'

And, to her surprise, Isla did enjoy the evening. The food was a stunning example of French cuisine at its best, and the table and ballroom decorations had a Marie Antoinette era look that gave the night a step-back-in-time feel.

Rafe was by her side until he got up to the podium to give his keynote speech. He spoke in fluent French as well as English on the importance of taking care of children in the community. *Every* community. The strategies he proposed for better care of the most vulnerable in the community were well-thought-out and practical, and Isla felt incredibly proud and deeply moved that he was so determined to bring about change.

When he came back to the table after rapturous applause, Rafe leaned down to kiss Isla on the lips before he sat back down. He took one of her hands and rested it on his thigh. 'I'm glad you came with me tonight. It wouldn't have been the same without you.'

'You were wonderful,' Isla said, leaning her head against his shoulder. 'I was so proud of you.'

He turned his head towards her and smiled and something in her stomach swooped. He stroked the curve of her cheek with a lazy finger, his eyes darkening. 'Dance with me?'

'I would love to.'

He drew her to her feet and led her to the dance floor just as the band began to play a romantic ballad. Isla melted into Rafe's arms and moved with him around the floor as if they were one person, not two. Dancing had never felt more graceful, more fluid, more natural than when in Rafe's arms. One song turned into two and then three, and then Isla lost count. She was captivated by the feel of his arms holding her close, the tangy scent of his aftershave teasing her nostrils, the sheer joy of being his entire focus.

Rafe looked down at her with a smile that made her legs weaken at the knees. 'We'll smash the bridal waltz next Saturday now we've had all this practice, *si*?'

A tiny tremor of unease tiptoed through her. *This time next week she would be Rafe's wife.* Was she doing the right thing by marrying him, even though he had never said he loved her? When all was said and done, it was nothing more than a duty marriage. Yes, it was convenient for him that he desired her and enjoyed her company. But he had never claimed to love her and had even intimated he wasn't capable of feeling that way about anyone. Was she being a fool for settling for care and concern and security instead of the love she desired and hungered for?

Isla fought to keep her features in neutral but he

must have sensed her disquiet and led her off the dance floor to a quieter area away from the other guests.

'What's wrong, *mio piccolo*?' His tone was full of concern. 'Are you not enjoying yourself?'

Isla smiled her lingering doubts away. She had to stop stressing over what she didn't have and enjoy what she did have. Rafe cared for her. He was prepared to provide for and protect her and their baby. 'I'm having a wonderful time. It's been a fabulous evening. I'm just feeling a little tired now, I guess.'

And in love. Hopelessly, stupidly in love.

He leaned down and gently kissed her forehead. 'Then it is time for me to take my beautiful Cinderella home from the ball.'

Rafe was relieved to leave the ball in any case. He didn't enjoy the spotlight at the best of times, and the last thing he wanted to do was make idle chat with people he didn't know when the only person he wanted to be with was Isla. That was one of the things he'd missed most when she'd left him three months ago. The emptiness at the end of the day when he returned home to his empty villa, when before he had looked forward to their lively debates and verbal tussles that made his blood tick with excitement. Dancing with her made him realise yet again how in tune they were with each other physically. It secretly thrilled him he had been the only lover who had satisfied her. But in some ways the reverse was also true. He had never felt with anyone else the intense level of satisfaction he felt with her.

Once they were back at his hotel penthouse bedroom, Rafe took Isla in his arms and kissed her softly on the mouth. 'You were the belle of the ball tonight.'

She linked her arms around his neck, her eyes as luminous as twin moonlit lakes. 'You don't do too badly in the handsome stakes yourself.' She moved against him, her pelvis setting fire to his. 'But it's time you took off that posh suit.'

Rafe raised a questioning eyebrow. 'Hey—I thought you were tired?'

She pressed herself even closer so he could feel every delicious curve of her body along every hard ridge of his. Her naughty girl smile sent a lightning strike of lust to his groin. 'Not *that* tired.' She stood on tiptoe and planted a series of kisses on his mouth. It was all he could do not to pull up her dress and take her against the wall.

He cupped her bottom in his hands, the smooth satin of her dress sliding against her curves with a sexy swish. 'You should be resting. I kept you on the dance floor way too long.'

Isla whipped off his bow-tie and tossed it to the floor, her eyes sparkling as bright as the diamonds and sapphires around her neck. 'Then you can take me to bed. Now. But you have to undress me first.'

'No problem.' Rafe tugged her dress down to reveal her breasts, the proud and ripe curves with their pregnancy darkened nipples sending every drop of his blood south. He pulled the dress further down and it fell to the floor at her feet, leaving her in nothing but her high heels, her jewels and a tiny lace thong. He cupped her breasts in his hands, feasting on their soft white creaminess against his olive-toned skin. 'You take my breath away every time I look at you.' His voice came out raspy and his need burned like fire in his groin.

She began to unbutton his shirt but she only got to button number three when Rafe took over the job himself. He hauled the shirt over his head and threw it aside, desperate to feel her hands on him. She was already on to it, her busy little fingers sliding down his zip and finding him. He shuddered at her touch, the play of her hand up and down his shaft driving him crazy with need.

He pulled her hand away, breathing heavily, searching for his self-control but finding it had gone into hiding. 'Let's slow down a bit—'

'Let's not.' Her mouth slammed into his, her tongue snaking between his lips and shooting fire into his mouth and into his blood. His pulse hammered, his heart raced, his lust roared.

One of his hands grasped her by the hip, the other dispensed with the tiny scrap of lace that was barely covering the secret heart of her. He caressed her hot wet centre with his fingers, teasing her into gasping cries of pleasure. He hitched one of her legs up so he could drive into her to experience the contractions of her orgasm around him, triggering his own powerful release. He gave a deep groan and lost himself in the star-exploding storm that shook and shuddered and shimmied through every inch of his body.

Isla ran her hands down his arms with a feather-light touch. 'That's more like the Rafe I know.'

Rafe was still trying to catch his breath. 'What do you mean?'

She circled one of his flat nipples with a teasing finger. 'Since I've been back, you've been making love to me as if I'm made of glass.' The edge of her mouth came up in a coy half-smile. 'I like it both ways.'

A shiver coursed over Rafe's body. No one could turn him on like her. A sultry glance from beneath those fan-like lashes, a flash of that knock-you-out-cold smile, the sexy scrape of her fingernails along his arm. Everything she did made molten heat flash along the network of his veins, sending his blood pumping, thumping, jumping in excitement.

He took her by the hips again and brought his mouth to just above hers. 'Let's see what I can do about that.'

Isla woke the next morning from a deep and restful sleep to find herself alone in the bed. Nothing unusual in that, for Rafe was an early riser—such an early riser he put most larks to shame. She pushed her hair away from her face and swung her legs over the edge of the bed, smiling when she felt tiny twinges in her inner core. Making love with Rafe had been the perfect way to finish the night of the ball. His compliments had made her glow with pleasure, his touch sending her into raptures time and time again.

She had made a bargain with herself last night to stop fretting about those wretched photos. Her worries about a public exposure of her past might never be re-alised and it was crazy to put herself under such stress over something she had no control over anyway. Rafe had told her to put it out of her mind—that it was not an issue for him. This time next week they would be man and wife. She had to focus on the future they had, together with their child. A future that might not be as perfect as she had dreamed of, but it would be secure and stable and she, of all people, knew there was a lot to be said for secure and stable.

Isla had a shower and, with her towel still wrapped on her head, came out of the bathroom to see Rafe standing by the bed with a newspaper folded up in his hand. His expression was inscrutable but there was a brooding energy that came off him in waves.

A shiver ran down Isla's spine like a small sticky-footed creature. 'You were up early.' She tried to disguise her worry by leaning to one side and rubbing the towel against her wet hair. 'Did you get some of those gorgeous fresh croissants from the bakery like the last time we were here?'

'Isla.' The note of gravitas in his voice chilled her blood. 'I want you to promise me something.'

She gulped and didn't try disguising it. She couldn't. 'Wh-what?'

'Promise me you won't look at the papers or anything online until this blows over. Okay?'

A cold hand clutched her heart and squeezed, squeezed, squeezed until she could only get enough breath to whisper, 'This?' Her eyes went to the folded newspaper under his arm. 'Oh, God…the photos?' The frozen hand around her heart suddenly let go and the trapped blood gushed and hammered so hard she thought her chest would explode.

A flash of pain went across his face and his eyes looked haunted. 'You have to let me deal with it, *cara*. Trust me. I will deal with it and you will *never* suffer this humiliation again. Understood?' The steely determination in his tone was as reassuring as if he had those dreadful negatives burning to smithereens in front of her right then and there.

If ever there was a man worthier of a white stallion and a suit of armour, Isla would like to see him. Rafe's promise to protect her, to keep her from harm no matter what, was as wonderful as if he had said *I love you*. Didn't that prove how much he cared for her? Why was she worrying about three little words that anyone could say but not always back up with actions?

'You'd do that? For me?' Her voice was just shy of breaking.

He threw the newspaper into the wastepaper bin and came to her and pulled her close against his chest. 'I'm sorry this has happened but we'll ride it out. Don't speak to the press, no matter what. It will only add fuel to the fire.'

Isla looked up at him with tears stinging her eyes. 'I'm so sorry.'

He kissed her forehead. 'You're not the one who should be apologising. I will not rest until I see justice served. You have my word on that.'

It took every ounce of willpower for Isla to walk past that wastepaper bin without pulling the newspaper out. It took willpower to turn her phone's Wi-Fi off so she couldn't look at anything online. It took even more willpower and fortitude to travel to the airport with Rafe and try and ignore the horde of press waiting for them wherever they went. But no amount of willpower could allow her to unhear the salacious questions fired at her like a rapid round of artillery. Each question hit her like a slap. She could feel her face on fire, shame raining down on her, weighing her down so she could barely walk in a straight line, her body hunched against the onslaught.

Rafe kept his arm around her, shepherding her through the knot of paparazzi to the waiting car. 'Don't respond. I'm with you. You have nothing to be ashamed of, *cara*. They are the ones who should be ashamed, not you.'

Rafe was so calm and controlled and yet she sensed he was simmering with an anger so intense she couldn't help pitying the person who'd posted the photos. She had given him all the details she could remember of the man who ran the club and Rafe had already set the legal wheels in motion.

A Sicilian's fierce pride was a potent thing and it thrilled her that Rafe cared enough about her that he would fight for justice no matter what it cost. For the first time, Isla thought that maybe there was a chance they could ride this out. Rafe was by her side and supporting her. Didn't that count for something? If it didn't matter to him, then why should it matter to her?

Once they were safely in the car, a mantle of peace settled over her. She no longer had to face this alone. He was with her every step of the way.

Rafe reached for her hand and drew it up to his mouth, kissing her bent knuckles. 'Together we will get through this, *mio piccolo*. I won't allow anyone to hurt you. You're safe with me.'

Safe. That was something Isla had never felt before now. 'You have no idea how much that means to me.' Her voice was soft with gratitude, her heart so full with love for him she was surprised he couldn't see it. So what if he didn't love her? She had enough love for both of them.

And maybe in time he would come to love her, as she was sure he would love their child.

They arrived back in Mondello, but they were barely in the door of the villa when Concetta came towards them with a worried look on her face. '*Signor*, you must hurry. Signora Bavetta has just been taken to hospital.'

Isla's heart sank. His *nonna* was ill?

Rafe dropped the bag he was carrying on the floor with a thud, his features tight with tension. 'Why didn't someone call me before now?'

'The call only just came in from her housekeeper, Maria,' Concetta said. 'They have taken her to the private hospital in Palermo where she went the last time she had a fall.'

'Did she fall again?' Rafe asked, rattling his car keys in impatience.

'No,' Concetta said, glancing briefly at Isla. 'She was reading something on her tablet and she suddenly collapsed.'

Ice-cold dread pooled in Isla's stomach. Had Rafe's grandmother seen the scandal of her past in the press? Was his *nonna*'s illness *her* fault? She looked at Rafe, her hand clutching her chest where her heart was thumping so jerkily she worried she might faint. Her past was never going to go away. It was always going to be a sticking point, if not for Rafe, then for his family and friends and business colleagues.

'Stay here, *cara*,' Rafe said, touching her lightly on the arm. 'You need to rest. I'll call you when I find out how she is.'

Isla grabbed at his wrist, tears already welling in her eyes. 'Why can't I come with you? I want to support you—'

The grim shadow in his eyes was only there for a moment before he blinked it away, but it was there long enough for Isla to know she had no place by his side. Not with him at his grandmother's bedside, given it was *her* scandal that had caused his *nonna* to collapse.

'No, Isla. You must stay here and rest.' His tone brooked no resistance. 'There isn't anything you can do right now.'

Yes, there is. Isla's heart plummeted. *I should have done it well before now.*

CHAPTER TWELVE

Isla packed a few things in an overnight bag and booked an online fare back to London rather than Edinburgh. She needed some time to herself before going back to Scotland to sort out the train wreck of her life. If Rafe found her before she had time to think about her future, she might be tempted to stay with him. But how could she stay, knowing it was *her* mess that had caused his grandmother to become ill?

Her past was not going to go away, no matter how much she wanted it to. No matter how much money Rafe spent on expensive lawyers. No matter how much he tried to reassure her. It was an ugly stain on a white sheet, an indelible stain that spread and spread until now it was tainting others. *Hurting* others. Hurting Rafe—the man she loved more than anyone in the world.

Rafe, whom she loved more than her own happiness.

Isla called a cab and waited in the foyer for it to arrive. Concetta appeared from behind one of the marble pillars with a frown on her weathered features.

'You are leaving? *Again?*' The housekeeper's voice contained a thread of worry. 'But you must not. The *signor* will be—'

'I'm sorry, Concetta, but I must go,' Isla said, fighting to hold her emotions in check. 'Surely you can see that? I don't belong in his life. You've always thought that. Deny it if you like, but we both know I'll only bring more trouble into his life.'

'I admit I didn't like you at first,' Concetta said. 'But that was because I didn't think you were being honest with him. I see now you are good for Signor Angeliri. You make him smile. You make him relax. He doesn't work such long hours when you are here. You cannot just leave him. The wedding is next Saturday.'

'There isn't going to be a wedding,' Isla said. 'I should never have said I would marry him.'

'You make promises and then you don't keep them.' Concetta's black button gaze was scathing. 'It is better not to make a promise in the first place so you don't get people's hopes up.'

Isla steepled her hands around her mouth and nose and let out a deep breath. So, it wasn't only Rafe and his grandmother she had hurt but his housekeeper too. She lowered her hands from her face and met the housekeeper's critical gaze. 'I haven't had much time yet to work on your daughter's portrait. But when it's finished I'll send it to you, I promise. And Rafe's grandmother's portrait too.'

'*Pah!*' Concetta's tone was as scathing as her gaze. 'If she lives to see it.'

The front door opened and Rafe stepped inside with a frown carved deep between his brows. 'What's going on? Why is there a cab waiting outside?'

'Your *fiancée*—' Concetta spat the word out like a lemon pip '—is leaving.'

Rafe's expression became as unreadable as a MI5

spy. 'Please excuse us, Concetta,' he addressed the housekeeper in a cool and formal tone. 'Isla. The salon. Now.'

He went to take her by the elbow to lead her in the direction of the salon but she stepped out of his reach.

'How is your grandmother? Is she…?' Isla couldn't go any further as dread and shame washed through her in sickening waves.

'She suffered a mild stroke but nothing to worry about. The geriatrician has put her on some blood-thinning medication. She'll be home in a day or two.' His voice remained calm on the surface but there was an undertone of tension. 'But it's you I'm worried about. What's going on? Has Concetta upset you?'

Isla picked up her tote bag from the chair near the hall table and hung it over her shoulder. 'I'm sorry, Rafe, but I have to go. This isn't going to work. I was stupid to think it ever would and I—'

'What's brought this about?' The tension in his voice went up another notch.

'It's me, Rafe,' Isla said. 'Me. You. Us. It can never work. I will only bring shame and disgrace to you and your family.'

He pinched the bridge of his nose—the first sign of a crack in his steely composure. He blew out a breath and locked his gaze on hers. 'I told you I'd handle the photo situation. I've got my people working on it as we speak. You have to trust me to deal with—'

'And what happens in the meantime?' Isla said, her throat tight and throbbing. 'Stand by and watch your grandmother have another stroke when she sees more of those awful photos splashed everywhere? I can't allow that to happen. I can't do it to her or to you.'

A flicker of something passed over his face—a tiny flinch of a muscle near the hinge of his jaw, a blink that lasted a little too long, as if he were mentally closing a blind on a distressing scene. 'Nonna would have had a mini-stroke regardless. The doctor said—'

'So, you're not denying that she saw the photos on her tablet and it caused her to get upset enough to—'

'Isla, it's not your fault.' The heavy chord in his tone told her the opposite. It confirmed everything she believed about herself.

'How can it *not* be my fault?' Isla asked. 'Next it will be your business taking a hit. Deals being cancelled because of me. The children's charity dumping you as chairman. I won't allow it to happen. I won't do that to you.'

'So, what you're doing now is okay, is it?' His top lip curled and his eyes flashed with sparks of anger. 'Running away again. Leaving because things got a little awkward. That's not how you handle stress that comes into your life, Isla. You have to face it head-on and deal with it.'

Isla raised her chin, determined not to be talked out of going. 'I *am* dealing with it *my* way.'

'Your way?' He gave a scornful laugh. 'Your way is childish and immature. You're having a child yourself. My child. You can't just run away when things don't work out the way you hoped.'

'I'm not running away. I'm removing myself from a situation that will hurt both of us and our child in the long run.' Isla was proud of the evenness of her tone, which belied the storm of emotion building in her chest.

His eyebrows were so tightly knitted there was no space between them. He opened and closed his mouth a couple of times as if searching for the right words. 'You're really serious about this.' It wasn't a question; it sounded more like a statement of resignation. Maybe he knew deep down how hopeless it was. How he might never be able to get rid of those wretched photos.

Isla tried to read his expression, looking for a clue, a hope to hold onto, to convince her he cared enough for her—*loved her enough*—to ride out any scandal, but his features were cast in marble. Impenetrable, unreadable, cold marble. 'I am serious. I'm flying home in a couple of hours. I'll keep you informed on the baby's progress and send you a copy of the next scan.'

'I want to be there when he or she is born.' There was a strange quality to his voice she hadn't heard before but his expression remained masklike.

She nodded and grasped the strap of the bag slung over her shoulder. 'Of course.'

He stepped forward to pick up her bag. 'I'll take you to the airport.'

Isla put a hand on his arm to stop him. 'No. I'd rather you didn't. I'm not a fan of lengthy goodbyes.'

The muscles in his arm bunched under the touch of her hand and he pulled it away as if she had wounded him. 'Yes, well, I should know that by now. I should be feeling grateful I caught you before you left. Or did you leave me a note like last time?'

Isla pressed her lips together, colour warming her cheeks. 'I was going to text you once I was on board.'

'Magnanimous of you.'

Isla let out a heavy breath and closed her eyes in a slow blink. 'Don't do this, Rafe.'

He gave another scornful laugh. 'Don't do what? My fiancée decides she's calling off our relationship within days of our wedding and I'm not supposed to be angry or upset?'

'I never wanted to be your fiancée in the first place,' Isla said, summoning up some anger of her own. It was either anger or reveal her love and that she was *not* going to do. Not to be rejected like every other time she had opened her heart to someone who didn't love her back. 'You were the one who insisted on marriage. You can still be a father without being a husband. And, I can assure you, you'll be a damn better father without me as your wife.'

'Is this your final decision?' The calm chill was back in his voice and his expression was as blank and cold as the marble pillar behind him.

'There's nothing you could say to change my mind, Rafe.'

One dark eyebrow went up in an arc over his eye. 'Nothing?'

Isla held his cynical look. How could she trust it were true if he said those three little words now? 'Nothing I would believe.'

He pushed his hands into his trouser pockets, rocking back on his heels as if he was waiting for a particularly annoying houseguest to get their act together and leave. 'I'll make sure there is plenty of money in your account to help with expenses.'

'You don't have to do—'

'Don't tell me what I have to do, Isla.' The chord of bitterness in his tone stung like a slap. 'I will provide for my own flesh and blood.' He removed his hands from his pockets and picked up her overnight bag. 'You'd better get going. You don't want to miss your flight.'

Isla walked out to the cab with her heart feeling as heavy as a tombstone. It was as if every sadness she had ever experienced, every disappointment, every rejection had gathered in her chest. Weighing her down with the reminder of how dangerous it was to love someone and then lose them.

She got in the cab and Rafe closed the door and stepped back, his hands going back into his trouser pockets, his spy face back on. 'Safe travels.'

Isla forced a polite on-off smile to her lips. 'Thank you.'

He turned and walked back into the villa and shut the door before the cab driver had even put the car in gear.

Rafe held his breath until he heard the cab drive off and then he swore. Loud and filthy and in three languages. There weren't enough words in all the languages in the world for him to express how angry he was feeling. Every muscle in his body was coiling with it, his guts burning and churning. He was angry that Isla had once again caught him off-guard and dropped a bomb on him. The *I'm leaving you* bomb. The bomb that exploded in his chest and made it impossible for him to breathe. An invisible steel band was around his heart, tightening, tightening, tightening until he was starved of oxygen. He had never had a panic attack in his life but this sure felt like it. What was wrong with him? He'd experienced Isla leaving before and got through it. He would get through it again.

He *had* to.

Rafe shoved a hand through his hair so hard he was surprised his fingers didn't come away dripping blood and hair roots. He wanted to punch the wall in frustration but he didn't think his hand would appreciate the contact with solid Italian marble. He pulled in a ragged breath and fought to calm himself. Okay, so the wedding would have to be cancelled. No problem. He had enough staff to take care of that. There were some tasks best left to others and that was one of them. He wanted no reminders of his failure to keep Isla by his side. He had offered her the world and she had rejected him.

Concetta appeared like a ghost, her face equally pale. 'She's gone?'

Rafe planted his hands on his hips and glared at her. 'I suppose you're happy now. You never liked her, did you?'

His housekeeper had the grace to look ashamed. 'It's true at first I didn't, but I came to realise she loves you and that's all that matters.'

Rafe stared at her as if she had suddenly started speaking in tongues. 'What?'

'She loves you, *signor*. You would have to be blind not to see it.'

'You're mistaken,' Rafe said. 'If she loves me then why the hell did she just leave in a cab for the airport? Huh? Tell me that. Why?'

'Did you tell her you love her?'

Rafe let out a frustrated breath. 'What is this female obsession with that word? I'm prepared to marry her, provide for her, and protect her and our baby. Why isn't that enough?'

Concetta folded her arms and shook her head, clearly disappointed in him. 'Loving someone isn't just about words, it's about actions. Your actions speak louder than any words but she still needs to hear you say it.'

His actions? What did his actions say other than he was prepared to take responsibility for the child he had helped conceive? He cared for Isla, wanted her, needed her like he needed his next breath...but love? That was a word he shied away from. It was a word that was used far too freely and easily. He had heard it throughout his childhood from his father, too many times to count. And yet, when forced to make a choice between his two families, his father's 'love' for Rafe had not lasted the distance. It had vaporised like a ghost in a cheap horror movie.

'You've still got time to catch her if you hurry.' Concetta's voice interrupted his thoughts.

Rafe shut the idea down quick-smart. Gone were the days when he would beg someone to stay with him. 'She's made her choice. For once, I'm going to respect it.'

Isla landed in London and found a cheap hotel to stay in but her heart was still back in Sicily. There was an emptiness in her chest that nothing could fill. Even her baby seemed overly restless, as if wondering where its father had gone. The one good thing about her trip back was there didn't seem to be any sign of her scandal following her. No paparazzi to hound her. No billboards or newsflash sheets outside shops documenting her shame. The newspapers here had other scandals to report but it was of small comfort.

She sat on the bed in her small hotel room and checked her phone. No missed calls and no messages from Rafe. She sighed and tossed the phone to one side and lay down, too weary to take off her travel-worn clothes and get into bed. She was just drifting off to sleep when she heard her phone buzzing and she snatched it up. 'Oh, hi, Layla…'

'Gosh, that was enthusiastic. Has someone died?' Layla said.

'Almost.' Isla sighed. 'And it was my fault.'

'Eek! What happened?'

Isla filled her friend in on Rafe's grandmother's health scare. 'So, you see, I had to leave because it will only happen again. I can't make my past go away.'

'No, but Rafe might be able to,' Layla said. 'It will cost him but if he loves you then what's a few million pounds here or there?'

'He doesn't love me.' Isla gave another sigh. 'He feels responsible for me. He cares about me and the baby, but love… I don't think so. If he did, why didn't he ever tell me?'

'You know what your problem is? I have the same problem so I should know,' Layla said. 'You haven't experienced a loving and secure childhood so you don't recognise love when it's right smack bang in front of you. You don't trust it even when you *can* see it. I reckon a man who spends squillions of pounds to protect you from humiliation is either completely nuts or madly in love.'

Could it be true? Did Rafe love her? 'But he never said he loved me,' Isla said.

'Did you tell him you loved him?'

'No, but—'

'Hah! There's your problem right there.' She imagined Layla snapping her fingers for effect. 'You're both too proud to fess up to how you feel. Someone has to make the first move to be vulnerable.'

'You sound like such an expert on relationships all of a sudden.'

'Och aye, I'm an expert all right.' Layla gave a self-deprecating laugh. 'Not that I've had any romantic relationships or ever likely to.'

Isla ended the call a short time later and got off the bed with her phone held against her chest. Should she call Rafe? She bit her lip and looked at the phone—she was a call away from adding even more pain to her life. Wasn't it better to leave things as they were? She had said all she needed to say. They would never have resumed their relationship if it hadn't been for the baby. She would just be another ex-lover he forgot about in time.

But she would need all the time in the world to forget about him.

CHAPTER THIRTEEN

RAFE DIDN'T EVEN bother going to bed to try and sleep. For the first three nights he avoided the bedroom he had shared with Isla and sat brooding in an armchair, occasionally drifting off out of sheer exhaustion, only to wake up and find himself back where he'd started three months ago.

But feeling worse.

Much worse.

It was like he had some sort of sickness. His muscles ached, his chest burned, his mouth was dry, his eyes bloodshot and sore. He'd stopped shaving two days ago because he couldn't stand the sight of himself when he looked in the mirror. He looked like a dog that had been kicked to the kerb one too many times.

He sat at his desk and put his head in his hands. As relationship hangovers went, this one was off the scale. Every bone in his skull was tightening against his brain like a clamp on a peach. He literally didn't know how he was going to function without Isla. She added colour to the bland palette of his life. His villa felt like a prison, his housekeeper a mean prison guard who kept shaking her head and tut-tutting not quite under her breath.

Rafe's phone buzzed with an incoming call and he snatched it up off the desk with his heart racing. But his stomach fell in disappointment when he saw his father's number come up on the screen. The last thing he needed right now was a call from his father. He turned the phone to silent and sought a perverse enjoyment watching it ring out. It was payback for all the times he'd wanted to speak to his father but his father had been 'too busy' to speak to him.

Childish of him, perhaps, but like father, like son as the saying went.

He pushed back his chair and walked over to the window, not one bit surprised to see it was raining. The gloomy weather suited his mood. It would be an insult to what he was suffering if the sun came out any time soon.

The phone rang again and he swore and turned around and picked it up. His father again. He sighed and answered. 'Father.' He never called him Dad or Papà. Not since he was thirteen.

'I heard about your broken engagement and I wanted to send my deepest sympathy,' his father said. 'You must be really hurting.'

'Deepest sympathy' was rather apt. It certainly felt like someone had died. 'Thank you but I'm fine. Not hurting at all.'

His father sighed. 'I know I made you this way and I'm sorry.'

Rafe frowned. 'Made me what way? What are you talking about? Look, I don't have time for this right now so—'

'I deserve that and more from you, Rafe. But please hear me out. I have always regretted needing your stepmother's money more than I needed your mother's love. It ruined everyone's life in the end. Yours, your mother's, your stepmother's and half-brothers'. And mine. I don't want you to end up like me. Surrounded by money and possessions but with no one who truly loves you. They only love the lifestyle I provide. Your mother loved me for me, with all my faults. It was a gift I threw away and I've regretted it ever since.'

'You've left it a bit late to air your regrets. Mamma has been dead for twenty years.' Rafe didn't strip back the bitterness in his tone; instead he laid it on thick.

'I know and that is an even bigger regret.' His father gave a ragged sigh. 'I thought I was making the right decision at the time. I could only provide for you and your mother and my other family if I stayed in the marriage. If I got a divorce it would have ruined us all. You wouldn't have had that private education in England for one. I would have had to sell your mother's apartment. Your half-brothers wouldn't have been able to achieve the things they've done without my financial backing. I weighed up the options and did what I thought was best under the circumstances. I never stopped loving you, Rafe. I felt ashamed of what I'd done to you and to your mother and it made me avoid you because I was too cowardly to face you. To see the derision and disgust you felt for me.'

Rafe leaned back in his chair and stretched his legs out like a bored teenager. 'It's a good speech since you've had twenty years to prepare it.' He knew he was being ungracious but the hurt was so much a part of him now he didn't know who he was without it.

'Don't make the same mistake by being too proud to accept when you've got it wrong,' his father said.

'Fight for love. Put everything on the line for it. Don't let it slip out of your hands because of stubborn pride.'

Rafe kicked a stack of paperwork beside his desk with his foot, watching it tumble to the floor. 'Look, I appreciate you taking the time to call but—'

'But you don't love her? Is that what you're saying?'

Rafe rubbed at the back of his neck where his muscles were clenched like a boxing champion's fists. What did he feel for Isla other than an ache deep in his chest because she wasn't here? An emptiness inside that prevented him from walking into the bedroom, where he could still smell her perfume. Where he could still see her jewellery and clothes in the wardrobe next to his. He would either have to move house or face up to what he was feeling. What he had been doing his best to ignore from the moment he'd met her.

He loved her.

He loved her so much it had terrified him into denying it. She had challenged him from day one to move out of emotional lockdown into emotional freedom but he had fought it every step of the way. But he could no longer hide his feelings. He had to tell her and hope she felt the same way about him. If she didn't, then he would have to deal with it, allow her the freedom to be the mother of his child without the pressure of being his wife. But he longed for her to be his wife. He longed for her to be by his side for the rest of his life.

'I do love her, Papà,' Rafe said. How strange that the first person he told was the last person he'd thought he would ever want to tell. 'I love her and I have to go and find her before it's too late. I'll call you, okay? Maybe we could meet up some time?'

'I would like that, Rafe.' There was a catch in his father's voice. 'I would like that very much.'

Isla was packed and ready to catch the train to Edinburgh once she checked out of her hotel. She was tired of the bustling energy of London when all she wanted to do was hide under a duvet and cry. There were too many reminders of happy couples walking hand in hand down the street or sitting in crowded cafés holding hands across the table. Even the weather she took as a personal insult. How dare the sun shine when she was feeling so wretched and lonely? It might as well be grey and dismal and rainy for the rest of her life.

Isla sighed and went to pick up her bag to make her way to the train station, but just then there was a knock on the door. She only had one overnight bag and her tote so hadn't called for a porter. She stepped past her bag on the floor and opened the door and her heart leapt into her throat. 'Rafe?'

'May I come in?'

She stepped aside and waved him in, not sure what to make of his expression. He looked like he hadn't slept since she left. The area underneath his eyes was as dark as a bruise and there were lines bracketing his mouth as if he had lost weight. She closed the door and faced him. 'How did you find me?'

He glanced at the bag on the floor. 'You're leaving?' His voice sounded hollow and his throat moved up and down as if something was caught in his gullet.

'I'm going back to Edinburgh on the overnight train.'

'Isla, don't go back to Scotland. Come home with me. Please. I shouldn't have let you leave without—'

'Rafe, we've already had this conversation,' Isla said, turning away with a sigh. 'I've made up my mind and you have to accept it. I'm not the right wife for you. I will only bring misery and suffering into your life.'

'I'm miserable and suffering without you,' Rafe said. 'I haven't slept. I haven't eaten. I miss you so much. I love you. I've been hiding from it all this time. I fell in love with you the moment I met you and I've been resisting acknowledging it ever since. Can you ever forgive me?'

Isla slowly turned back to face him. 'You love me? Are you sure you're not just saying that to get your way?'

He gave a humourless laugh. 'I guess I deserve that. The first time I've ever told a woman I love her and she thinks I don't mean it. I love you and I want to spend the rest of my life proving it to you. I can't bear the thought of spending another day without you. You're everything to me. I'm only half a person without you.'

Isla tried to control the tremble of her bottom lip but couldn't quite manage it. Tears sprang from her eyes and she brushed at them with the back of her hand. 'Why have you waited until now to tell me? Why didn't you tell me four days ago?'

'Has it only been four days?' He took her by the hands and drew her closer. 'It felt like four decades. I was a fool back then and an even bigger fool three months ago by not finding you when you left and telling you how I feel.' He held her gaze with his own shining with tenderness. 'When we first met you rocked me out of my emotional deep freeze. I fought it, denied it for as long as I could. Loving someone terrified me because it gave them the power to hurt me if they left. I felt that when my father left all those years ago and I made a promise to myself to never experience that pain again. And yet, I ended up losing you—the love of my life.'

Isla wound her arms around his neck and pressed close to his body. 'You haven't lost me, darling. I'm right here. I love you too. Like you, I've been hiding from it, too frightened to be rejected like all those times when I was a kid.'

He kissed her soundly, his arms wrapped around her as if he never wanted to let her go. After a long moment, he drew back to look down at her. 'I have something to tell you. That lowlife creep will never harass you again. There are a number of charges against him on other matters that will put him away for a long time. I can't guarantee the photos won't surface some other time but this time we will face it together. We will ride it out because we are a team that can't be disbanded. No scandal or misstep in the past will be big enough to tear us apart.'

Could it be true? She would never have to face the shame of her past alone? Isla suddenly felt stronger than she had ever felt. She knew she could face anything with Rafe by her side. 'Oh, Rafe, I don't know how to thank you.'

He cradled her face in his hands, looking deeply into her eyes, his own eyes glistening with moisture. 'When you left the second time, I didn't realise the significance of what you said until later. You said, *"You'll be a damn better father without me as your wife,"* and it made me realise how much you tried to protect me from your past. That you acted in what you thought were my best interests. I'm sorry I didn't see that at the

time. My father said something similar to me yesterday about why he did what he did and I realised I've
been a bit blind and stubborn about him too. I allowed
my anger to overshadow everything else. Can you ever
forgive me for letting you go, not once, but twice?'

'Of course, I forgive you.' Isla pressed a series of
kisses to his lips. 'I love you.'

'I love you too, you probably have no idea how
much.' He gave another wry laugh. 'I'm only starting
to realise it myself. I can't believe I was so blind to my
own feelings. It's like I was a robot walking through
life before I met you. I didn't feel much for anyone. I
didn't allow myself to get close to people. But a few
minutes in your company and all that changed. And
it freaked me out so much I denied it.' Rafe hugged
her close to his chest. 'My stubbornness nearly ruined
both our lives. I will do everything I can to make it up
to you. You'll just need to give me the next fifty or so
years to do it, okay?'

Isla looked up at him with a smile so wide she
thought her face would crack. 'You're on.'

* * * * *

COMING SOON!

We really hope you enjoyed reading this book. If you're looking for more romance, be sure to head to the shops when new books are available on

Thursday 31st October

To see which titles are coming soon, please visit

millsandboon.co.uk/nextmonth

MILLS & BOON

Coming next month

HIS CONTRACT CHRISTMAS BRIDE
Sharon Kendrick

He remembered seeing her swimming in his pool, her strong arms arcing through the turquoise water in a graceful display of strength and power. Length after length he had watched her swim and when she'd eventually surfaced and blinked droplets of water from her eyes, she had looked genuinely surprised—and pleased—to see him. He shouldn't have been turned on by her plain and practical swim-suit but he had been, though maybe because he'd never seen someone of her age wearing something so old-fashioned. Just as he shouldn't have been unexpectedly charmed by the way she made him laugh—which was rare enough to be noteworthy. He'd found himself staying on for dinner, even though he hadn't planned to—and even though he'd told himself that her dress was cheap, that hadn't stopped him from being unable to tear his eyes away from the way the dark material had clung to her fleshy curves, had it?

Maybe it was inevitable that they had started kissing—and just as inevitable that they'd ended up having sex. The unexpected and unwanted factor had been encountering her intact hymen and realising he was the first man she'd ever been intimate with. At the time he'd been irritated by the fact she hadn't told him because, according to friends who knew about such things, taking a woman's virginity brought with it all kinds of problems—not least the kind of mindless devotion which was the last thing he needed. In fact, he despised it, for reasons which still made him shudder. His mouth hardened. He had enough difficulty keeping women at arm's length as it was, without some idealistic innocent longing for rose petals and wedding bells.

But his irritation had lasted no longer than it took to resume his powerful rhythm inside her. And she had surprised him. Not just because she had proved to be an energetic and enthusiastic lover who had kissed more sweetly than any other woman he'd ever known. No. Because she seemed to have realised herself the limitations of their brief affair and to have accepted the fact that he had ghosted her from his life afterwards. She hadn't made any awkward phone calls or sent texts carefully constructed in order to appear 'casual'. And if his abundantly healthy ego had been fleetingly dented by her apparent eagerness to put what had happened behind her, the feeling had soon left him, because it was entirely mutual. But it made him realise that in many ways Lucy Phillips was exceptional. Emotionally independent, a trained midwife and, thus, the perfect candidate for what he needed...

He felt his mouth dry as he studied her earnest face and the clothes which failed to flatter her curvy shape. It was hard now to believe that she had choked out her fulfilment as he had driven into her firm body or to imagine the way he had fingered her nipples in the blazing Greek sunshine so that they had puckered into tight little nubs just ripe for sucking. But when you stopped to think about it, *all* of this was hard to believe and he needed to present his case so that she would receive it sympathetically. Rising to his feet, he addressed her stumbled question as he slowly approached her fireside chair. 'I'm telling you because I need your help, Lucy.'

'*My* help?' she echoed, her bright eyes looking up at him in surprise as his shadow enveloped her in darkness. 'Are you kidding? How on earth can I help someone like you when you're one of the richest men in the world and I have practically nothing?'

'No, I'm not kidding,' he negated firmly. 'And, far from having nothing, you have something I need very badly. Niko's baby needs security and continuity. He needs a home and I'm in a position to offer him one. But not on my own. Not as a single man whose work takes him to opposite sides of the world and who has no experience of babies, or children. And that's why I'm asking you to marry me, Lucy. To be my wife and the mother of my orphaned nephew.'

Continue reading
HIS CONTRACT CHRISTMAS BRIDE
Sharon Kendrick

Available next month
www.millsandboon.co.uk

LET'S TALK
Romance

For exclusive extracts, competitions
and special offers, find us online:

MILLS & BOON

THE HEART OF ROMANCE

A ROMANCE FOR EVERY KIND OF READER

MODERN

Prepare to be swept off your feet by sophisticated, sexy and seductive heroes, in some of the world's most glamourous and romantic locations, where power and passion collide.
8 stories per month.

HISTORICAL

Escape with historical heroes from time gone by. Whether your passion is for wicked Regency Rakes, muscled Vikings or rugged Highlanders, awaken the romance of the past.
6 stories per month.

MEDICAL

Set your pulse racing with dedicated, delectable doctors in the high-pressure world of medicine, where emotions run high and passion, comfort and love are the best medicine.
6 stories per month.

True Love

Celebrate true love with tender stories of heartfelt romance, from the rush of falling in love to the joy a new baby can bring, and focus on the emotional heart of a relationship.
8 stories per month.

Desire

Indulge in secrets and scandal, intense drama and plenty of sizzling hot action with powerful and passionate heroes who have it all: wealth, status, good looks…everything but the right woman.
6 stories per month.

HEROES

Experience all the excitement of a gripping thriller, with an intense romance at its heart. Resourceful, true-to-life women and strong, fearless men face danger and desire - a killer combination!
8 stories per month.

DARE

Sensual love stories featuring smart, sassy heroines you'd want as a best friend, and compelling intense heroes who are worthy of them.
4 stories per month.

To see which titles are coming soon, please visit

millsandboon.co.uk/nextmonth

JOIN US ON SOCIAL MEDIA!

Stay up to date with our latest releases, author
news and gossip, special offers and discounts, and
all the behind-the-scenes action
from Mills & Boon...

 millsandboon

 millsandboonuk

 millsandboon

might just be true love...